Dog Days

Dog Days

Ericka Waller

ST. MARTIN'S GRIFFIN
NEW YORK

First published in the United States by St. Martin's Griffin, an imprint of St. Martin's Publishing Group

DOG DAYS. Copyright © 2021 by Ericka Waller. All rights reserved. Printed in the United States of America. For information, address St. Martin's Publishing Group, 120 Broadway, New York, NY 10271.

www.stmartins.com

Illustrations by Beci Kelly

Lyrics on p. 188 from "I Said My Pajamas (And Put On My Prayers)" words and music by George Wyle & Edward Pola, copyright © 1949 MCA Ltd. Universal/ MCA Music Ltd. All rights reserved. International copyright secured. Used by permission of Hal Leonard Europe Limited.

Library of Congress Cataloging-in-Publication Data

Names: Waller, Ericka, author.
Title: Dog days / Ericka Waller.
Description: First U.S. edition. | New York : St. Martin's Griffin, 2021. | "Originally published in Great Britain by Doubleday, an imprint of Transworld Publishers, a Penguin Random House company"—Title page verso.
Identifiers: LCCN 2020056363 | ISBN 9781250817730 (hardcover) | ISBN 9781250274731 (trade paperback) | ISBN 9781250274748 (ebook)
Subjects: LCSH: Dogs—Fiction. | Dog owners—Fiction. | Human-animal relationships—Fiction.
Classification: LCC PR6123.A45475 D64 2021 | DDC 823/.92—dc23
LC record available at https://lccn.loc.gov/2020056363

Our books may be purchased in bulk for promotional, educational, or business use. Please contact your local bookseller or the Macmillan Corporate and Premium Sales Department at 1-800-221-7945, extension 5442, or by email at MacmillanSpecialMarkets@macmillan.com.

Originally published in Great Britain by Doubleday, an imprint of Transworld Publishers, a Penguin Random House company

First U.S. Edition: 2021

10 9 8 7 6 5 4 3 2 1

To Grace, Daisy and Bliss
(remember, anything is possible)

and to James,
for always believing in my writing

Prelude

I T's ONE OF THOSE spring mornings you get down on the coast, a scene so brilliant it reminds you of a child's painting: the sky a solid block of Crayola blue, the sun scrubbed to a radiant beam. On the horizon, crisp white clips of sails like petticoats, like maids curtsying to the shore. The Beacon winks with buttercups and dandelions. The grass does silent t'ai chi in a breeze that may adjust a hat to a jaunty angle, but would never be so rude as to whip it off your head. And there is the windmill, casting its shadow on the bodies of Luke and Lizzie, Dan and Atticus, on George and Betty and their dogs.

Even from this distance, it's easy to spot who belongs to whom. That Fitz and Wolfie belong to Dan and Luke, striding over the mound. Fitz's tongue is too long and his tail too waggy to be perfect, but you'd struggle to find a more decent creature, just like his owner. Wolfie – the flirt, the airhead, the poor simple beast – is distracted from chasing a squirrel by Maud. Lizzie is supposed to be walking her, but it's always the other way round. Betty and George are on the bench with Poppy, who is licking the salt from George's fingers as he eats. Betty is knitting another hideous jumper for her rescue greyhound, Lucky – a coat-hanger of a dog who always looks embarrassed but never leaves her side.

The rain comes out of nowhere, as it can so close to the

sea. The first dollop of water lands on George's thin hair. He tuts. Fucking weather. Poppy barks. Fitz and Wolfie roll in something dead and smelly. Lucky's woollen coat starts to itch.

They all look up at the rain, heads tipped back, pale necks exposed to the elements, like birds waiting to be fed. They stay that way for a minute, before Betty covers her head with her newspaper and George packs away his lunch. Before Luke worries about his hair. Before Atticus takes off his coat to give to Dan, who, says Lizzie, needs it more.

There is a brief moment when time pauses itself, and we can see the fragile threads between them glittering like gold in the rain. From a finger here to an elbow there. From the corner of Atticus's smile to Dan's beating heart. From paw to person and back again.

George

(Where is Ellen?)

I T'S SEVEN SIXTEEN ON Wednesday night and Ellen still isn't home from her book club. George hasn't had his dinner, which Ellen always cooks from scratch and always has ready on the table with his half-glass of beer at five forty-five.

After she serves something warm and British (George doesn't believe in any seasoning other than salt and lots of it, always sprinkling some liberally before checking the dish needs it), Ellen does the washing-up, dries the dishes, then lays the tea-towel over the tea-towel holder he made for her thirty years before. She snaps the cloth out before she hangs it, three times quickly, then once again. It will dry in the slow breeze that comes from the back door, which they always leave ajar for this reason. It will be ready to polish the plates after the boiled egg, and marmalade on toast they will have for breakfast the next morning at seven thirty. It will be washed that afternoon and hung on the line, which George put up five years earlier, after the first one collapsed in a storm. (George was cross about this. He'd planned for that washing line to see him out.) The tea-towel will hang alongside the sheets, towels and George's white underpants, which Ellen washes on Thursdays.

On Wednesdays, Ellen leaves for her six o'clock book club at five fifty-four because it's at Sue's house, only three doors down. Sometimes they hold it at Barbara's house, ten doors down, and then Ellen leaves at five fifty. They never hold it at George and Ellen's house because George hates Ellen's loud, opinionated friends, and he hates books even more. He also hates the nibbles Ellen makes that he is not allowed to eat because of his cholesterol. George doesn't believe in cholesterol, global warming or baseball caps.

Ellen's book club finishes at seven. George sits in his chair and his stomach hurts and now it's seven eighteen and Ellen still isn't home. Sometimes George stands at the bay window and watches her walk back towards him, sees her stop to say hello to next-door's cat, which George wants to shoot because it shits on his shingle.

Today, he doesn't go to the bay window to watch Ellen walk back to him, because Ellen won't be walking back. Ellen died eight days ago. Her book-club book is on the walnut side table next to the beige sofa. George made her that table, dovetailed joints she'd cooed over. *Eleanor Oliphant Is Completely Fine*. George hates this book most of all, and the fact that Ellen was often reading it instead of cooking his dinner, and now she's dead and there's no one to look after him.

The clock ticks. The early-spring evening sky tie-dyes itself yellow, orange and red. George ignores the glorious sun setting outside the window and continues to stare at the dining table where his dinner won't appear. Finally, he gets up and slow-shuffles to the kitchen.

Before the funeral, he'd been living off the Tupperware boxes that were placed quietly on his doorstep by neighbours who couldn't stand him but loved his wife. George had watched them tiptoeing up the path, then scurrying back down it before he could get to the door. As if he'd thank them.

He had eaten the soggy stews in his pants and vest, flicking out bits of broccoli along with anything pink and suspicious. He had washed down claggy mashed potato, and thick gravy skin with gulps of water from the tap, cupping the liquid in his hands after he'd realized he couldn't fit his head under it. He soaked the front of his vest, his sagging brown nipples visible. He didn't care.

At the funeral, Barbara-from-the-fucking-church-and-the-fucking-book-club had plied him with two curled-up egg-and-cress sandwiches. He had put them into his mouth to stop himself telling Barbara how much he disliked her and what she could do with her patronizing smiles and arm pats. God works in mysterious ways, she had told him. God could fuck off, as far as George was concerned, and he let Barbara know as much once he'd swallowed the second sandwich.

George thinks perhaps he should eat something now. It might make him feel better. He's at the age where his diabetes is controlled with tablets, but the threat of injections looms. He knows he needs to sort out his blood sugar, although he doesn't know what blood sugar is because he doesn't listen at the doctor's appointments. That's Ellen's job. He's sure it means he should eat something sweet.

He opens the bread bin and this is where he spots the letter. He has to look twice to make sure he's not seeing things. It's really there, though, with his name on it, in Ellen's handwriting.

She's never written him a letter before. She's never needed to. Sometimes she left him notes: *Didn't want to wake you. Remember to pay the milkman when he comes. I'll be at Knit and Natter. Money on the side. Be home at 3.35 p.m.*

This is a *letter*, though, in an envelope that looks thick and expensive.

The bread bin also houses a single green bread roll. George pokes it and powdery mould stains his finger. He goes to the fridge and pulls out a tin-foiled box of what might well be shepherd's pie, which George has on Mondays and which Ellen makes with a fake meat called Quorn that George hates. He once read that the mould used in Quorn was developed to feed the Germans in the First World War. It's not true, but George has never let the truth ruin an opportunity to vent his vast opinions on what is wrong with society. Every time Ellen serves him this shit, he gives her a Nazi salute. She always ignores him, and hunger wins.

He leaves the pie on the counter and picks up the letter. His glasses are on the side table along with the remote control and his pill box, which is empty because Ellen sets up his medicine on Sunday nights and she's been dead for over a week. He opens the envelope and reads.

George,

Please make sure you eat regularly and that you take your pills. I've restocked them for the next three weeks. The boxes are in the bathroom cabinet and I've written a note on how to do it yourself when you run out. If you have any problems, that nice girl Sophie from the pharmacy can help. You can have a biscuit from the tin if you're feeling whizzy. There's a shepherd's pie in the fridge that you can microwave and there's more food in the freezer. Don't forget to feed and walk Poppy. She needs you.

Love, Ellen

George finishes reading the note, screws it up and tosses it at the bin. He misses. The time is now 8.01 p.m. and the sky is navy blue. George shouts, 'FUCK,' as loudly as he can, then stomps into the kitchen to retrieve the meal. He hasn't turned on any lights and fumbles with the tin-foil lid. When he finally prises it off, he's hit with the sweet smell of fermentation. He drops the container on the floor by the back door, then makes his way to the laundry room, where Poppy has been impounded. Barbara still comes in to walk her twice a day and pick up the piss-stained newspaper, but she's told him it can't carry on much longer. He'll have to start doing things himself.

George keeps his radio on loud enough to ignore Poppy's crying and barking. The smell is harder, but he gave up washing a week ago, so the stench could be coming from either of them. He closed the windows when Ellen died and hasn't opened them since.

Poppy scrambles out, tail wagging, short legs slipping, long body wiggling. She stops by George's feet and looks up at him. He points to the food. She barks. He pushes her with his slipper towards her supper. She barks again, three sharp yelps that make George clench his jaw. He hasn't got his teeth in, though, and all he makes is a wet noise, like a baby.

'Eat,' he tells the dog, 'eat, you ugly mutt. Eat and shut up.'

Poppy rolls onto her back and gazes at George with sorrowful eyes, like she pities him. Her long pink belly is exposed. Bald, save for the odd bristly black hair and uneven nipples, like the skin tags under George's armpits. She is more piglet than dog, her pencil-thin tail swinging like a pendulum between her stubby legs. If a dog could smile, that's what she was doing, smiling at him, coquettishly, like a lady of the night trying to pick up a punter, 'Like what you see, sir?' as she shimmies on the floor, her body curving into a question mark. 'Go on,' her raised ginger eyebrow says. 'Give me a tickle. You know you want to.'

George watches her in disgust. He's never liked flirty women, and flirty dogs are no better.

'Filthy strumpet,' he says, and staggers to his straight-backed chair. His ship in the storm. When he is sitting in it, he is a captain, capable of conquering the stormiest of seas. He's Scott of the Antarctic in that chair. It won't leave him when he's not looking. Won't drop dead on him with no warning. It creaks now and again, as old things do. When it does, George takes it gently down to his shed to glue and fix, and straighten and polish, and then he brings it back again. Sits it in the grooves the angled feet have indented in the shell-patterned carpet that was not his choice. His chair is reliable, not like Ellen. George imagines himself spraying her with WD40, with wood oil. Imagines he's going mad. Clutches the walnut arm rests and shouts at the dog.

'Don't eat, then,' he says. 'Don't matter to me.' Poppy stops gyrating and gets to her paws, evidently realizing she's *not* going to get a belly rub. On the way back to her room she pauses by the food. George watches her recoil at the smell and back away, leaving a trail of wee. I'm the boss round here, George thinks, not you.

Ellen came home with the dachshund puppy three weeks ago. She didn't tell George she was getting a dog. Didn't ask him first. Ellen knew George hates dogs. Especially small ones. It was the first thing she had ever done without consulting George first. And then she died, which was the second.

Dan

(Enter Atticus, stage right)

D AN'S *STAR WARS* ALARM clock wakes him at 6.30 a.m. He rolls over and punches Darth Vader on the head, then climbs out of bed and stretches. In the corner, his yellow Labrador, Fitz, yawns, and it sounds like Chewbacca, which always makes Dan laugh. Together they pad downstairs, Fitz's tail drumming a beat on Dan's bare legs as they go. Fitz checks that the garden is as he left it while Dan fires up the coffee machine. Dan counts the whirs and ticks but manages to turn the tap on and off only four times. Fitz comes back in time to hear the hiss of hot water, then sits and waits for the milk from Dan's cereal bowl.

Dan has a new client today and that makes him nervous. It takes him longer than normal to button up his shirt and he sweats with the effort. He thinks about having another shower but doesn't have time. This makes him sweat more. He knows the only way to stop the sweating is to start the counting. He tells himself it won't really stop the sweating. The left side of his brain knows he's being stupid. The right side tells him this three times, then three times more. On the second set of threes he turns the light switch on and off. On the third set he counts his vinyl records. He wants to reorganize them by era, not colour, but he knows this would make him very, very late.

He pats Fitz sixty times instead. Fitz licks his nose with a wide pink tongue. Dan breathes him in deeply, fur and dog and friend, and says he'll walk him later. Fitz offers a paw, which Dan shakes. 'Deal,' he says, and Fitz gives a single solemn bark in return, then lumbers back out to the garden. 'Don't chase that seagull,' Dan says. 'It's not just *your* garden. You need to share it with the birds,' but it's too late. Fitz is already haring down the narrow pathway to yip and yap a symphony at the trespasser.

Dan is seven minutes late to work. His new patient isn't due until ten, but he likes to have a full hour to study the referral notes beforehand and he worries he might miss something vital with the seven minutes he's lost. Even after two years and seven months, Dan is still waiting for someone to realize that he is entirely unsuited to being a counsellor. Waiting makes him nervous. It always has. His mother called him an impatient child, but it wasn't that. It was the not-knowing, the unforeseen in any circumstance. He was not impatient, he was uneasy.

He's twenty-five now, and still fears what might lie ahead, beyond the next bend. The sooner Alan, the owner of the practice Dan works for, realizes that Dan is masquerading as a compos-mentis professional and fires him, the better.

The door opens at 10.02 a.m. and in walks Atticus, without knocking. Dan knows he should stand up and introduce himself, protocol, professionalism, but the order of the universe flips over in a second too brief for him to count. Dan thinks it might have something to do with Atticus's shoes. A man confident enough to wear tongue-pink tasselled suede loafers cannot possibly require any of the knowledge Dan has gleaned from his person-centred counselling degree. The shoes have spoken, have clicked their heels together three times, and, without a word, Dan is the patient and Atticus the counsellor. Because of this, Atticus does the introductions.

'Daniel James, I'm Atticus. Your ten o'clock.'

It's just a sentence, but the way he speaks makes it a state-ment, a question and a suggestion all at the same time. Dan jumps up in the same instant that Atticus flops down onto the sofa, kicks off his loafers and flings his arms above his head. One shoe hits an ornamental Chinese vase that sits inside the disused fireplace. It wobbles, and they both watch to see if it will fall. Dan tells himself that if it smashes he will have reasonable grounds to refuse to offer therapy to Atticus.

'Prone to aggression,' he'll tell Alan. 'Best referred to Anger Management.' It's not Dan's speciality.

As the vase quivers, Dan practises the line 'Sorry, I can't be your therapist. Here's a referral to a colleague I trust' in his head so that it won't sound too forced. Or relieved.

The vase finally stops vacillating, choosing to remain erect and intact. Dan tells himself to make eye contact. He feels like he's been shot when they look at one another that first time. He has to glance down at his clipboard just so that he can breathe. He had clutched it to his chest when he stood up and knows he looks awkward now but doesn't know how to be anything else.

He tries to commit to a seat. Normally, he would take the blue chair next to the sofa, but today there doesn't seem to be enough space between the two pieces of furniture. Atticus is sprawled out, long limbs stretching into the middle of the room. Dan has to walk carefully around them as he makes his way to the red chair in the corner, which is only there to cover the damp on the wall. NHS. Cuts. Lack of funding. Old buildings.

Dan knows Atticus is studying him from his spot on the sofa. He dips an eyebrow at Dan's socks as if to say, '*Star Wars?* How very cool of you,' but by the time his gaze drifts back to Dan's face the smirk has been replaced with a lazy grin that Dan instantly understands is his trademark.

'So, tell me, Daniel James,' he says, from under unusually long eyelashes, 'how exactly are you going to fix me?'

The notes Dan has been given on Atticus are brief. Male. Thirty-two. Seeking help for generalized anxiety. Has attended counselling various times. Never stayed for the whole six weeks.

Dan repeats these snippets in his head and tries to work out the best way to respond. Atticus has done this before so he must know how counselling works. He is aware that Dan cannot fix him. Dan doesn't offer cognitive behavioural therapy, or any other kind of therapy, really. He is simply a counsellor. People talk and he listens. Rephrases their words and offers them back, carefully, with soft hands. His patients receive them like pebbles, smooth and warm in their palms.

Dan organizes people's brains. That is what he does. That is what he is good at. He is a gentle gardener, concise as he prunes his way through their thoughts. He parts their words like leaves, finds the fronds and petioles. Digs, careful of flints, until he hits milky root. Dan removes the bindweed, tugs at scutch grass, churns the mud until it is rich, chocolatey earth again.

But Dan has no idea what to do with, or for, Atticus, can't think while his long bare feet are pointed at him, like an accusation.

Dan thinks of Fitz, and counting, and dominoes falling in perfect rows. He thinks of ironed creases in white shirts and his sparkling cutlery drawer, spoons all facing the same way. He thinks of books that have yet to be opened, straight spines, his apple-cutter and the perfect eights it makes.

He says none of this, though. Instead he says, 'I can't fix you, Atticus. That bit is up to you,' then pauses for a beat too long. Atticus makes all the colours in the room bleed. He makes Dan glottalize his 't's. Dan never does that. Missing 't's in words is as bad as skipping over numbers when counting.

The chair squeaks in protest at being sat on after a year spent acting as a prop. Dan has to speak louder. 'I'm here to help you on your journey.' He groans inwardly and wonders if he always sounds so clichéd and cringy. He's got nothing else, though, so has to keep going. 'This is your fifty minutes. You can talk, and I will listen. Anything you say will be kept within this room, unless you tell me something that puts yourself or others at risk, and then I am obliged to report it to your doctor and any other relevant healthcare professionals.'

Normally this speech comes out smoother. Normally Dan smiles reassuringly as he says it, and the patient smiles back confidently to assure him it will never come to that. Then they say something like, 'Oh, I'd never hurt myself or anyone else. It's nothing like that,' before launching into a rambling speech about why they have come and Dan pictures secateurs in his hands, bends down and starts pruning. By the third session, Dan will realize the first reason the patient gave for needing counselling was not the real reason. Nor was the second. He's been pulling out begonias, not the weeds, bird's-foot and moss.

'Why are you in counselling, Atticus?' Dan asks suddenly, needing to know, more than ever before, why he's been given the privilege of asking personal questions of a stranger without having to give anything of himself away.

Atticus shrugs and spreads his hands, palms facing up, long fingers curled slightly at the tip. Dan looks at them, briefly wishing he was a fortune-teller.

'I was lonely,' Atticus says simply.

Dan didn't expect an answer. He didn't know what he was expecting, but it was not loneliness.

'And now?' he asks. There is a beat of silence. A meeting of eyes. A tectonic shift in the universe. Day-blind stars are realigned.

'And now I am not,' Atticus says, and it is as simple and as complicated as that. Dan knows that six weeks will never be enough for Atticus. Nothing Dan can do will ever be enough for Atticus.

Counselling sessions are fifty minutes long. Dan gives himself at least ten minutes between clients. Always, when a session ends, Dan closes the door softly, then lightly mists the sofa with a lavender spray and opens the window to air the room. His nan always used to do that when people left her house, especially ones she didn't like. Dan likes to think it makes the atmosphere clean and fresh for the next patient – him, too. Then he drinks a glass of water while he records notes to type up in detail later. Sometimes, he adds in the odd 'Good boy, Fitz,' because they'll listen to the recording together, Dan frowning and scribbling, Fitz wagging his tail with joy that he hasn't been forgotten. Dan does all this as quickly as he can so he has enough time left to straighten his socks, plump the cushion and line up his pencil before there is a knock on the door.

After Atticus, though, Dan does none of these things. He just stands, staring blindly into space, and would have carried on doing so all morning had his next client not arrived, pulling him from his reverie.

Lizzie

(Maud refuses to listen)

Lizzie is wearing too many clothes. This is nothing new, but dog-walking is and she's sweating in the thick fluffy socks from Lost Property. None of it is actually lost, it's donated, but that doesn't roll off the tongue as nicely. Lizzie finds it easier to wear a lost pair of socks than a pair given to her out of pity.

Lizzie doesn't trust the dog. She's not used to them. Never wanted to walk it in the first place. She can't understand why people bring animals into their home, with their fangs and claws and potential violence. They could kill you for looking at them in the wrong way, for approaching them as they eat. Are a wet nose and wagging tail really signs of happiness? And when has happiness meant safety? There is so little people can control, not even themselves, yet they still place faith in the flesh-eating descendants of wolves, leave them alone with babies, and let them think they are in charge.

Lizzie has no choice, though. Tess took her in, when she needed succour, and in return she must take out Tess's dog. It was on her list of jobs – 'Take out Maud'. Initially she thought Maud was an old, or mentally impaired, woman. When she found out Maud was a dog, she felt briefly relieved. Then

Maud sniffed at her, investigated her with her snout, and Lizzie froze.

Lizzie shudders as she clips on the lead and tells herself Maud is probably too old to do more than bark. Two brown eyes stare up at her crossly. Lizzie once read you should never look a dog in the eye, but neither of them can seem to break contact.

Lizzie also read up on what to do if a dog attacks you while she was researching them at the library. Forewarned is forearmed, after all. Lizzie, an excellent scholar, now knows that a bloodhound's sense of smell is so finely tuned that it has been cited in court as evidence. She also knows that up to 30 per cent of Dalmatians are deaf in one ear, and that all dogs have three eyelids.

Maud's eyes remind her of the teddy bear she had as a child. Lizzie wonders how many mites live in the dog's long black eyelashes, remembers the delighted squeals of disgust when she taught her class that in a science lesson – how we are slowly being eaten alive by infinitesimal insects gorging on our skin. How they spend their whole lives travelling the planet of our face, mating on our nose, laying eggs in our eyebrows, dying on our lips. How they love the dark and secret places, the moist holes and hidden folds. The children scrubbed at their eyes with tiny fists, their faces screwed up in appalled disbelief. She had them then, in the palm of her hand. You could have two thousand follicle mites eating the dead skin around your eyelashes and you'd feel nothing. Lizzie quite likes the idea of oblivion, leaving things to Fate, although she doesn't trust Fate any more than she trusts dogs.

She walks up the steep path to the Beacon, with Maud pulling on her lead. Lizzie checks that she has the sausages in her pocket, then finally lets the dog off. 'Come back when I tell you,' she commands, trying and failing to channel Barbara Woodhouse.

The Beacon is too vast, too open for Lizzie. A constant wind blows off the tile-grey sea, forcing her coat open and her scarf to flap, as if it's trying to shake secrets out of her. She doesn't like the tiny paths winding here and there, leading nowhere. No exit routes. The long, brittle grass whispers about her as she walks past. The trees, bent and weathered with age, stretch out long spindly fingers that reach for her bobble hat. They want to snare her in their arms, imprison her. There are dips and holes disguised by moss and bracken. The Beacon is dangerous, nowhere to hide. These are stupid thoughts, paranoid, paranormal. Not like Lizzie at all.

Maud sprints in circles, yapping with joy at being free. Lizzie feels she should do the same but can't. Maud simply lets herself go. Her back legs flail as she runs. Her gait is lopsided, and there is a bulge at the end of her back. There is no dignity in her, yet she doesn't care. Lizzie holds herself like a pack of cards, close to her own chest.

She tracks Maud along the Beacon, distracted now and then by the glittering sea laid out in front of her. If she were in teacher mode, she'd describe it as *terribly* exciting. Terribly. It scares her. She's not been down to the beach yet. It's too overwhelming. If the sea is too bright, Lizzie is too faded. A sepia version of herself. Even after a month, the bags remain under her eyes. The cuts have healed, and her shoulder doesn't hurt any more, but she's careful with it. As she's careful with everything.

They wander like this for a while, Maud darting here and

there, Lizzie sticking to the paths, head down. Maud needs to do more darting. She is fat and needs exercise. The average Jack Russell should weigh between thirteen and seventeen pounds and needs four to six hundred calories a day. Maud gets that much in custard creams alone, given by Tess with a 'Who's a pretty poppet, then?'

Lizzie tries to 'lose herself in nature', like Tess told her to, but all she hears is violence. The wind whips and wails, the seagulls screech and scream.

She walks to the bench, dedicated to someone she'll never know, so it doesn't matter, but she polishes the bronze plaque with her sleeve anyway, as if asking permission before sitting down. Her word-search book is in her pocket, her pencil in her hair. The wind calms as her fingers run up and down the rows that hide the world's largest cities. Lizzie finds Shanghai straight away then looks for Jakarta, her heart slowing with each 'a'. There is a moment of panic when she can't find Tokyo, but she reminds herself it's in there somewhere. All the answers are there: she doesn't have to think. Doesn't have to work anything out. All she has to do is follow the vowels and the words will appear.

She is distracted by Maud's strangled bark. Shoving the word-search book back into her pocket, Lizzie chases after her, scrabbling for the sausages she keeps in the pocket of her jeans. She finally catches up with Maud, who is dancing round a lanky wolfhound.

'Maud! Lizzie pants, out of breath from running. She tries to get hold of the dog, but Maud has no intention of going back on the lead. She swerves between Lizzie's legs, barking and squirming.

'It's fine,' the owner says. 'Wolfie's friendly, aren't you, mate? He wouldn't hurt a fly.' He bends and strokes his dog's ears. Wolfie wags his shabby tail and sniffs at the air. 'What's your dog called?' the man asks Lizzie, straightening up.

He's tall, Lizzie thinks irrelevantly. 'She's not mine,' she says quickly, 'but her name is Maud.'

Maud yaps in response, as if introducing herself. She's clever, Lizzie thinks suddenly.

'Hi, Maud. Nice to meet you,' Wolfie's owner says, then, 'I'm Luke.'

He looks at Lizzie, waiting for her to offer something back, but she doesn't. What will come after her name? A suggestion they walk together? A chat? Questions. Lizzie can't. She just can't. There is a moment of uneasy silence. Wolfie breaks it by sniffing Maud's bum and Lizzie finally gets a finger under her collar and clips her back on the lead.

'Wolfhounds make terrible guard dogs,' Lizzie says awkwardly, nodding at Wolfie. 'They're not at all suspicious of strangers.'

Luke grins at that, neat white teeth inside a smile bracketed by dimples. Far more dangerous than any dog, that smile of his, Lizzie thinks idly.

'Should he be suspicious of you, then?' Luke asks. Before she can answer, 'Yes,' Maud barks again and strains at the leash. Lizzie takes this as an excuse to turn and bolt.

She stops, out of breath, at the bottom of the Beacon. Hates herself for running away. Thinks about her son. Seven. Small. Perfect. The sun shines in his heart, bright and pure. Just the thought of him warms her up, calms her down.

George

(George tries to stop time and fails)

GEORGE HAS TAKEN TO sleeping in his armchair. The bed seems too far away and the sheets smell sour. George smells sour. The whole house smells sour. The dog certainly smells sour. Barbara has stopped coming. On her last visit she dropped off twelve tins of puppy food and a pile of old newspapers. She knew better than to ask him to reimburse her. George leaves the back door open now and lets the dog do what it likes.

After a visit to the pantry and a perusal of the empty shelves that he made years ago but hasn't looked at since (because pantries are for women), George is living on beer, tinned meat and stomach acid. He did an excellent job on those shelves. He even made tiny boxes for Ellen's spices. Took him bloody ages. She had told him not to go to too much trouble, but he did. Of course he did.

The dog barks incessantly. George hopes it will wear itself out but, so far, no luck. He calls it all the names he can think of and it just wags its tail at him in gratitude.

He'd kick it out, set it loose, if only he had the energy. If only Ellen would stop leaving her bloody sanctimonious notes. If only Ellen would just come back. George needs his wife, like a snail needs its shell, but she's gone and now he's exposed to everything.

He found the second note the day he ran out of pants, which was also the day he stopped wearing them. It was in the bottom of his underwear drawer. That neat handwriting telling him how to load the washing-machine. The amount of fabric softener to use. Fabric softener! George's hands are riddled with calluses, chunks of fingernail missing from years of sanding. Nothing about him is soft and that's just the way he likes it.

Hello George,

I know you will not be finding it easy. ['Who does she think she is? A fucking ghost?' he'd said to Poppy, who barked and went on a hunt for him, dogs being better than humans at sensing the supernatural.] *I wish I'd had time to do more for you before it all kicked off.* [She made it sound like a fight in a chip shop.] *Things will get easier. You always said the washing-machine couldn't be rocket science if I could work it out. Remember when one of your braces got trapped in the rubber seal and it sounded like someone was trying to break in? You mended it, no problem. It's just a couple of knobs and dials, nothing to it. Think of all the parquet flooring you used to lay. Now that was a puzzle. You used to come home smelling of tar and your work trousers were a nightmare to wash. These days they only need a quick rinse and spin. Not your undies. They need a hot wash at 60. If you hang them on the line, the sun will help bleach the stains.* [It was torture. He could hear her talking, hear her voice, but she wasn't there.] *The pegs are in the little jumper-shaped holder at the end of the washing line. If you hang your trousers neatly, they shouldn't need ironing, and really, George, do a couple of creases really matter? You don't go out much and wrinkles are the privilege of getting older. I never told you this, but I hated ironing. The steam made my face red and my hair frizzy, and the iron would hiss at me without warning, like it wanted to attack.*

The note went on to food shopping, complete with a list. Three oranges. Two tins of beans. Sliced ham. A pint of milk (red label). One head of broccoli (*you need the fibre*). A small pack of cheese (*to last a week, George*). Margarine (*not butter!*). Frozen pies, with instructions for cooking them. (*Insert a fork in the middle to make sure they are done.*) He had to stop for breath before he could continue.

You could get meals delivered. Oh, I can imagine your face as you read this. Don't be cross with me, my darling George. Death comes to us all. You might like some of the meals on wheels anyway. Hetty swears by their spotted dick – no jokes, please. [George tells the joke to Poppy. She barks and wees a bit.] *Righto, must get on. Do wash your pants, George. Braces and trousers are not enough.*

Love, your Ellen
PS Kisses to Poppy

George had decided to ignore the note, the washing, the shopping and the doorbell. The telephone, too.

The food parcels have stopped coming. Ellen's friends have paid their dues. Letters pile up on the doormat. Poppy piddles on them and hopes for praise. Ellen always gave her a titbit if she did it in the right place but George doesn't care. Poppy has tried weeing on other things – the carpet, George's slippers – but all she got in return was a dry nose from dehydration.

Grease clings now to unwashed cutlery. Dust slithers through cracks and breeds like cancer. Everywhere is infected. Everywhere is tacky and smudged and stale. George sits in his chair, with the cricket on the radio, ploughing through his tins, like a sailor in a shipwreck. He eats until he sleeps, and wakes up to piss and shit, avoiding the dog's piles and puddles as he goes. His prostate is failing him, like everything else. He holds his limp, shrivelled dick, willing it to work.

On one visit to the toilet, he opens the back door and orders the dog to leave. She seems to contemplate the idea then chooses to remain, an unwelcome guest. She invites the breeze in to join her, bringing with it the sounds and smells of life not on hold. High heels clicking. Cars braking. Children singing. School mums chatting, and the postman's cheery whistle. All mixed in with the smell of next-door's Wednesday roast – George has always envied this: he only got a roast on Sundays – and the earthy smell of spring.

George swears at it all. Beer cans collect by the door where he has taken aim and missed his targets (delivery men and neighbours, asking him *please* to stop the dog barking). He'd kill himself, but Ellen isn't there to do it for him.

Poppy takes herself away until she is sure George is asleep, then creeps onto his slippered feet, curls herself into a ball and shuts her eyes. She is perfectly content. The smell doesn't bother her at all.

Dan

(Dan is never going to wear those
Star Wars socks again)

Dan and Atticus's second counselling session passes painfully. When Dan asks Atticus why he feels he needs counselling for his loneliness, Atticus tells him, 'An unexamined life is not worth living,' while studying his fingernails. When Atticus asks Dan why he became a counsellor, Dan tells him the sessions are not about, or for, him. They are for Atticus.

Dan knows that personal questions are a typical response to pull the focus away from the client when things get uncomfortable. Some people hide their insecurities by exposing those of others. They are masters of what Alan loves to call 'projection'.

Atticus's eyes are fixed on the small green Yoda on Dan's socks, and Dan feels he may as well be naked. 'Is there something specific you'd like to examine in your life?' Dan asks, while discreetly trying to tug his trouser legs down.

Atticus rolls his eyes at him and says, 'Something lost, inside yourself. That which you seek, inside you will find.'

From Socrates to *Star Wars*, Dan thinks. Whatever Atticus

is or isn't, he's definitely not stupid. '*Return of the Jedi*,' Dan says in response. 'I take it you like *Star Wars*?'

'Not as much as you, obviously,' Atticus replies, waggling his toes.

And that is how the session continues. Dan and Atticus playing ping-pong. Dan asks him if he is happy and Atticus tells him, 'Most folks are happy so long as they make up their minds to be.' Dan asks him if work is stressful, and Atticus says, 'My father is an art dealer,' as if no more explanation is required. Dan doesn't know why his father being an art dealer should have anything to do with Atticus's work but feels probing would make him look ignorant and judgemental.

Dan's nan wouldn't like the self-assured look on Atticus's face, or those shoes. She'd tut loudly and say, 'He thinks he's *something*.' For some absurd reason, the thought of his nan meeting Atticus makes Dan want to smile.

His nan understood him in a way his parents and sister never did. When he was with her, everything felt a little bit safer. He thinks of her going out in her slippers – 'Give the neighbours something to talk about, eh? Me going senile.'

His mouth twitches. Dan turns it into a cough, drums his fingers three times on his clipboard, then tells himself to take control. 'Are *you* an artist?' he asks.

It comes out like a chat-up line, and Atticus laughs and says, 'I'm permanently dissatisfied. That's probably the same thing.'

Atticus has a great laugh. Dan tells himself not to be distracted by an open mouth and a row of white pearly teeth. He swallows a sigh, girds his loins, and says, 'What made you book the appointment to come here? Did something specific happen?'

Atticus looks at him for a long moment, then says, 'I'd been working on a gallery opening for a long time. It ended and I felt . . . bereft.'

'Bereft as in missing something or someone?'

'Yes,' Atticus says, not answering the question.

'Do you still feel that way?'

Something flashes across Atticus's face then, but it's gone too quickly for Dan to decipher it. 'Not right now, no.'

Sometimes conversations have a rhythm that Dan can spot and count. A cadence, a staccato beat. Right now, this one is taking a pause, while the string section draws back their bows and the saxophonist takes a deep breath before his final solo. Dan wishes he could stay here in the silence. Wishes he could be the bird-flute in Prokofiev's *Peter and the Wolf*, light and cheerful. But Dan has a job to do: Dan has a grave to dig for Atticus to bury his ghosts in. Dan has to be the French-horn wolf.

'Have you ever taken medication for depression?'

Atticus looks at him so sadly then, as if Dan has somehow let him down. 'You want me to take pills? Find fake happiness in plastic placebos and push me out of the door? How very disappointing.'

'No!' Dan jumps up, surprised by his vehemence. 'Not at all. I don't believe in medicine, not unless everything else has failed. I believe in . . .' He almost says 'you' but switches to 'keep fit, and dogs' at the last minute. Where the fuck did 'keep fit' come from? Dan wonders. He imagines his cousin Luke saying, 'Dude, the eighties just called. They want their language back.' He looks down at his notepad and writes, *Where is my mind?* then circles it to look like he's had some profound insight about his patient.

His training seems to have deserted him. Nothing in any of the many books he has read has prepared him for what to do when you had a client like Atticus. A client who made you want to check you didn't have any traces of lunch between your teeth. Dan racks his brains for tactics on how to pull the session back on track. What he needs is a nice stock question.

Atticus hums in the awkward silence, then says, 'And how *do* you?' When Dan looks up Atticus is smiling again, a smile that says, 'You like me. I know you know you like me.'

'How do I what?'

'Keep so very fit?' Atticus says, his face a picture of innocence.

'I run,' Dan says, flushing furiously, then adds, 'and I encourage my patients to do the same.'

'Sounds great. Perhaps I'll try it.'

Dan thinks of the husbands he has counselled, after they had taken up road cycling, lost weight and had the affair with their secretary. After they had moved into a one-bedroom flat littered with takeaway boxes, cheap underwear and silence where their family should have been. After they had crawled back, tails between their toned thighs, and begged their wives to forgive them, offering to go and 'see someone'. Like Fitz, when he thinks he's been forgiven before the stolen sausage has even been swallowed, the husbands would come, full of remorse, but quickly decide they'd repented enough. Then there would be the moment when they shrugged their shoulders, looked at Dan and said, 'I know it was a stupid thing to do, but, *Jesus*, man, she was something, know what I mean? No one could have said no to her.' For a moment the wife was forgotten again as their face lit up with a dreamlike sheen. Dan, loyal as his Labrador and prim as a schoolmistress, would clear his throat and say something like, 'How did you meet your wife?'

But there is something about Atticus. Something in the way the air bends around him, about the shape of his spine. Dan has a premonition that one day he could be in counselling with a dreamlike sheen on his face, trying and failing to regret whatever is about to happen.

Because something is going to happen. Dan can feel it, feel the universe holding its breath. A wrinkle in time, when the clocks stop and traffic halts. Birds pause in mid-flight and boats perch atop static waves. Dan panics under the pressure. 'I don't think I can help you, Atticus,' he says quickly.

Atticus's eyes are Fitz-like when they look at him. 'I know. But please can you try? Just for a little while?'

Dan's answer, after a pause, is a single nod.

The universe can't wait for them any longer.

Lizzie

(I don't wanna talk about it)

THE AIR INSIDE IS pea-soup thick. Dust spirals in shafts of sunlight. Some of the women call it magical, but Lizzie thinks the place just needs a good vacuuming. It's a big house and must have been beautiful once. Now it's like the women who live inside it – bruised, used, dressed in items scavenged from rummage sales and charity shops. There is the odd bit of glamour, a starburst mirror in the entrance hall and a sheepskin rug spread over a chaise longue. The windows, though smeared, are large and topped with art deco panels of yellow and red. The banister has ornate spindles and a newel cap shaped like a giant acorn. The floorboards are the colour of honey, covered with home-made rag rugs in rainbow colours. Someone seems to be doing an experiment on how much water orchids need. Some fall lopsidedly in dry soil, while others float in yellowing water that smells of rot.

Lizzie distributes the water evenly between the orchids, hangs her coat on a hook shaped like a dog's tail, and puts her borrowed wellies on a pile of newspapers to dry. She stops in the small bathroom near the front door, the one papered with roses and graffitied with women's names, to wash her hands before she goes in search of Tess, who is buried in paperwork but looks up at her with a smile as she enters.

'Aha, there she is! How was the walk?' Tess puts down her pen, pushes up her glasses and gestures at the chair opposite, an invitation for Lizzie to sit. To talk.

Lizzie remains standing, her hands bunched inside her oversized jumper. She doesn't want to talk. She just wants Lenny. Her boy. Her sun. 'It was okay. Maud came back when she was called.'

'She's a good egg, that old dog,' Tess says, and Maud gives an indignant yip from the other room – she's neither old nor an egg. 'I bet the fresh air felt wonderful. Nothing like a windy walk to blow away the cobwebs. Won't you sit?' Tess flaps a bloused sleeve at her.

'I need to pick Lenny up from Kids' Club.' It's true, but it sounds like an excuse. A part of her is missing when they are not together. Without the constant anxiety that comes with a daredevil seven-year-old boy, Lizzie's brain becomes full of the things she doesn't want to think about. Decisions she's not ready to make. She is crocheted without him, full of holes.

Tess's eyes are bright and quick as they assess her. Lizzie knows she's not doing what Tess wants. Tess wants her to *share* her feelings. *Talk* about the vastness of the sea and how *wonderful* it was to 'go out without fear'. But Lizzie will never go out without taking fear with her. It's her constant companion, faithful as a dog. Lizzie knows Tess wants her to explain the bags under her eyes and the flesh missing from round her nails, where she picks and peels until she bleeds. Tess wants to know why Lizzie favours one arm.

Lizzie imagines Tess thinking that Lizzie couldn't tell her anything she's not heard before, couldn't show her any bruise or scar she hasn't already seen. Tess is wrong.

'So, can I go now?' Lizzie says, then tacks 'please' onto the end. She sounds like Lenny. Sounds like the kids she used to teach. Now she feels like one herself.

'You don't have to ask permission to come and go, Lizzie. I'm not your keeper. This is your home now, remember? I did just want to have a quick chat with you before you collect Lenny, though, about you speaking with the police. It's standard procedure for all my ladies and I only agreed to let you in when you promised me you would.'

Tess had wanted Lizzie to ring them the morning after she'd arrived, but Lizzie had managed to stop her. 'Not yet, please,' she'd said. 'Soon, I promise. I just need to rest for a bit first. I've not slept in so long.'

It was on that first day at the shelter that Tess had shown her the list of chores the women shared, with the line 'Take Maud out'. Her name had also been put next to 'Fill bird feeders' and 'Tuesday breakfast duty'.

Lizzie had added her name next to all the cleaning and cooking slots. She'd happily take out the bins and scrub lentil curry from battered pans used by battered women, but group sessions were a no. A hard-fist no.

Lizzie couldn't have been the first woman to come to the shelter who didn't want to *talk*. All that shame and guilt, anger and resentment. Who wanted to lift the lid on that? How many women would say, with such passionate vehemence, that they'd never let a man hit them, and then did? And then let them do it over and over again? A black eye meant the blood was already draining away: the event had already happened. Where had it really started for these women, who all thought they were different? Lizzie knows her own stories, fact and fiction, but they are lost inside her sentences, her word searches, under her clothes, and she is too tired to find them.

Tess had offered to make her a doctor's appointment for a prescription. Antidepressants, maybe antibiotics, too ('That burn looks jolly nasty'), but Lizzie didn't want to be zoned out. Now she sweeps floors with a zeal not seen in the shelter, where women sag, like bags of flour, on sofas and chairs, pecked scarecrows with their insides on their outsides. Although not all of them. Some are wound up taut, elastic bands, who jump and snap at the slightest sound. Others sit staring, as blank as walls. Meanwhile Lizzie scours and steams and scrubs, her old life playing like a newsreel inside her head. Black and white, an era she can't go back to. There was a time when her biggest challenge was how to get a reluctant reader to try. Spread-sheets and lesson plans used to keep her up at night. How she had longed for sleep, for peace and quiet. She could doze with her face pressed against the steamed-up window of a bus.

Now she can't sleep anywhere. Now she bleaches the kitchen instead of marking papers. Now she digs the eyes out of greening potatoes instead of turning them into clocks. She used to command her class like a conductor, could make the children gasp and cheer with her chemistry set. Now she commands a cleaning rota that no one except her seems to care about.

'Maybe I'll meet with the police next week,' she says finally, her jaw tense.

Tess knows she's lying. 'You remember the old saying, Lizzie, "Why put off till tomorrow what could be done today?" It's been a month!' Tess sing-songs and smiles, and Lizzie thinks how manipulative she is under all that Mary Poppins-ness.

'Next week would be better. I'm still settling Lenny into school.'

'I see,' Tess says, in a voice that says she obviously doesn't see at all. They have a silent, passive-aggressive conversation through body language, Tess tilting her head, Lizzie shuffling her feet. Finally, after an offer of tea and a quick perusal of Lizzie's room – under the pretence of checking the radiator – Tess surrenders. 'I'll leave you to it, then.' She stomps out in remedial-looking shoes, leaving the door open.

Lizzie shuts it behind her and sighs into the silence. Most of the women keep their doors ajar and invite one another in for a chat. They congregate in the corridor before *EastEnders* and *Coronation Street*. 'You coming down, hon? Want a cuppa? I've got some choccy in the fridge.' They gather in clusters, like wasps around a jam jar, discussing developments in their court cases and vowing they'll 'not let that bastard take another strip' from them.

One of them knocked on Lizzie's door the first couple of nights. They wanted to know if she was like them, if her story was as bad, or worse.

Lizzie knew she came across as cold when she said no. She didn't like it, but she couldn't help it.

'Ask Lizzie a science question and she's grand,' her mother had said to her primary-school teacher on Lizzie's first day. 'Socializing? Not so much.'

Her mother didn't know the name for her daughter's detached, frustrated outlook on life. Her fascination with numbers and trains. She just thought she had a difficult child, probably due to the 11.30 a.m. nip of sherry she never stopped taking through her pregnancy, with two Embassy cigarettes, or maybe that fall in the seventh month when she was running for the bus. Lizzie's mother was in denial and defended her only child with unassailable vehemence. Guilt is a wonderful decision-maker.

'Nowt wrong with her,' she'd told the teachers with a sniff, her too-tight headscarf making her chins wobble as she nodded. The hem of her best coat undone at the back. A wonky American-tan stocking sagging down her shapeless shin. 'Just likes what she likes, that's all. And bright? She could teach you a thing or two. Just you ask her about seahorses – she'll chunter on for hours.'

The teacher, who'd been educating kids for thirty years and had never met a girl like Lizzie, and who just wanted an easy freefall into retirement with a nap in the afternoon, had frowned and shoved Lizzie into a corner with a book. Subsequent teachers had kept her separated and given her work they never even marked, just put in the bin at the end of the day. Sometimes Lizzie, bored with facts about pandas or volcanoes, would shout out the answers to spelling tests or, worse, correct her teacher. Even her brain, which was more mechanical than most, could deduce she wasn't liked, wanted or understood.

Making friends was a long, hard battle. Lizzie had to force herself to ask questions, share toys, not be bossy. Tamsin, a tiny child with a squint who wore a built-up shoe, was obsessed with horses but struggled with reading. Lizzie had amazed her with facts. Horses can sleep standing up or lying down. Horses can run shortly after birth. Horses have bigger eyes than most other mammals that live on land.

'Really?' Tamsin used to say, her one good eye bulging in its fleshy socket.

'Really,' Lizzie would reply, and Tamsin would beam at her, and briefly Lizzie had felt like the fastest racehorse in the world.

In return for this equestrian knowledge, Tamsin would sit with her at lunch, and trot next to her in the playground, where they played *Black Beauty*.

But Tamsin's eyesight deteriorated and eventually she was sent to a special school. Lizzie spent a sad season alone, looking for conkers, until Michelle adopted her in return for some help with homework. Lizzie preferred Tamsin, who didn't want to pluck her eyebrows or experiment with blue eyeshadow, but her dad had a computer that he'd sometimes let Lizzie and Michelle play on.

Michelle and Lizzie's friendship lasted until the end of secondary school. Then Michelle went to hairdressing college, and Lizzie went to study science. She had more in common with her new classmates, but missed Michelle and Tamsin.

She went to parties and on study dates, on political marches and camping trips, but was always on the outside, somehow, until she met Greg.

And then came Lenny, who is nothing like her. Who shows her another way of viewing the world. She doesn't have to feed him facts in return for friendship, or have her hair permed and plaited. She just needs to be herself.

Since they've been in the shelter, they're tighter than ever. They eat dinner with elbows touching. Finish their water at the same time. Rush up the stairs, where, in the privacy of their shabby pink room, he makes up worlds and possibilities that warp and stretch the walls. He tells her how, when he's older, he'll find the Loch Ness monster, and Lizzie can almost see it. Lizzie, who can't watch *Jurassic Park*, can picture herself packing her son's bag with a compass and a net.

And when he finally gives in to slumber, when his baby face reappears with the moon, Lizzie writes his name into a grid of letters that will hide him and keep him safe.

George

(Betty, by the way)

GEORGE IS WOKEN FROM his lunchtime nap by someone clearing their throat loudly. Briefly, he thinks it might be Ellen, then remembers that's impossible, and no one else matters.

'What-ho!'

He opens one eye and sees a pair of neon-green leggings. He lifts his groggy head and spies a matching green top. The owner is lumpy, the Lycra making hillocks over her sagging stomach. He carries on looking up till he finds her face. Pink and shiny. White-grey hair held back from her face by a sweatband.

'Howdy! I'm Betty. Your dog has been barking for weeks.'

'Fuck off,' says George, closing his eyes again.

'No can do, Sweary Mary.' Her voice is deep for a woman. Well spoken. She sounds like a Radio 4 presenter imparting bad news. 'I'm the head of the Neighbourhood Watch. We've had sixteen complaints about your dog in the last week. Two new recruits off the back of it, mind you. Every cloud . . .'

'So take the dog with you when you fuck off.' George tips his head back, wanting to return to the custard-thick oblivion he'd found when he closed his eyes. Phosphenes dancing like fireflies. He was a Boy Scout again in that inky darkness, not a wasted old bastard in a wing chair. A leather-clad foot taps him, making him jump.

'Mother of pearl, your house smells! You need to open some windows.' The woman flaps a hand in front of her nose. 'Phooey.'

'Your clobber is worse. Get out.'

The foot taps him again, harder. 'Oh, go fry an egg. I'm not here to take your dog. I'm here to tell you to look after it better, poor thing.' On cue, Poppy dramatically slumps to the floor and lays her head on George's slipper.

'You can't come in here and tell me what to do,' George roars, rising from his chair. Slightly drunk, definitely dehydrated, and very, *very* pungent.

'I just did. I'd shake your hand, but you smell too bad. Christ on a cracker, when did you last wash?'

'Get out of my house, or I'll call the police.' The living room tilts slightly, and George suddenly feels seasick.

'Please do. I work closely with them as part of the Neighbourhood Watch. I'm sure they'd be happy to pop in. When they see the state of this place, they'll happily contact social services. Is that what you want, Larry Layabout? Nurses in to wipe your bottom and feed you meals on wheels?'

'No one is coming into my house,' George hisses.

'That's the spirit! We can sort this place out ourselves in a jiffy.'

Who is this overbearing, nosy neon Nazi standing in *his* house, demanding he clean? George wonders if he's dreaming. He's been feeling dicky for days. His tongue is thick and furry, his head is spinning and his hands shake. He hears footsteps leaving the room, then the kitchen tap running. A glass of water is passed to him.

'If it's not whisky, I don't want it.'

'It will make you feel better.'

'No, it won't. My wife is dead. I've got a sausage-shaped dog I don't want, and an ugly cow ranting on at me. Nothing will make me feel better.'

'Just drink it, Doubting Thomas. Slowly.'

George snatches the water, fully intending to throw it in her face, glass and all, but then he relents and gulps it down. It tastes like nectar, like a cup of Ellen's tea after he's been chopping kindling in the hot sun.

'Someone was a Thirsty Kirsty. Now then, just sit there. I'll get you some food.'

The heavy feet plod off again. Good luck with that, George thinks. He might have said it out loud, but he's not sure. He falls unconscious again just as the piss he's been wanting to take all night finally seeps out and trickles warmly down his leg.

When he wakes again, he's still in the chair but his feet are on the stool he made for Ellen after she twisted her ankle at Step class, and someone is wrapping a cuff round his arm. 'Get off me!' George slurs, trying to pull away.

'It's all right, Mr Dempsey. I'm your doctor. I just want to check you over.'

Head throbbing, too weak to fight, George finally lets himself be pulled and prodded. A cold stethoscope on his chest. Lights in his eyes, thermometer in his mouth. Needles. He is aware that the doctor is asking him questions, but before he can call him a nosy cunt, another voice pipes up.

'I found him like this when I arrived this morning. He must have been here a while, if the smell is anything to go by. I'm Betty Keller, head of the Neighbourhood Watch. You know me already, of course. We've had sixteen complaints about his dog barking. If that doesn't beat the band! The postman had tins of Spam thrown at him. Imagine! And he's a vegetarian. I'd have come round sooner, but I've been helping gather donations for the refugees in Calais. Dreadful business.'

George has to strain to hear the next part as the old cow is whispering.

'He's known to be rather crotchety, but I'm not scared of the old blockhead. I'll just give him a prod in the right direction. Jesus wept, I nursed my Bill for three years before the cancer took him. Well, you remember, Doctor. Now, let me think, tea with no sugar and a dash of milk, semi-skimmed, am I right? Partial to a slice of cake at about three thirty. Nasty business. The cancer, I mean, not the cake. I bet you've missed my brews . . .'

Maybe George is dying. Maybe he's already dead and living in Hell, being looked after by a gasbag who helps dirty immigrants and wants to see him naked. He misses Ellen with a ferocity that voices itself as 'Fuck off, you Nazi cunt,' but then the energy leaves him and a clammy sleep claims him once more.

When he wakes, he's in his bed at the back of the bungalow and the roaring in his ears turns out to be the vacuum cleaner. Looking down, he sees he's been put into some pyjamas that are too small for him and he's not wearing any pants. He tries to get out of bed and knocks a glass of water off the Formica side table. 'Shit.'

The vacuum cleaner stops. For a minute he forgets, then Betty appears, shattering his hopes with her tight curls and her shire-horse stomp. Ellen was so light-footed. If it weren't for the fact she was always humming, she would've made him jump. But the lark ascending always preceded her arrival, as she swept in and out like the cello in 'The Blue Danube'.

Ellen.

'Welcome back! We were almost worried about you. Hadn't you got yourself into a state? Well, never mind. The *dashing* doctor has fixed you up and told me which pills you need to take and when. You'll be capital again before you know it. I found a very informative note from Ellen with the same instructions while I was cleaning the bathroom. I've put it next to your bed with all your tablets lined up. I – Oh dear, have we had a little accident?'

Betty is looking at George's damp pyjamas and trying not to smile. George hates her more in that second than he's ever hated Barbara. 'No, "we" fucking haven't. I spilled the water you brought, which I never asked for.'

'Crikey O'Reilly, you are a Gloomy Gus when you wake up. I'm just waiting for the washing-machine to finish. Then I've got to go and pick up a lasagne the church ladies have made you in their cooking session.'

'I don't eat foreign shite. I don't go to fucking church and I don't want your help.' George is so cross he gets back into bed and pulls the covers up as high as they'll go.

'Well, I'll eat the lasagne, then. You can have one of the meals I found in the freezer. Strike a light, your Ellen was some woman. And weren't you a spoiled lad? It's going to be a big adjustment, looking after yourself. Like she said, though, time to pull your socks up.'

'Don't you go reading her fucking letters. Don't snoop round my home. Take your do-goodery and arse like a bag of custard out of my house and don't come back.' As the curses roll off his dry lips, George realizes he's feeling better than he has in days.

As she's walking out of the door, Betty-the-battleaxe tuts and says, 'I took your lovely dog out earlier. Such a poppet.'

'Take her. Take her and never come back.'

Poppy barks then, as if she's heard and is hurt. George can see her sad little face in his mind and pulls the covers so high that only his Humpty Dumpty head pokes out. He listens for the slam of the front door, but instead he hears the click of the kettle and she's back moments later, pulling down the blanket he's hiding under, a cup of tea in hand and the dog under her arm. 'Here you go then, a nice cup of tea. Just what the doctor ordered.' She drops the dog onto the bed and puts the teacup just out of reach. Poppy, who has never been on a bed before, is slightly nervous of the uneven terrain. Her paws get caught up in the orange waffle blanket and she growls at it, digging her claws into the wool.

'Hey. Pack that in!'

Poppy stops and cocks an ear, then carries on regardless. It takes another shout and glare from George before she stops trying to fit her long nose through one of the small holes in the blanket. Instead she turns round carefully three times, then curls into a tiny black-and-tan ball by George's knee. He moves it away, and she moves with it. He does it twice more before he gives up. Poppy sighs and burrows in closer. Betty watches the exchange with a smirk, then bustles over to straighten his blanket.

'I don't need tucking in! I'm not ten! And get this bloody dog off me.'

'Don't be such a Hard-hearted Hannah. She needs the company. It'll stop her barking, might stop you, too. Ha! Rightho, I'm away then, back soon. Try and stay out of mischief.'

George is so cross he can't get the words out and just splutters at her retreating back. The tea looks like it's been made in a pot. That perfect shade of brown, a toffee, a polished conker. As soon as he hears the front door slam George gulps it down and licks the sugar from the bottom. Poppy snores quietly by his right knee and the sound is a siren call, irresistible. George joins her.

Dan

(The dog ate my homework)

THE REST OF DAN'S clients are easy in comparison to Atticus. A woman who wants to talk about her mother-in-law. A teenager referred for panic attacks during her GCSEs. An ex-policeman who can't get a knife-fight out of his brain six months after the funeral of the child he couldn't save. Easy, compared to Atticus. Dan sees patients with anxiety every day. He talks them through fight or flight. Tells them it's a redundant survival instinct and they should stand their ground. Imagine roots under their feet, their own strength. Now it's Dan's turn to panic and he can't take his own advice. He won't survive Atticus. He needs to run away. His life is neat and tidy. He has his dog, his job, his mum, his sister and Luke. And that's just how he likes it. Atticus is a page full of scribbles. Everything about him is messy and chaotic. Yet Dan can't stop thinking about him.

So he makes a decision. At the end of the day he types up his notes, tidies the room, taps the light switch three times, three times again, then goes to knock on Alan's door. He tries to do it only once but can't.

'Come in! Ah, Dan. How are you? Have a seat. Good day?'

'Hello. Thanks. Um, yes and no.' Dan stops himself adding 'sir' at the end of his sentence and lurks by the door instead of sitting. 'I'd like to refer Atticus to someone else in the practice. Please.' There, he's said it.

Alan sets his pen down on his desk and smiles. 'I'm assuming you know him, or a relative of his?'

'Um, no.' Don't wring your hands like that, Dan, he tells himself.

'Have you worked with him in the past?'

'No.'

'Then what is your reason?'

Dan thinks of new white shirts in cellophane packets. Tins in the supermarket, labels facing front. The pink of Fitz's paws after a bath.

'A personality clash?' Dan's voice goes up at the end.

'Dan,' Alan takes off his glasses and rubs his eyes, 'I think you're a good counsellor. We've had nothing but praise for you from your clients. I think you could go on to be a great counsellor. But you won't be able to do that until you've dealt with tricky cases.'

'Like Atticus?' Dan feels everything inside him crumple.

'Like Atticus.'

'Do you think he even needs to be in counselling?' Dan knows this is very bad advertising.

'Dan, I think everyone needs to be in counselling. We both attend counselling ourselves, do we not?'

'The unexamined mind . . .' Dan murmurs, thinking of Atticus.

'Exactly! Atticus is an interesting case. Someone you can sink your teeth into. His notes are brief, but he's been in and out of therapy for years. Something keeps bringing him back so it's up to you to find out what that is. Relish the opportunity.'

Years? Dan thinks. That's even worse. If no one else has been able to get to the root of Atticus's problem, Dan certainly won't manage it. Atticus makes his mind go blank and his mouth go dry. Atticus makes him aware of the position he's sitting in, how tight his jeans are. These are not helpful or illuminating observations.

Dan sighs and looks at his watch. He wants to be on the bus, on his way home to Fitz. 'I don't think I can,' Dan admits, wondering if he's really prepared to lose his job over some pink suede loafers. All that money he saved and spent on his training.

'I think you can. I think you just don't *want* to.' Alan peers at him. 'Is it because you're attracted to Atticus?'

Dan's head shoots up in alarm, denial bleeding from every pore. 'What? No. Of course not.'

'Can I remind you that a relationship between a counsellor and their client is completely unacceptable?'

'Of course!' Dan says. 'It's not that.' In his head he hears Atticus murmur, 'Methinks the lady doth protest too much.'

'Nothing like that,' Dan says.

'Okay, Dan,' Alan says finally. 'Here's what we'll do. You'll continue to see Atticus for two more sessions. If, after that, you've made no progress or you still feel *uncomfortable*' – he says the word with an emphasis that makes Dan blush – 'then I'll take him on as a client. You'll have to tell him why, though.' Dan wants to gulp. Instead he scrunches his toes in his trainers till they hurt. 'And I'd like to meet with you twice a week to debrief on all your cases.'

'Have I done something wrong?' Dan asks. Alan had said he was doing well, hadn't he?

'Not at all. Learning to detach from your clients and their concerns is a hard skill to master. There are cases that get under my skin even now. I want to make sure you're not holding your client's emotions after they've left the session. Think of it as a ritual cleansing. Burning the sage.'

Dan knows there's no point in arguing. No point in trying to say more. He thanks Alan for his time and closes the door behind him.

The Beacon is one of Dan's favourite places in the world. Even in the rain, it welcomes you. The windmill is always there and always will be. Dan doesn't need to count its arms. There are six, and always will be. Six arms splayed out, like sunbeams. It always has its hat on. Dan and Fitz have explored every inch, every nook and cranny of the Beacon. They have had Famous Five-worthy picnics with lashings of ginger beer. Dan has sped down every hump on his BMX. He knows every dip of his happy place. Here the wind dries him out, like laundry on a line, pushes his hair from his eyes, washes him clean.

It was his mother who first introduced him to the Beacon, and the village of Rottingdean, where he now lives. A quieter seafront, just along the road from Brighton, a hidden gem, centred round a pond and a church, with a village green that hosts village fetes. Rottingdean is also the site of Kipling Gardens, maintained by the locals and named after the man himself. Rudyard Kipling rented a house in the town, and there is a crumbly old museum upstairs in the library with a not-at-all-lifelike waxwork of an old man.

When they used to visit, Dan's mother would park her car by the Beacon and catch the bus into the centre of Brighton. Dan wanted to tell her he was happy where he was. That he liked how deserted the beach was, and the lollies sold in the shop on the corner. His cousin Luke, who liked to be a big fish in a small pond, was similarly infatuated with the place, and with the local girls, their sunburned shoulders. He dived into the waves, cycled with no hands along the promenade, flirted with the daughters of the fish-and-chip man. As they grew older, and wanted to move away from their home town, Rottingdean was a natural choice.

While he pauses for Fitz to poo, Dan thinks back to his conversation with Alan and wants to kick himself. What was he thinking, running to the teacher like a schoolboy? He should have known Alan would turn it into something. He's a counsellor. That is what they do. Now Alan is going to keep asking Dan how he feels. Like a fraud, Dan thinks. Like an idiot. Fitz finishes, then walks three feet away to dig up the earth nearby, his pants puffs of steam. His yellow fur glints in the evening light and his muscles ripple under his slight (cheese lovers, the pair of them) fat roll. He was made for running. His legs are pistons, his haunches the shape of tennis racquets as he canters, mouth agape, tongue lolling.

Fitz fills Dan with the simplest form of love. Comfort. Fitz is nursery food, coddled eggs, honey and milk. Dan admires his dog chasing an abandoned crisp packet as men in flat caps appreciate thoroughbred horses trotting out at the Grand National. There is no better dog, never could be.

Yet Fitz was a risk. Dogs are messy and uncontrollable, need a lot of time and effort. Spread hair and mud, and dribble. They force you to be sociable with others when out walking. Dan hadn't wanted a dog, but then Luke got Wolfie and Dan found himself falling to his knees to ruffle the dog's furry ears. Dirty jeans be damned. Dan would laugh out loud when the oversized dog scrambled into his lap, knocking him backwards onto his heels, covering him with wet laps of his tongue.

It was not long before Luke turned up at Dan's with a bundle of fluff. A pink nose poked out, and two brown eyes appeared from the wrinkles in its face. Dan had never seen such kind eyes.

'Oh,' he had said, backing away as his heart and resolve melted, like candle wax. 'Ah.'

The dog had slipped from Luke's grasp and wobbled over to Dan, who found his arms were already outstretched, waiting, like the windmill, to welcome his boy home.

'All done, fella? Good to go?' Dan asks now. Fitz answers with a head-back howl. They complete their final lap, then head home, nodding to the evening regulars carrying the ubiquitous little black bags that swing in the evening wind. Since Atticus, though, nothing feels regular any more.

At home Dan cooks spaghetti for twelve minutes, slices tomato and prepares a smoothie for the morning. Fitz paces up and down with Dan's running sock until he's ordered to put it back in the washing, which he carefully does.

Dan calls his mother, who tells him what she had for dinner and describes the neighbours' various ailments. 'He's got that disabled badge, Dan, but I've seen him jogging from the car to the loo.'

'Have you?' Dan says indulgently.

'I have, Dan. It's all that funny food she cooks. The smells that come out of her kitchen window. I worry about my washing.'

Dan hums and tuts and asks about his sister. 'Do you think Dave is going to pop the question while they're away in Tenerife?'

'I hope so, Dan, I really do. They've been together four years now. Your dad would've liked that . . . What a shame he won't be here to see her get married . . .'

Dan changes the subject before the tears start.

Lizzie

(Fancy seeing you here)

'LENNY, SCHOOL IS GOING to be fun. You'll make lots of new friends.' Lizzie is trying to convince herself as much as him. She doesn't want Lenny to go. She wants to keep him by her side, tuck him under her arm, cling to his hand. Fill her lungs with his sunshine. She wants to be his only friend, like he is hers.

Instead she adjusts the collar of his second-hand polo shirt and sweeps his too-long hair out of his eyes. He refuses to let her cut it. 'Don't want to go.'

This is a lie. Lizzie knows Lenny is bored, and desperate to get out of the shelter, and his loyalty makes her heart ache so much she has to cover it briefly with her hand. 'You've been out of school too long. It's been over a month now. You need to get back in the classroom. I wish I got to go to school! Just think of the football in the playground and I'll be there afterwards with a Mars bar and I'll ask Tess if we can make cupcakes later.' Lizzie watches Lenny pretending to waver. There are no boys his age in the shelter and she is rubbish in goal. She's always too afraid to dive.

Lenny lets her waffle on about all the fun he's going to

have as she walks him across the blustery Beacon. Maud trots along beside them, peering left and right. Lizzie wonders what or who for.

Taking Maud with her on her walks has become second nature now. Tess is always grateful. 'Thank you, Lizzie, always so much to do. I'd love to have time to wander over hills and dales with the old girl, but duties prevail.' Tess is certainly married to her job, but her adoration of Maud is obvious. The Jack Russell has baskets and blankets all over the place, and a chicken breast of her own cooked on Sundays. 'Saved my life, that dog,' Tess says. 'All she has to do is wag her tail.'

Maud seems to understand her elevated status in the house, and occasionally climbs, Siamese-cat-like, atop a pile of clean washing. 'Hey, Lady Muck, get off,' Tess says, with mock sternness, then to Lizzie, 'Only a bit of dog hair, no harm done.'

Lenny forgets himself in the breeze, as only children and kites can. He takes his arms out of the sleeves of his coat, does up the top button and lets his cape fly him across the hill. 'Look, Mum! I'm Superman!'

Lizzie chases him until they are red-cheeked, still catching their breath as they walk up the lane to school, which, Lizzie is relieved to see, is hidden away up a dirt track. Giant conifers shield the playgrounds, and wooden doors, too high to see over, are locked shut. 'That'll do, Pig,' she says to Lenny, who snorts on cue.

She presses the buzzer and waits until a tinny voice says, 'St Jude's. How can I help?'

Lizzie gives her name and Lenny's and they stand back as the doors creak open. A gravel path leads down to a glass-fronted dining room next to the main entrance, where pot plants break up the red-brick walls. Lizzie, not sure on their dog policy, or what dogs think about being held, asks, 'Can I pick you up, Maud?' The dog sits down, which Lizzie takes as a yes. 'Thank you. It's only for a second.'

'See? Isn't this nice?' Lizzie says to Lenny in a chirpy voice as she signs them in. 'Lunch smells good, too.'

It doesn't. It smells of every school dinner in the world. Chips and spilled milk. Lizzie moves on into the foyer, following her nose. Shoe polish and nit shampoo. Sun cream and Dettol. Moth-eaten beanbags. Sweaty plimsolls. Herself. Lizzie can smell her old self in here. Wishes she was behind one of those closed doors, with a class of children in front of her and a whiteboard behind. Armed with her marker pen, her projector and the curriculum.

Children appear from corridors like ants, dressed in hats and scarves although spring is here. Lizzie remembers the damp smell of wool on radiators, the warmth she drew from being with children. She was never awkward with them. She didn't need to be their friend, she needed to be their teacher, but she became both. Her notice-board was always full of cards from her class. 'To the best teacher in the whole (infinite) universe' and 'You are even cleverer than *The Guinness Book of Records*.'

Lenny says nothing, but cranes his head, taking it all in. He's small for his age, the borrowed clothes too big. Lizzie wants to scoop him up in her long cardigan and take him home. She wants his nose in her neck. A shelter is no place for a kid, Lizzie. She knows that. He needs to be at school. Making friends. Learning. He wants to eat the whole world and she can only offer him the tiniest sliver, a waning crescent. She feeds him encyclopaedias. Sets the timer on his T-Rex watch, five facts in ten seconds. She fills his brain with statistics and trivia. Did you know pigs can't look up? Monkeys go bald in old age? Kangaroos can't walk backwards? She tells him that you can make dynamite with peanuts. The word 'muscle' means 'little mouse' in Latin, because that is what ancient Romans thought biceps looked like. Bodies give off a light too weak for the eye to see.

The details fall through him, like water in a sieve. Hey, Lenny, your heart is the same size as your fist. Lenny's fist is tiny, but his heart is huge, and there is a tear in the muscle, a mouse hole, that only his dad can fill.

'Ah, Lenny,' says an overly made-up receptionist wearing a badge that says *Linda*, 'I've been looking forward to meeting you. I hear you like football.' She gives him a conspiratorial wink and adds, 'I know some boys who badly need a good left-footer.'

'I'm left-footed!' Lenny blurts out. Linda smiles over his head at Lizzie, who mouths, 'Thank you,' and breathes slightly easier.

'How about that, then?' Linda says. 'Come on, kiddo, it's almost time for break. Mum will be back to pick you up at three fifteen, okay?'

A quick kiss and a hard sniff of his minty shampoo. It will have to last Lizzie the day. As she walks out of the door, she hears the sound of paper ripping and realizes it's her heart being torn in two, so part of it can stay with her boy. Maud licks her cheek and she squeezes the dog briefly, before she realizes what she's done, remembers dogs' tongues can carry

Capnocytophaga, a bacteria that can cause all sorts of disease and infection. She sets Maud on the floor and the dog whimpers in the direction of the gate. 'I know,' Lizzie says, 'but it's for the best.'

She's first in the queue at pick-up time. Maud had trotted out and stood by the door as Lizzie was preparing to leave, but Lizzie said no. This was her special time with Lenny. She sees him before he sees her: messy hair, grin splitting his face in two. Then she tracks the arm around his shoulders up to its owner. And there, smiling broadly, is Luke-from-the-Beacon. Their eyes meet briefly before Lizzie looks down and rushes over. Lenny ducks under Luke's arm with a 'Bye, Mr Williams. See you tomorrow,' and races towards his mum.

'Mum! Mum! I'm on a football team already! They're reading *Goodnight Mister Tom* in class, but I've read it already, so I'm reading another book of hers called *Back Home* and—' The rest of his sentence is lost inside Lizzie's cardigan as she wraps him in her arms, then fits her palm around his bony shoulder and steers him out of the playground.

Lenny waffles on about his day and how much fun he's had as they walk home. He's all 'Mr Williams this' and 'Mr Williams that' and each time he says the name Lizzie flinches slightly and doesn't know why.

She picks up Lenny's star-shaped hand. 'It sounds great, your teacher too.' The thought of Lenny being happy without her hurts, like a stitch. She plasters over the wince of pain with a smile. She can't be his only happiness. She knows this, but it still stings.

Back at the shelter Lenny undresses and folds his uniform

ready for the next day. There is already a scuff in the knee of his too-long trousers and a button missing from his coat. 'Sorry, Mum, I scored a goal, though!'

Lizzie grins. 'Don't worry about it. Nothing a needle and thread can't fix. Did you know there's a story that buttons on shirts were invented by Napoleon? He was sick of seeing his soldiers wipe their noses on their sleeves.'

'A button won't stop me,' Lenny says, with pride, and Lizzie laughs.

'Come on, Tess is calling us.'

Stella has cooked the dinner, though Deb's name was down. No one sticks to the rota except Lizzie. The person cooking is supposed to make a list of what they've used and what needs replacing, which also rarely happens. The person who cooks doesn't do the washing-up. Stella never makes dessert. When Sandra cooks, she makes sure all the items are separated by an inch: the peas don't touch the carrots and the potato shrinks back from the chicken, the way she used to for her husband. Tess always makes a big deal about mashing her meal together.

Lenny wolfs down his dinner, even though tonight it's veggie curry. Full of vegetables, mostly peas, and the odd chunk of pineapple. It's overcooked and sloppy, but he doesn't seem to mind. The second he's through, he shouts, 'FINISHED!', which he has done ever since he could talk, and she used to do too, once, a long time ago.

Lenny wipes his orange-stained mouth and pulls back his chair from the table with a screech that scares Maud, who had been lurking around for scraps but would never admit she ate things from the floor. 'Delicious. What were the yellow bits? Please can I go and kick the ball outside, Mum?'

Worry about his day has exhausted Lizzie. All she wants to do is wash him clean, tuck him into bed, read to him until he falls asleep, then lose herself in her word searches. 'Oh, Len, haven't you played enough today? You'll be back at school tomorrow. You can have a kickabout then.'

'Mum, that's not *fair!*' He brushes his fringe out of his eyes angrily, swiping away a fat tear.

He's tired, Lizzie thinks, but he'll never admit it. No one denies exhaustion like a boy needing his bed. Lizzie feels tears of her own prickle in a Pavlovian response to his, and starts to backtrack, but Tess puts a hand on her shoulder and says, 'Stay there and finish your supper, Lizzie. I'll take Lenny out with the ball for half an hour. I'm no Daniel Beckham but I'll give it a go.'

Lenny is too excited to remember that he doesn't like Tess because she smells funny. 'David Beckham,' he corrects, then says, 'He's, like, ancient. It's all about Dele Alli now.'

'After you're done, go on up and have a nice bath, Lizzie. You've been cleaning all day! There are some posh bubbles on the side. Frankie went shopping earlier. Add a dollop of them – and take up a cup of tea. I'll play with this rascal out-side for a bit and he can jump in after you.'

Lizzie knows when she's beaten. She thanks Tess quietly, lowers her head and forces down a lump of indistinguishable vegetable. Lenny is too happy to protest the bit about the bath. He's already waiting at the back door, doing keepie-uppies with the ball.

Once Lenny and Tess have gone, Lizzie scrapes her plate

and makes her way upstairs. She'd love to bathe with Lenny, like she used to, but her body is a map of scars that he cannot see. She counts them as she soaks herself in water not quite warm enough to be relaxing and jumps out when she hears him bound up the stairs, quickly wrapping herself in her dressing-gown. It's cheap, the itchy nylon sticking to her damp flesh. She had a towelling one at home. Penance.

'Come on, Lenny, hop in,' she says, topping up the bath with the last of the hot water.

'Tess is all right in goal,' Lenny says, as he pulls his jumper over his head. 'She even saved a couple.' He pulls down his trousers and pants at the same time and would have got into the bath with his socks on if Lizzie hadn't stopped him.

She kneels by the bath and makes him a long beard with the bubbles. 'They are always round because of surface tension. Their shell is made from a layer of water between two layers of soap. Bubbles can be frozen, just like water. Snapping shrimp kill their prey with bubbles.'

'Never.'

'True fact.'

'Cool.' Lenny pretends to kill her with his pincers and, after some persuasion, lets her wash his hair.

He falls asleep halfway through 'Jabberwocky'. She doesn't sleep, though. Instead she opens the curtains slightly, so the light from the brillig moon shines on her son and her slithy toves, as she watches him breathe in, and out, and in again.

George

(George lays it out on the table)

'M ORNING, POPPY! HOW ARE you today?'
            'She's hardly going to answer you, is she, daft mare?'
'Dogs have their own way of communicating. You just have to be able to understand them,' Betty says, bending down to kiss the fur between Poppy's eyes.

'I don't want to own a dog, let alone understand the poxy thing. What next? Tea leaves and Tarot cards?'

'I thought I'd run the vacuum round first.' Betty stands up painfully slowly and says, 'Takes a while for my psychic abilities to kick in. And don't say those things about Poppy. She understands more than you think.'

'She's as bad at taking a hint as you are,' George says, briefly wondering if Betty has a walking stick, then deciding he doesn't care. He made Ellen a fine pikestaff with a smart brass cap that tapped like a hobnail boot. Far too good for Betty: she'd only bend it.

'Hang on, I'm sensing something.' Betty waggles her head. 'I'm picturing a bacon sandwich. Does that mean anything to you?'

'Humph,' George says, and snatches the newspaper from the side table. 'Four slices, as crispy as your hair.'

She's brought her own dog along today, an ugly old rescue greyhound called Lucky. Betty covers his ears as she walks him through the house to the back garden. 'I can take your potty mouth, but my poor boy's been through enough and he doesn't need to hear it.'

George laughs. 'Ha! I bet *he* doesn't think he's lucky!' Then: 'And what the fuck is he wearing?'

'It's a coat I knitted for him. Don't listen to him, Lucky. You look hotsy totsy.'

'He looks like one of those piss bottles men get given in hospital.'

'Nonsense. He looks lovely and smart, don't you, Pipperoo? He needs it, anyway. He gets cold, don't you, Lucky?' Betty says, rubbing the dog's ears as Lucky cowers in the itchy polyester.

'He's not cold, he's embarrassed,' George says, and Lucky's tail moves to the left by a couple of inches, then back again. 'Look, his tail's moving. He agrees with me.'

'I thought dogs couldn't communicate?' Betty asks innocently.

George raises his finger in response and Betty chortles with delight.

'A point to me,' she says to Poppy, holding up her hand for a high-five, which Poppy loyally ignores.

'Would take more than a coat to smarten up your mongrel anyway. He's got teeth like a bag of burned chips.'

'Rude. I did knit a little one for Poppy . . .' Betty says, pulling out something pink with bobbles on it.

'No. Absolutely not. She's not wearing a coat. She looks ridiculous enough as it is.' George wonders, again, why Ellen chose to punish him with a dog. What *was* she thinking? Bloody Poppy. What does the dog want from him? He has nothing to give her. He's never once tossed her a scrap of his toast, let alone a bone, yet there she is, every mealtime, looking at him as if he's hung the moon, or invented Pedigree Chum. He doesn't even feed her. Betty does that, and she takes her for walks with Lucky.

No matter how hard George tries, he can't shake them off. Poppy and Betty seem to be here to stay. The other day Betty found the spare key when she was cleaning the kitchen (nosing about in the tins), and now she simply appears every morning.

He's sworn at her, ignored her, pretended to be asleep. Once he even tried being dead, but she just stepped over him, said, 'Great Scott,' and put the kettle on, then let the dog out and sang a song about waggy bones.

Never once has George asked her for anything nicely or thanked her for her help. It would take too much from him, and his dignity is all he has left. Realizing that the doctor had undressed him that first morning, not Betty, had gone some way to reassuring him he had not completely lost control, but for a while it was close.

Now Betty is his alarm clock. He gets up when he hears the key turn. He ignores her greeting, but shuffles into the kitchen for the tea he knows she'll bring to his bedside if he doesn't rise. 'Stay out of my bedroom.' If he's told her once, he's told her a million times, but she keeps walking in anyway, a feather duster in one hand and Shake n' Vac in the other. He used to say, 'Stay out of my house.' Now George just demands she stay out of specific rooms, namely his bedroom and the spare room. So far, she seems to have sensed there is no lee-way on the latter, mostly because George guards it when she's on the prowl for things to clean. After the funeral, Barbara put away all Ellen's things in the spare room. Knowing Betty, she'd march in and come out wearing Ellen's wedding dress, then expect George to take her for a turn round the rug.

A part of him he refuses to acknowledge feels cramp-like guilt when he sees Betty washing Ellen's crockery. The fruit bowl they got as a wedding present from her mother. The plates with fish on them that she won in a raffle and raved over all the way home, and which she only ever used on spe-cial occasions. George wants to tell Betty to use the brown-and-white swirl ones, the everydays. He wants to tell her the posh plates belong to Ellen, but he can't get the words out. He'd rather Betty see him naked than watch him strug-gling to say his wife's name.

He tells himself that Betty isn't quite as good a cook as Ellen. He tried to refuse her food at first, he really did. He watched fluffy scrambled eggs congeal on a fish-patterned plate for a week before giving in (okay, two days).

Ellen was a little sparrow, who pecked at her food and flit-ted with a quiet voice and even quieter feet through their house. Her laugh was a tinkle and she smelt of Dove soap. George wonders how something so light could weigh on him so heavily.

Now George eats his bacon sandwich in angry silence, while Betty crunches her way through a third slice of toast, slath-ered in Ellen's blackberry jam. (It's got Ellen's name on, for fuck's sake. Has Betty no shame?)

'Come on, Sad Sam, the day is young, even if we aren't.' Betty brushes the crumbs off her hands and removes her pinny, then uses the mirror on the windowsill to reapply her lipstick. 'Let's go out for a walk.'

'No, thanks. People might think we're friends. Your lips have gone all blue. Are you ill?'

'Tut. It's frosty shimmer from Avon. What *do* you fancy doing, then?'

'I'm going to listen to the cricket. You are going to bugger off and annoy someone else.'

Betty just laughs and says, 'God's socks, you are grumpy!' then lays out the cards for them to play Patience.

'You'll need a lot of bloody patience if you think I'm playing fucking card games. Plus, it's a one-player game. Play it yourself.'

Eventually, she gives up and picks up her knitting, the clacking of her needles receiving little rounds of applause every few minutes. The cricket plays loudly on the radio and George is being lulled to sleep by the sound of leather on willow, except then Betty suddenly switches over to Radio 2.

'What are you doing, you harridan? I've just missed a wicket.'

As soon as the cricket is back on, George goes back to snoring and Betty goes back to her scarves for the homeless.

George is woken by his stomach announcing it's time for lunch.

'We only had breakfast two hours ago!'

'Pah. One measly sandwich for a man like me?'

Betty sighs, puts away her knitting, and goes to the kitchen.

'Why don't you come along to bowls with me this week?' she says, a short while later, as she brings over a plate laden with food.

'I wouldn't be caught dead on a bowls pitch.' George raps his knife on the top of a boiled egg.

'Why not? It's the same costume as cricket.'

George looks up as he stabs at the top of the egg. 'It's not a fucking costume. It's a kit. A kit. And bowls is played by old bastards with nothing better to do. Cricket is a game of skill. It requires finesse and subtlety. Something you'll never understand.'

'Merlin's beard, George! It's only hitting a ball with a bat! Here, let me do that.' Betty tries to take George's knife from him. 'You're scalping the poor thing.'

'I want to scalp it, you daft cow. Then I want to eat it! It's an egg, for fuck's sake, not one of your hopeless cases. Why do you have to save everything? I bet you say sorry to the shitting teabags before pouring boiling water on them.'

Betty drops the knife and steps back, faltering slightly. 'I was only trying to help you, George.'

George sighs but relents. 'Fine. The thing was burning my fingers anyway.' Betty off-kilter makes him feel a bit fuzzy. He thinks of apologizing but swallows the words.

Betty decapitates the egg with a quick sweep of the knife and blows the steam away. George grits his teeth but lets her fuck about removing the 'snot' and lining up the soldiers neatly before hunger beats patience. 'Enough!' he says, pouring a pyramid of salt into the open brains of his egg, then very quietly adds, 'You're a good cook.'

Her hand wobbles slightly at the compliment. He knows

she's pleased because after lunch she serves him lemon drizzle cake just out of the oven.

'This was supposed to be for afternoon tea, not lunch.'

'Says who?'

'Well . . . decorum?'

'Bollocks. Give me the first slice.' George munches away in bliss.

'Good?'

The cake is warm and sweet, but tart. There are crunchy bits and moist bits and his tongue tingles with it all. He finishes it too soon and licks the plate. 'Mmm. You know I have diabetes. Are you trying to kill me?' George still can't bring himself to say, 'Thank you.'

'You don't have to eat it,' Betty says, shovelling in a mouthful and spilling crumbs.

'Say it, don't spray it. I asked for the news, not the weather,' George says, then winces at her barky laugh, hates that it warms him slightly each time he manages to coax it from her. She's a tough crowd, Betty.

Ellen used to think George was hilarious. Once, he'd put on a hat she'd brought home from the church bring-and-buy sale. It was pink and had a ring of fake fruit round the rim. He'd said nothing, just walked in wearing it, sat down and started eating. Ellen had laughed so much she'd had to run off for a wee. 'Oh, George,' she'd gasped, wiping her eyes with a hankie, 'you'll be the death of me.'

'Lovely table, this one,' Betty calls from the kitchen, wiping it down after she's cleared everything away. 'Mine is broken. One of the leaves snapped. I overloaded it, re-covering the church's hymn books.'

'Oh,' George says.

'Hardly worth replacing now there's only me.'

Ellen used to take her friends' hands in hers when they said such things. She'd comfort strangers she saw crying in church. George mulls it over for a bit and decides mending Betty's table is the perfect way to pay her back for all the cooking and cleaning (and dog-walking, tablet-collecting, sorting and doling-out) she does. He won't even charge for his time, or tools, which is unheard of for George.

'I'll fix your table,' he says abruptly. Even Lucky looks surprised. Poppy slinks off under the armchair with her worried face on. 'No charge,' he adds.

'Strike me pink!' Betty says. 'How kind.'

'No, it's not. You cook for me. I'll fix your table. I'll do a bloody good job too.'

'I wash your clothes for you as well,' Betty says, smiling.

'I've never asked you to do anything for me!' George feels his temper, which had been having a long, carb-induced lunchtime nap, wake and stretch. Bloody women. Why did they have to be so complicated? Why couldn't life be innings and runs and wickets and fast bowling? At least he understood that.

'I know you haven't. I happily help from the charity of my heart.'

'Well, you don't *have* to.' George wants to kick her.

'I *want* to, you old rattlepate.'

'Don't you have anything better to do?'

'Not really, and neither do you. I live at sixteen Lenham Road. Come tomorrow and bring your drill. My clock has fallen down, and the radiator in my bedroom leaks.'

Dan

(Anyone for a game of Cluedo?)

D AN DUTIFULLY ATTENDS A catch-up session with Alan
and goes through all his cases in detail. He uses
words like 'tickety-boo' when Alan asks how he's feeling,
and slaps his palms on his knees before he stands up, like
his dad used to. The whole thing feels forced and awkward
and nothing like his debriefing session with Fitz, when they
watched Bob Ross paint winter scenes. When Bob added
in a second tree, because everyone needs a friend, Dan
and Fitz nodded at one another and Dan told Fitz about
Atticus.

'He's like one of those dogs from Crufts, Fitz. Well groomed,
his hair all shiny.'

Fitz had put his head on one side and yawned quietly, not
in boredom, but in his best tell-me-more voice.

'But I do think he's hiding something and I want to know
what it is. I want to help him. I think he's sad.'

Another curious look from Fitz.

'I do like him, Fitzy,' Dan confessed. 'I don't know why, but
I can't stop thinking about him.'

Dan slumped back on the sofa. Fitz pushed his nose into

Dan's hands, and gave him a solemn lick. *I hear you. I understand. Your secret is safe with me.*

They stayed like that for a moment, sharing the silent man-and-beast bond, then Dan made them a tower of Ritz crackers and cheese with his enviable opposable thumbs and Fitz did a perfect Scooby Doo impression by eating the whole thing in one gulp.

Now Dan is pacing round his room waiting for Atticus to knock or walk in without knocking. He wants to look as if he's beavering away at his desk, *professional*, but is too full of nervous energy to sit still. On his tenth rotation, he stops to look out of the window and across the Brighton rooftops, where seagulls strut like kings and students smoke with their Dr Martens dangling off ledges. A heavy cloud sits low in the sky, the colour of a day-three bruise. Someone somewhere is playing a trumpet. The whole world seems to understand how to be itself – everyone except him. *Control the controllable, Dan*, he reminds himself, as the door opens and Atticus breezes in, smelling of spring and leather.

'Sorry I'm late. Stopped to get caffeine.' He waves a cardboard coffee cup at Dan, who has been picturing nothing but Atticus's face since he last saw him.

He realizes he was wrong, and Atticus is more beautiful than he remembered, and all he can do is open his mouth and close it again.

'Oh dear, does coffee offend your sensitive palate?'

Dan realizes his face must show his discomfort and he forces himself to make a noise that could be a laugh or perhaps a sort of sob. 'Not at all. Please sit,' he says, and gestures vaguely at the sofa before parking himself, with slightly weak knees, in the chair.

'So you do like coffee?' Atticus says, as he unwinds a long grey scarf from his neck.

'I'm a tea man.' Dan groans inwardly the moment he says it. What was that? A lie, for one thing. His coffee machine, bought with his first month's wages, is one of his most treasured possessions. He polishes it daily and sometimes, only sometimes, says, 'Coffee to go? Thanks, love,' in a northern accent, because inside Dan is another Dan entirely, one who dances to the radio and sings into his potato masher and can do a cracking impersonation of Alan Rickman.

'Oh, I say. A tea man!' Atticus is delighted. 'Please forgive me for bringing this black poison into your sacred space. Can you bear to have the cup in your bin, or shall I take it with me?'

Too scared to open his mouth in case he says something ridiculous, Dan just nods. A braver Dan, the one who dances to Kate Bush with Fitz ('It's me, Fitzy, I'm home now'), would say, 'Have at it, sailor.'

Atticus tosses the cup with a flick of his wrist and it lands in the bin, right way up. He shrugs at Dan and says, 'Don't tell my parents I'm good at throwing. They were desperate for me to play sports. When I told them I batted for the other team, my dad thought I meant Worthing.'

Dan wonders if Atticus is giving him something he can get hold of at last. His mind pirouettes with information. Questions line up, one behind another. He hears each one drop like the whir of a projector reel.

'Is your relationship with your father affected by your lack of interest in playing sports?' Dan asks, inwardly congratulating himself for sounding in control as he reaches for his clipboard.

'Not at all,' Atticus says airily. 'He was gutted I'm queer, though. Lord knows why, when he raised me in an industry stuffed with fags and prima donnas.' Atticus says this with jazz hands, but Dan is not going to be put off. Not this time.

'So, you have a good relationship with your father?'

'Yes. I just have to leave the pink loafers at home and not feel up Cousin Monty when we play pass-the-parcel at family parties. I've told my father I've no desire to pin my tail on *that* donkey, but he won't believe me.' Dan blushes and Atticus says, 'Anyway, enough about me. Tell me more about you being a "tea man".' He says this with quote marks. 'What's your poison? Darjeeling, Assam, Earl Grey, Lapsang Souchong?'

Dan squirms in his seat. Anger at his body's reaction to Atticus and a splash of shame make his voice snitty when he says, 'This session is not about me, it's about you. You were the one who booked counselling, Atticus.'

It's the first time Dan has ever said his name out loud and the word is a wedge of lemon in his mouth.

Atticus sighs. 'Oh, fine. I don't sleep well, okay? Caffeine and I go way back. It's an intense relationship. Not quite as passionate as your love affair with tea, obviously.' He grins at Dan with a look that says, 'You'll forgive me for being audacious because I'm so bloody handsome,' and Dan does, but refuses to make the eye contact Atticus is aiming for.

Instead he pretends to be writing a profound insight on his clipboard. He's actually just written his dog's name six times in a row. 'How long have you had trouble sleeping?' Dan asks, thinking of Atticus staring at a blank ceiling. It makes his heart thump once in sorrow.

'I've never slept well. My mother used to drive me over humps in the road at three a.m. to try to get me to settle.'

'Did it work?'

'Nope, but it stopped me crying, or so I'm told, and I still like being out late at night, when the world isn't watching.' Atticus's voice is matter-of-fact, but Dan's heart rabbits again in sympathy at the idea of Atticus being out alone, with no one to admire him except the streetlamps.

'Do you get on well with your mother?' Dan says, hoping so badly he will say yes. He wants Atticus's mum to have spoiled him rotten, pinched his cheeks. For her to let him for ever be a little boy round her. He has a feeling that Atticus needs that kind of unconditional love. The kind his own mother and late father showed him. Dan's early childhood was guarded by a large pair of hands, his falls softened, his tears dried.

'Well enough. She wanted me to be a girl so she could plait my hair and take me shoe shopping.'

Dan rubs his palm over his heart to ease the ache Atticus's words have put there. Atticus, apparently sensing Dan might be getting somewhere, waggles his feet. Today's choice of footwear is a pair of brown brogues, with purple laces. They both take a moment to admire them. 'Shoes are another weakness, along with coffee,' Atticus says, 'although from now on I shall drink only Black Ivory beans, consumed by elephants and collected from their waste. Or perhaps I'll switch to Tetley.'

Damn you, Atticus. Dan almost smirks. He hides his reaction by looking down at his Jordan high tops and hates himself for hoping Atticus likes them. 'At least get Twinings,' Dan says, and realizes he's being pulled off track. He clears his throat and carries on: 'Your file suggests you suffer from anxiety. I'm looking for a trigger. Work stress can be a big factor.'

'I don't find art stressful, I find it boring, mostly. I help set up the exhibitions, but other than that, my father doesn't ask too much of me. As long as I go and visit Mummy every now and again, I'm golden. Not that she even notices I'm there, the old lush.'

Dan wonders if Atticus is also an alcoholic. He once had a client who kept talking about her mother's drinking problem. It took a couple of weeks and the smell of brandy for him to realize she was talking about herself. He makes a note on his clipboard. Now it reads *Fitz Fitz Fitz Fitz Fitz Fitz, drinking problem?*

When he looks up Atticus smiles almost shyly and says, 'Are you unravelling my mystery so soon, Daniel? Do share your findings. Was it Professor Plum in the study with the candlestick?'

Dan blushes again, writes *Grow up, you numpty* on his clipboard. He needs to pursue the drinking comment. It was a throwaway, but Dan noticed a crease in Atticus's eyebrow as he said it. A momentary distance in his eyes. Maybe he felt guilty about transferring his drinking problem to his mother. Or maybe he was speaking the truth and there was more to come out. Atticus alone in a big house. No one to pick him up from school or cook him dinner. Perhaps he had to put his mother to bed each night from a young age, his dad too busy hobnobbing in the art world.

Dan needs to tread carefully. He's trying to figure out the perfect approach when Atticus interrupts his thoughts.

'Let me guess what you're thinking . . . I'm a spoiled brat who gets to dress up rooms and fanny about with lighting. I pick the nibbles and shout at the waiting staff for drinking the champagne, which I obviously want all for myself, because I'm an alcoholic, right?' He says it while trying to peek at Dan's clipboard. Dan hugs it to his chest like a fourteen-year-old schoolgirl hiding her lack of breasts with a book.

'No. I'm not thinking that.' Dan is shocked by Atticus's momentary self-loathing. The counsellor in him says, 'Explore this. Ask him why he hates himself,' but his heart says, 'Be kind. He needs a friend.'

Dan is not supposed to be friends with his clients. He is supposed to chase the clues they leave and help them confront their fears. He knows this, gets paid for this, but for the first time in his career, he doesn't do it. Instead he says, 'Are you working on an exhibition now?'

Their eyes meet. Dan could have pushed. Atticus might have confessed. They read this on each other's face. Atticus looks so grateful he didn't that Dan cannot regret his decision. All he can do is hope he gets another chance.

'I'm working with the Pavilion. They've been given back some paintings removed by Queen Victoria when dear old Albert died. I'm advising the trust on what the room would have looked like when the paintings were originally hung,' Atticus says, his voice loud again, equilibrium restored.

'Interesting.'

Dan loves the Pavilion. He's been known to lie on the floor of the music room and stare at the giant lotus-shaped chandeliers for hours. The tour guide recommends it, as long as shoes are removed, and no photos are taken. For one crazy second Dan imagines himself and Atticus side by side on their backs, trying to count the gold cockleshells that make up the domed ceiling.

'*Very* interesting. I get access to the underground tunnels George used to sneak off and see his mistress.' Atticus pulls a shocked face.

'He didn't!' Dan almost shouts. At last! Something he knows more about than Atticus does. 'The tunnels were built after George got fat. He didn't want to be spotted on his way to visit his horses. It was never about Maria.'

Atticus smiles broadly.

'You already knew that, didn't you?' Dan says flatly.

'Of course, but your knowledge is charming. Have you been down the tunnel yourself?'

Dan doesn't know if Atticus intends the innuendo and decides he probably does. 'No, I've not.' Dan's curt voice returns and cuts toenails. Clip, clip, clip.

'Well, any time you want to go exploring, do let me know.' Atticus is definitely flirting.

Dan is going to remain professional and not be sucked in. He writes, *Focus Daniel, you utter twat,* on his clipboard then asks, again, 'So why did you come to counselling? You haven't really answered me.'

Atticus sighs and says nothing for a while. His mouth makes the shape of words, but nothing comes out. Finally, he mutters, 'Okay. Art imitates life, yes?'

'Okay,' Dan says, wondering where this is going.

'So sometimes I feel like Tracey Emin.' Atticus shrugs, as if he's answered the question and there is nothing more to say.

Tracey Emin. A bell rings in a recess of Dan's mind. Didn't she do something about an unmade bed? How does this explain Atticus? Silence normally draws more words from patients, but Atticus won't be played. Dan is forced to do the exposing.

'I'm sorry, I don't know much about her work. Didn't she do something about her bed?' Dan feels his cheeks redden as he says the word. What is he – ten?

'She did. Had a breakdown in it and didn't get up for four days. Just lay in her own piss and blood among condoms and empty bottles. When she finally emerged, she crawled to the sink for water. On her way back, she looked at the bed she'd left and didn't see a place where she'd almost died. She saw a place that had kept her alive. How fucking brilliant is that?'

'You find that brilliant?' Dan asks, trying not to look appalled. All he can think is how unhygienic it must have been, how repulsed it makes him feel.

'Don't you? It's incredible. She's amazing. She also sewed the names of everyone she ever slept with into a tent.'

Atticus shakes his head in wonder while Dan wonders why. How is that something that Atticus, who smells of cologne from an old-fashioned bottle with a French name, can relate to? He worries how many names Atticus could sew into a tent.

Dan's would be startlingly blank. It has never bothered him before. Exploring his sexuality always seemed too expos- ing. A minefield of potential embarrassment, revealing his inexperience. Dan was happy to stay celibate. Now he wishes he'd smiled back at some of the men who'd nodded at him. Tried talking to one in a club. Fumbled in the corner of a darkened cloakroom with a stranger he'd never see again.

Anything. His naivety seems pathetic now. Atticus exudes carnal knowledge and, in comparison, Dan feels like a badgeless Boy Scout.

As a child, being chronically shy was hard enough, especially when he spent some time around his naturally gregarious cousin, Luke. Then came his obsessive disorder. Dan always preferred lining up the *Star Wars* characters neatly as opposed to playing with them. Luke would laugh as he knocked over Dan's figurines, but Dan knew from a young age that he was always going to struggle not to tidy up the world. He always wanted to tell strangers if their coat was buttoned up wrongly, or if their scarf didn't lie just so, but his shyness stopped him. So it made him anxious instead. Dan had had enough to contend with, without realizing he liked boys. He didn't want to. Didn't want the limelight, the stress. There was no bad experience: he just wanted his life to be easier. He didn't want to spot the cracks in the pavement, didn't want to have to pull the rug tassels straight before he could walk over them, and he didn't want to be gay.

Dan has worked hard on the shyness. Now he's quite friendly, even if he does say so himself. But afterwards, how he checks himself. Rewinds it all. Did he stand too close? Did he stay too long? Did he smell okay? Were they desperate to leave?

He is not shy at work, where his patients pay him to analyse them in the way he normally analyses himself. He knows they want to spend another fifty minutes with him because they book another session at the end of the last one. Dan feels crisp and clean at work, efficient as a freshly emptied Hoover.

He did, that is. Until Atticus.

'Tell me more about Tracey Emin,' Dan says. 'Tell me everything.'

And that is how the rest of the session goes, with Atticus's feet up on the couch, ankles crossed, and Dan's head tipped back to receive his words, his plummy voice.

When the clock ends their session and Atticus is halfway out of the door, Dan says, 'Is this helping?'

And Atticus says, 'Yes,' so quietly Dan isn't sure he said it at all.

Lizzie

(Give peas a chance)

LIZZIE IS CLEANING/HIDING in the kitchen again when Tess comes to find her.

'Ah, there she is. Morning. How are you today, Lizzie?'

'Fine,' Lizzie says, her voice muffled. She's on her knees, using the back of a scrubbing brush to cleave ice from the giant freezer. She doesn't turn around.

'What are you doing?' Tess says, bending down to join her.

'I'm defrosting the freezer,' Lizzie says, straining to reach in deeper.

'Well, stop it at once. Your poor knees.' Tess puts a hand on Lizzie's back and Lizzie wants to shake it off. Doesn't Tess know not to touch?

Lizzie fishes out a blackened pea. 'I like cleaning. Pathogenic bacteria cause most food-borne illnesses.' She raises her arm so Tess's hand slides off. 'They can still thrive in cold temperatures. They could be on this spatula.' Lizzie peers at it, missing her microscope.

Lenny would find this fascinating but Tess just harrumphs. 'Those peas have lived happily in the freezer, doing no harm for the last seven years. Leave them be. Give peas a chance. Ha!'

Lizzie wishes she could jest like Tess does. See the funny side of things. She used to laugh more, used to care less about things being 'just so'. But now she can't. Her guard has been up for so long, she doesn't know how to let it down. Maybe if she puts the kitchen in order, her life will follow suit.

Lizzie looks round and sees that Tess is waiting for her to laugh too, so she says, 'Ha,' weakly, then adds, 'Listeria is probably growing all over the food. It presents as flu, and often people have no idea until it's too late. It's a silent killer.'

'A bit of bacteria never hurt anyone, Lizzie. Instead of trying to free the peas, why not think about freeing yourself?'

Lizzie says, 'Ha,' again, but Tess isn't joking any more, so she moves on to the recycling box instead.

'You won't find self-realization or self-worth in the bottom of that recycling box either, no matter how hard you scrub it. You don't always need to be *doing* something, Lizzie. Why not use this time while Lenny is at school to think about preparing your statement and looking at career workshops?'

Lizzie is thinking all the time. She thinks so much her brain hurts. She wishes she could sleep the day away. Would welcome the break from herself. She can't tell Tess that, though, so she says, 'Right,' instead, and stands awkwardly, scrubbing brush in hand. Tess smiles and takes the brush from her with an 'I'll have that,' then walks over to put the kettle on.

'Now then, which tea-cosy will we have today?' Tess holds up two, a crocheted replica of the Pavilion and a knitted trifle. Lizzie wonders if it's a test and her choice will mean something. She picks the Pavilion.

Tess leans over her to get to the cupboard. 'Now, I've got a present for you.' She pulls out a plain white mug. 'There are paints in the dresser drawer. I'd like you to decorate it in any way you like. All my women have one.' She points above the kettle, where a rack of graffitied cups hangs, like a row of Salem witches. Lizzie casts her eye over the crudely painted words. *Still I rise, I am. I am. I am.* She has no idea what to put on hers. *I hate mugs with stupid slogans on them* maybe?

'You probably think it's a daft idea.'

'Can Lenny have one too?'

'Of course!' Tess gets another out of the cupboard and puts it next to Lizzie's. 'You can paint them this weekend. Now then, let's take this tea into the office. I need some help with the filing.' Tess bustles past with the tray and Lizzie trails behind. 'Right.' Tess claps her hands together and Lizzie jumps. 'Can you organize these by surname and pop them into this folder for me?' She holds out a sheaf of papers and a bright pink lever arch file. Lizzie nods and takes the stack of papers being handed to her. The surname is at the top right-hand corner. It's the only place she needs to look, but words keep jumping off the page at her. *Fist . . . broken . . . burn.* It's like a word search and she can't stop her brain finding more: *trauma, dislocated, infection.*

Lizzie's hands are shaking slightly, but she files the first letter under B and forces herself to continue, until she sees the words *baby* and *skull fracture.* Then she stands abruptly and drops the folder. 'I've got a bit of a headache. Can I take Maud out?'

'Now?' Tess looks surprised.

'Yes. I need some fresh air. Also, Maud is at least five pounds overweight, probably from all the custard creams. Obesity in dogs can lead to anything from infected fat folds to breathing problems. And it's almost time to get Lenny from school. I'll take her with me.'

'It's only two.' Tess makes a show of looking at her watch, but before she can say anything else, Lizzie calls for Maud, who comes trotting in looking utterly furious, as if she has understood every word Lizzie said and is thinking, *Infected fat folds indeed!* How very dare you?

'Lizzie, I think maybe we need to talk about—'

Lizzie is saved by one of the new arrivals coming down the stairs, balled-up sheets in her hands and shame painting her face a menstrual-blood red. 'Sorry, Tess,' she says, 'bit of an accident.'

Tess bustles about, crooning, 'Don't worry, sweetheart, happens to the best of us. Give them here. We'll leave them to soak. It'll all come out in the wash.' She says this last bit while looking at Lizzie, who busies herself checking for the lead and poo-bags.

Maud stays close to Lizzie on the Beacon. So close Lizzie worries she'll trip over her. 'Go on,' she says, throwing a tennis ball she'd found in Maud's basket, 'run after it.' But Maud just pads along silently.

'Why aren't you weeing on everything and rolling in dead starlings?'

Maud stops and looks at her then, head tipped to one side.

'Not that you need to. Your ancestors did it to mask their scent. It protected them from predators, helped them sneak up on their prey. You don't have to catch your prey. You just have to waddle to your food bowl and Pedigree Chum appears.'

Maud seems fascinated, so Lizzie carries on: 'I've been

looking into a better diet for you. Canagan mimics the diet your ancestors would have eaten in the wild.'

Maud barks and Lizzie says, 'They have lots of flavours. Salmon. Chicken. Highland Feast.' Maud barks twice at that and Lizzie says, 'I'll get the Highland Feast.'

She gazes at Maud in admiration. She knew about guide dogs and sniffer dogs, but she thought those dogs had all been specially bred for the jobs. She hadn't realized any dog could be trained, potentially. Lizzie feels the fizz of an experiment bubble up inside her. Words like 'hypothesis' and 'testable explanation' whisper in her mind. Her hand opens and closes on empty air, as if she's reaching for something already gone.

The sudden lump in Lizzie's throat is painful. She walks to the bench, Maud half running to keep up with her. The sobs feel as if they're choking her and her ribcage spasms. It feels like her heart is cracking, but her heart has nothing to do with it.

Maud licks her hand. It's oddly comforting, even though Lizzie will have to wash her hands immediately after they get home. 'There are three types of tears, Maud. Psychic, basal and reflex. Psychic tears are caused by emotions. Basal tears keep the eyes lubricated. Reflex tears are in response to something else.'

Maud carries on licking.

'If the first tear comes from the right eye, it's happiness. The first tear from the left means pain. They all look different underneath a microscope. Tears of joy look like a map of a city. Grief looks like boats on the sea. Onion tears look like fern leaves.' Lizzie strokes the soft fur of Maud's ears. They're dappled, like they've been dipped in a cup of tea. 'I don't know which type of tears these are.'

George

(Cadbury's and Kleenex)

GEORGE DRESSES WITH CARE on Saturday. He wears a shirt with a collar, which Betty now irons for him ('George, this iron is awful. It hisses! *However* did Ellen manage?'), and George wonders how he has let Betty wheedle herself so far into his life. He's nursing a viper at his breast. He teams his pressed shirt with his best brown braces and his brown buckled shoes, the ones that had made Betty ask him if he'd had to wear callipers as a child. She knows nothing about fashion, and he told her so. She just laughed and smoothed down her purple silk shirt.

He's not been out and about since the funeral and the trousers are tighter than he'd like. The doctor will be on at him about diabetes again. He'll have to do some exercise. Ellen used to drag him round the shops with her each week. Sometimes she'd even convince him to go for a walk on the Beacon. He'd only go if she made a proper cricket tea, from scratch. Would lurk around the kitchen reminding her not to forget to pack the mustard, and had she added extra bacon to the quiche? (Always yes and yes again.)

Once they got there, George carrying the wicker basket, as

a man should, she'd witter on about swallows and flowers, nests and nature. He'd roll his eyes, and when she'd finally decided on the perfect spot, he'd park the picnic, make a pillow out of his cardigan, turn up the radio, and moan about the dog shit. Only for Ellen would he do this.

Last summer, someone had started a campaign called CRAP – Community Ramblers Against Poo. A self-appointed man in a self-important hat and high-vis had circled dog shit with spray paint. George would wait till the man was bent as low to the poo as possible, then shout, 'While you're there, you might as well pick it up, you sad bastard.'

Ellen would tut at him and wave in apology. 'Stop it, George, it's got nothing to do with you. We don't even have a dog.' She had said this wistfully, George remembers. CRAP folded soon after – citing a lack of community support – and she had never mentioned a dog again.

He would never understand why Ellen had liked it so bloody much up there. It was boring and there was only one bench to sit on. It was always windy, and down on the far side, where the Beacon borders the home for blind veterans, there was a constant smell of beef stew. The smell annoyed George as, not being a blind veteran, he wasn't entitled to any. 'I did my bit,' he used to tell Ellen. 'I did my bloody bit.'

George would stick to the paths, but Ellen had walked in the long grass, at risk from sheep and shit, and never seemed to care. She was too busy collecting her tiny conical snails. They were always falling out of her pockets and George would stomp on them with childish glee, till he saw her flinch. He felt dreadful then, and had made her a box with a magnifying-glass set in the top. 'Here, you can peer at your snails till the cows come home.'

'Oh, George.' How many times had she said his name like that? In exasperation, in gratitude? How much would he give to hear it one more time?

George thinks about his wife on the Beacon, skirt flirting with the wind, sniffing the salt on the air. 'Breathe it in, George. Doesn't it make you feel alive?'

The realization hits him as he puts on his cardigan and can't do up the buttons. Ellen bought Poppy not for company but to keep him fit. She didn't pity him. She *knew* this would happen, this weight gain, this sedentary settling of fat under his skin. He didn't notice and wouldn't have cared when she first died. He had fully intended to sit in his chair and eat processed meat from the tin until it was time to join her in the grave he never went to visit. Fat wouldn't bring back his wife.

But something has changed. He's been getting up at seven thirty to greet the morning with a long squeaky fart en route to the toilet. He sometimes tells Poppy, 'Listen to this – too good to miss,' before he does so.

His dog-for-fitness theory is proven correct when he stops at the pharmacy and Sophie takes out his medication, together with a note from Ellen. 'She brought this in a while ago.' Her spider-leg lashes blink away a tear as she says it. 'Such a lovely lady. We all miss her.'

George wants to ask Sophie how she thinks it feels for him, the stupid, dozy tart, but she's holding his medication and a letter from his wife. He wants the first and needs the latter, so nods his head and goes to pay, but Sophie smiles and tells him not to worry about it, prescriptions are free to the over-sixties. George didn't even know that. Ellen did all of this for him. His wife had thought of everything, it seems, except how to say, 'I'm dying. Goodbye.'

Hello George [reads the note in her neat cursive swirl]

Isn't Sophie lovely? Don't judge her by her nose piercing. I rather like it! The fact you are out and about means you've managed to feed and dress yourself and you are not sitting in a diabetic coma at home with the radio on. Well done! I hope Barbara hasn't been driving you mad. I told her to pop in until she was sure you'd manage and not pester you too much. She tries her best. I hope you brought Poppy with you. Why don't you take her to the Beacon after? It's lovely up there. Get yourself a Scotch egg from the baker's. It's time to confess – I used to buy them, not make them at home. I'm sorry, but you were so explicit about your cricket tea. Corned-beef sandwiches, Scotch eggs, quiche and all those cakes. It used to take me hours, and the raw sausage meat stuck in my engagement ring. Poppy will need a check-up at the vet's. Sharon, the receptionist, is lovely and knows all about her. [Who isn't fucking lovely, according to you? thought George.] *She'll need her second jabs done too. I've paid already but do be nice to her. She's only little. Well, not as little now. I bet she's a beauty.*

You know the drill with your medication. The current order will be waiting for you, but you'll have to ring the surgery in four weeks for repeat prescriptions. Jenny on

Reception there is less lovely, but I'm sure you'll be able to cope.

I'm sorry I didn't tell you I was dying. But there was nothing you could have done. It wasn't like Fred, three doors down, with his cancer of the ear. Remember how he misheard the doctor and came round to tell us he'd won Cancer of the Year? Mine is not that type of cancer. There's nothing funny about it. It's going to kill me, but it doesn't have to kill you too. Walk Poppy, twice a day. Eat less cheese.

With love,
Ellen

George reads the letter on the bench overlooking the bowls pitch. The bench has an inscription on it that reads: *To Pat, who never liked this view.* George has always found it funny, until today. He can't find anything amusing right now.

He allows himself to wallow in misery and guilt. He'd only left the house to get his pills and fix another woman's table. He hadn't even considered the dog. The dog has nothing to do with anything. Just because Ellen bought it to keep him fit doesn't mean he intends to walk it. Now he feels bad for leaving Poppy at home. Shit. George rubs his balding head. Thin white hairs stick up like dandelion fluff. A pathetic sight, but George never looks in the mirror, so he will never know.

Betty's house is small, tidy and covered with thank-you cards. There are no frills or cushions, and the whole place is much plainer and colder than he was expecting. The Formica counters smell of bleach. The kettle is white, and the toaster matches. There is a small packet of the fake sugar that George hates on a tray next to a fruit bowl that only has big pithy oranges in it that no one could like.

He spots a handsome-looking armchair in one corner of the living room, sporting a dent that would have taken years of carb-induced naps to achieve. George knows this because his own armchair has a similar imprint. Above an electric fire, a row of photos sits gleaming in gilt frames. George scans them as quickly and surreptitiously as he can.

'My daughter, Ann, and her husband Andrew. They have two children, David and Lisa. That's them in the second photo.' Betty is suddenly right beside him. She can be stealthy for such a sturdy lass. George says nothing. 'They moved to Australia four years ago. Andrew was offered a job too good to pass up. We Skype every week.' George has no idea what Skype is, so just nods. 'And that's my son, Joseph.' George flicks his eyes to a photo of a boy in woollen socks with scratched knees and a stick in his hand, then to the other photos, then back again, like windscreen wipers on the slow setting. The photo of the boy looks old. The boy looks pale.

'He died when he was ten. Car accident.' Betty reaches past George and strokes the photo with a knobbly, arthritic finger, just once, then snatches it back. George notices that she is still wearing her wedding ring, but there is no photo of her husband. 'Such a beautiful boy, apple of my eye.' Betty's voice is tinged with sadness. 'He'd have been fifty-six this September.' He's been dead forty-six years, thinks George. Does she picture him as he was, or does he grow each year in her mind? Has Betty given him a wife and a job and a beard? Are those dog-jumpers really for the ghosts of her grandchildren?

George considers the ghost of Joseph briefly, then goes back to thinking about himself and how this news affects him. It explains why she's never said sorry his wife died. If Betty pities him, she folds it into her cake batter, or the crisp lines of his linen, but she never says it out loud.

George and Ellen never managed to have children. They didn't discuss the absence of noise around the table or the lack of tiny shoes lined up in the hall. George could talk for hours about cricket, or which wood was good for which project, but when it came to feelings, he was mute.

Ellen had cried about it secretly in the first few years of their marriage. George knew this because there were tissues everywhere at 'that time of the month', and because it was only then that she'd eat chocolate. Every four weeks, her pinny would be stuffed with Kleenex and Bournville wrappers, and she'd be unable to look George in the eye. A couple of days later, she'd be fine again, humming along to her classical music.

Once, the tissues didn't appear after four weeks, and then eight. Ellen had beamed then, moving like she was in slow motion. She had sat with George in the evenings, feet up on the sofa. But then they were back, the tissues, like birds coming home to roost. The first day Ellen hadn't moved at all, not even in slow motion. It was the only time George didn't get a cooked dinner, just a cold Spam sandwich. Wet pink meat and claggy bread. Ellen's tears.

George should have gone to her, but instead he had taken his radio down to his shed and shut the door. Ellen had her

DOG DAYS

tissues and her chocolate. George had nothing else to give her. He had wanted to hold their child. Instead he gripped a tea-tray he was making, as he carved, curved and sanded. Tattooing his grief into the pale wood.

And so, because George has never been a father, has never lost a living child, he cannot conjure up a living Joseph, forever ten, or the man he might have been. He can only imagine tiny bones in dry soil, and it makes him think of graves, which makes him think of Ellen. Another person would have said, 'Sorry for your loss,' or some other trite platitude. George says nothing, just marches into the dining room and starts looking at the table, very closely, as if it's about to sneak off somewhere.

He wonders how Betty can believe in God when all He's ever done is shaft her. George has never had to question his faith. He never had any to start with.

Dan

(Any old iron)

WHEN HE FINALLY GETS home after his session with Atticus, Dan is exhausted, but Fitz needs a walk and Dan needs to run away the day, so he laces up his New Balances and whistles to Fitz, who beats a tattoo on his leg. Dan thinks, not for the first time, how much easier it would be if he could give dogs therapy. He imagines Fitz sitting on his work sofa, paws together, ears pricked.

'So, how was your day, Fitz?' he'd ask politely, pen poised to take notes.

'Well,' Fitz would say slowly, 'a leaf fell off the tree in the garden. I barked at it and scared myself. Cats are stupid. I had a piece of grass poking out of my bum. It made me feel bad. I'm cutting back on the cheese. I missed you.'

The thought makes Dan laugh out loud.

They set off along the seafront, past the candy-coloured huts and the tiny café set into the cliff that looks idyllic but sells stale buns, before tackling the spiralling stairs that take them up to the Beacon, and on which Dan can do little more than count his breaths. Then they hit the windmill and Fitz bounds ahead, weeing on every bush in sight, and Dan feels the world begin to right itself again. Fresh air and exercise, Dan, not gold-plated ceilings and naked games of Cluedo.

When they reach the middle of the Beacon, Dan spots Luke running towards him. They wave hello and round the last curve of the Beacon together. Luke and Dan are first cousins and best friends. They had a happy childhood kicking balls, making dens and setting low-key fires. They have always been close, and always will be, and both enjoy the benefits that being related brings to their relationship.

They run together once or twice a week. Luke plays football on Thursday nights and Sunday mornings. Sometimes Dan plays too, though he feels out of place in the changing rooms and often hides in the toilet. He never knows where to look, or what might make him seem suspicious. Luke doesn't have any problem stripping off. He marches round with his willy flapping, chatting about offside rules and missed goals.

To the untrained eye and a mind given to stereotypes, Luke might be the gay one. He uses beard oil and is a primary-school teacher. He wears skinny jeans at the weekend and knows how to do the Charleston, which he does with abandon when he beats Dan in a race. Their nan summed up Luke perfectly when she said, 'Luke is the kind of man you couldn't trust to go out and buy a sensible hat.' Dan wonders how perfectly Nan summed him up to Luke but has never dared ask.

Dan envies his cousin. Flirting comes easily to Luke. He is always about to embark on, midway through, or lamenting the end of a relationship. Part of Dan wants to be Luke and part of him wants to tell Luke to grow up. But while Luke is still acting like a teenager, Dan can too.

The counsellor in Dan knows they are both 'enablers' and their relationship is not always healthy, but when Dan is with Luke he doesn't need to think. Luke doesn't push him out of his comfort zone and Dan doesn't tell Luke he needs to stop making the same mistakes and get serious. They get to be the innocent, slightly daft boys they always were.

They don't talk about Dan's sexuality. Dan knows Luke wouldn't care what he is or isn't, but Luke knows not to go there. It's not that they aren't close enough for deep and meaningful conversation. When their dads both died of prostate cancer only a year apart, they spent many long nights together, putting their shattered world back to rights over craft beers. Then they would hit the brandy and carry on.

'The hokey-pokey, dude,' Luke said, during one of these sessions. 'What else can it really be about?'

'I think it's the hokey-*cokey*.'

Luke had snorted and said, 'Don't be ridiculous,' then burst into tears because Luke had always believed things were better out than in.

Dan doesn't. He's a Russian doll of himself, over and over again on repeat. The tiny one at the centre can never get out.

If Dan did want to talk to anyone, it would be Luke. But he doesn't want to talk at all. He doesn't want to be 'anything'. Well, heterosexual, perhaps, but the thought of finding girls attractive is impossible. While eleven-year-old Luke mooned over Princess Leia, Dan couldn't stop looking at Han Solo. Now he can't stop thinking about Atticus Finch, his client. His bloody client!

Atticus jokes that his childhood shaped his sexuality. Dan grew up in a semi-detached in suburbia. His mum was a teacher, and his dad a hesitant accountant, who hid behind newspapers and spreadsheets. Maybe Dan can blame his father for his obsession with numbers, but he can't pin any homophobia on him. His nan loved Fred Astaire, even though he was as 'camp as Christmas'.

Dan has never had a specific crush on anyone or anything since his geography teacher's beard. He's found aspects of certain men attractive, arousing even, but never the whole package. Luke's former flatmate, Michael, had hairy forearms that made Dan want to stroke them. One of the men on his counselling course had a moustache that looked soft and smelt wonderful. There is a regular on Dan's bus whose jeans fit so well over his thighs that Dan can't look at them for too long without feeling giddy.

Overall, Dan found it pretty easy to be celibate, until Atticus walked in. He was the forearms, the stubble, the smell, the height, the exact shade of pale that Dan had never known he'd been looking for or avoiding all his life. In bloody pink suede loafers. Dan can't stop himself counting – that was bad enough – but now he also can't stop himself picturing Atticus next to him, at night, opposite him at breakfast.

Luke speeds up for the last five hundred metres and Dan pushes to keep pace with him. They both flat-out sprint towards the windmill, their dogs at their heels, laughing but determined to win. Fitz and Wolfie are panting heavily. They're a competitive pair. Wolfie has longer legs but is prone to distraction. Fitz wants to grab the finish line and bring it back to Dan in his teeth, then drop it at his feet, like a prize.

Luke pips Dan to the post as Fitz beats Wolfie by a clear paw. Exhausted and elated from the exercise, Luke and Dan bend over, panting and wheezing, while Fitz and Wolfie lick the damp grass.

'How far did you run before you met me?' Luke huffs, using the bench to stretch out his legs.

'The normal,' Dan replies, taking a drink from his water bottle.

'Saw your Strava time the other day. A *personal best*, no less!' Luke grins, and bows at him.

Dan remembers that he was running away from Atticus at the time. He's pleased his already red face hides his blush. 'The wind was behind me.'

'Always so modest.'

Dan shrugs and says, 'Hey, are we doing the Brighton marathon this year?' He and Luke have run it for the last four years, raising money for the Macmillan nurses, who helped their respective fathers. Dan loves the training. All those numbers and segments to study. Luke loves all the extra carbs, and the women cheering from the sides.

'Dunno, dude. I fancy something different.' Luke drops to the ground for a set of push-ups. 'I'm thinking . . . Ironman. We're pretty fit and it looks like fun.'

'It looks horrible,' Dan says flatly, dropping to join him.

'Hideous. Run, swim, bike. Fucking disgusting. So, you're in?'

'Obviously,' Dan says, on a groan, as he finishes his set. They high-five, adding the finger waggle they made up when they were ten and can't seem to drop.

'We're going to have to be *super*-disciplined. I'll start a training schedule.' Dan thinks of spreadsheets and formulae, all that restriction. An Ironman suddenly seems like the best idea Luke's ever had.

Lizzie

(How can she say no?)

HAVING LEFT FAR TOO early for school pick-up, Lizzie has time to kill, so she goes into the post office to get a Mars bar for Lenny. The woman behind the till recognizes Maud and Lizzie stiffens, wondering if she's guessed Lizzie is one of Tess's refugees.

'Hello, Duchess, how are you today?' the woman says to Maud, who rolls over and wiggles her slightly wonky nipples in delight. Lizzie thinks 'Duchess' is an ambitious nickname.

If the woman suspects Lizzie is a 'battered woman', she never mentions it. Just pets Maud, asks if the Mars bar is all she wants ('Two for one on Murray Mints') and compliments her scarf. 'Such a lovely colour, all autumnal. Did you knit it yourself?'

'No.' Lizzie knows she's being rude – her mother has told her a million times – but she can't help it. Small-talk with strangers always seems to choke her. She'd got better at it *before*. Had gone to the same cashier each week when she did her food shopping, enjoyed their chats about recycled packaging. They'd even begun to share the odd recipe.

Then there were the school mums, with a son or a

daughter who didn't fit in. Another Tamsin, another Lizzie. She'd understood those mums, pressed tea into their wringing hands, reassured them about their brilliant children. The wonderful futures that lay ahead. Lizzie's throat burns with longing for her old life, her old self. That hard-won confidence is long gone. Now everyone is dangerous to her.

She contemplates just taking off the scarf and giving it to the woman. 'I can't knit. Someone else made it.'

She didn't know who. She had taken it from the peg at the shelter. No doubt it was crafted by a woman who deserved the warmth far more than she did.

'Well, it's lovely. Does she sell them too?'

'I don't know. I didn't ask,' Lizzie says, wanting to bolt.

'Maybe you could ask her. I'd love one for my niece. She needs to cover herself up a bit more.'

'Oh.' Lizzie fights a wave of panic and squishes the Mars bar in her sweaty fist.

'I've told her no one will want to buy the ice-cream van if she's giving away the lollies for free, but she won't listen.' The woman laughs at her own joke.

'Bye, then.' Lizzie does her best attempt at a smiling face and the woman beams back, eyes magnified by her thick glasses. Lizzie wants to feel a connection again, badly, but she can't let her guard down. She did it before and look what happened. No. Her and Lenny's safety is more important than making friends, for now. Lizzie hopes it won't be for ever.

'So, you'll ask her, then?'

'Yes.' Another lie. She pulls open the heavy door, and a gust of sea air slaps her in the face. Cold, sharp and salty. She has one foot on the pavement outside, and is tugging at Maud, who's growling at some wrapping paper with cats on it, when the woman says, 'When will you pop back in? It's her birthday soon, my niece, and it might take a while to make.'

'I don't know.' Lizzie thinks about Lenny and his creative excuses. 'She's very busy. Knitting takes a long time, and she has arthritis, although knitting is good for arthritis.'

'Right. Well. You just let me know, then.'

'The first knitting union was for men only. When it was first started in Paris, in 1527, no women were allowed.'

'Is that a fact?'

'Yes.' Lizzie never lies about facts.

'Well I never. You learn something new every day.' The woman beams at Lizzie now, her rheumy eyes squinting behind those specs.

Once out of the shop, Lizzie rips off the scarf and shoves it into her bag. She's cold again within seconds, but wearing it is risky. A small-talking point.

She marches up to the school, faster than Maud would like, and lurks at the back of the playground, hoping to grab Lenny and go. Not wanting to see Mr Williams and not sure why. 'No dogs allowed,' comes a voice from behind her, and Lizzie turns to see the caretaker. 'You'll have to tie her to the gate, love, same as everyone else.' No doubt he sees Lizzie as another overly precious mother, a law unto herself.

'But she's not mine,' Lizzie says. 'Statistically, there is a high chance she'll run off if I leave her. Or someone could take her. I'm currently testing her abilities. She's more intelligent than she appears.'

The caretaker looks at Maud briefly, then tuts and tells Lizzie she'll have to stay back until the playground is empty. Then she can take the dog to the door. From a duchess to a pariah in less than ten minutes, Lizzie thinks. Welcome to my world.

'Or I can send your son out to you. What does he look like?'

Lizzie can see that he wants to help, knows she's being awkward again, but she can't help it. 'No.' Lenny wouldn't like that at all. He'll want to see her face in the crowd. He'll be looking out for her. 'I'll wait till the end.'

The caretaker shrugs and Lizzie waits anxiously until the playground clears, cursing the mothers who stand around laughing and gossiping. Go home, she thinks. Go home and let me get to my son.

She sees them surreptitiously appraising her, just like the women at the shelter did. They eye her up and down, her shoes, hair, eyebrows, waistline, nails, handbag. A million pit-falls, tests with no answers you can learn beforehand. Lizzie knows she's got it all wrong. She's got naturally thick hair that doesn't need dyeing, enviable eyebrows and a small waist. Greg had told her that when she asked why women hated her. 'And that brain. So sharp it's a weapon.'

Greg was equally smart. Could keep up with her fact for fact, would lie in bed with her on Sundays and test her on marine biology. She had to take off a piece of clothing for every fact she got wrong. It was the only time she deliberately flunked a test.

'True or false. Jellyfish have been around longer than dino-saurs.' His hand was warm on her stomach.

Lizzie had pretended to think. 'False?'

'Lose the shirt.'

Lizzie is used to mums carrying an extra half-stone of digestive biscuits and leftover fish-fingers looking at her like it's her fault they can't lose weight. She wants to tell them WeightWatchers doesn't work. Portion control and calorie counting does, but she can't, not till she's asked why she's so thin, and even then, women don't like her answer: 'I simply consume eighteen hundred calories each day.'

Some women radiate warmth. If they were planets, those women would be Venus. Lizzie would be Neptune now, the inhospitable ice giant. Once she was the moon. Full of mystery and intrigue.

Once she had students who loved her. She got top marks, was on track to be deputy head. She was never supposed to be here, this mismatched version of herself, all loopholes and loose seams.

Lizzie cannot remember exactly when the two roads diverged in the wood of her life. She cannot pin it down so easily. Not like Alice in her Wonderland, though they do have something in common. She can't go back to yesterday either. She was a different person then.

Now only Lenny draws warmth from her. He found a secret garden inside her. A disused well she never knew about. His heart, a bucket on a string.

At last the playground is empty of scooters and buggies. Crisp packets and letters-home-to-parents are all that remain as they cartwheel across the hopscotched tarmac and pin themselves to the climbing frame.

Lizzie runs to the door, where Lenny is scowling next to a slightly anxious-looking Luke. 'I'm sorry, Lenny,' Lizzie says, as she pulls out the battered Mars bar. 'I wasn't allowed to bring the dog in, and I was worried someone would steal her. I wasn't late. I was just over there the whole time.'

The scowl slides off Lenny's face as he reaches for the Mars bar. ' 'S okay, Mum.'

'Don't worry. It's fine,' Luke says, smiling at her, with a row of perfect white teeth. 'We were having a lovely chat, weren't we, mate?' He ruffles Lenny's hair and Lenny looks up and widens his grin.

'Want some of my Mars bar?' He has already taken a bite. There is chocolate round his mouth and caramel on his teeth, and it's so sweet it hurts Lizzie to look at him.

'No, thanks. I'm training for an Ironman.' Luke pats his flat tummy and smiles at Lizzie. It's altogether too much teeth and exposed gums. Her eye is drawn to the top pearl button on his black shirt. It looks like an eye, winking at her. Lizzie notices he's doing something odd with his hands as he talks. Is he nervous? Because of her? Curiouser and curiouser, she thinks.

'Come on, Lenny.' Lizzie feels a headache starting, above her right eyebrow. She rubs at it. 'Time to go.'

Luke, who seems to be blushing, straightens and says, 'Ah, um. Oh, yes. We have a Lego club after school on Tuesdays. I wanted to ask if Lenny would like to come along.'

Before she can decline, Lenny chimes in: 'Can I, Mum?'

'I don't know,' Lizzie says. 'You want to do every after-school club going. Multi-sports. Football. Karate. You'd do the sewing course if it meant you didn't have to go back to—' She stops then, catching herself just in time.

'Back where?' Luke says.

'To the house, to our house,' Lenny replies quickly, looking at his mum and frowning. He doesn't want anyone to know where they live either. 'It's so boring there.' He yawns dramatically, over the top, and Lizzie can't help but smile.

'I just don't want you getting tired, Lenny,' she says, unable to stop herself reaching out and stroking his sticky cheek.

'Lenny, tired?' Luke says. 'I've never known anyone with more energy.'

'I could do the Iron Man with you!' Lenny shouts. 'I love Marvel!'

Luke laughs and it is the hum of a faulty machine coming to life, the fizz of a can opening, a fire crackling. He claps Lenny on the shoulder. 'Maybe when you're a bit older, mate.'

Lizzie looks at the two of them and bites her lip. There's something between them already, she can see it.

'It's only Lego club, Mum. I can still get all my homework done, and I did super-well in my spellings, didn't I?'

'Nine out of ten,' Luke says, in an American accent, and offers him a high-five, and Lizzie has been beaten again.

'Okay. Lego club it is.'

Lenny dives in for a quick, hard hug, which she holds for a beat too long.

'Terrific,' Luke says, and bends down to give Maud three long strokes from ear to tail, and Maud, being Maud, lowers herself to the ground, rolls over with her legs akimbo and grins at him, overbite on display. 'Oh, yes. One thing before you go,' Luke says, standing back up, with something in his voice that makes Lizzie think he's prepared his next sentence. 'We're supposed to be going on a school walk up to the Beacon next week. The kids are going to be looking for nests and plants. They might do some scrub-bashing, too. The thing is, we *really* need some parent volunteers. Can I put your name down?'

'Please come along, Mum,' Lenny says. 'We're allowed to bring money for an ice-cream!'

Lizzie wants to say no. She wants to grab Lenny and run away, away from Maud and Tess and Luke and this village. But she can't. And if she doesn't start doing something other than cleaning all day, Tess will keep pushing her, keep appearing with cups of tea and inedible rock cakes and that you-can-talk-to-me face, which hides a will of granite. The school trip is a good idea: Lenny spending time with a man and not going on about his dad is a good thing. Shut up, Lizzie, she says, to the bell that tolls quietly in her head. 'What time?'

'Ace! It's ten a.m. on Thursday. We'll meet here, at the school. That's great, awesome. Thanks so much.' Luke produces a form from nowhere and a pen from behind his ear and Lizzie takes a long time carefully signing her name.

Lenny grabs her hand on the way home. His is sweaty and slightly sticky. He swings it high in the air, and Lizzie remembers when she and Greg used to walk like this, Lenny in the middle, them like bookends on either side, swinging him together. Making him say, 'Wheee!'

She remembers before Lenny was born, when Greg used to hold her hand on Sunday walks and say, 'One day, we'll be doing this with our children.' Lizzie had been scared at the time. Greg had been so sure of her, and their future. Right from the day they met.

Tess is delighted when Lizzie announces she's helping with the school trip. It's as if Lizzie has declared she's off to sort out the peace talks in the Middle East single-handedly.

'Brillo! It's lovely up there at this time of year. Will you be doing some *scrub*-bashing? Such fun. How many are in the class? Will Lenny be in your group?'

'Yes.' Lizzie takes a big sip of her coffee and says, 'I used to be a teacher. Before.' Tess's ears prick up, like Maud's do when she hears the word 'ham'. She's a bit deaf, though, so they also prick up when she hears 'jam', 'Pam' (a frequent visitor to the shelter, who donates tins and is petrified of dogs), and 'flan', which Frankie makes and no one likes, not even Maud.

'Primary?'

'Yes.'

'Do you miss it?'

'Painfully.' She misses her old job almost as much as she misses the person she used to be when she was doing it. She could say more. Could talk about the smell of the store cupboard, yellowing pages, crisp-lined notebooks. Sharpened pencils and the look on kids' faces when she'd sing 'The Periodic Table Song' to them and they'd try to keep up but never quite manage it. Lizzie made kids want to prove her wrong. 'Surely you can't know this,' she'd say, and arms would shoot up like arrows. Lizzie used to stretch imaginations; now she cowers in corners. Her mum always told her she was tireless, that she expected too much: 'You want to crack the world like an egg, tip it upside down. Always wanting to know why, why, why. Here's a question for you, my girl. Why can't you just let things be?'

Now Lizzie has been cracked and tipped, poured out like sand, and for the first time, she wishes she'd listened to her mother.

George

(Currying favours)

GEORGE HAS MENDED BETTY's table and radiator, and hung up her clock. He's fixed some trellis and repaired an old stool he found in the shed so she can sit as she cuts up her vegetables. 'Or you could just eat less, then your feet wouldn't swell up.'

'Tut. If I didn't have to cook for you, Lazy Louie, I wouldn't get so sore.'

That shuts George up. He won't bite the hands that feed him. Jobs done, he tells himself. The debt is paid and he can go home, but instead he fixes a loose window and puts new felt on her summerhouse roof while Betty cooks and sings along to the radio. George has his own with him, turned up loud to block out Radio 2.

He used to love making Ellen furniture. The way her eyes would sparkle at him. He seemed to grow an inch taller each time she said, 'Did you make this all by yourself?' and another inch on top when she said, 'Did you copy it from a book?'

The bedside table with a little dip the size of her water glass. 'That way it won't spill in the night, when you fumble around for the light.' The bureau with all its slots and the leather-topped desk that slid down on silent hinges: 'For all those letters you love writing for the church.' The first thing she had written was a thank-you card, tucked between two jam tarts, still warm.

Betty calls George in for lunch. She's made him a cheese, ham and pickle sandwich. A huge mug of tea sits next to it. George has pissed more since he met Betty than he has in years. The sandwich is too big to fit in his mouth, just as a proper sandwich should be.

'It's a beautiful day,' Betty says, as she bites into her own doorstop. 'I thought we'd take the dogs for a romp.'

'Nope.'

'Blooming Nora, George!' Betty puts down the sandwich. 'You need to walk your dog and you *also* need to lose weight.'

'How's that going to happen with you stuffing me to the gills with sandwiches?' George scoffs.

'You can walk them off, nitwit. It would be good for you. We could try stick walking.'

'You can stick your walking up your arse. I know what's good for me.'

'Really? That's why I found you in a chair, is it? Unable even to speak.' Betty has never before mentioned what happened the first day they met. George didn't know what he'd do if she did. He does now. He jumps up from the table and grabs his coat.

'Don't strop off, dunderhead. Sit down.' Betty tuts and pours more tea.

'So you can feed me, then call me fat and tell me what to do? Not bloody likely. I never—'

'—asked me to butt in. Heavens to Betsy, don't I know it. You tell me that all the time. I just thought a walk might be fun.' Betty adds two lumps of sugar to her cup and stirs, tapping the teaspoon on the side. She treats George like a naughty schoolboy and makes him act like one.

'Fun?' George loads the word with scorn.

'Yes, fun. I need to go into the village anyway. I thought I might make a curry.' Betty gets up to rifle through her cupboards, muttering about spices.

'Disgusting stuff. Shouldn't be allowed.' George is still standing and holding his coat, but his hot air has cooled, and he wants to sit down and drink his tea before it gets cold, too. Poppy doesn't know if she's coming or going. She looks at Lucky, whose gaze flits between the coat in one of George's hands and the cup of tea in the other. Lucky sits down and scratches an ear, like he's trying to work it out.

'You don't eat curry?' Betty turns to look at George, cumin in one hand and coriander in the other.

'The only way I'd eat a curry is if Sachin Tendulkar came to my house and cooked it himself.'

'Ooh, is he the one off *The Great British Bake Off*?' Betty shakes the spices, like mini maracas.

'*British* bloody *Bake Off*? Jesus Christ! He's the greatest batsman of all time. Well, him and Alastair Cook.'

'Oh, cricket again. How interesting.' She yawns, so George can see all her grey fillings. 'Well, you could at least come and help me carry the tins.' After a bit of effing and jeffing, George concedes that carrying heavy tins is a man's job. The tins may also be required for his non-curry dinner.

'Fine.'

'And we'll take the dogs?' Poppy and Lucky look up at this and scramble to their feet on the shiny tiled floor.

'Fine. So, we agreed, no curry?' George needs to be clear on this.

'No curry. I'll make a proper steak-and-kidney pie instead. Come on, Lucky. Where's your woolly pully?'

Lucky makes a sound like a groan and Poppy's yap sounds like laughter.

'Steak and kidney . . . That'll help me lose weight,' George says, downing his tea.

'You don't want one, then?' Betty stops writing the list she's started and looks up at him, pencil poised.

'I never said that, did I?'

George won't admit that he enjoys bickering with Betty. Neither will he admit that he's started to lift Poppy up when he goes to bed so she can curl up next to him on his pillow, warm breath fanning his face. She wakes a few times in the night, to lick him on the nose in gratitude and wag happy farts into his ear. He doesn't even mind.

They stop at the local grocer's, which George thinks is a rip-off. 'Two pounds for a cabbage. I could grow them for pennies.'

'Why don't you, then?' Betty says, studying two heads of broccoli. 'The church has an allotment that we barely have time to manage.'

'I've told you. I'm not bloody religious.'

'Neither are cabbages. It might be fun for you.'

'Ooh, I know . . . Maybe I could walk there with a stick. Then it would be double the fun.'

'Get knotted.'

'*Fun* is sitting at home listening to the cricket without *you* bleating in my ear.'

'You mean fun is sleeping,' Betty says, rootling deeper into the crate of vegetables. 'They might pay you.'

George's ears prick up at this. 'Oh, aye?'

'I'll ask.' Betty finally commits to her broccoli and adds it to her wicker basket along with apples and potatoes, suet and flour. George insists on paying and pulls out a crisp fifty-pound note.

'Look at Charlie Big Potatoes,' Betty caws, when the cashier doesn't have enough change and has to run to the bank.

'Shut up, wench, and don't nick anything while the shop is unattended.'

Betty laughs. George almost does, too, then wonders what on earth he's doing.

When the cashier comes back, he takes the bags and marches out of the shop ahead of Betty, uncomfortable at the thought of someone seeing them together. The village is full of nosy fuckers with nothing better to do than spread gossip.

He parks Betty and the dogs by a bench then stomps off to the hardware store for bin bags and dog food, passing the paper shop, which is selling daffodils outside in dirty buckets. For a second, he wants to buy some for Ellen's grave. The thought leaves as quickly as it arrives. He hasn't been there since the funeral. She isn't there anyway. She's dead and he'll soon be dead too.

Ellen.

He had found another letter in the shed when he was looking for his chisel.

Hello George,

I'm so happy you are using your tools again. Maybe you can make Poppy a basket. I didn't buy her one as they are so expensive, and I'm sure you could make something even lovelier than what's in the shops. You could use one of the old wooden crates I stored jam in. Speaking of which, there should still be some left in the pantry. Maybe give a few jars to the people who have been helping you. I know you well enough to know that someone will be feeding you: you'd never learn to cook, and ready meals aren't your style. If it's Barbara, maybe you could thank her by taking your toolkit into the church and looking at the pews. They need some TLC. Also, the manger the school uses for the Nativity broke last year. One of the children got in it with a tea-towel on her head. She fell right through the back and the Vicar said, 'Jesus Christ . . .' but managed to add, '. . . is born,' before anyone realized what was going on. Maybe you could fix that while you are at it. I hope Poppy is doing well.

Don't forget to book your review with the diabetes nurse.

Love,
your Ellen

How did she know he'd find the letters in this order? It was as if she'd turned into God, but George doesn't believe in God.

A sudden bout of missing his wife had hit him then like a bullet and he'd had to sit down on an upturned jam crate and stare at a jar of nails for five minutes until he could stand again.

George had sat in his armchair for the rest of that day. He had turned up the cricket as loud as possible and tried to lose himself in runs, innings and the banal chatter of the commentators, but his eyes kept straying to the clock on the mantelpiece, to the half-hours and quarter-hours, the slices of time that used to bring his wife in and out with her chatter and her tea-towel.

Dan

(Hide-and-seek)

D AN CANNOT STOP THINKING about Atticus. He doesn't
want to, which of course makes him think about him
all the more. He thinks about things that don't matter, wonders if Atticus drinks the milk from the bottom of his cereal
bowl. Wonders if he lines up his suede loafers at night, just
so. Dan has never thought about someone else in this
way. He wants to put Atticus inside a snow globe and shake
him up and down. Is that a normal thing to want to do to
someone?

He can't remember what used to fill his brain before those
pink suede loafers. Atticus is Dan's last thought at night and
his first in the morning. Midnight feasts with Fitz are ruined
by what Atticus might think of him, eating cheese and jam
crackers in his pants by the light of the fridge.

Dan wonders if this is how Luke feels when he gets a
crush. The realization that he has a crush makes him slightly
giddy. He wants to ask Luke about it. Deep down, Dan knows
he wouldn't be shocked, but Dan can't. Luke would love it too
much, would crow with delight, 'He wears pink slippers!'

Not happening. He'll have to make do with Fitz, who is

great but sometimes gets distracted by his tail while Dan is talking.

Having a crush is distracting. Yesterday Dan put the milk in the cereal cupboard and forgot to lock the back door. Fitz had to remind him with his yowling bark. In bed, instead of sleeping, he imagines Atticus on his sofa downstairs with Fitz, playing video games, or running alongside him on the Beacon, tasselled suede loafers getting covered with mud.

There is nothing possible about Dan and Atticus. Atticus is an art deco mirrored dressing-table, indulgent and expensive. Curves for curves' sake. Slightly tarnished, which only serves to make it more beautiful. Handmade for a siren of the silver screen. Betty Grable, Rita Hayworth. Atticus is James Dean. Next to him, Dan is a white fridge, buzzing, with a socket that stutters and trips. What does it matter anyway? Atticus is just a client. A job. Wages. A resource so Dan can buy bones for his dog. So why, then, can't Dan stop thinking about him?

He's wrong, anyway, about those shoes. When Atticus appears on the Beacon one cold Tuesday evening, he's not wearing his loafers. He's wearing some battered old New Balances and strides up to Dan with a casualness that suggests it's perfectly normal for him to be there.

Dan fights a childish urge to put Fitz on his lead and run away. Instead he waits and watches the details of Atticus as he approaches, hair blown about by the wind, lapel of his tartan shirt flapping. Hands in pockets. That smirk. 'Lovely evening for it,' Atticus says, stopping so close that his trainers almost bump against Dan's Nikes.

Dan wonders if that's all he's going to say. Is he really going to pretend that appearing here, on Dan's Beacon, in Dan's village, is normal? Dan glances round for Luke, then remembers he has football training. 'It's amazing up here,' Atticus says, 'so quiet I can't even hear myself. Christ, how long has it been since I looked at this view?'

Dan doesn't know so he can't answer. Instead he takes in Atticus as Atticus tips his head back, then breathes in and out as if he's just learned how. Below, to the left of them, is the marina, white-tipped waves licking at the walls, and further still, gaudy lights from the pier winking in neon colours. To the right, seven miles of sea and then the wind farm. A row of red lights that flash at Dan in warning.

'What are you doing here, Atticus?' Dan says quietly, but there is no surprise in his voice, and he realizes he knew this was coming, was waiting for it, has been holding his breath all these years.

'I thought I'd take an evening stroll.' Atticus shrugs. Dan sighs and practises the art of silence. Seconds pass. Seventy-five of them. And finally, irritated that Dan won't play his game, Atticus says, 'I saw the photo of you and him,' he points at Fitz, 'on your desk. The windmill was behind you. I did some research. Incidentally, they use it for art exhibitions. I might rent it out.'

Dan refuses to be moved off topic. 'You can't be here. You can't do this.' He wishes he sounded more forceful.

'Do what?' Atticus says. A smirk reappears. 'What am I doing that's so wrong? I didn't bring any coffee with me or anything.'

'You can't follow me. Research me.'

'You left the photo out.'

'Not as a clue!'

'It felt like a clue to me.'

'It's just a photo!' Dan protests, though he sees now that it wasn't just a photo, and when he looks back on it all, he'll wonder how something so colossal could have started with something so small and insignificant.

'What's your dog called?'

'No.'

'No? Funny name for a dog. Rather negative. Hello, No.'

Fitz, the traitor, wags his shaggy tail and rushes in to be petted. Atticus solemnly shakes the proffered paw, then pats him on the head. Fitz smiles widely, with all his teeth.

Fitz is loving this, Dan thinks, looking at his dog. He's enjoying seeing me wrong-footed for once. I'm like him when he nears a red post-box and he goes all low and slinky and weird. 'It's only a post-box, boy. Nothing to be scared of. Silly dog.'

Well, look how the tables have turned. *It's only a man, Dan. Nothing to be scared of!*

'What a perfectly lovely beast. Manners of a true gent,' Atticus says, like he's just tasted a fine wine. Fitz runs off to find a stick to drop at his feet.

'Atticus. You need to go.'

'Do I?'

'You know this isn't right. You're my client.' Dan's hands are fists at his sides. His heart is beating too fast, like he's been running.

'What? Me being here, on this Beacon, walking along next to you? How is that wrong? We've merely bumped into one another.'

'Yes, but . . .' Dan scrabbles for words. 'You don't even have a dog.' It's pathetic and, for the first time, they both smile. At one another, at the same time, like a string is pulling their cheeks up round their ears. There is Atticus's slightly wonky front tooth and Dan's dimple that Atticus is going to kiss one day. Dan feels his mouth stretching, unstoppable. So wide it hurts.

'I'll get a dog.'

'Don't.'

'Why not? Dogs love me. Look at No.' They both turn to see Fitz on his back, legs in the air, tail wagging at Atticus as though he's made of cheese. 'It might be good for me. Stroking dogs reduces stress.'

'That's cats, or llamas.'

'So I'll get a llama.' Dan can picture it. He tries to think of a way to end this ridiculous conversation while Atticus stands there, looking like James Dean, smelling like Christmas. Atticus takes his silence as weakness and says, 'There's nothing wrong with two people walking dogs – or llamas – together, Daniel.'

'Atticus.' Dan wipes a sweaty hand across his sweaty brow.

'Daniel.' Atticus caresses the word.

Time stops as the two of them study one another. Dan doesn't know how long they stand like that. Trainer to trainer. Too close, too far apart. The evening wind sends orange-tinted clouds scudding across the sky. The windmill is bathed in light and Dan, who is not religious, prays for a sign.

He wants to fall to his knees and count the blades of grass. He wants to beg Atticus to leave and stay at the same time. He is mute with all the words he cannot say.

Eventually Atticus taps him with a long, pale finger. 'You're getting cold.' Dan's skin has goose bumps. Atticus goes to take off his leather jacket but Dan shakes his head vehemently. 'Then walk with me. Let's warm you up.'

Dan nods and Fitz barks, wanting to go home for dinner. They take a slow loop of the Beacon together, Atticus's legs making bigger strides than Dan's. Nothing about them fits. In the last of the sunlight, their shadows look ridiculous together. They look perfect.

On the third lap of silence, Dan says, 'Not here next time,' and holds out his phone for Atticus to type in his number. As they bend their heads together, the first line is crossed and their shadows blur into one.

Lizzie

(Maybe we could be friends)

LIZZIE CURSES HERSELF, AGAIN, for agreeing to the school trip. Why did Luke ask her? Surely there were other parents available. But she can't cancel now, because Lenny is so excited about having her there. They spent the evening learning the names of coastal plants. Lenny has plans to pick the edible ones and cook Tess dinner. Marsh samphire, sea buckthorn and *Crambe maritima*, which makes even sea kale sound more appetizing. Lizzie used to study etymology. Loved to learn the roots of things. Now she can't go back that far. She tells Lenny 'samphire' is a corruption of 'St Pierre', the patron saint of fishermen. Lizzie wonders how her brain remembers these useless facts, but not the second her life detonated like an atomic bomb. Everyone knows the date of Hiroshima, or where they were the exact second a plane flew into the Twin Towers. Why can't she remember when she slipped behind the glass, down the rabbit hole? Why can't she remember the day she died?

'You look nice, Mum,' Lenny says now, as she twists and folds her hair into a knot on her head. She's going to wear a tiny bit of make-up, just enough so she doesn't look washed out, so grey. Just enough to look nice for Luke. The thought comes from nowhere and she wills it back there.

'Thank you,' she says. Guilt at the fact she's dressing for another man, not her husband, makes her awkward and flustered, so she does what she always does and reverts to the encyclopaedia inside her. 'The word "beacon" comes from the old German word *baukna*, meaning "signal". We stole our language from all over the place.'

'How *interesting*,' Lenny says, just like Tess, and despite herself, Lizzie laughs.

'Fine. A jumping flea can accelerate faster than the Space Shuttle.'

'No way.'

'Way. Stomach acid is strong enough to dissolve stainless steel.'

'Shut the front door.' Lenny pulls his most impressed face. 'Is that a new cool saying I should know about?'

'Yep.'

'Right,' Lizzie says. Then: 'Polar bears can't be detected by infrared cameras.'

'You are so cool, Mum.'

Lizzie smiles and tries not to cry.

She drops Lenny off with a kiss, which he squirms away from at first, but then grins. She has an hour to kill before she needs to be back for the trip. There is a crumpled five-pound note in her wallet, so after doing a word search by the duck pond (months of the year, far too easy, but she still struggled with June), she heads to the tiny bakery on the high street and orders hot chocolate and a Scotch egg.

'Sorry, none left,' says the girl behind the till, and she nods to an old man in the corner, with thin white hair and a red face. He is scowling into breadcrumb-covered hands and muttering to himself. 'Croissant do you?'

Lizzie eats the pastry slowly, like she used to when she was a child, layer by layer. Afterwards she takes the plate to the counter. 'That was delicious. Thank you.'

The cashier, a curvy girl with rhubarb-and-custard colouring, looks up and grins. 'Pleased you liked it. Fresh out of the oven this morning.'

'Do you make them?' Lizzie says.

'Yes. Well, I don't. I just work here.' The cashier leans over and whispers, '*She* does all the baking. Two batches of Scotch eggs a day and we still run out.' She thumbs to a stern-looking woman in the back room, who is frowning at a row of minced-beef patties as if they are misbehaving children.

The woman claps flour off her hands loudly, then looks up at Lizzie and barks, 'No, you cannae have the recipe, been in my family for years. Will stay that way,' in a thick Scottish accent.

'Scotch eggs aren't from Scotland. One story is that they came from Yorkshire,' Lizzie says, before she can stop herself, 'and they used to be covered with fish paste, not sausage meat. The name comes from the restaurant that served them.'

'Jesus, have you got a death wish or something?' the cashier whispers. 'She's famous round here for her traditional Scotch eggs. The recipe has never been written down, in case it's stolen. She says it's more coveted than the secret ingredient in Irn-Bru.'

'No, I—' Lizzie goes to say more but the cashier snorts,

'Fish paste,' quietly. From nowhere, a gurgle of laughter bubbles up Lizzie's throat and they share a high-pitched giggle,
which makes both the baker and the old man in the corner
glare at them.

'Croissants aren't French either,' Lizzie says. 'They're Austrian. Can I have a couple of those gingerbread men?'

'Fucking women, rabbit fucking rabbit. Nothing better to
do,' the man says, killing the moment, like a popped balloon.

George

(Angry man)

BETTY IS GOING AWAY for the weekend to visit a 'friend' and she's taking Lucky with her. She offered to make pies for George's freezer, but he is too cross to accept them. He's furious with Ellen for dying, and Betty for sticking her beak in and getting involved, important, essential. He's incandescent about the lack of pie. He feels old and bitter. His belly is full of lemons.

When he goes out to do his shopping with Poppy, people smile at him and say hello.

'Is she a puppy? Isn't she lovely? How old is she?' He's tried dragging Poppy on, but dogs are like their owners, and Poppy is stubborn. She rolls over on the pavement and offers her belly to anyone who'll touch her. That must have come from all the time she's spent with Betty, George thinks.

George hates Poppy's neediness. Hates the way Sophie-from-the-chemist's talks about Ellen as if she were still alive, then realizes her mistake and covers her mouth. He hates that the church called because Betty gave them his number and they want him to go and look at the allotment.

Ellen would have put Poppy into her handbag with a bloody

bow round her neck and let strangers stroke her, wasting hours of a life she was racing to the end of. Ellen would have made him do things to help other people. Box up books, or sand down chairs. Now she's dead, he doesn't have to care. He doesn't want to bloody care.

Ellen.

Betty leaves his house spotless before she goes. She's cleaned it so many times now, not even a particle of his wife remains. No half-moon fingernail under the sofa, or strand of hair on the rug. Betty has vacuumed her all up, and now his house smells of Dettol, cheap perfume and dogs.

George spends his Betty-less morning searching his house for a piece of dried skin from the sole of Ellen's foot, for one of her screwed-up tissues, for anything.

There might be some of her in the spare room. Maybe he didn't wash her favourite mug, with the thin gold-rimmed lip, before ordering Barbara to 'get it out of his sight'. It might still hold the faintest trace of the Vaseline she would tap on her lip with a fingertip. Her kiss print, like a fossil, like proof that something incredible used to walk the earth.

George stands next to the spare-room door, but he can't open it. He is not ready to realize she won't be in there, whole and quietly smelling of lavender and rose.

The knowledge makes him angry. He curses and Poppy hides under his chair. Her trembling body, the idea that he would hurt her, makes him even angrier. He smashes Ellen's favourite fish plate, holds it high in the air and watches it shatter. Then he picks up each splinter of smashed china carefully, using his magnifying-glass so there's no danger of one piercing Poppy's paws, and the acknowledgement that he cares about the dog exhausts him. She creeps out from under the chair and crawls into his outstretched arms. They sleep in his armchair, and when he wakes, he decides to go to the shop for bread and beer.

Before he leaves, he throws his old patched-elbow cardigan over Poppy. 'See you soon,' he tells her, then, 'I'll bring you back some ham.'

He refuses to acknowledge anyone who says hello to him in the local shop. Instead he clicks his fingers at the spotty youth behind the till. 'Oi, you. Serve me.'

The boy stutters and presses the bell for his manager, who knew Ellen and therefore George. When the man arrives, he whispers something in the boy's ear, then approaches George carefully with a bright smile and hands held high in surrender. 'Hello, George, what can I help you with?' What George wants is a row. He wants to shout, 'Cunt!' loudly and shock old ladies. He wants to swipe packets of cereal off the shelves and stamp on them, sling eggs at the windows and pour milk in crevices where it will dry and leave a sickly odour. He wants to make people hurt.

But the manager just smiles at him in a way that promises no resistance. He'll help George, and then later in the staff-room he'll say to the spotty boy from the till, 'Poor old dear lost his wife. He's probably going a bit senile too. If he comes in again, let me deal with him.'

It won't do. George doesn't want pity, he wants a fucking war. He wants to throw bags of flour, like grenades from trenches. He wants to smash bottles and see blood. He wants to leave the shop the way he has been left. Broken.

He wants the manager to punch him and stop his pain. He

won't, though. He'll call the police or the doctor instead, then firm hands and firm voices will restrain George; he'll piss himself in the street and people will swim past him on floats of pity.

Outside, he scans the street for where to go next and sees the bakery. Before he can think better of it, he marches in, stumbling slightly on the step.

The girl behind the till doesn't even have time to ask him what he fancies before George grabs two Scotch eggs, the last ones, and stuffs most of the first into his mouth. Ignoring the offer of a plate, he stomps over to the bench by the window and slumps into the seat. The window is cold at his back and he regrets giving the dog his cardigan.

Crumbs and egg and sausage meat cover his chin, like whiskers, and spill down his brown shirt. Till-girl has the audacity to bring him a cup of tea. She places it next to him carefully and backs away slowly. She's scared of him and it makes him feel awful.

George wants her to call him a miserable old bastard. He wants to squash the raspberry tarts on the counter. Stick in his thumb and pull out a plum.

He wants to apologize but he can't.

Instead he glares at the girl on the till from his spot in the window, kicking his sandalled foot loudly against the table leg. She ignores him and carries on sticking Jelly Tot eyes to gingerbread men. After a moment, she wipes her hands on her apron and brings over the bill and an envelope with his name on it.

Ellen's handwriting knocks the wind from his sails and his cheeks flame with remorse. She held this envelope. He brings it to his mouth and sniffs, pretends he can smell her roses. 'Thank you,' he whispers, and doesn't know if he's talking to the till-girl or to Ellen.

George,

I'm sure you'll be feeling angry now. No doubt taking it out on anyone within ten feet of you. If I know you, and I do know you, George, you'll be stomping round the village being a grumpy bugger.

Don't. Please. I know you can't handle grief, but don't take it out on people who are only trying to help you. Show them there is more to you than swearing and foot-stamping.

I'm not asking you to skip around the village doffing your hat and helping old ladies into church on Sundays. I'm just asking you to accept that I'm gone. No amount of raging or using your beloved C-word can change that. The awful poem that Barbara will want to read at my funeral claims 'death is nothing at all' but we both know that's a lie. I have not just slipped away to the next room, and life will not still mean all that it ever meant. There is no absolute unbroken continuity, but if you are out eating Scotch eggs, you are still going somehow. You've not starved and you're taking your medication. Take your anger too, and bury it. Walk it off, hammer it away. Break cricket bats if you must, but let it out, and let me go. You are still alive, George, for the rest of your life. I know you have a beautiful soul under all that pomp and bluster, but others might not be so generous. Don't burn all your bridges.

Be nice to Lucy (the girl who handed you this letter) and don't short-change her. She's lovely.

I love you,
your Ellen

PS How was the Scotch egg?

How did Ellen know? Did she take the bereavement course Betty always bangs on about?

'Grief is a journey and I've ridden that son of a jackal to the end. Denial, anger, bargaining, depression, acceptance.' Betty had counted them on her fingers, rattled them off, like she was giving him directions.

The Scotch eggs twist in his guts and his head pounds. He wants to rest it on the table and sleep. Wants to wake up at home in his chair with his dog and the sound of cricket. Suddenly he can't remember how he got here, and shame stains his face, like a slap, like a damp patch on his crotch.

He folds the letter, exactly as it was, puts it into his pocket and goes to pay the bill. He's not been charged for the tea, and Till-girl, *Lucy*, tries to press a brown bag into his hands, but he pushes it away and leaves the shop before the first tear he's cried in over sixty years falls.

When George gets home, he stops and rests his weary head on the spare-room door, pressing his fingers on the wood. He stands there until Poppy rubs her nose against his leg and brings him back to himself and his shit day. Then he goes to bed and sleeps in his clothes on top of the covers, Poppy by his side.

He's woken the next morning by Betty letting herself in.

Over a breakfast of kippers on toast, she asks him how he got on alone all weekend.

'Fine. What did you think? That I'd die without you, you old windbag?'

'Tut, tut, of course not. I thought you'd be out clubbing down West Street, a card like you.'

George thinks the only thing he'd wanted to club was the manager of the shop, but he says nothing. Ellen's letter is still in his pocket and he closes his fingers around it. The paper whispers against his leg.

And, for once, he doesn't reply.

Dan

(*Sesame Street*)

DAN AND ATTICUS HAVE reached their last counselling session. Dan is sitting on the sofa and Atticus is in Dan's chair. It works better this way because Dan is always slightly light-headed around Atticus. And the sofa is very comfy. If Dan were the kind of person who napped in the day, he'd do it here, with sunlight falling on his face and the clock ticking.

Dan knows this final session will not be the last time he sees Atticus, but it may be his last chance to counsel him. He is determined to try, again, to see if he can get anything out of Atticus. If he can do what he was meant to do, which was help him. This time, he tries a different approach. He gives away a weakness of his own.

'I count,' he says. 'I've always done it, and it drives me mad. Probably a sign of a bigger issue. I know this, and still I count.'

'You count, eh? Existentially? Or is that a title?' Atticus says, sounding amused. 'Like Count Dracula, or the Count from *Sesame Street*? A-one ha-ha-ha, a-two, ha-ha-ha . . .' He swivels slightly in the chair as he says this. A wheel squeaks in time.

Dan sits up and rubs his forehead. He's trying to share something real here, which is more than Atticus has ever done. 'I count, like the folds of the curtains, and if the number isn't even, I have to rearrange the material. Even when I know it's even, I have to count again to make sure I've counted correctly.'

When Atticus says nothing, Dan keeps talking. 'I even pat my dog a certain number of times. I have this job where I'm supposed to know all the answers, to be sorted, but I count everything. It makes me feel like a fraud.'

'We're all frauds,' Atticus murmurs, as he squeaks left and right.

'What?' Dan looks up at him.

'I said, how awful for you. Do you want to talk about it?' Atticus toys with the height adjuster on the seat.

Dan wonders why he thought Atticus might take him seriously. He's batted away any attempt at serious conversation for the last six weeks and all his explanations have been anaemic, full of watery holes. Dan's trying to *tell* Atticus something, trying to give a part of himself, but Atticus dodges left, and feints right on that chair, avoiding the ball. He doesn't want to hold the weight of Dan's problems and hides the pulse of his own. Trying to help Atticus is like having a roof full of leaks and only one bucket.

The only time Dan felt he was getting anywhere near the truth was when they met on the Beacon and they'd shared that look. Atticus's pupils, two globes of unexplored territory, like bombs dropping on Dan's defences. In that moment, he'd felt authentic.

They've met a few times since then, but never back at the

Beacon. Too open, too conspicuous. Luke might see them. So Dan has met Atticus at the sprawling grounds of Stanmer Park instead. They have walked across lattices of fields in the dying light, Dan's elongated shadow so much braver than he is as it blurred into Atticus's.

Occasionally Atticus would brush his hand against Dan's as they walked, and once he had bent to tie up Dan's lace when they were sitting on a log, but other than that, he hasn't touched him. Dan had both prayed he would and hoped he wouldn't.

Atticus always carries a notebook in his jacket. Dan had spotted it peeking out, like a pocket square. He was desperate to read it. Once, when the grass was damp, Atticus laid down his jacket for Dan to sit on. Dan had been charmed and embarrassed in equal parts. When Atticus went off to 'relieve himself', Dan had pulled out the book (after sniffing the collar of the jacket for three giddy and arousing seconds, then three more) and flicked guiltily through the pages, which were filled with Atticus's spidery scrawl. He couldn't make out much, but one sentence, underlined twice, stood out: *'My whole life has been pledged to this meeting with you'* – *Pushkin*. He had read that line again, committing it to memory. Is that how Atticus felt too? He had frantically searched for more, but the rest was illegible, and the sound of bracken snapping underfoot alerted him that Atticus was inbound.

He had shoved the book back into Atticus's pocket and pretended to be fascinated by a squirrel. Atticus came whistling over, and plonked himself down next to Dan. Thigh to thigh, arm nudging arm. Dan had wanted to lay his head on Atticus's shoulder but didn't. Fitz had barked at the squirrel and it scarpered, but Dan kept staring at the tree in front of him, instead of turning towards Atticus and the kiss he knew would come.

'Dangerous things, trees. You need to keep an eye on them – they could attack at any second,' Atticus had said into the silence, and Dan's heart constricted. *My whole life,* he thought, *has been pledged to this meeting with you.*

The squeak of the chair pulls Dan back into the room, into the puzzle the pair of them make.

'I want to stop needing to count, Atticus,' Dan says. 'That's what *I* need help with.'

Atticus's response, which comes after fifteen seconds and seven and a half turns on the chair, is not a confession. 'It sounds onions.'

Dan sighs and goes along with Atticus's latest diversion tactic. Realizes, in that second, that he always will and feels failure grow, like bindweed, around his best intentions. 'Onions?'

'Yes. Onions. Awful things, evil. If Hitler were a vegetable, he'd be an onion.'

'You don't like onions?' Dan says, slightly incredulous. Inwardly he cradles this small truth that Atticus has given him, like a child clutches a pebble on a beach with a thousand more. This is something, isn't it, Dan? No, not really, but it's all you've been given.

'You *do*?' Atticus pulls a dramatic face.

'They're all right.' In fact, Dan loves them. He and Fitz often share a packet of Pickled Onion Monster Munch at the weekend. Sometimes Dan, the other Dan, tries to wedge them onto Fitz's paws, like ornate rings.

'Well, don't eat any before I kiss you.'

Atticus says it so casually that Dan thinks he might have misheard him. He wants to ask him to repeat himself but isn't brave enough. Instead he sits and wonders how the conversation went from Dan's counting to *Sesame Street* to onions to kissing. Because this is Atticus, Dan realizes, and this is what he does, and this is why Dan likes him, and doesn't like him, and is, and is not, desperate for Atticus to kiss him.

'Have you gone red? You're adorable.' Atticus is peering at him. His hair is messy, and his eyes bright, and Dan thinks, I'm not the adorable one.

Then the clock chimes, the one he used to wish would make their sessions pass as quickly as possible, and Atticus stands up and smooths down his shirt. It's periwinkle today. 'Well,' he says, towering over Dan on the sofa, 'that was the last second of the last minute of our last counselling. I feel entirely healed. I sleep like a baby and don't even need caffeine any more. I shall review you most wondrously on TripAdvisor or Checkatrade. Now you are no longer my patient, or the other way around.' He kneels, so that he is at eye-level. 'Count Danula, please, please, may I take you out to dinner?'

'Please will you tell me, once and for all, why you came to counselling?' Dan says quietly, in return. 'Please.'

They look at one another in silence for a moment. The expression on Atticus's face is so sad that Dan wishes he hadn't spoken.

'Can I try?' Atticus says, his voice also quiet, almost faltering. 'One day? Would that be enough, Daniel? If I promise to try?'

Dan cannot breathe. The counsellor in him can see Atticus's ice is growing thin. Dan could break through it now, if he wanted to. One hard push and he'd be in. Dan silently weighs his options. Wrong or right. Counsellor or companion.

'I don't know,' he says slowly, finally. 'This all puts me in rather a pickle.'

Atticus grins and it's a perfect banana curve. 'Daniel James, did you just make a *joke*?'

Dan blushes and feels like he's just won the marathon, scored a goal *and* completed his Rubik's Cube in a record time.

'So you'll let me take you out?' Atticus says again, more seriously. More seriously than anything he's said so far. Too overwhelmed to speak, Dan nods, and lets Atticus pull him up to standing, where they grin together, banana shenanigans, until Dan remembers his two o'clock must be waiting outside.

Lizzie

(Flirting and football)

WHEN SHE GETS BACK to the school, Mr Williams (call me Luke) is waiting for her in the office. There is an awkward moment when he peels the sticker, with her name and *School helper* on it, off the strip and obviously doesn't know whether he should attach it to her cardigan or pass it to her. Lizzie can't help him, because she doesn't know either. While he's deciding, hand hovering near Lizzie's breast, the ends curl and stick together and they both blush. The receptionist watches with one eyebrow raised.

Lizzie is in charge of Lenny and three other boys, whose names she knows she is going to forget because she wants to remember them so much. Luke is in full teacher mode. 'Come on, kids, coats on, zipped up. Arms *inside* your sleeves, Sebastian. Whose packed lunch is that? I'm not carrying it.' He turns to Lizzie and grins. 'They'd forget their heads if they weren't screwed on. I do hope you've remembered *your* packed lunch.'

Lizzie, who doesn't normally eat much but doesn't want to appear as anything other than normal, panics at this simple question and mumbles something about an Austrian croissant. Luke must notice her discomfort because he leans in and says, 'Don't worry, you can share mine.' Lizzie wants to tell him it's not because they're poor that she's come empty-handed, but a voice in her head tells her not to.

In her group, Sebastian turns to Henry and says, 'Ooh, Henny-poo, you can share *my* packed lunch,' and Henry swoons in return, bats his eyelashes and croons, 'Why, *thank* you, good sir.'

They carry on like this and Sebastian is halfway through a sentence about laying down his coat over a puddle when Luke finally snaps, 'One more word from you and no ice-cream. Outside, now.' His voice has lost its playful tone and Lizzie can see the tops of his ears are pink. He soon recovers himself, however, and within minutes the group is marching along to his version of the hymn 'Bringing In The Sheaves': '*Macaroni* cheese, *macaroni* cheese, we shall come rejoicing, macaroni cheeeeeese.' Then, in a quiet voice, he says to Lizzie, 'What are sheaves anyway?'

'Bundles of corn.'

'Oh,' Luke says, not expecting an answer.

'Did you know that an ear of corn is actually female?' Lizzie adds.

Luke looks impressed. 'You're really clever.'

'I know.'

Luke smiles at her and says, 'So—' but he's interrupted by Lenny, who marches over, shouting, 'Macaroni cheeeeeese!' as loudly as he can.

Luke rolls his eyes and shrugs, then moves to the front of the group to break up a scuffle. As he breezes past her, Lizzie notices that he smells nice. She hasn't noticed how anyone smells in ages. Only herself and Lenny, who smells of boy-sweat and Marmite and her heart. Why have her nostrils noticed Luke? Why does she want to inhale him deeper, chase that woodsy peppermint?

She hangs at the back with her boys. They are loud and swing their lunch boxes wildly around their heads, disturbing the wildlife they're supposed to be looking out for. Lizzie can't bring herself to tell them off. She wants them to like her, wants them to think Lenny's mum is cool. So, instead of telling them to calm down and stop swearing, she tells them Lenny's favourite facts. Rabbits and parrots can see behind themselves without moving their heads. Most of the dust in the school hall is dead skin. Butterflies taste with their feet. Some tumours can grow hair and teeth. The first thing a human embryo develops is its bumhole.

It must be working, because Lenny catches her eye and grins from ear to ear. He looks so like his dad when he does that that Lizzie feels sick. As if Greg is still there with them. The thought makes her shiver in her clothes.

Lenny keeps a picture of his dad inside his football-sticker book, stuck wonkily between Jermain Defoe and Étienne Capoue. Lizzie wants to rip it out and burn it, but she can't. She's not supposed to know it's there.

Greg had taught their son how to tackle, how to carve a place inside him that could only be filled by a football. Their back garden at home had muddy patches where a lawn should have been. They'd stay out dribbling through a haze of late-afternoon sun as it rotated into half-light, crisp twilight, then finally bled into a black too thick to see in. They'd finally come inside, red-nosed, pink-cheeked, and make giant sandwiches stuffed with crisps and cheese, layers of ham and coleslaw.

Lizzie would tut and tell them their dinner would be ruined, but they were too lost inside their football to care. They'd eat in the living room, spitting feathers over *Match of the Day*. That innocuous theme tune, spewing out of the speakers. Lenny, an origami bird under his dad's crane of an arm, identical grins turning to identical scowls as Spurs made and lost chances. Lizzie would try to lesson-plan, blocking out the noise, but it was impossible.

The group is still chanting 'We shall come rejoicing' when they get to the windmill and stop for a break. Luke pushes Sebastian out of the way with a 'Run around and wear yourself out,' then plonks himself next to Lizzie on the bench.

'Want my apple?' He unzips his lunch box and proffers the contents to her.

'That's not fair, Mr Williams. How come you and *her* get to have your lunch now and we don't?'

'First, her name is Mrs Robbins, and second, because I'm in charge. Plus, I already saw you eating your sandwich on the way here.'

'And I'm *still* hungry,' Sebastian grumbles. Lenny offers him half of his sandwich and Lizzie reminds him he isn't allowed to eat his yet either. Lenny and Sebastian sigh and roll their eyes, making her smile and Luke laugh loudly and freely.

She'll lie awake for hours that night, wondering what she thought she was doing. She knows how stupid, how dangerous this is. It's too soon and she's too scared and her trust has gone. She's risking everything, and for what? A smile from a stranger who'd run a mile if he knew who he was sitting next to and what she hid beneath her clothes. But those thoughts are for later. For now they just eat lunch together. She nibbles the head of a gingerbread man, while Luke wolfs down an overloaded wrap.

After they are 'finally' allowed lunch, Lenny and Sebastian go off and get ice-cream. The spring sunshine makes the grass look greener than it really is, so Lizzie offers Luke an arm of her biscuit and a crumb of her life. 'I used to be a teacher too.'

'Really? Where? Down here? What year?' So many questions, it makes her head spin.

'Not here. Primary, same as you. Year Six mostly.'

'God. Now I feel like you've been assessing me the whole time.' Luke blushes shyly.

'You're a good teacher. I've seen Lenny's half-term booklet. Interesting choice of topics. Lenny is looking forward to making a submarine.'

'He's a good lad, that one. Dojo point for him when we get back.' Luke swallows the ginger arm and bites into the apple Lizzie refused. 'You going back to it, teaching?'

Lizzie nods at Lenny, who is chasing Sebastian with his ice-cream. 'I went back when Lenny was a year old but trying to get the kids through SATs with a baby who doesn't let you sleep was too hard.' She's very pleased with this sentence and how plausible it sounds. She tells herself not to touch her mouth, a sure sign someone is lying.

'Do you miss it?' Luke has finished his apple and throws the core into the bush behind them. He cuts off Sebastian's 'Sir, that's littering' with 'It's biodegradable. Concentrate on writing up your report before I make you spell that.' Sebastian drops down and grabs his exercise book.

'I do miss it,' Lizzie says slowly, 'but I'm too far out of the loop to go back right now, and Lenny wouldn't want me at his school.'

'Yes, he would. He adores you. He talks about you all the time.' Lizzie is so pleased, tears sting her eyes and she has to wipe them away quickly before they fall.

'There's always the other school in the village, Our Lady of Lourdes.'

'The Catholic one?'

'Yes. Not your thing?' Luke's eyes are all the colours grass can be in this light.

'No.' Lizzie winces at the thought of confession.

'Well, I hope you do come back to education. We need more great teachers.'

'I could be awful!' Lizzie's not flirting, but she's not *not* flirting either.

'Impossible. I teach Lenny, remember? He's the smartest kid I know.'

'Thank you.' Lizzie clings to his words as reassurance she's doing the right thing. Proof she's a good mum. Who needs a dad when you can read and write? she thinks sarcastically. 'I have to force him to do that stuff. All he wants to do is play football.'

Luke stuffs his wrappers back into his lunch box (*Star Wars*) and stands up, brushing lettuce off his jeans and stretching, arms out at his sides, like the windmill behind him. 'Well, my team play at the park on Sunday mornings. I'd be happy to hang about afterwards and have a kickabout with him. I'm in charge of the nets and cones so we can use them.' He flushes and says, 'I wasn't, you know, showing off when I said that.'

This is where not *not* flirting gets you, Lizzie thinks, as her lips twitch again. 'I can't pay you, for your time,' she says, twisting the brown-paper bag from the baker's in her hands. She's trying to take back control, weasel out of it, but her argument is weak, and she knows it.

'Are you joking? I don't want paying! I'd love to do it,' Luke says, offering her a hand up, which she takes without thinking. He briefly curls his fingers round hers and the warmth she feels makes her marvel. All that boiling water and bleach hadn't killed the feeling in them after all. They look at one another for a moment. Lizzie knows what's going to happen, but how can she say no to someone offering to play football with her son?

'Maybe,' she mumbles, snatching her hand back and shoving it into her pocket, hoping she's bought herself some time. Lenny approaches a second later to tell Luke that Sebastian is locked in the toilet and can't get out.

'I'd best go and sort that out. Back in a sec.' He turns to Lenny and says, 'Looks like we have a kickabout booked at the park on Sunday morning. Bring your football boots. I'll bring the Mars bars.'

George

(More rabbit than Sainsbury's)

G EORGE IS IN BETTY'S spare room, trying to fix the slats on the bed that her friend Jean broke when she last came to visit.

'Hell's bells, she likes her food. The only time she's missed a meal was when a seagull snatched a doughnut out of her hand on a trip to the pier.' Betty giggles herself out of the room.

George is under the bed, swearing. He crawls out to wipe his brow and notices that, apart from the bed and a wardrobe, the room is empty. He wonders what Betty has done with her husband's clothes and belongings. George has an irrational urge to search her attic for proof the man ever existed.

George thinks of his spare room, packed full of Ellen's clothes and shoes, her hats and best coat. Her half-finished art projects and the hideous china dogs she used to collect. He thinks of giving it all away and feels sick. Her hands had polished those porcelain tails. There might be a strand or two of her hair left inside that hat, the one she used to wear to church on Sundays. They are all he has left. If he opens that door, he imagines all her belongings coming together, a magnet drawing the scattered particles of her into a pile, a person, a ghost. He's too scared to open the door and find out he's right. He is even more scared of opening the door and finding out he's wrong.

Betty comes in with a cup of tea, which he drinks as he peers out of the window that overlooks a spotlessly tidy, soulless back yard.

'Don't you like gardening?' George blurts out before he can stop himself.

'Bill used to.' Betty's voice is flat. A Keep Out sign.

George looks again and sees pots lining the back wall. They probably used to be planted up each spring. Betty obviously loves colours – her outfit combinations give George a headache. Why wouldn't she have flowers in her garden? He knows she does them for the church, and she's not lazy. She's many, many irritating things, but not that. She's so full of energy that sometimes just watching her exhausts George.

'You don't fancy planting some bulbs?'

It comes out like a question, like he's offering to get his hands dirty. But he doesn't want to plant her bulbs. He hasn't planted his, and doesn't plan to, so why should he care about Betty's?

Betty sighs and says, 'Nosy Nora today, aren't you? Bill took to this room when his cancer got worse. I used to plant all sorts outside, so he'd have something to look at. I ordered them from a magazine that came through the door. He picked them for their names. Goldenrods and larkspur. Stargazers and dancing ladies. Since he's been gone there doesn't seem much point. Time I could give to someone else.'

George tells himself he couldn't care less either way. He just wants to mend the bed and eat the chicken-and-leek pie Betty made this morning. Then he wants to go home, listen to the cricket and fall asleep in his chair. He thinks this, then says, 'You don't always have to give your time to other people. What have they ever done for you?'

George remembers the trite thank-you cards in Betty's kitchen and wonders if they're enough to make her feel all the knitting and gathering and cleaning and sorting is worth it. Money talks, as far as George is concerned. Cards can fuck off. He didn't open any of the ones sent after Ellen died.

'Everyone did a lot for me when Bill was sick.' Betty wipes at some dust on the windowsill with the corner of her cardigan. 'There was always someone coming or going. The doorbell never stopped buzzing.'

Betty sounds as wobbly as the bed. George needs to change the subject, because he can't glue her back together. He means to ask her how the pie is doing but it comes out as 'How long was he ill for?'

'Three years. Starve the lizards, eh? For a while we thought he was going to get better, but he never did. He took to his bed one Sunday and never got out of it on the Monday, or ever again.'

George tries to imagine Ellen in their spare room, rotting away slowly over three years while the doorbell rang on repeat. All the people, the smells, the hopelessness. Doctors and nurses and tablets and blood. Bed sores and bruises from veins collapsing with overuse. The pity George refuses to acknowledge for Betty pokes him just under the ribcage.

They stand in a silence that other people might fill with a hug. Poppy realizes someone needs to do something, so goes and lies by Betty's feet. Lucky, slow on the uptake, drags an ugly jumper from his basket and runs around half-heartedly with it in his mouth.

Over lunch Betty is quiet. Normally she prattles on about any old crap and talks to the dogs in a high-pitched voice.

'Good pie,' George says, to break the odd silence.

'A compliment! Excuse me while I drop to the floor in shock!'

'Funny. Did Bill used to like it?' George's voice no longer seems to belong to him.

'Stone the crows. Aren't you interested, all of a sudden?' Betty is joking, but there is an edge to her voice, and it brings out the serrated knife that chafes inside George.

'Couldn't care less. Cook, don't cook.'

He means to continue, to call her a pest, a blight on his peaceful life, a meddling lumpy old gasbag, but something about her face stops him. Her eyes are too shiny.

'He loved his food,' she nods at George's waistband, 'like you. The cancer drugs made him feel sick. He didn't want to eat much, just custard and jellies and soup. I tried puréeing stuff, but he hated it. And there was always so much to do. Making sure he had all his tablets and his checks. Rolling him over for the bed baths. I started to buy ready-made meals for me, and baby-food for him. Banana and avocado. Apple, spinach and pear.'

George can imagine Betty with her ready meals. Italian one night, Chinese the next. He wonders if that's what she eats on the days they don't see one another. Another dig to his ribs. Maybe cooking Bill's old food makes her sad, but George knows he won't stop her. She needs it. Needs to flour and roll and crimp pastry, fill her sterile house with stew and steam, just like he needs to moan and tut and rant and rail. They understand one another, George and Betty.

Dan

(My my my, said the spider to the fly)

ATTICUS WANTS TO COOK Dan dinner. He should just text Atticus back and say no and that would be the end of it. Then he can move on with his life. The problem is, the other Dan, the one who lives inside this one, really wants to see Atticus. He's desperate to go to his house, where there may be clues about him. He wants to turn up in a deerstalker hat and Inverness cape, puffing on a calabash pipe. Wants to say, 'Never trust to general impressions, my boy, but concentrate yourself upon details,' then study every inch, every nook and cranny with a giant magnifying glass.

Dan cannot count the other Dan out of his head or scrub him off in the shower. In fact, the other Dan gets all *sorts* of ideas when he's in the shower and he comes out feeling dirtier than when he went in.

Dan has dreamed about his teeth falling out, about missing trains and spilling coffee. He has woken in the night with the rusty taste of his heart in his throat and reached for his phone to read the text over and over again, and it's always the same.

COUNT DANULA. DINNER AT MINE. 14 MADEIRA DRIVE. WEDNESDAY 8 P.M. FITZ MOST WELCOME.

It's as if Atticus is shouting at him, as if Dan's in trouble. Is dating supposed to feel like this? He wants to delete the text and hide, but there's no point. The words are branded on his brain. The text came on Sunday night and now it's Wednesday morning. What is he going to do?

He goes to call Luke more than once, but what will he say? 'Hello, buddy. I've got a date with my client this week and I need some tips. By the way, he's a man.'

He paces round and round the living room, occasionally slapping his forehead. When he puts on his coat but doesn't grab the lead, Fitz snorts and turns away. Dan wants to shake paws. Needs the constant unconditional love of his four-legged friend. But Fitz curls in his basket with his back to Dan and sighs as if his problems are bigger. Dan feels guilty. You can't look like you're going to take a dog for a walk and then not do it. Fitz would never do that to him.

'Fitz, old pal, I'm sorry. Come on, say bye to me. I'll come back at lunchtime to walk you,' Dan says, stroking the silky fur behind his ears. Fitz, who normally groans with joy when having his ears touched, pretends to be asleep.

'Come on, Fitzeroo, don't do this to me. I need you, buddy.'

The dog finally opens an eye and wags his tail once.

'Thank you. Sorry. Sausages for dinner,' Dan says, and Fitz wags his tail three times, which clearly means, 'Yes, please.'

At work Dan is all over the place. He forgets the name of his client and calls her Clare Lacy instead of Lacy Clare. He drops his notes and lets silences go on for too long, because he is lost in his own world. Lacy interprets this to mean her answers are not good enough and repeats herself.

'I said, it's not fair. My mother-in-law undermines me every time she comes into the house and my husband refuses to see it. Now she wants to come to the birth!' She wraps her hands round her belly as she says this. 'I've tried telling Matt how I feel, but he just says I'm being paranoid and sensitive and I'm lucky to have his mum around. I'm not lucky at all. I lost my mum when I was twenty-one. If I can't have her at the birth, I don't want anyone, not even Matt.'

Dan nods and says it must be hard. He's doing counselling for dummies because his mind is walking up Atticus's steps and knocking on his door and, shit, is he holding flowers in his sweaty hands?

'She checks to see if my plants have water. If they're dry, she jokes about how she hopes I won't forget to feed the baby. They're *cacti*, Dan. They're *supposed* to be dry.' Dan nods again.

'Not that she thinks I'm going to be able to feed the baby myself. She's already told me I'll be lucky to get anything out of my boobs.' She moves her hands to her breasts as she says it, thrusting them towards Dan for inspection. Dan looks at them and thinks how much easier life would be if he found women arousing.

Lacy Clare is crying now, big, fat emotional tears, her belly moving up and down with the force of her pain and frustration. Dan grabs the box of tissues and proffers them to her. He tells her everything is going to be okay, which is number one on the list of things *not* to say to your client. It trivializes their problems and gives them false hope. Having walked the plank of professionalism and jumped off, Dan carries on making up new rules.

'Here's what we're going to do, Lacy. We're going to take control of the situation.' Lacy looks up at his words, at the way he's made them a team, and listens. Lacy Clare is going to go home that night and tell her husband that his mother is an interfering *cow*, and if she doesn't back off, Lacy will move in with her sister until the birth. She's going to tell him that cacti are supposed to be dry and that her breasts are more than good enough. They are bloody marvellous. They are bad-ass baby-feeders. She's going to tell him to stop being a Mummy's boy and start being a husband.

And Dan is going to pick up his phone the second she leaves and text Atticus: *SEE YOU THERE.*

'Right, Fitz. Am I going or am I not?' Dan says, hands out in front of him, fists closed. 'Pick one.'

He's holding a sausage in his 'going' hand, so the question is unfairly weighted.

'I'm going.'

Fitz yawns.

'I want to go, Fitz. I'm scared and shy and nervous, but I really want to go.'

Fitz eats the sausage and wags his tail.

'I might make a twat of myself, but you'll still love me, right?'

Fitz sits up and offers a paw.

'Right. I'd best get ready.'

Dan washes his hair twice, until it looks like a fluffy duck on top of his head. The opposite of the look he was hoping for. He tries on three different pairs of jeans, two shirts and a jumper, and nothing looks good. He stands in his black pants and *Star Wars* socks, feeling sick as a pig, and now it's seven thirty-five p.m. and he's going to be late, even if he leaves as he is currently dressed.

A line of sweat drips down his back. Seven thirty-six p.m. Come on, Dan. He pulls on the first pair of jeans, a black pair, and a plain blue T-shirt. He adds a green belt, his high tops, and rubs a tiny bit of wax that smells of coconut into his fringe. He sprays Tom Ford on his neck and pulls on his Harrington jacket. He doesn't look at himself as he passes the mirror.

There are no parking spaces outside Atticus's house and Dan's watch reads 8.08 p.m. when he finally rings the buzzer. Atticus answers at once, his deep voice distorted by the intercom. 'You're late.'

'Sorry, I couldn't find anywhere to park.'

'Humph, come on up.'

Atticus is waiting in the open door, meaning Dan doesn't have time for one final sweaty hand rub on his jeans *and* Atticus catches him counting the treads on the staircase. He is barefoot, in dark-blue jeans and a long-sleeved black woollen top that looks expensive enough not to be itchy. There is a spicy smell coming from the flat and music throbs in the background.

'Welcome.' Atticus holds the door open but doesn't move out of the way so Dan is forced to duck his head under Atticus's arm. 'You smell delicious,' Atticus says quietly, into his ear, as Dan squeezes past.

Dan doesn't answer. He is too busy looking around Atticus's apartment in wonder. It's all peeling wallpaper and crumbling art deco curves and huge crystal chandeliers. Of course it is, Dan realizes. How else would it be? An overstuffed velvet sofa sits under the window, piles of books scattered on the floor next to it: Kurt Vonnegut, Graham Greene. There's no TV, Dan notices, but a record player has pride of place next to the fireside. He hears the soft hiss of the needle as he approaches and sees a Rufus Wainwright album cover.

In time, Dan will listen to the same record on the same player and know every single word, but for now he just walks past it and carries on looking around.

Eventually, when he's had enough of the faded seaside glamour of it all, has counted the hearth tiles (a pleasing twelve in all) and sniffed the curtains around the bay window, which are covered with peacocks and palm trees, he turns around and hands Atticus the Turkish Delight he's been clutching. He bought it on Sunday afternoon, after traipsing round Brighton for three hours. The box is pink, and the lid is a red fez with a tassel on it. Dan told himself that it was a pointless purchase as he wouldn't even be going to the dinner, but the other Dan had squealed in delight when he stumbled across it. 'It reminded me of your shoes.' Dan is blushing now, but that's okay: it's reasonably dark here.

Atticus laughs and flips the tassel. 'I love it, thank you.'

Two places have been laid at the table. The cutlery is old and losing its sheen. For some reason, the sight of it makes Dan sad. The plates are heavy slabs of taupe. Upon them linen napkins are perfectly pressed, in orange holders. They are an anomaly in the otherwise messy space. Dan wonders if Atticus ironed them especially for him and feels giddy and guilty at the same time. Two wine glasses are sitting next to a bottle of red that has been left open to breathe. The rest of the table is covered with paperwork and pencils and half-melted candles.

'Nice plates.' Dan nods and tells himself he's an idiot.

'You like them? My mother will be pleased. This is my parents' place. I moved in when they went up to London.'

'Oh.' Dan looks around again, disappointed that he's not sitting at a table Atticus picked. He counts the gouges and scratches in the wood while Atticus flits round the kitchen adding pepper and spices to the pot, stopping to taste the contents every so often. Dan wonders how many times he's cooked this dish and for whom. He imagines lots of arty types around the table, smoking and arguing till the candles have burned down and the wine has gone. He cannot see himself in the scene, not even the other Dan. He wonders where Atticus lived before now, and why he left, and if he'd decorate a place like this if he could choose. Dan wants to ask but he's gone all shy, like Fitz does around the pretty lady with the red shoes and the Afghan hound that is so posh it wears a silk scarf around its ears.

Atticus opens a cupboard and his top rides up and Dan can see a white streak of flesh. Atticus is so slim his hip bones jut out. Dan looks down at the table quickly. From under lowered lashes, he watches as Atticus dollops something from a bottle into the pot, stirs it, then puts the lid back on. 'Ten minutes or so,' he announces, then plonks himself down next to Dan with a plate of bread and dips. 'Are you in a hurry?'

'No,' Dan says quickly. Atticus raises one eyebrow and smiles slightly as he pours them both a drink.

'None for me, I'm driving.'

Atticus stops mid-pour. 'One won't hurt.' He looks at Dan all wide-eyed and adds, 'Or . . . you could stay the night?'

Dan briefly imagines what sleeping over might entail. How it would highlight his inexperience. He's watched porn – of course he's watched porn. He's shy, he's not a saint, but they don't show this bit on film. They don't tell him how to get from the table to the bedroom, at which point you remove your clothes. How often you ask if the other one is okay, enjoying themselves, even.

At college, when people had started talking about their sex lives, he'd always changed the subject, feeling chronically shy and unsure of himself.

Dan shakes his head firmly and says, 'Fitz.'

'Is that your safe word? Where is he anyway? Washing his hair?' Atticus says, filling his glass to the brim.

'He's at home.'

'He's welcome here,' Atticus says, taking a sip of wine.

'He's happy,' Dan says. 'He's probably hogging the sofa and eating all the cheese.'

'And you like to have an excuse to bolt.' It's not a question, it's a fact. Dan twiddles the stem of his wine glass as Atticus loads a pitta sliver with hummus and places it delicately in his mouth.

Dan feels out of his depth, clumsy and awkward. Why did he agree to come? Why does Atticus want him here? Surely he could have anyone. Someone who knows all about woody red wine and art and how to do this. How to drink and flirt and move from the dining table to the couch.

Atticus has been watching him, and when he looks up, they lock eyes and Dan jolts, like he's touched an electric fence. Atticus smiles and puts down his wine glass. 'Relax, Daniel. I'm not going to ravish you before the main course. I've spent all afternoon cooking it.' The joke is supposed to relax Dan, but he only feels worse. The wine, the carefully prepared stew. The best plates. What does Atticus want in return? It can't just be Dan's company. Atticus didn't do all this just to sit and watch Dan gulp nervously.

Dan takes a sip of the wine before he realizes what he's doing. It's thick and rich and no doubt cost more than anything Dan has drunk before. The flavour coats his tongue and he worries his teeth will stain. He plants his feet on the floor, ready to push his chair back, make an excuse, pull out his wallet and offer to pay for the food, when Atticus stops him with a hand on his thigh. It's heavy and warm. His long fingers curl round the side of Dan's quad and squeeze gently.

'Don't go, Daniel, please.'

'I don't know how to do this, Atticus,' he confesses, to the fingers on the leg of his black jeans.

'There is nothing to do, Daniel. I don't have a plan for how this evening is supposed to go. You don't like the meal, we get a takeaway. You don't want red wine, I'll go and get you a beer. You don't want this –' he nods to his hand on Dan's leg – 'and it doesn't happen. I just want you here, in my house, around my table. I'm happy enough just to watch you frowning and counting under your breath. There is no script, no expectation. Just. Be. With. Me.' He punctuates each word with a squeeze that shoots up Dan's leg. Unable to speak, Dan just nods, then takes another gulp of wine. Atticus gives his leg one last press and gets up to take the pot off the stove.

The dinner is quietly delicious and accompanied by the clink of cutlery as a late-spring evening breeze wafts in from the open window above the sink. When they finish, Dan tells Atticus he's training for the Ironman with his cousin Luke as he keys his calories into his phone.

'Sounds onions. Is your cousin as handsome as you?' Atticus asks, as he collects the plates and stacks them in the sink.

'Much better-looking,' Dan says, pocketing his phone, grabbing the pot and taking it to the stove.

'Impossible,' Atticus says, and then, more quietly, almost to himself, 'That fucking blush.' Dan obliges him with another and goes to start the washing-up, but Atticus bats him away. 'Leave it. I'll do it tomorrow.'

'Please,' Dan says, 'let me do this. It helps me relax.'

'If cleaning is what relaxes you, go mad.' Atticus casts an arm around the kitchen and grins. 'Have at it, sailor.' Dan settles for washing up and wiping the sides.

When the tea-towel is hanging neatly over the oven door and the sauce is blotted from the table, Atticus takes Dan's hand and the rest of the wine and leads him into the living room. He turns the record over and lowers the needle, then pulls Dan with him onto the couch.

Lizzie

(The offside rule)

LATE LAST NIGHT A new girl arrived at the shelter. Lizzie had been in the kitchen when Tess came in to make soup for her, as she always did for new arrivals. 'Good for the soul,' she'd say, but they never wanted it. Even the ones with missing teeth usually turned it down.

'You must come and meet Sarah,' she'd said, but Lizzie kept finding jobs that didn't need doing, until there was nothing left for it but to walk into the living room and say her awkward hello.

Sarah had the beginnings of a black eye. She'd been lost inside the comfortable sofa, a mug of tea clamped between her bony knuckles, muddy fingers leaving traces on the polar-white china. Lizzie wondered what slogan she'd paint on her mug one day.

'You did the right thing. He'll never change. Next time he'll kill you,' Frankie had said, on repeat, while others pulled up sleeves to show scars, regaling the new girl with tales of the last beating they'd taken.

'Nothing bad can happen now,' Frankie had said, and Lizzie thought how wrong she was. Maybe it showed on her face, because Sarah had looked at Lizzie then. She was expecting her to share her own story.

They all were. Frankie, Stella, Tess. She knew, if she did confess, it would break down the walls between them. In this place, a human-rights lawyer could become best friends with a beautician because they both bore the same hidden scars. They had both married men who always avoided hitting their face.

Here, in Tess's tarnished old house, full of tarnished women, it didn't matter if your blood was red or blue. It didn't matter if you worked in a shop or on the stage. All religions were accepted here. No one envied anybody. The bodies in this home came with abuse. No one would choose that. Here, no one bothered with fad diets, and the only beautifying done was when someone wanted to disguise themselves with hair dye, or swap glasses for contact lenses. Here, people knocked before they entered, trod quietly on the stairs, never shouted.

Lizzie was living in a sanctuary. These women had lost everything – their jobs, their independence, their friends and their dignity – and still they bled human kindness. With nothing left to give, they offered immunity.

If only Lizzie could be as brave. If only she could open her mouth. If only she didn't have as much to lose.

Lizzie had avoided Sarah's eye, and busied herself folding blankets and tidying books, but inside, the pressure was piling up.

Tess had marched in then, with her tinned chicken soup for the soul and bread with the crusts off. After plonking down the tray, she swept Sarah's hair from her forehead without asking and turned her face to check the swelling eyelid. 'Oh, that's nasty. What a rat he is.'

Lizzie had wanted to tell them all to leave the girl alone. Even she could see Sarah was uncomfortable, and sick of people touching her. Instead she said, 'Emotional tears are more watery than other types. That's why your eyes swell so much when you cry.'

She'd known it was the wrong thing to say even before Frankie had looked at her with her standard what-the-fuck? expression. She'd done it again, been a scientist when they wanted a woman. Marie Curie, Lizzie's idol, had been both, but it had killed her in the end. In exposing radium and polonium, she had also exposed herself.

'Nothing in life is to be feared,' Lizzie added quickly. 'It is only to be understood.' Also the wrong thing to say in front of a roomful of women beaten by men for no reason at all. But that was Lizzie, always outside the circle looking in. She gave facts when they wanted feelings, statistics when they wanted advice, nothing when they needed comfort. It had been all right when she was a kid, and facts had been impressive, but as she'd got older, friendships had become more complicated. Both liking horses was no longer enough. People had wanted more than Lizzie's IQ. They wanted her opinion, her emotional response. They wanted the locked-away parts of her.

Briefly, Lizzie allowed herself to think about the teaching assistant she'd had before it all started. Bright-eyed, early and eager. A brilliant mathematician. Always willing to stay late. Brought in cakes on a Friday. She had asked Lizzie about her weekend plans and met Lizzie's eye during the daily breakthroughs and heartbreaks of being a teacher. Laughed with her about those little triumphs. Lizzie missed her, and the friendship they'd slowly built.

And then there was Greg. Funny, smart, sexy Greg. Quick as a whip, ridiculously well read, decent to a fault and so incredibly patient. He'd peeled away Lizzie's brusqueness with the painstaking tenderness of a conservator dabbing at a timeless masterpiece. He'd taken her out again and again, until her brief, frustrated responses had become sentences and her hands had written symbols in the air. 'I'm hard, Greg,' she told him, the first time he went to kiss her. 'I'm not good at this. I . . .'

Greg had stopped the end of her sentence by delivering the kiss.

'See?' he'd said to her, a few dates later, as she lay naked in his denim-coloured sheets, hair like a mermaid's tail, red mouth swollen, chest still heaving. 'Nothing cold about you.'

'I lost the baby,' Sarah said to no one in particular, but the words had pulled Lizzie from her thoughts and her heart had stopped for a second in sympathy.

'I'm so sorry,' Lizzie said, and for once it didn't sound wooden, or insincere.

Last night Lizzie slept deeply. So deeply she has woken forgetting where she is. Half asleep, she thinks she is late for work. Her mind whirs with lesson plans and permission slips; her hands, automatically going to cradle her huge belly, find the flatness of her abdomen instead, and her eyes notice the too-small curtains of the shelter's bedroom. Then she remembers.

She gets up for her morning wee, and there it is. What she'd been dreaming about, why her back felt bowed. A bright smear of blood. Proof.

George

(Forget-me-not)

G EORGE WOULDN'T HAVE GONE to the allotment if it was on the church grounds, because Ellen has a headstone in the graveyard and he never wants to see it. He didn't want the funeral at the church, or the headstone, but stopping either of those things would have meant getting up and doing something and at the time he was incapable.

He let other people make the decisions. They wanted to pick her coffin and her flowers. They wanted to stand up at the front of a damp church she loved and tell each other their versions of his wife. He let them. None of it was going to bring her back. A diamond-encrusted coffin wouldn't wake her, so what did it matter? She'd never smell the roses or hear their words and muffled-by-embroidered-handkerchief sniffles. It made no difference to him. A better man might have eulogized his wife, but George was still frozen in the shock that had shrouded him as he walked out of the hospital carrying a bag of his wife's clothes while she lay naked in a morgue.

Ellen had told him she was feeling 'peaky' the day before she called for an ambulance. George had frowned at her and told her to stop being so dramatic. It was while he was telling her it was because of hypochondriacs like her that the NHS was up shit creek that he had noticed how grey her skin was. A colleague of his had broken his hand at work once, trapped it in a vice, and he'd seen the same greyness on his face. A waxy sheen. He remembered asking Ellen if she'd broken anything. Later he'd realize that she'd broken everything, including him.

He might have noticed her sudden deterioration sooner if he'd thought to look, but she'd been keeping herself busy with the housework and the cooking and phone calls in her bedroom. At the time, he'd thought she was organizing another raffle for the church. Now, he knew she'd been putting his life in order before she died. Spending her last days making his easier. Of all the things he resented his wife for, he resented her most for that. She'd remembered the pills and the appointments, the letters and the cooking, but she'd never thought to tell him she'd been diagnosed with pancreatic cancer.

She didn't tell him she'd been to the doctor about agonizing back and abdominal pain, had undergone blood tests, had been sat down and told she had weeks to live. And George had only found that out from the doctors after she'd died in front of him. At the time he'd still thought it was just a bladder infection.

If she hadn't bought Poppy, she might not have died. There is no logic in this, but there is a chance for blame, for absolution. George had been so cross with her when she brought the puppy home.

'Take that dog back where it came from.'

'No. Shan't.' Ellen's chin had quivered with a stubbornness George had never seen before.

It was stalemate. He didn't acknowledge the dinners she

made him, or the cups of tea. He didn't thank her, didn't lock the door she kept opening and closing to praise the fucking dog every ten seconds.

The dog had taught her how to bark back. His afternoon tea was lacking a biscuit, but he found crumbs on the floor by the newspaper Poppy pissed on. It was as if George was the pet and Poppy the husband. He got fed three times a day, and Ellen opened the window to give him fresh air, but all her chatter, all her sunshine, had gone to the puppy.

She would pick it up and tell it how pretty and clever it was. She slept in the spare room with it. She got up during the night and stood in the garden in her nightgown and curlers while it sniffed round for the perfect place to shit. George would get up and watch them from the window, the moon for a torch, Ellen cradling a ball of fur and teeth, like it was a newborn, while the early-morning dew soaked her velvet slippers.

It was Ellen who finally broke the silence, as George had known she would. She had offered to slice the cheese. He'd been hacking at a block of Cheddar, having not received his pre-bedtime supper. She'd been cooking sausages for the dog to train her to come back. 'What a fucking waste of sausages,' George had muttered, under his breath. 'Let me have them and the dog can bugger off.'

Ellen had turned to him then, before her face had gone as grey as her hair. 'No, George. The dog stays.' She hadn't broken eye contact, hadn't added 'please'. Hadn't ever looked as beautiful as she did in that moment, putting him in his place in her old blue dressing-gown. 'Now then,' she'd gone on to say, 'would you like me to slice you some cheese, or do you just want to gnaw on the block?'

'Slices,' he'd said, 'and an apple, too . . . please.' In their marriage, 'please' often meant 'sorry'.

That was at eleven p.m. When they awoke the next morning, it was as if they'd never rowed. For a few days she'd scurried around, her industrious ant-like self, carrying George's world on her back. Then the morning came when she wasn't up before him. He woke to find her curled up on the pillow next to him – she'd come back from the spare room – asleep with her small mouth open, smelling faintly of rot. The kettle hadn't been about to boil. He couldn't hear the clink of cups or the sound of the toaster popping, just his wife's shallow breathing.

George had thought she might be going mad. First the dog, then the telling-off, now the sleeping in. What next? he'd wondered. Within a couple of days, he'd found out.

What came next was Ellen asking for an ambulance, collapsing before it arrived. She was barely coherent in the hospital. She looked blurry, like she did when George didn't have his glasses on, except he did. She was bleeding round the edges, flooding his bleeding heart. He was pleased to be sent home with a 'Nothing you can do here, best go home and rest.'

He knew he should have felt worried, but seeing her there, all floppy and flaccid, had scared him and so he had run away, his tail between his legs. Had been pleased to get home, where life felt normal, apart from the fucking dog, which he'd promptly locked in the laundry room with a bowl of water and some Bonio biscuits.

He'd got a taxi to see Ellen the next day, full of ire about the cost of it, and the bloody foreigner who'd driven him in a cab stinking of flowers. He'd been hungry and hadn't found the shirt he wore on Tuesdays. He'd marched down dimly lit corridors that made his shoes squeak, looking forward to having a good old moan to his wife, but she'd been asleep when he arrived, and when she woke, she was full of morphine. Her eyes couldn't focus, had lost all their blue. They'd already died, and the rest of her went later that afternoon.

It hadn't been dramatic. No beeping machines or people rushing in. The room didn't seem emptier once her heart had stopped beating. Her soul didn't rise from her body and ride on white wings through the ceiling. She was just alive, and then dead. Wires were removed and her body was wheeled away, pushed down the corridor by two orderlies discussing *EastEnders*, and George had been pushed out of the door with a plastic bag containing her clothes.

He didn't remember getting home. His next memory was the innings being interrupted by the phone ringing. It was after eight o'clock and George ignored it, and the first couple of timid knocks on the door. The phone didn't stop, though, and the knocks grew more insistent. They forced him from his chair, propelled him to the door, where he yelled, 'She's not here. She's dead. Now fuck off.' It had been Barbara, wondering why Ellen hadn't come to their weekly Knit and Natter.

George had watched her run, for the first time in twenty years, down the road to Sue's and pound on the door. When Sue finally opened it, Barbara had panted, 'Quick! Call the police! He's finally done it. George has murdered Ellen.'

Dan

(Crossing the line)

THEY SIT ON THE sofa in silence as Rufus sings about a 'Foolish Love', and Dan has to close his eyes because the lyrics are too close to home. He can feel Atticus looking at him, watching for the green light to make a move. From so close, Dan can make out a small scar by his left ear. He wants to put his finger on it. He wants to be the other Dan, who is brave enough to close the gap between them and kiss Atticus, but it's late, and he's tired, and the Elvis Dan has left the building.

'I'd better go.' He pulls back and jumps up, almost knocking over the bottle of wine in his haste. Atticus says nothing but discreetly adjusts his crotch before standing. Dan tries and fails not to notice. Instead, he babbles into the awkward silence. 'Fitz is home alone. He'll need a wee-wee soon, and I have work tomorrow. Thanks for dinner and the food and . . .' He doesn't know what else to say. He can't believe he just said the word 'wee-wee'. Oh, God, what a car crash, and all Dan can think is wee-wee, wee-wee, wee-wee, over and over in his head, like a stuck record.

When Atticus opens the door to let Dan escape, he doesn't

manoeuvre himself so that Dan has to duck under his arm. He opens it wide and the smell of the candles and dinner and their mutual disappointment seeps out into the hall.

Dan takes the stairs two at a time, still wee-weeing as he goes. He forces himself not to run until he is out of sight, then he sprints. The food and the wine churn in his gut and he wants to be sick almost as much as he wants to go home.

He unlocks the car with shaking fingers and dives in.

The image of Atticus adjusting his crotch makes it hard for Dan to catch his breath and it takes him two attempts to start the car.

When he gets home, Fitz looks up at him and raises an eyebrow. But then he registers Dan's distraught face, and gets to work trying to lick away his frown. Dan pushes him weakly and Fitz has to settle for sniffing his hand instead, which is his version of saying, 'There, there,' just like Dan does when Fitz has got himself overexcited about something.

Dan takes off his clothes and gets into the shower, leans his head against the cold white tiles and lets himself sag. He ran away, like Fitz does from the vacuum cleaner. Like his patients do from their problems and fears. He thinks of what might have happened if he'd stayed. Thinks of his cousin, who throws himself into anything and everything with gusto. How he'll always dance, no matter where he is, whenever his favourite song is played. Dan doesn't want to be here. He wants to be at Atticus's house. He wants to be somebody else.

He reaches for peppermint shower gel and scrubs at his skin until it's red, until he's exfoliated something of himself away, scrubbed off some of the shyness. He brushes his teeth till his gums bleed. Washes his clean hair until it squeaks.

When he gets out, he puts on his running shorts and a long-sleeved Nike T-shirt, then adds his bike helmet.

'Fitz. I've got to go back. You understand.'

Fitz is fine with it all. He's had his quick wee outside and is happy to be at home, with his sock.

He curls round, head on his paws, and is soon dreaming of seagulls and squirrels, his tail occasionally wagging, legs twitching.

It's cold and it's dark and there are no lights along the sea-front as Dan cycles. He forgot his music in his hurry, but he can hear Rufus Wainwright in his head and his feet pound a rhythm on the pedals.

By the time he gets to Atticus's door the sweat has cooled and steam rises from his shirt. He doesn't speak when he presses the buzzer and abandons his bike in the narrow hallway. The door is already open when he gets to the top of the stairs. Atticus is there, barefoot, wearing the same clothes, his shoulders slightly sagging.

Dan jogs the last three steps and doesn't stop until he hits Atticus's chest. The force of him pushes Atticus back through the door and they crash into the hat stand. Before he can right himself, Dan is pulling Atticus over the finish line, completing his first Ironman. Finally, he crosses the ocean between them.

Their noses bump, but Atticus's exclamation is swallowed by Dan's kiss. Atticus keeps his arms by his sides, not responding until Dan tugs at his hair and tilts his face to the side. 'Please.'

Then Atticus groans slightly, turns Dan so his back is against the wall and parts his lips with his tongue.

'What are we doing, Atticus?' Dan asks him, when they pull away, slightly panting.

'We are turning into ourselves,' Atticus replies, and kisses him again.

Lizzie

(Let sleeping dogs lie)

WITHIN MINUTES OF THEM leaving the shelter the rain starts, but the match is still going when they arrive. A thin drizzle hangs over everything and the pitch is a mudbath. Lizzie spots Luke easily. He grins and waves at them before going to tackle someone. Lenny cheers him on, running up and down the sidelines and bringing back the ball every time it goes out of play. Mud splats up his legs like camouflage, blending him into the scene. Lizzie stands out in her red coat and her yellow scarf. She is a traffic light.

Finally, the whistle blows, and everyone gathers in soggy clumps to shake hands and gulp water. Luke approaches, high-fiving team members on his way. Lizzie goes to say it's far too wet and cold for them to play, but Luke is already kicking a ball to Lenny and saying, 'Come on, mate, I'll go in goal.' The ball hits Lenny in the chest. He bounces it off with practised skill and does keepie-uppies with his knees. His smile must hurt his cheeks.

Luke laughs at him, then turns back to Lizzie. 'Hello. You look nice.' He blushes, then points to a door behind the toilets. 'It's dry and warm in there – you can make coffee and listen to the radio.'

Lizzie dashes inside, where she sees that Luke has brought Mars bars, milk, teabags, coffee, and shortbread biscuits in the shape of dogs. He's also brought a blanket, which Lizzie gratefully wraps around herself. She watches them through the window as she drinks her tea, their sliding tackles and shots on goal. It's so small in the storage shed, so warm and strangely safe, that Lizzie drifts off to sleep under the drum-beat of drizzle, her hands on her aching stomach.

She's woken by Lenny and Luke barging into the room, jostling together, all wet hair and red cheeks. Luke pulls a couple of towels from a kitbag on the floor and hands one to Lenny. 'Amazing game! You've some serious skill. You really need proper football boots, though.' Lizzie looks down and sees Lenny's trainers are ruined. They are his only pair and he'll need them for PE on Monday.

'Lenny, take them off and let me warm you up. Did you know it's impossible to fall asleep if your feet are below a certain temperature?'

Lenny is not listening: he's singing another of Luke's stupid songs – 'We're picking our nose, picking our nose, picking our nose by the fire.' It's irritating and Lizzie wants to tell him to stop. Greg taught Lenny ridiculous football songs – 'Tottenham are the greatest team the world has ever seen,' they'd crow, back in the good days.

Her back aches and her head feels thick. She wants to be in bed with a hot-water bottle and her books, Lenny under one arm reading a comic. Not here, with Luke looking at her with pity because she can't afford football boots for her son.

Once, she was one of the best-paid teachers in her school. Their Ofsted scores were the highest in the area, largely thanks to her. It was still a modest salary at best, but she'd earned it. She used to get job offers from schools up and down the country. Private schools that could pay her triple, not that she'd ever consider it. At heart, Lizzie was a fierce socialist. She used to be part of a union. She used to have a voice. Now she scrabbles for lint-covered coins in the bottom of her pockets.

She forces herself to breathe slowly, paints on a smile and says, 'Come on, Lenny, we'd better get going.'

'Oh. I was hoping you might want to come back to mine and meet Wolfie,' Luke says, when he emerges from the towel. His hair is sticking up all over the place. She knew it was coming. Of course she did. Men don't just play football with other men's kids. They always want something in return. The blanket, the teabags. The posh biscuits. She sees Greg in her head and feels sick.

Lizzie says, 'No,' at the same time as Lenny says, 'Yes, please!' and the look he gives her says he knows he'll be in trouble when they get home, but it will be worth it. The football and the Mars bar and going to Mr Williams's house to watch the greatest goals of all time on his no doubt giant flat-screen TV. He squeezes his mum's hand as they walk towards Luke's car, hoping it will take the tightness out of her smile.

Lizzie knows she needs to stop this, whatever it is, now, but her feet follow Luke's, as if she's trailing prints left in the snow. She never did learn the offside rule, but this must be it.

*

On their way to Luke's house they listen to the radio. Luke sings and taps the steering wheel. Lenny joins in, not knowing any of the words. Lizzie is pleased they're not talking. She doesn't want to know why Luke decided to be a teacher, or where he grew up. She doesn't want to know that he has a mum and dad who love him, or an annoying little sister. She doesn't want him to be whole and real. She needs him to stay patchy and translucent. The more real he becomes, the more real she needs to be.

The car pulls up in front of a neat block of flats and Luke announces they're home. He sounds nervous, fumbles with the key, and when they finally get inside, he stands with his hands by his sides looking awkward. The flat is spotless and smells of cleaning products. Lizzie knows that if she looks at him his face will admit he'd planned for this outcome.

Wolfie comes bounding out of the kitchen and launches himself at Luke. Lenny's eyes bulge in delight and, within seconds, he's rolling around on the floor with the dog. Luke grins down at him and Wolfie, then casts his eyes sideways at Lizzie, who feels her pulse quicken.

There is an attraction between them. It's undeniable, but it's science. Just science, she tells herself. Some people are drawn to one another like magnets. It's not love or anything like that, it's pheromones, the phantom scent of a stronger immune system. A subconscious hunt for good mating material. It's not *personal*. There's no magic, no spark. It's all about survival and procreation.

Lizzie isn't looking for a mate. She's not looking for anything at all. She needs to tell Luke this, and tell him now, before it goes too far. She bumps into Wolfie, who sniffs at her tentatively. Does he remember her, from the Beacon?

'Hello, Wolfie, nice to see you again,' she says formally, putting out her hand for him to sniff.

Dogs have over three hundred million olfactory receptors in their nose, compared to the six million humans possess. The part of their brain devoted to analysing smells is forty times bigger than humans'.

Lizzie wonders what Wolfie's superior nose can detect. Her rose-oil perfume and bathroom bleach must be obvious, but what about the layer under that? Blood and bone? Can he smell her marrow? Her white blood cells? Her endocrine system? She considers the perfume of fear. Is it tailored to each individual? Would Lenny's smell of spiders and slugs and thin iron needles? The idea of never seeing his dad again? And what about Lizzie? Does her fear smell of her shedding womb and Tess's hairspray? Of Greg's leather belt?

If she were a dog, she would submit to Wolfie. She has power over Luke, but Wolfie has power over her. He sniffs once more, his tail low but not tucked under his legs. His ears are not flat against his head, but his body language is unsure. He licks her hand once, tasting her, and then walks away. Lizzie wonders if he senses there is something under all those chemicals and roses that is already weak and broken.

George

(Knit and Natter)

GEORGE IS WORKING ON the allotment. Betty is prattling on about something, but George has his radio turned up to drown her out. Poppy is snuffling through the mud and Lucky is trying to wriggle out of his latest jumper.

George will stop soon to eat the sausage sandwich with lashings of brown sauce that Betty has made and is keeping warm next to a flask of tea. Betty loves food almost as much as George does. She's like a hamster, cheeks always padded out with a toffee or a piece of cheese. It makes him think of Ellen's cheeks, the soft, powdery down on them. How did he never notice how thin his wife had become?

He turns over the soil, adding fertilizer until it's rich and filled with luscious pink worms that he tosses at Betty when she tells him to put his back into it. She knits as she watches, and her latest project is starting to look suspiciously like a man-sized jumper.

George likes gardening. Forks and spades don't talk back. The bulbs light up the trenches he ploughs like glow-worms, and he likes how strong he feels when he pokes them down, hiding them under a blanket of earth, knowing they'll reappear.

If he were a singing man he'd warble 'We'll Meet Again' by Vera Lynn. He's not, though, so he just pushes each bulb in with a 'humph' and moves on to the next.

Ellen's ashes lie under a bed of earth, but she's not coming back. She won't grow roots and layers of skin, like his onions. She won't poke her head up one day. They won't meet again. He doesn't like to think of Ellen in this way. It makes him need to sit down and catch his breath. To distract himself he asks Betty if her husband was buried or cremated.

She finishes counting her row of stitches, then looks up from her knitting. 'He wanted to be buried. Lord knows why. I wouldn't want to be stuck in the ground being eaten by worms. That's what he wanted, though, so that's what we did.'

'Was it a big funeral?' George doesn't know why he cares, but something about the way Betty talks about Bill makes him feel a bit itchy, right in the middle of his back where he can't quite scratch it.

'Aren't you a nosy parker? It was big enough. He'd been poorly for years. Lots of the nurses and carers came. They'd grown fond of him.' Betty has her head back in her knitting now. She's talking to an uneven row of purl stitches in a diarrhoea brown.

'I thought you said you nursed him yourself.' George takes a handkerchief out of his pocket to mop his brow, then stuffs it back up his sleeve. He's wearing a vest under his shirt and jumper.

'Strike a light, George! I did, but you can't do it all alone. There are machines and medication and all sorts.' Betty sounds defensive, like she does when George asks her where the last bit of pie went. He wonders why he's pushing her but he can't stop himself.

'Yes, but you could have learned how to use the machines and when to give the medication.' Ellen knew the names of all of his tablets and what they did. She could rattle off side effects and dosages like a pharmacist. Better than a pharmacist.

George can tell from Betty's face that his forked tongue has hit a root, or maybe a piece of flint. She wrings the knitting, like she wishes it were his neck, and speaks to him in a voice he's never heard her use before, her teeth clenched.

'For crying out loud! I sat by his side from the day he took to his bed until the day he died. I made four thousand three hundred cups of tea and one hundred and seven Victoria sponge cakes. I know this because I kept count. I know exactly how much I did. I know every medicine that man took, alphabetically. Aspirin. Bisacodyl. Diazepam. Epirubicin. Feroglobin . . .'

'All right, enough already. No need to overegg the fucking pudding. You're a modern-day marvel. A real-life Mother Teresa.'

'No, I wasn't. I was just his wife. I changed his sheets every single day, with two nurses helping me to lift him. I cleaned the carpet on my hands and knees so the vacuum wouldn't wake him up. Towards the end, I made him fourteen bowls of custard a week. I made cakes and cards and scarves for every single person who came in to help us. I spent three hundred pounds on merino wool, you old dumb-cluck. So don't you *dare*, for one second, tell me I didn't do my best. I was there, watching him die, and die and die a bit more every day, for three years. You didn't even notice your Ellen had cancer.'

Betty is almost crying by now, and even though George was not the one ranting, they are both out of breath. The spring air is cool, but anger and indignation have made them puff steam at one another, like two bulls about to charge. Their eyes flash with accusations and denials. George wants to break something over her head. In the end he settles for snatching her knitting and unravelling it in long handfuls. 'You can't knit for shit. Fucking poxy ugly shite I'll never wear.'

'Give it back. It wasn't for you.'

'What?'

George is still tugging at the wool, enjoying the way all her hard work is coming undone in his hands. He stamps on the strands as they hit the ground, covering them with clots of mud from his boots.

'That jumper wasn't for you.' Betty's voice is calmer now.

'Well, which poor unsuspecting fucker was it for, then?'

'It was for Don at the church. His wife died last month, and she always knitted him a jumper for the spring. Nothing too heavy. I had to go into town on the bus to get that wool from a special shop.'

George tugs so hard that the last bit of wool snaps. He stumbles backwards on the uneven mud, almost losing his footing.

'Fuck!' He bends and grabs at the crinkly mass on the ground, but it's all just a knot now and the jumper wasn't for him anyway. It was for Don, another sad bastard with no wife who Betty has taken in to look after, like a stray dog.

Does she go to Don's house and cook for him? Do they sit together and eat cake? Does she do his ironing – and why the fuck does George care? Betty will only ever be a home help to him. If she wants to go and clean for the whole fucking village, what does it matter to him? He doesn't envy Don, or any other unfortunate sod she's knitting for. He doesn't want her for himself: he doesn't want her at all.

Except that Betty fills in the quiet spaces. She's noisy and loud and she annoys George. She's so annoying he feels ten years younger. She fills him with insults and sarcasm, and it pumps like oxygenated blood through his veins. He digs better when she's watching. She can take the shit that no one else will tolerate. Even now, after all the things he's said and what he's done to Don's jumper, she'll forgive him. For some reason, Betty needs this too.

One day, when he's ready to face the consequences and be totally alone, he'll squeeze it out of her. He'll get to the bottom of the woman who never cries for her husband and doesn't have a single reminder of him around the house. The woman who remembers everyone's birthday, and their fucking dog's birthday, when her friend's great-niece's exam results are due. She volunteers in the charity shop, at the WRVS. She sends boxes full of pants and socks and soap to the forces at Christmas. She knits blankets for babies in the Trevor Mann ICU. She leaks compassion and thoughtfulness. It drips out of the TENA Lady urine-control pads that George knows she wears because he saw her try to hide them in the trolley when they went shopping.

She cries over a broken cup, a 'lonely robin'. She sobs when she spills milk, so why the fuck doesn't she cry for her dead husband? Why doesn't she ever go to his grave and weep, and where are all the photos? Where is her wedding ring? Where is any proof he was ever there at all?

That is what George wants to unravel, not the jumper. Not today, though. He's hot and hungry and he wants a cup of tea and a piece of fruit loaf after his sandwich. He wants to go back to his gardening.

How can he fix this? He can't knit them back to where they were ten minutes ago. He can't say sorry. All he can do is stand there awkwardly.

Poppy sighs from her nest on top of Betty's coat. Super-sausage-dog to the rescue once again. She gets up with a yap, then trots over and starts attacking the remains of Don's jumper. She growls at it and tugs at it with her teeth. She barks at Lucky, who stops licking his paw and comes over for a sniff, before cocking his leg and doing a long, steaming piss over the remains of one sleeve. It goes on and on and on and all George can do is watch.

Betty snorts first, slaps her hand over her mouth to stifle it, but it's there and it's marvellous. George tries to choke back his mirth as it rises and erupts from inside, a volcano bursting lava. Within seconds they are both bent double, George leaning on his spade for support while Betty dabs at her eyes with the bottom of her Hawaiian shirt. 'Oh, stone me, strike me pink,' Betty wheezes. 'Bring in the dancing lobsters.'

Dan

(The morning after the night before)

DAN CAN'T SLEEP AFTER the kiss. He lies awake and replays it, his heart thudding along in time. Atticus's lips on his own. No space between them, passing air back and forth. Tonsil tennis, Luke used to call it when they were kids. Seven minutes in Heaven. Dan touches his lips in wonder and smiles. Was it seven minutes? For once he had forgotten to count.

Maybe next time. He hopes there'll be a next time. With more kissing and more than kissing. He can feel molecules of Atticus in his body osmosing. He used to be only in Dan's head, but now he can feel Atticus in his fingers and toes. He can feel Atticus in his pounding heart.

As always, Dan's thoughts dip and dive like a rollercoaster, from dizzying euphoria to dread. Maybe Atticus thought he was a substandard kisser and won't want to see him again. He's probably used to rich boys who can tie cherry stalks into knots with their tongues. Dan is tongue-tied, but in all the wrong ways. Once again, he curses his lack of experience. Why hadn't he ever slipped off to a nightclub where he could peer and peruse, and practise on a stranger in the dark? He has nothing except the noise Atticus made to reassure him he was doing it right.

Fitz stretches and arches his back, then gets up to start his morning dog yoga (doga). He doesn't stay in his downward pose as long as normal, because Dan and Fitz are perfectly osmosed. Because of this Fitz knows Dan is feeling uneven, so he pads over and licks his hand solemnly. One, two, three, four, his tail goes against Dan's shin. One, two, three, four. Fitz is his metronome, his balance, his best pal.

'Hello, Fitzy,' Dan says, after a couple of rounds of counting along. 'Let's get this day on the road.' He's distracted, though, and Fitz has to keep nudging him in the right direction. Towards the back door and the bin where his dried food lives. The treats drawer, in case Dan is so distracted he might not realize it isn't treat time.

Dan has a cold shower, and gulps at the cold coffee he forgot about because he was too busy staring at his phone. No message from Atticus. Instead there's a message from his mum on the answerphone telling him that Dave did indeed propose to Helen in Tenerife, which means there'll be a family wedding to go to. Great. Dan dresses in black and tosses Fitz ham as he makes his sandwich. He listens to the news and tries to care about the 160 people who died in an earthquake.

By the time he gets to his office and sprays his morning lavender, he's in a bad mood. In what his nan would call 'a funk'.

Lacy Clare isn't. She's euphoric. 'He did it, Dan! He told his mother to back off,' she tells him. 'He was kind, but firm, so firm, and manly.' Her mother-in-law left 'with a bee in her bonnet and she took her Bundt cake with her, which would have been dry anyway'. Dan smiles weakly, encouraging her to carry on.

'When the phone call from my father-in-law came to say, "Mummy isn't feeling well. She worries it's her heart. Perhaps you'll call her," he didn't. He didn't do it, Dan! He told his father she'd be better off getting some rest and he'd call them in the week.' Lacy was so pleased with her husband that they'd had awkward but very satisfying sex – 'Truly wonderful, Dan' – in one of the positions recommended in her yoga-for-pregnancy book.

Dan is glad for her but riddled with jealousy, which is not like him. He sees his clients as little seedlings. His aromatherapy-scented office is a warm little propagator in which they can germinate. He keeps the thermostat set at the exact same temperature. Offers them water as he sits them in the patch of sunlight refracted off the sea. He creates a bubble, a green-house in which they can throw their angry stones, break their little bell jars and bloom.

Not today, though. He is not enjoying Lacy Clare's efflorescence. He wants to snatch her happiness and take it for himself. He is Morticia Addams, snipping the heads of roses in bloom. He wants to lie on the couch and have someone listen to him talk about how confused and angry *he's* feeling.

His next client is significantly less happy. Dan is relieved – and disgusted with himself for that. He tells the bullied teenager that often the way people treat you is more about themselves than it is about you. 'No one has the power to make you feel anything. You have a choice and you can choose not to believe the names you're being called. You can choose to believe your own version of yourself, not other people's. You are the one with the power.'

Dan feels like a fraud as the trite words fall out of his mouth, like broken teeth. How can he sit there and say the power is hers when Atticus has him in his fucking pocket? Dan is there, in his phone under contacts, and he hasn't called, hasn't texted.

Whenever anything happened to Dan as a child, whether it was a bad fall, score or disappointment, his nan would always say, 'Some people have no legs, Daniel. Think about that and then how bad your problem is.' That was the reason he wanted to become a counsellor. His nan was wrong. Pain and suffering *are* personal and incomparable. A lost leg is no more distinguished than a lost lover or a dying dog.

But now it is Dan who is wrong. People do have power over other people. They always have done, and they always will. He tells others to be brave and have courage, but he is a coward. He can call it shyness if he likes, but the truth is he's scared. He's in his own little bell jar, fingers pressed up against the glass.

When Dan was twelve and his friends started talking about girls, Dan was confused, but not embarrassed. Why waste time looking at silly girls when they could be playing *Star Wars* or armies? It wasn't until he started staring at the boys while they stared at the girls that he began to worry. At home he'd ponder his weakness for Adam's apples as his mother sliced fruit for his break-time snack.

She always had textbooks lying around the house. He normally didn't notice them, but one day she came home with a book called *Why Be Happy When You Could Be Normal?* by Jeanette Winterson. Dan was thirteen, at that age when he didn't need to read a book to get the gist of it. This one felt like an omen. It wasn't *normal* for boys to want to kiss boys, not in his small town anyway. It was normal for boys to like girls. Dan was already the shortest in the year, and late to the puberty party. He was still without a single armpit hair, while Barry Tanner had bum-fluff above his top lip and was so tall he could rest his elbow on Dan's shoulder. At school they named Dan after a tiny jockey with a lisp. 'Hey, Lester Piggott, pass the ball.' Dan was already on the back foot. Already had to fight to overcome his shyness, his shortness, his self-doubt. Being gay was simply too much to contend with.

And so the die was cast. Dan had chosen normal over happy. Some people have no legs. Dan has no courage, like the lion in *The Wizard of Oz*. Atticus is Dorothy, wanting to lead him to the Emerald City, but Dan has seen the ending, and he isn't altogether sure it's a happy one.

His client leaves feeling worse about herself than she did before she arrived. She'll go home and tell her diary she isn't strong enough not to believe them when they call her fat and ugly. She'll call in sick for the next counselling session and beg her mum not to make her go. Her mother, who wishes her daughter would lose fifteen pounds and get braces, will sigh and tell her she's not helping herself.

Dan makes a note to phone her and tell her she needs to reinforce the messages being discussed in their sessions. The old Dan would have run down the stairs, caught up with the girl at the door and made eye-contact with her. He would have told her she was doing really well and deserved happiness. He'd have pressed an acorn from the stash he keeps inside an old marbles bag into her hand and said, 'Remember. Before the acorn can bring forth the oak, it must itself become a wreck.'

Dan has photos of saplings in pots on windowsills. They live in houses belonging to people he will never see again. He doesn't need to. He can see they're growing just fine without him.

Where is that Dan now? This version of him feels made up of the Seven Deadly Sins.

The phone finally pings at twelve thirty, as Dan is looking at his sandwich and thinking he's never felt less hungry. He tries not to lunge across the desk to reach it.

ATTICUS: *I climbed up the door. And opened the stairs. I said my pyjamas. And put on my pray'rs. I turned off the bed. And crawled into the light. And all because you kissed me goodnight. Xxx*

Dan has to google the lyrics, and in the break between his afternoon patients, he puts his feet up on the sofa and listens to Doris Day crooning at him that ' 'twas midnight and yet, the sun was shining bright, and all because you kissed me last night'.

Dan's afternoon flies by and he's soaring. He finally manages to convince a long-standing patient who needs cit- alopram, not counselling, to go to the doctor. 'You deserve a better life. You deserve not to carry this anxiety around with you. You deserve to arrive in St Pancras station and see nothing but the best bits, not spend your time frantically searching for escape routes. I want you to stand next to the piano as someone plays and listen to them while you miss your train.'

What a speech, Dan! He's so buoyed up when she leaves, tears in her eyes, that he calls the mother of his last patient and gives her a list of books to order and tells her to make sure her daughter attends the next session, along with his personal phone number, which is entirely against the rules.

When he walks out of the building at six p.m., Atticus is standing outside, leaning against the wall. Dan is happy, embarrassed and aroused all at once. He can't help but smile, though. Atticus pushes himself off the wall and says, 'Hello, Daniel-sun,' with such open affection that Dan's head whips around to make sure no one can see them. The light in Alan's office is off. He'll probably be walking out of the door in a minute. Dan grabs hold of Atticus and drags him around the corner.

'Oh, hello, sailor,' Atticus says, surprised at Dan handling him so roughly. 'This is a pleasant surprise.'

Dan wriggles out of his embrace and sets off at a brisk pace that most people would call a jog, Atticus included.

'Why are we running? Are you that keen for me?'

'Atticus!' Dan says, in the voice he uses when Fitz won't come back to have his lead put on. 'Someone might see us.' He marches them down to towards Queen's Park.

'So what? We live in Brighton. The gay capital. I don't think anyone will be too surprised at two men walking along together. It's pretty normal down here.' Atticus reaches for Dan's hand and clasps it, sliding his cool fingers between Dan's sweaty ones.

Dan snatches it back as if he's been burned. 'It's not normal for *me*,' he hisses, tucking his hand into his jacket pocket. Poor Dan. All morning he waited to hear from Atticus and now he wishes he hadn't. Kissing him was the boldest, most outrageous thing Dan has ever done. He needs time to process it. He briefly wishes only his leg was gay so he could cut it off.

Atticus stops suddenly and touches the back of Dan's jacket. When Dan tries to walk on, Atticus says, 'One minute, please.'

Dan has never heard him sound so serious, so reluctantly he plants his feet and turns to look at Atticus. A vein is pulsing in his neck and Dan wants to trace it. Fuck. No, he doesn't. He wants to go home and see his dog.

'I'm sorry, okay? Last night was . . . amazing, and you've been on my mind all day and I just wanted to see you. I won't come to your work again.'

Dan sighs, the breath whooshing out of him in relief. Out, too, comes, 'It can't have been all day. You didn't even text me until lunchtime.' Dan cannot believe he said that out loud. He sounds like a petulant child.

'Is that why you're cross with me? Because I didn't text you sooner?' Atticus grins. 'Daniel, after your kiss, which left me more aroused than the first time I watched David Bowie performing as Ziggy Stardust, I spent most of the night trying and failing to get to sleep. I don't think you're ready to hear about what I was thinking, or wanting, for the rest of the night, so I'll just say it took me a long, long time to get any sleep. I texted you as soon as I woke up.'

Dan flushes and stutters and carries on walking, but there

is no pace to it now. He finally gets the courage to glance at Atticus, who is trying to look contrite and failing, and they share a smile that is an entire conversation, a whole new solar system. When they get to the taxi rank by the station, Atticus opens the door for him, and Dan gives the driver his address in a slightly breathless voice.

George

(George's marvellous medicine)

GEORGE'S DOCTOR IS SURPRISED. He'd expected George to be too fat or too thin. He'd predicted his diabetes would be off the chart and was worried about convincing him it was time to start the injections.

The diabetes nurse also admitted she'd been dreading it. She'd given up speaking to George about his health years ago, when she realized all he was ever going to do was scowl at her pink hair. Ellen was always kind, though. She used to write down everything the nurse and doctor said, and bring baskets of jam and hand-knitted scarves at Christmas. She remembered their names and sent thank-you cards.

This is the first time George has seen the doctor since the day of his home visit and, despite the odds (the doctor is secretly a betting man), he is coping. Well, his body is anyway. He looks healthy. There is colour in his cheeks and his gut protrudes no more, or no less, than it always has. The braces he wears are clipped to clean, pressed trousers and his cardigan smells of laundry powder.

The doctor wonders if he has underestimated George.

Somehow, he's managing to get by. He'd been sure George would follow his wife into the grave very soon after, before the grass could even grow over the mounded earth.

When he'd visited George's house, the sight of him in his chair had reminded the doctor of a bird who'd lost its mate and was lying on the floor of its cage, waiting to join it. As a doctor, he believes in medicine and facts, but the heart is the most vital organ, and in old people death can be contagious.

Yet here is George and he's in a hurry because he 'has lots to be getting on with'. The doctor weighs and pokes him and asks about his prostate and his bowels, and George is as indignant as always and asks what the hell it has to do with him. The doctor chuckles and wishes cantankerousness and indignation could be bottled and given to people who are fading. He imagines injecting his elderly patients with a fizzing shot of George, right in the backside. His marvellous medicine would make them leap off the examination table, keen to complain about the service.

He writes George a repeat prescription for the maximum length of time possible, and for the first time it's not because he doesn't want to see him. He signs his name with a flourish and in a moment of madness he goes to shake George's hand. George just stares at it, of course, and his face suggests the doctor has dropped his trousers and pulled out his penis for George to greet.

Betty has an appointment after George.

'Need another prescription to cure your mad cow disease?' he says.

'Ha-di-ha-ha,' Betty says. 'You need a trip to Specsavers,

Mucky Malcolm.' She points to a splotch of egg yolk on his shirt.

'Don't forget to tell him about your flatulence.'

'I won't. Did you show him your piles?'

'I don't have piles!' George roars, loud enough for the whole waiting room to hear.

'Oh dear, George, any louder and we'll all start dancing.'

'Dozy tart.'

'Debbie Downer.'

'Greedy pig.'

'Billy Bullshit.'

A laugh blasts out of him before he can stop it. Betty's face lights up in victory, just as her name is being called.

George sits in the waiting room, and tells himself he's not waiting for Betty, just having a break before he braves the bus home. He stands up as she ambles towards him in her matching ill-fitted livery, stumbling slightly on the ridiculous stacked trainers she wears that she claims help weight loss and balance. ('They saw you coming,' he told her, when she brought them round to show him.)

'Still not been committed to the funny farm, then?' he says now, as he wrestles himself into his coat.

'No. They don't know I spend time with you so they think I'm completely normal.'

George scoffs so hard he almost spits out his teeth.

The receptionist watches them walk off and thinks how quickly George has replaced his lovely wife, and how sad it is that she dedicated her life to a man who didn't seem to care about her at all.

Dan

(Come out when you're ready)

ATTICUS IS AS ENCHANTED with Dan's house as Dan was with his. There's not as much to see, though. Dan is neat and tidy, contained. Fitz's personality is more prevalent. His red parrot chew toy is on the living-room rug. In the corner of the kitchen, his basket is full of balls and the driftwood he brings back from the beach in his gentle mouth, like the retriever he is. He takes Dan's odd socks from the laundry to hide and for Dan to pair again later. There are drifts of hair on the patches of floor he likes to lie on, by the patio window, where he guards his garden, on the end of the sofa, by the front door, where he waits for hours for his owner. For his daily reunion, a dog's form of holy sacrament.

As for clues about Dan, a vintage *Star Wars* mug and a framed film poster lend a splash of colour to the living room. He has a sheepskin cushion, which his sister bought him, on his grey woollen sofa, and a framed photo of himself and his dad finishing a run together sits on his mantelpiece above a wood-burner, lined on both sides with perfectly stacked kindling and logs. It is so beautiful, so satisfying to look at, that Dan isn't even embarrassed at the amount of time it obviously took. 'Like a piece of art,' Atticus says, nodding at the neat rows, and Dan blushes with pleasure.

Dan offers Atticus coffee from his beautiful machine. Atticus asks if it's new and Dan says no. Atticus says, 'I thought you were a tea man,' and Dan says, 'Maybe my taste is changing.'

He wonders if Atticus is going to kiss him again, although he's just drunk an espresso, and maybe his mouth will taste weird. 'Back in a sec,' Dan says, and he runs upstairs to rub some toothpaste into his gums, just in case.

When he comes back downstairs, wearing a new T-shirt to suggest he was just getting changed, Atticus is reading a message on his phone. 'Someone called "Luke Solo" just texted you. Apparently, you're supposed to be meeting him at the windmill for a ten-mile run.' Atticus frowns. 'Is that code for something better, and who is this Luke Solo, who plans to "angry truck-man your ass all the way to Woken, Tennessee, Wallace and Gromit style"?'

Atticus looks from the phone to Dan, the skin above his eyebrows rippling like a wave. 'Not much surprises me, Daniel, but this is most unexpected. Even I don't know what Wallace and Gromit style is.'

Dan groans and tries to snatch his phone, his face red. 'Shit. Luke's my cousin, and an idiot, obviously. It's this thing we do together, the running. With our dogs. We're training for an Ironman. I can't let him down. I won't be long, if you want to stay.' Dan trails off when he sees Atticus frown.

'You're really going to go and leave me?'

What else can Dan do? He can't tell Luke he's busy,

because Dan is never busy. Luke will want to know what he's doing, and Dan can hardly say, 'I've got my ex-patient on the couch and I'm hoping he'll kiss me.'

Not knowing if Atticus is being serious, Dan says carefully, 'We're training. We can't skip sessions.' Just the thought of it makes him flinch. 'I won't be long, and I'll cook dinner when I get back. I'm sorry.'

Atticus still looks a little unsure. 'Will you be going all the way to Woken, Tennessee, tonight or just Shoreham?'

'Oh, God. I'm sorry. Luke always talks like that. He's a primary-school teacher. Being a grown-up all day is hard for him.'

'Just him?' Atticus asks, scrolling up the messages with a long, pale finger. 'It seems you struggle too.'

Dan tries again to grab the phone, but Atticus raises it higher. 'Careful, Daniel, or I may be forced to beat you so hard you say Uncle—'

'Atticus. If you don't stop, I may die.' Dan gives a final lunge and snatches the phone back. Embarrassment has made him angry. 'You shouldn't go through people's phones. It's illegal. A violation of their privacy.'

'Sorry,' Atticus says, looking and sounding genuinely contrite.

'That's okay.'

Atticus silences whatever Dan was going to say next with a kiss. 'I'll cook dinner,' he adds, as he lets Dan go.

Luke is fiddling with his phone when Dan gets to the Beacon, accompanied by Fitz. He doesn't even notice Dan approaching till he clasps his shoulder.

'Shit! You made me jump!' Luke twists the phone back onto his armband and smiles at him. 'Ready, Eddie?'

'Let's do this,' Dan says. He's talking about the run, but he's thinking about Atticus. If Luke notices he is quieter than normal, he doesn't mention it. He thinks Luke seems slightly preoccupied too. Meanwhile, Fitz and Wolfie bend and scratch out a warm-up.

They start out slowly, letting legs that have been sitting behind desks all day warm up and loosen. Dan likes to imagine each muscle in his body stretching out, starting with his toes. Normally, by the time he gets to his head, his mind is an empty church on a rainy day, and his legs are machines that pistol and pump. Not tonight. Tonight he can't stop thinking about his virginity.

Dan knows what his body is physically capable of, the extent to which he can push it, yet at the same time, he has no idea at all. His body is a stranger that's never been used for sex, to give or receive pleasure. 'Please don't let me be shit at it,' he chants silently, as he runs. 'Please don't let me disappoint Atticus.' He wonders who he's praying to, wonders if this is what the sky will look like the first time he has sex. Will those tiny fluffy clouds still be hovering in the last of the light? He wants to take a photo. Keep this moment as a solid piece of evidence in his wallet.

They finish on a sprint so punishing that he can think of nothing except breathing.

'Aren't you going to cool down?' Luke says, when Dan doesn't drop to the floor for some yoga-like limbering. 'Not like you to forget.'

Dan blushes and says, 'I was just about to,' and drops into the most painful warrior pose possible.

Fitz and Wolfie toss out a sun salute and a cobra.

'Don't make it too obvious, but there is an S-Q-U-I-R-R-E-L at ten o'clock,' Luke hisses, from the side of his mouth.

There is nothing Fitz and Wolfie love more than to chase squirrels, for hours if they can. But Dan needs to be getting back home, to Atticus.

'Hey, Fitz, what's this, boy? What's this?' Wolfie bounds over immediately. He's never learned that Dan doesn't carry treats in his pocket, he just pretends to. Fitz, however, is a wiser sort of dog, and instead scans the vicinity. He knows Dan often uses diversionary tactics when there are foxes about, or badgers, or . . .

Fitz's barks are a staccato Morse code to Wolfie, who looks to eight o'clock, nine o'clock. Fitz barks again and finally Wolfie spots their ginger-and-grey nemesis. And they're off. The squirrel, which Luke names Jerry, waits until the last possible moment before shimmying up a nearby beech tree.

Atticus is still in the kitchen when Dan and Fitz get home. He's lit the candles Dan keeps in the fireplace by the burner, and laid the table. Dan can hear the sound of the bath running. Atticus must have been standing by the window, waiting for him. For the first time, Dan acknowledges how very lonely he has been.

After the meal, they wash up together, occasionally bumping hips or brushing arms, and Dan doesn't know how it happens but suddenly they are on his pristine sofa, cushions askew, kissing. Buttons pop and zips purr as half-undone cloth-ing is hurriedly tugged off.

And then they are naked, and Dan looks out of the window at the sky to make sure he remembers exactly what shade it is. He's decided to paint his whole house that colour, but then Atticus halts, presses his forehead to Dan's briefly before roll-ing off and saying, 'Sorry. I got carried away.'

Dan wants to say, 'It's fine. Better than fine. Better than anything in the world. Carry on,' but he can't because those lines belong to the Dan who lives inside him, so he says, 'Oh, right, yes. Sorry. Me too.' And then there is the slightly awk-ward re-dressing dance, buttons that moments ago were wrenched from holes now being carefully re-done. Off-balance hopping on the spot as jeans are tugged up. Zips too loud in the silence as Dan wonders what he did wrong.

'Nothing,' Atticus says, taking Dan's face in his hands. 'You did nothing wrong. I just need to know you're sure.'

'I am,' Dan says, not sounding it, and Atticus laughs, kisses him once and says, 'I'll know you are when you *demand* I carry on.'

He heads out of the door and Dan locks it behind him, knees still knocked, ego, too. Then he blows out the candles, whistles for Fitz and goes to bed, where sleep doesn't come.

Lizzie

(I don't know what to tell you)

Lizzie dreams she's in her classroom, an autumn wind plastering russet-brown leaves against the large windows. The children have their heads down, working. Pencils scraping a symphony. She's drowsy after lunch, hands on bulbous stomach, swollen feet resting on an upturned wastepaper bin, when she feels arms and feet thrashing inside her, the movements frantic. It feels as if her baby is drowning, is attacking her. This pain has teeth. She pulls up her blouse and watches elbows and knees protruding through her Plasticine stomach. She can almost see the baby, kicking and punching inside its globe of amniotic soup, tugging on the cord, ringing a bell. Stopping the world.

Eventually the seas inside her calm. Lizzie waits for her baby boat to right itself again, but she feels the head has become dislodged from her pelvis. From where it should be. Outside the sky darkens quickly and without warning, late September dying dramatically. She'd only fallen asleep for a moment and suddenly everything has changed.

Fear wakes her now, visceral and suffocating. Lizzie lies

listening to her heartbeat, feels her sweat cool. Breathes in for four and out again. Pictures a square in her mind.

She's dreamed this dream over and over, the details never changing. Sometimes it's so bad she wakes Lenny with her cries, her pleas for it to stop. She turns to face him now and sees he's snoring lightly next to her, one pale leg over the covers, arms above his head.

She gets up carefully and wraps herself in a robe, before creeping out of the door and down to the bathroom, where she splashes herself repeatedly with cold water to wash away the memories.

They'd gone back to Luke's house after school and Luke's dog had stared at her again.

'Wolfie, what's the matter, mate? You've met Lizzie before. She's a friend.' Luke had bent down to stroke his ears. 'He's never been like this with anyone before.' He started patting his dog, like it was a baby who needed winding, and added, 'I think he's jealous of you!'

Luke had laughed and told Wolfie what a handsome, special dog he was in a sing-song voice. Wolfie's tail had wagged on autopilot, but his eyes remained wide and locked on Lizzie.

He knows who I am, Lizzie realized. The woman who didn't give him any sausage. The woman who only thought about herself and smelt like a dog who'd rolled in dead fish to cover its scent. There was no jealousy here.

Luke had sent Wolfie outside with a bone and 'Here you are, champ,' and Wolfie had gone, snaking his long, bristly fur past Lizzie's legs, leaving goose bumps.

Luke had cooked them dinner. Carbs and chicken and far too much. It had sat in her stomach and weighed her down. She liked to pick and graze. A handful of nuts here, a raw carrot there. Maybe the dregs of Lenny's cereal if he didn't want it. 'Brown pasta helps lower cholesterol, even though it actually has more calories than white,' Lizzie had said, making a volcano of her leftovers.

'Don't play with your food,' Lenny said smartly, and Luke laughed. 'Brown stuff doesn't taste as nice.'

'No, but your body needs more than just empty calories.'

'We know, Mum,' Lenny said, then rolled his eyes at Luke. 'She's obsessed with brown. Brown bread, brown rice, brown pasta—'

'Brown-ie for dessert?' Luke interrupted, and Lenny grinned and offered him a high-five.

While she was washing up, Luke had tossed a box to Lenny. She'd watched from the sink as Lenny opened it and pulled out a pair of football boots. She didn't know which make they were, but she knew from Lenny's face that they were good. The ones he wanted, the ones she couldn't afford. Lenny had jumped up to throw his arms around Luke, who sounded slightly choked up when he told Lenny how welcome he was and he should try them on to make sure they fitted. Lenny went one better and demanded to go outside into the garden to practise his kicking. It was dark, but the garden was tiny and the light from the kitchen glowed brightly enough to allow him to see the ball.

Luke had come in to join her just as she finished drying the dishes. 'You shouldn't have done that,' she'd said.

'It was nothing.' Luke moved closer, so he could watch

Lenny cheering and skidding on his knees, jumper pulled up over his head.

'It wasn't.' Lizzie's voice was quiet and detached. Luke was too distracted to notice that the mood had changed until she added, 'We don't need your pity, or your charity.'

He'd turned to look at her then, surprise and hurt on his face. 'I don't think that at all. I bought him the boots because he needs a pair, and I wanted to do it.' Luke had sounded nervous.

'You should have asked me first. Do you know how hard it's going to be to persuade him to give them back?'

'Why would you give them back?' Luke said slowly, trying to catch up. Two red spots had appeared on his high cheekbones.

'It wasn't your place to buy them.' She looked at Lenny, sitting on the damp lawn, running his fingers over the boots in wonder. Greg's ghost stood behind him in the shadows, watching her through the window. She shivered.

'He's happy, though, Lizzie,' Luke had said, shrugging. He didn't understand what the big deal was. 'He deserves someone who will encourage him, buy him the gear.'

She'd whipped round then and hissed, 'Don't tell me what my son deserves. I know what's best for him.' Her hands had started shaking and tears had sprung to her eyes. She'd had to take a deep breath and dig her nails into her palms to calm herself.

Luke had been contrite, realization dawning. He'd touched her arm gently and said, 'I'm sorry. I was just trying to help.'

Lizzie sighed then, and all her anger had whooshed out, leaving her nothing but tired. 'I overreacted. It's hard . . . sometimes.'

'You didn't. I'm to blame, come here.' He'd reached for her wrist and must have seen her flinch, but before she could turn away, remove his hand, he'd pulled up her sleeve and seen the mark, the perfect shape of a cigarette butt. The wound had mostly healed, but a spot in the middle was still damp and sticky.

'Lizzie, what the fuck?' Luke had said, staring at her wrist lying limply in his palm. The skin around the burn was pale. He'd studied it in silence, his cheeks getting redder and redder. Lizzie had shaken her head but said nothing and, in slow motion, he'd carefully eased her sleeve up higher, until he found the next, and the next. A constellation of pain. An atlas of her past.

'Who did this to you, Lizzie?' Luke's voice had been quiet, but she still said nothing. 'Was it his dad?' Luke had nodded to the window. Outside, Lenny had taken off his boots and was wiping the mud and wet grass off them with his T-shirt. Wolfie sat next to him, giving him the odd lick here and there.

Lizzie couldn't find her voice and Luke had taken her silence as a confession.

'Are you safe,' Luke had asked her gently, 'when you go home?'

'We ran away. We live in a shelter. Some of the cuts are just slow to heal,' Lizzie had said into his chest, into the warmth of another body, after such a long time of being the strong one. She'd held Lenny like this so many times. How wonderful it felt to be the one being comforted, being held, just this once. Just for a little while.

Now, back at the shelter, alone in the bathroom, she keeps on splashing her face with water, but it's incapable of washing anything away. When the door creaks she assumes it's Lenny, come to find her, missing the shape of her next to him in the bed. 'Night, Lenny,' she says each night, as he is pulled into slumber, away from her. 'I'll meet you in my dreams.' It never happens, though. She dreams of things that have already happened and – thankfully – Lenny is never there.

Her visitor is not her son. It's a wet nose, followed by two pointy ears. Maud walks in slowly, her paws making a clicking noise. She stops near Lizzie's ankle and gives it a lick. Her tongue is warm and wet, and Lizzie isn't sure she likes it, but Maud won't stop.

'Why won't you leave me alone?' she whispers to Maud, but Maud carries on licking the patches of skin she can find, and it's stupid but Lizzie almost feels like she's being cleansed somehow. She slides to the floor and tips her head back against the wall, letting Maud complete her expurgation.

George

(How could you do this to me?)

GEORGE IS AT BETTY'S house. She's finally decided to do some work on her garden and has asked George to help. Nothing flash or too tricky to manage. Just pots of bright colour here and there – she points to the exact spots. She doesn't have time for anything more, she tells George, almost apologetically, as if he's desperate to do it.

He's in the little shed in the garden, marvelling at how neatly her husband's tools are lined up, how clean they look. He's searching for a screwdriver to make holes in a hanging basket, digging through the old dresser drawer, when he finds it.

The letter is tucked under an elastic band along with two packets of sunflower seeds. He recognizes the handwriting immediately. This letter doesn't have his name on the front. It's addressed to Betty. It has been opened then resealed with a piece of tape, which George rips off with his teeth and spits out onto the clean floor.

Betty,

I'm sorry to write to you like this out of the blue. We have met before, but only briefly. We both helped with the

Christmas tree exhibition at church for the local school-children. I loved the tree you decorated using recycled plastic. I think I told you that at the time, and you said you loved my knitted tinsel. The tree hadn't come out quite the way I wanted it, and my dried oranges smelt slightly of mould, but thank you. I really appreciated your kind words. Obviously, I'm not writing to you to thank you for liking my Christmas tree, it's just hard to broach the subject and I fear I'm making a hash of it already. I am not very well, Betty, and my husband doesn't know. I can't tell him because there's nothing he can do to stop it (cancer of the pancreas, stage four). He will show his sadness as anger and I don't have the energy for that. I only have enough left to make some of his favourite meals and sort out his appointments. I don't think you've met my husband, but you may have heard about him. Forget what Barbara says. She means well, but she and George don't get on. I've been married to him for over forty years and I know him better.

I wish we could be having this chat over a cup of tea. Time is nothing until you have none. The things I want to tell you should come after years of friendship, but I don't even have weeks, so I hope you don't mind.

To understand George I need to tell you a story. It's about my dad. He used to go to the pub every night smelling of coal-tar soap and a peppery cologne. My mother used to dust the bottle, stopping every time to sniff the lid. She didn't have a bottle of her own perfume to dust, just that cut-glass bottle with the red metal cap.

I could smell it each time I was sent to collect him, when eight o'clock passed and then nine and his dinner *was cold on the table . . . My mum would never go herself. She would pat her hair and smooth her pinny and say, 'Look at me, love, in my slippers!' and I'd think that all she needed to do was put on her coat and dab on some lipstick. It wasn't about other people seeing her, I finally realized. It was about what she would see herself. Her husband sitting in the corner booth of the local, the light of a single candle making him seem like a single man. Next to him a lady, always a different one. He loved them all, and they seemed to love him, but none more than my faded mother in her washed-out aprons.*

My mum cried all the time, over a man who could only ever really love himself.

Fast-forward a few years, to the day I met George. I was at the Saturday market, getting fabric. It was hot and busy, so I decided to buy a punnet of strawberries to eat on the bus. The fruit-and-veg stall was crowded. I stood back, fanning myself with my shopping. A woman pushed past me and started picking peaches. She was tall and pretty, and her stockings were ruler-straight down the back of her legs. She went to pass the bagged fruit to the seller when a man said, 'Oi, I was first. Wait your turn.' The woman looked shocked. A face like that didn't normally have to wait. George pushed her out of the way and paid for his bag of Brussels. That was when I knew he was the one for me. He'd never have his head turned by a pretty woman. Forget the pub, he'd be at the table before dinner was served, banging his knife and fork with impatience. He was rude and awkward and no one else would want him.

As soon as I got to know him, though, I knew I'd picked more than just a loyal man. I'd picked a decent, hard-working one. I never wanted for anything. Each year, he demanded I get a new coat, new hat, whatever I needed, whatever I fancied. George tries to hide it, but he's thoughtful. He's honest, too, and he's funny, Betty. He'll make you laugh like no one else. He's kind, when he thinks you can't see it, and he cares about doing a good job. About making something better, making something that will last.

I used to joke that if we were Jack and Rose on the Titanic, *he'd push me off the bit of wood into the sea. He always said, 'No need. I'd have made the bloody ship better in the first place.'*

And we were happy, Betty. In a way other people won't understand. Our marriage ran like the Singer sewing-machine George bought me instead of a honeymoon. Sometimes it needed a belt replacing or a new bobbin winder, but we spooled on like my original 66 straight stitch. It never broke down, no matter the material I fed it or what I threaded it with. I pressed the pedal and it sewed. After all this time it has never stopped working and the original mechanism still shows no sign of wear. It could go on for years. Alas, I have only days. That sewing-machine is yours now. Please keep an eye on my George.

He's going to need someone when I go, and I think that person might be you. It feels odd to sit here, at the table he made for us, and ask a stranger to look after my husband because I'm not going to be here to do it myself. I'm not scared of dying, but I'm scared for George.

I know you lost your lovely husband, Bill, a while back. I'm sorry I didn't get to meet him, he sounded wonderful. So was the way you picked yourself up after he passed. It was nothing short of remarkable. Every time I went to put my name down for something, yours was already there.

I know you're busy, with all your (wonderful) projects, and I'm certainly not asking for my husband to be your next one, but would you please, if you have the time, or the inclination, maybe check on him now and again? He won't like it and he'll be rude, but I saw how you handled those children when they tried to steal the prayer cushions to make a fort and I think you can handle him. I'm not asking you to do much, maybe just push him in the right direction. My George is never going to sing from hymn sheets and he's not the neighbour you'd call on for milk or sugar, but he is a good man, Betty. We were never blessed with children to go round this table George spent months making. We only ever had one another. It's all right for me, I get to go first. I don't have to live in a world without him. I'm sorry, Betty, I need a minute to get a clean hanky. This dying business is so messy. Right, I've blown my nose and made a fresh pot of tea, so where was I? Oh, yes, he loves gardening and woodwork. Maybe, with enough nagging, he'll tackle the church allotment. He needs something to do other than listen to his beloved cricket. I hope getting Poppy was a good idea. She's a lovely dog. George doesn't agree but, in time, he will. She's sitting next to me as I write this, her dear little nose on my arm. I feel so sad I won't see her grow up. Anyway, I'd best get on. I've a funeral to plan. I do hope Barbara doesn't go too mad with the flowers and hymns. George hates the poem 'Death Is Nothing At All' so no doubt she'll kick off with that. Sorry, again, to lay this on you. Feel free to ignore this letter, but please, never tell George I wrote it. He's a proud and private man. Oh, and please do help yourself to any of my things. I know George will hoard all of me in the spare room. I don't have much, but if any of it could be of use to anyone, then please pass it on. I know the charity shop in the village is always asking for donations.

With gratitude,
Ellen Dempsey

George is so angry he can't speak. He's so angry he's forgotten all his favourite swear words. All he can do is stare at the letter while betrayal and humiliation stab at him like a thousand knives.

Ellen had asked Betty to befriend him. Betty had known his wife was dying before he did. The more he thinks about it, the crosser George gets. He can feel his heart racing and hopes he's having a heart attack. He hopes it's the end for him, right here in another man's shed. He wants Betty to find him, to know she killed him with her lies and deceit and her fucking greasy cooking. And why did Ellen tell Betty all that stuff about *them*? What on earth had got into her? She never used to be so loose-lipped. Likening him to her Singer. That bit about her mum and dad. No one else would want him? The words hit him like gunfire. Stomach, legs, temple, a round of bullets in his heart.

George tries to stop breathing. He wants to choke and flail

his arms as he falls. He wants to smash the plant pots, land on their spikes and make a bloody mess for Betty to slip in. The blood would be on her hands then. Maybe people will think she killed him. The idea is so wonderful he considers slashing his wrists with a jagged piece of pottery if this heart attack doesn't finish him off first.

After five minutes of trying to cut off his air supply with his bare hands, George admits defeat. His heart will not stop fucking beating. He can feel it pounding like a machine-gun in his chest, firing him up.

His wife knew when she was dying, had it all planned out. George isn't so lucky: he's still here and, according to the doctor, he's as fit as a fucking fiddle. Not even this shock can carry him off.

He sits down and wonders what to do next.

Dan

(Picture perfect)

D AN HAS STUBBLE RASH from kissing. Last night he and Atticus had been repeating the dinner and make-out session, and just as Dan was about to say, 'Stay,' Atticus pulled away. Dan wanted to demand that he carry on, but he couldn't find the words.

'You're not ready,' Atticus said, when Dan sighed in frustration.

'I am,' Dan had said shyly.

'Trust me, Dan,' Atticus replied. 'Please.'

So they had parted, pink and rosy. Fitz had looked at Dan and something he saw made him bark, as if he could sense Dan's frustration. Dan thought of the meat-filled bones he got Fitz from the butcher, which the dog loved but which also drove him mad. Fitz could never get to the jelly in the middle, no matter how hard he tried.

'I'm not about tomorrow. It's the opening night of an exhibition I'm running at the Barbican,' Atticus had said, on the doorstep. 'It opens at eight. Smart dress. You're very welcome to come along.' He'd looked at Dan hopefully, but

Dan had just said, 'Oh. Cool. Good luck,' and swallowed his disappointment.

All the next day Dan is sullen, distracted and irritable. His nan would have described it as 'feeling vinegary'.

At five o'clock, he goes running with Luke. They both push themselves hard and don't talk, and it's not until he blurts out that he would like Luke to have Fitz overnight for him that Dan realizes he's going to the gallery, to Atticus.

Luke raises an eyebrow and demands to know who the lucky lady is. Dan blushes and says, 'No one,' and Luke laughs.

'Must be someone if you're going to make a night of it,' he says.

'It's not like that. It's just a thing in London that I can't easily get out of and it's to do with work and I won't be staying over. I just don't want Fitz to be left alone for too long. If it's going to be a problem, I won't go.'

'No. Go you must. Will you be bringing her to the wedding?' Luke said innocently.

It had been all Dan's mum and sister could talk about since the proposal, Dan's bi-weekly phone calls to his mum saturated with hotel names and hat colours. She'd asked him, overly casually, if he'd be bringing anyone special along. 'Maybe, probably,' he'd blustered. 'I'll be too busy making sure Luke doesn't hit on any of the bridesmaids.'

'Forget the wedding,' Dan says. 'We've got to survive Dave's stag night first.'

So far, they'd been told to expect 'shooting, fishing, go-karting and a club night'. Dave had a mate who could 'sort them out with anything'. The same mate also knew 'a cracking stripper', apparently.

'Fuck. How can we get out of it?' Luke says.

'We can't. Helen will kill us.' She'd already messaged them both, a stern warning that they *had* to go, and be nice, and not let Dave get too drunk.

They sigh in miserable unison.

'Anything could happen before then anyway. Helen might realize what an utter dickhead he is,' Luke says. 'Well, you go and have fun anyway. I want to hear all about it when you get back, though!'

On the way home, Dan wishes he could peel off his skin and hide it in a bin. Luke isn't going to let this drop. He'll want to see photos and know names and details. He's going to want to meet her. Shit, he's going to tell Dan's sister and his cousin about her. He's going to tell his mother and then she is going to want to meet her too.

And it's not her. It's him. Atticus.

By the time Dan hops on the train, in the only suit he owns, the one he bought for a funeral, he's convinced himself that he's going to tell Atticus it's over. It's all far too complicated being this new Dan who goes on dates with men. He's only going so he can come back the way he used to be. He's leaving Atticus and all that jazz in London where it belongs and he's going to come back as the old Dan. The Dan who got frustrated by impossible jigsaws and uneven numbers.

But the second he sees Atticus reflected in the glass of a painting, Dan knows he won't tell him it's over: he'll never be able to say those words. Not when Atticus is wearing a plum velvet jacket and a black bow tie with his hair swept back and, Christ, he's even got a silk handkerchief poking out of the pocket of his shirt.

Dan spends a few minutes admiring him before Atticus looks up and their eyes meet. Atticus immediately stops talking to the couple next to him and marches over, pausing to take two glasses of champagne on his way. Dan watches him approach and wonders how much Atticus just lost on the sale he was making and decides he would pay it over and over again to see Atticus swagger towards him like that.

'You came.' Atticus's eyes are as bright as his trousers. Surely, it can't be him, Dan thinks as they stand, beaming at one another. Surely Dan can't be the reason for the unbridled joy on Atticus's face right now. 'Can I introduce you? Can I take you around and show you to the paintings?'

'I think you got that the wrong way around, Atticus,' Dan says, smiling.

'No, I haven't. I want to explain you to them all in detail. I want to tell them all about your colour and composition. I want them to gaze at you in wonder as I do.'

Atticus doesn't leave his side for the rest of the night. He escorts Dan to each painting with his hand pressing lightly on the bottom of his spine and Dan, who's never really 'got' art, gets it at last. How can he not when Atticus is so close to him, murmuring about composition and light, reflections and single brush strokes?

The gallery sells ten paintings that night, a new record, and afterwards people will say the real masterpiece was Atticus himself, though he isn't aware of anything but Dan.

Tomorrow, when he wakes up, his phone will be full of

messages and voicemails from the gallery and his father. Artists will have emailed him, asking what they need to do to get
him to exhibit their work. But that's for tomorrow, and tonight
is still young.

When the gallery finally empties, Dan grabs the last two
glasses of fizz and hands one to Atticus. 'A toast – to you. You
are . . . That was amazing.'

Dan tips his glass to drink but Atticus stops him. 'No. A
toast to you, Daniel. The most beautiful thing in the room
tonight, and in all the rooms, always.' Atticus kisses him before
he has time to swallow the champagne, and the bubbles fizz
and pop on his tongue. Staff are cleaning up around them but
tonight Dan doesn't care that they have an audience.

'Are you sure?' Atticus asks later that night, when they are
in the ridiculously plush hotel room that Atticus had booked
to 'stare out the window and miss Dan in'.

'Yes, don't stop.' Dan pulls off Atticus's bow tie and lays it
carefully on the dresser, along with his dinosaur cufflinks.
He's finally given in, has surrendered himself to lust, to desire,
is letting it guide his hands, his mouth. All he has to do is
stop thinking and feel his way.

It's just as they are both naked and Atticus reaches for him
that Dan sees it. The smallest dot and curve of ink, on the
underside of his bicep.

'Why have you got a tattoo of a semi-colon?'

Atticus shakes his head to dismiss the question, his fingers
darting over Dan's bare chest, but Dan takes his hands and
squeezes his fingers gently. 'Why?'

Atticus takes a breath, then says, 'To remind me that I
could stop, but I choose to carry on.'

Dan knows this is important. A puzzle piece in the jigsaw. He needs to write down what Atticus just said, look at it from all angles, but there is no time, because Atticus's fingers are on him again and with each touch Dan is losing his voice, his breath, his mind.

'Do you want to stop?' Atticus whispers in his ear.

'No. I choose to carry on.'

Lizzie

(Moon whale song)

LIZZIE HAS BEEN THINKING about Luke. Late at night when only the stars can hear her. About how he's still coated in boyhood. How life hasn't tarnished him at all. She thinks about how he smiles at anything – Lenny kicking a ball, a patch of sunlight that comes out of nowhere. He's the kind of teacher the school fears losing. The kind of person who makes everything better just for being there.

She can picture him in the staffroom, making the tea for everyone, bringing in cakes on Fridays. Lizzie found that side of teaching difficult. She preferred to spend her time in the staffroom working so she could spend her free time with Lenny and Greg. In happier times, she would want to rush home, would wedge herself between them on the sofa.

'Come on. Turn the TV off and get outside. Why don't we be mycophagists? That's someone who eats wild mushrooms,' she'd say, and Lenny and Greg would roll their eyes and Lenny would go back to the TV and Greg would kiss her forehead and reply, 'You don't have to teach everyone all the time, hon.' But then, after half an hour, he'd say, 'Right. Wellies on, Lenny. I'll make the sandwiches.'

Lizzie would clap her hands and rush to pack chocolate and her book of things to spot outside, and they'd be off, Greg and Lenny pretending not to be impressed with all her facts, even though Lizzie knew they were listening.

'How much potassium does a single portobello mushroom contain, Lenny?'

'More than a whole banana, Mum.'

It was so easy to be happy then. They lived in their own bubble, her and Greg and Lenny. Until it popped.

She can't keep doing this, foraging back in her past, looking for the versions of who she used to be. She's got to keep moving forward. She's begun doing some paperwork for Tess, who pays her a pittance, but it's a start. She spent her first wages on organic fruit and veg for the shelter, Lenny's football stickers and an issue of her much-missed *New Scientist*. With the change, she bought a bag of oranges and a bunch of bananas for the homeless man outside the shop. 'I'll bring you some socks next time,' she said. 'Feet are representative of the state of your whole body. The salt water from the sea would help clean out some of those cuts. Just make sure you keep them as dry as you can afterwards.'

'Thank you,' the man said, looking shocked. Most people bought him the three-pound meal deal. All-day-breakfast sandwiches, salty crisps and fizzy drinks.

'The bananas will boost your serotonin, and the oranges will help your gout.' She nodded at the swollen red lumps on his feet. 'Drinking less grain-based alcohol would help too.'

He smiled at her then and asked, 'Are you a doctor?'

'No. I just know things.'

He took the oranges and bananas and set them down on his filthy blanket. 'You *should* be a doctor, lady.'

As a child Lizzie had dreamed of wearing a white coat, and a stethoscope round her neck, but she soon realized she lacked the bedside manner needed for that profession. She didn't mean her words to come out detached and flat, as they did at times. It was just the way she was. Those who can't, teach, her mother had said, so she did.

'Thank you,' she'd said to the man now, and walked away feeling slightly taller.

Tess uses today's paid time with Lizzie to give her well-rehearsed recovering-from-domestic-abuse speech. 'Communication, communication, communication, Lizzie! Look at Sarah. She's blooming. You must spend some time with her, Lizzie. I'm sure you'll have so much in common. Why don't you come to our Friday film night?'

Lizzie had gone to a film night a couple of weeks previously, and it hadn't gone well. They'd let her pick the film and she'd put a David Attenborough documentary on, which was turned off immediately.

'*Boooring*,' one of the women had said, switching to a soap.

Lizzie had wanted to tell them they might like the programme if they gave it a chance. It was the one about the birds of paradise, and their ridiculous mating dances. 'He has all the moves, fancy footwork, the whirling dervish,' Attenborough said, as if he was commentating on *Strictly Come Dancing*. She had wanted to show the women that males in the animal world were no better than humans. They dazzled their prey into submission.

She wanted to help them, to teach them things, but she didn't know where to start. They all seemed so comfortable together, wedged arm to arm on the sofa, while Lizzie struggled with personal space.

She'd said sorry. Tried to watch the soap, but had no idea about any of the characters, or the storyline. She'd gone to bed feeling as if she'd failed an important test. One that she couldn't re-sit.

Tess waffles on. It's not until she says that they might soon need the room for someone else that Lizzie sits up and starts paying attention. 'What?'

'I said that at some point we're going to have to think about your rehabilitation. You can't stay in the shelter for ever.'

'But I'm not ready to go.'

'You won't be ready to leave until you start working through the programmes we offer, darling girl. The counselling, the group chats. The writing sessions. The employment talks. You need to put your name down.'

She's smiling, but Lizzie can tell from the tight lines around her mouth that Tess isn't prepared to give her this speech many more times. 'You need to start communicating, Lizzie!'

'I want to work for a charity.' The idea comes suddenly, ignited by her conversation with the homeless man, but she means it. She wants the feel-good buzz he gave her with his 'You should be a doctor, lady.'

'And that's great, but how are you going to work for a charity? Do you want to go back to college and get a qualification?

Do you want to work in a shop? I can help you, I *want* to help you, but only if you start talking.'

'Change is hard. The transtheoretical model of behaviour identifies it as a six-stage process. Precontemplation, contemplation, preparation, action, maintenance and termination. The pathways of our brain are formed at—'

'Lizzie,' Tess takes her hand, 'forget science for a second. None of us is ever ready to reveal our secrets. Who wants to tell people about their shame and hurt? Who wants to admit the things they've been subjected to? It's the twenty-first century and we women are still having to fight.'

Tess is on a roll now. Lizzie knows she's about to be given examples of women's suffering throughout history. She'll start with Sylvia Pankhurst (not Emmeline, Lizzie, she only wanted votes for the middle class), then she'll talk about Maya Angelou, eventually she'll move on to Frankie's story, and finish with her own. Lizzie knows this because Tess tells her the same thing all the time, like a sermon. 'That rat, Lizzie. That rat I married.'

Lizzie sits silently through the story of the first time Frankie had her arm broken. She doesn't fidget as Tess tells her about the time her husband cut off her clothes with a pair of scissors and locked her in the garden shed for twelve hours. When Lizzie's tears come, they're full of frustration and resentment, but Tess doesn't notice. She just takes Lizzie in her arms and rocks her like a child.

'There, there, pet. It's okay. Let it all out.'

Lizzie, trapped and anxious, agrees to attend the group session once a week. She even offers to make some beaded bracelets with the women on film night. Friendship bracelets to buy for friends. It's childish, but Tess smiles and rubs Lizzie's arm, coos like a pigeon.

That Friday night, Tess lends Lenny the shelter's iPad and Lizzie makes a nest for him in their room. 'I've got to go downstairs for a bit, lovely boy. Will you be okay?' Lenny, lost in YouTube clips of his favourite footballers, waves her away without a word, and Lizzie feels a flash of resentment. 'I want ten facts on the origins of football when I come back,' she warns him sternly.

Downstairs, she sits, alert like a meerkat, with the lemon biscuits she made earlier. Maud jumps onto her lap and Lizzie is grateful her hands have something to do as they stroke her. They are the only two in the room. Lizzie is about to give up and go back to Lenny when she hears hissing from the corridor. 'Just for ten minutes, please, Frankie. No, she's not, not when you get to know her.'

Lizzie hears Frankie groan loudly. Then she shuffles in, her motley crew behind her, and Lizzie moves to the far corner of the sofa to make room for them.

Moments later, Tess bustles in with a tray of tea, and a 'There, isn't this nice? All my girls together.'

Lizzie opens the beads she brought and the others watch as she sorts them into DNA strands of colour. Sarah cracks first and begins a bracelet, her fingers slim and nimble. There is a white scar on her knuckle that moves as she twists a bead onto the nylon.

'The turquoise is good next to the white. You need light in order to see colours,' Lizzie says, passing her a handful of beads.

Sarah smiles shyly, not showing any teeth, and, encouraged, Lizzie carries on. 'Aristotle thought colours came from mixing black and white together. Then Isaac Newton did his prism experiment and the theory changed.'

Sarah says, 'I didn't know that,' which is Lizzie's favourite sentence. She beams, and Sarah, who knows nothing about Aristotle or colour spectrums, tells her she's from Crawley and she misses her mum but is too scared to go back to visit, in case *he* finds her.

Lizzie misses her mother, too, but can't admit that out loud. Instead, she digs in her supplies for the nicest beads to pass to Sarah. 'Blue means protection, and in China red represents happiness. Maybe you can make your mother one too.'

Sarah smiles at her, as does Tess. Even Frankie has stopped glaring.

It's hot and Lizzie is stuck in the corner of the sofa. Panic dances at the edge of her vision. She pinches her thigh hard and thinks of Lenny, her port in the storm, and her feet twitch with her need to flock to him. Maud's wet nose is cold when it nudges her. The shock brings her back to the present. Lizzie moves her wrist away, but Maud finds it again and gives it a hard nudge, with the gentlest hint of teeth. Do it, Lizzie. Stop running away.

She takes a deep breath, and carefully rolls up her sleeves so the scars and burns emerge. The conversation withers, like the wrinkled patches on her skin. Lizzie says nothing, just carries on digging for beads, her fingers shaking, while Maud sighs on her lap in quiet approval.

After a moment, Lizzie feels a hand on her shoulder and turns to see Tess, who is so happy that Lizzie is sharing, opening up, she's actually twitching with joy. Around her, the women start to hum, like energy-saving light bulbs. Not conversation, more like whales communicating across the sea, filling the room with pulses and gentle clicks. Orcas are as capable of feeling loss as humans. Some have been known to carry their dead calves on their snouts for days. They are Lizzie's favourite creatures.

She says nothing, but everything has changed, and when she goes up to bed later that night, after staying behind to tidy up, she finds all the bracelets she helped the women make lying on her bed with tags that say, 'For you, Lizzie'. They are all blue, for protection. They were listening to her after all.

George

(You are dead to me)

Letter in hand, George marches out of the shed to find Betty, who's singing 'If I'd Known You Were Coming, I'd've Baked a Cake' in the kitchen as she drops glacé cherries into scone mixture. She turns when she hears him approach.

'Ah, there you are. I was—' But whatever she was going to say is forgotten when he thrusts the letter into her chest.

'Ah, about that . . .' She wipes her hands on her pinny nervously.

'About what, Betty?' George is going to make her say it. He wants to hear her tell him she's a liar.

'Christ wept, George, how could I tell you? I didn't even know you. I couldn't just go to your house and tell you your wife was dying.' Betty's voice squeaks in panic, turkey neck flapping.

'Yes. Yes, you fucking could have.'

'You read the letter. She didn't want me to. She didn't want you to know.'

'It wasn't for her – or you – to decide to keep it from me. As if I'm a child, or deranged!' George is on fire with rage. It's burning him up.

'George, she was doing what she thought best.' Betty smooths out the letter, as if she's about to start reading from it, but George can't ever hear those words again. Never.

He snatches it back. 'Did she pay you to go to my house and look after me?'

'What?' Betty looks horrified.

'Did she *pay* you? Is that why you won't take my money? Had you already had a lump sum off her, or just the sewing-machine? Where is it? Did you sell it?'

'Christ on a bike! No, she didn't pay me and I don't want your money. You know that. I spend time with you because I want to, you thickwit.'

'Bollocks. You spend time with me because my lying, dying wife begged you to.' Oh, Ellen, how could you do this to me? thinks George, falling into a kitchen chair and wiping at his brow. How could you make such a fool of me?

He hears Betty putting the kettle on, no doubt thinking that's the end of the row and a teabag will brew them back to the way they were before. She's wrong.

'This whole time, you've been coming to see me out of pity. Out of duty to my wife. I bet they're all in on it. All of them up at the church. I bet you're all laughing at me behind my back.'

'George, no one is laughing at you, you great clot. People are just starting to like you! Father Anthony is so delighted with the allotment, he wants you to join the choir.'

'I don't care about being liked and Father fucking Agony can shove his choir up his arse. In fact, he can shove it up yours.' George has found the energy to get to his feet and is reaching for his cap.

'George, please sit down. You've gone all shiny. I was going to tell you about the letter. I just—'

'Just what? When were you going to tell me?'

'I don't know. Soon.'

Poppy and Lucky, who have been watching from the corner until this point, their long noses going from George to Betty and back again, like tennis umpires, slink into the garden and cower behind the compost bin.

Back in the kitchen, Hurricane George rages on. 'What stopped you? Did you want to see how far you could lead me up the fucking garden path?'

'No, I didn't. I enjoy your company. I don't want to stop seeing you.'

'Oh, God, you're in love with me.' Betty goes to protest, but George speaks over her. 'You sad old windbag.'

Betty, who normally bats away his insults, looks hurt. Her eyes are glistening, and her fat cheeks are wobbling. Encouraged by this, George carries on. 'I wouldn't touch you with a barge pole.'

Betty finds her voice and forces her words to sound calm. 'I. Am. Not. In. Love. With. You. Didn't you read the letter? Ellen might have wanted you for your rudeness, but I don't. Yes. I admit. I came to see you because Ellen asked me to. She dropped the letter in at the church for me, three days before she died. The Neighbourhood Watch thing wasn't a lie, though. I'd had complaints about your dog. And when I got there and saw you . . .' She trails off, and George remembers that afternoon. How drunk he'd been. How she'd called the doctor. Oh, the shame of it. How he wants to die from the shame of it all. 'I did what anyone would do. I called the doctor and had a quick whizz round.'

'I wouldn't have done it.' George is by the back door now, talking to the frosted glass, his face a pink blur.

'Well, I did, and I'd do it again. I thought we'd become friends. I thought we had a bit of fun together.'

George turns to look at her and deep-fries her with his words. 'You are *not* my friend. You never were, and you never will be. You were just someone who could walk my dog, clean my toilet and cook my dinner. You could have been anyone, and so could I. I don't know what the fuck happened to your old man, but I know there's a reason why you don't talk about him. Why you don't even have one fucking photo up of him.' George twists and casts a hand wildly round the spotless house. 'But I'm no surrogate husband. I'm no replacement.'

'George! How *dare* you? I . . .'

Betty is as cross as he is now. He knows he's about to get the spiel about how many cups of tea she's made and how many cakes she's baked. She's probably got a booklet all about George somewhere. How many eggs she's boiled. How many Marmite soldiers she's prepared. How many bottles of bleach she's squirted down his loo.

George can't bear it. He needs to go home. He needs to sit in his chair and turn up the cricket and think of nothing and no one. 'Not one word, Betty. I swear to fucking God, not one more word out of that lying cakehole of yours.'

Betty says nothing. She just nods, once, and it's a sad sight, seeing the old battleaxe deflate, like a withered balloon. She's got none of her daft sayings for him now. No 'What's this banana shenanigans?' banter to butter him up. He's stripped her like willow bark.

George's anger fuels him all the way home, to the pantry for his beer and then to his armchair. When the cricket is over, and he's finally managed to piss out the three bottles he's drunk on a hungry stomach, he goes to the door of the spare room. It takes him a minute to open it – he's all fingers and thumbs, and drunk enough to cling to the dream that Ellen might be in there somewhere. What was that fucking awful poem from the funeral? 'Death is nothing at all. I am merely in the next room.'

Another of her lies. Ellen is not in the room, and neither are her possessions. Everything has gone. Every item of clothing, every pair of shoes. All the perfumes and powders and pots from the dressing-table. The hangers in the wardrobe. Her brown knitting bag and her parrot umbrella. The set of Basildon Bond writing paper that George now knows she bought to write to him and others from beyond the grave, playing them like chess pieces against one another. Her dressing-gown with the missing belt is missing. The faded blue slippers. Her hairbrush and rollers, that antique mirror with the brass handle that used to belong to her mother. The scarves she wore over her head on windy days and hairdresser days. Her record collection: Elvis Presley, Fats Domino and old swing classics. The china dogs, and the fake roses in a chipped vase that George stole from the hotel they stayed at on their first holiday together. The jar of buttons. Even the scented drawer liners had been taken, along with her socks and pants, and bras and stockings.

George tells himself he's imagining things. Tells himself it's the beer. Tells himself to go to bed, and in the morning everything will be normal again. He backs out of the room, staggers down the hall, then passes out on his bed with his shoes on. Poppy has to settle for sleeping on the floor, occasionally licking at the flaky patch of skin above his sock and below his trouser leg.

George sleeps for ten hours, and wakes confused and dehydrated. After a quick check that he hasn't wet the bed (it happens), he sits up slowly and groans as the room tilts and spins. Poppy barks and his brain pulses. He'd be sick, if only he had something inside him. An image of scones pops into his head again, cherries glowing like rubies. George remembers the rest and sees red.

Ellen's letter. The row with Betty. He gets off the bed too quickly and has to lean against the wall on the way to the spare room to keep his balance. He throws open the door, telling himself it was all just a dream, but he knows he's wrong before he even turns the handle. The spare room is as empty as it was the night before. Every single trace of Ellen is gone. George does a slow scan of the room to make one last check. Behind the open door is a cardboard box. George lifts it and underneath it is the Singer sewing-machine.

George sinks to the floor and reaches out for Poppy, who's followed him. He brings her little black-and-tan body towards his face, and for the first time since Ellen died, George sobs for his wife.

Dan

(I've heard that one before)

'ASK LUKE TO HAVE Fitz again,' Atticus implores Dan. 'I want to take you away. We could go to Paris.'

'I can't. I have work, and the Ironman training.' Dan smiles and tries to get out of bed, but Atticus pulls him back.

'Just for a couple of nights. I'm sure Luke can train on his own for two days.'

It's the morning after the previous night, when they became one mass of molecules for the first time. After the sex had ended but they were still combined, carbon and hydrogen, yet to re-form as two separate entities, Dan had realized he wanted to know all of Atticus. Nothing could be more exposing, more intimate, than the experience they had shared. Dan had given Atticus his body, his virginity. His trust. He hoped, in return, that Atticus might give him some honesty.

And so he asked, once more, for the truth: 'You never did tell me. Why did you come to counselling?'

But instead of the truth, Atticus had looked at him, stroked a finger down his face and, in a voice that sounded almost sad, had said, 'To find you, of course.'

'But you didn't know you'd find me.'

'But I *did*. Now, nothing else matters.' Atticus had combed his long fingers through Dan's hair, and it felt like walking into a room with an open fire after missing the bus and walking home in a storm.

'So, there *was* something else, some matter?' Dan pushed sleepily.

'If there was, it's all gone now. It's been replaced by you,' Atticus said, and the next thing Dan remembered was waking up curled around another person for the first time in his life. Then the delight of naked flesh and Atticus's morning growl.

Over the next week, Atticus keeps talking about French food, the Louvre and the Parisian boutiques. Keeps reading him restaurant reviews. The other Dan who lives inside him is rather keen to go shopping. Would rather like a plum velvet jacket and expensive scented candles. He wants to buy aftershave that they will both wear and a silk dressing-gown for Atticus.

'Maybe,' he says to Atticus. 'Maybe.'

The other Dan wants it so much that he finally asks Luke. They've just finished a bike ride and are both cleaning their wheels. The miles are adding up. They're getting fitter and the calorie-counting has been wonderful. Dan feels strong and in control.

'Can you have Fitz again?' he asks, as Luke sprays his wheels with Muc-Off.

'Yeah, sure.' Luke sounds distracted and Dan is instantly worried. Where are the questions about why? Where is the cheeky grin?

'You okay?'

Dan can't believe he's asking for a ribbing, but he's never seen Luke act this way before and he doesn't like it. It's like the rare times when Fitz doesn't eat his breakfast and Dan's world tilts sideways, making him seasick.

'Yeah, just knackered.'

He looks exhausted, Dan realizes, examining him properly for the first time in ages. 'Do you want to stop? We don't have to do this Ironman. We could do one another time.'

'No, of course not. I'll be fine.' Luke is paying more attention to cleaning his bike than normal. Usually Dan is the one who insists on all the spraying and wiping. Normally he has nothing else to do. He does now, though, and wants to get on with it, but he can't leave Fitz with Luke when he's in this mood. He wouldn't be able to relax.

He needs to do a bit of digging, but he can't use his counsellor voice on Luke because when he was doing his training, Luke was his guinea pig. He probably knows as much about counselling as Dan does. He'd dutifully made up scenarios (I think I'm related to Darth Vader; I've been abducted by aliens) and let Dan practise on him for hours. Dan, in turn, had been there for Luke when he was doing his teacher training.

Dan realizes they don't talk like they used to, and he's missed his cousin, even though he's sitting next to him and sees him almost every day. He wants to be able to share Atticus with him, but talking about it might make it real and Dan doesn't want to wake up yet, so he has told Luke he's going away on a weekend course for work. The lie tastes sour on his tongue and he sees Atticus in his mind, shaking his head sadly. Denied. Closeted. He pictures him wedged in Dan's wardrobe.

He's wittering on about not being back late when Luke says, 'I've met someone, but it's new and it's tricky, and I'm not sure what's going to happen. She's a parent at the school.'

The old Dan would have raised an eyebrow at the parent thing, but he's sleeping with a former client, so he says nothing, and Luke carries on: 'She's . . . It's . . . I don't know. She's something.'

'You always say that,' Dan says, with affection, and cuffs Luke on the shoulder.

'No, man, I mean it. This one is different. She's special.'

'That's exactly what you said about the tiny girl with the blue hair who worked at the library. You said, and I quote, "She's so perfect. You know how long I've been looking for my Smurfette." Remember?'

'Yes, but I didn't mean it then,' Luke says, sounding sulky.

'And you said the same thing about your teaching assistant with the long hair. You said she was the perfect Princess Leia and smelt of pick 'n' mix.'

Luke grins at that. 'Ah, sweet Lydia and her long Leia hair.' He shakes his head. 'But seriously, dude, Lizzie is not like them. She's super-clever – she knows the most random stuff. She's grown-up. She's hot.'

Dan smiles indulgently and pats his cousin's arm. 'Okay, buddy. Enjoy your serial killer. I'll give it a week.'

'I'm being serious, Dan. She's different. She's not trying to be anybody else, you know? She doesn't care about impressing people, even though she's a crazy genius. She's not . . . performing for anyone. She makes me think I don't need to perform either.'

Luke is hurt and immediately Dan feels contrite. 'Sorry,' he says, while the cogs inside whirl. Luke is a natural performer: he seems to love being centre stage, on display. Has that all been an act? Has Luke been hiding in plain sight?

'We haven't even slept together yet. I want it to mean something when we do. If she even wants to . . . She's got scars, from her ex-husband, on her arms. She ran away from him. I don't know much and I don't want to push her, you know?'

'Wow.' Dan's face creases with concern. He hadn't expected that. 'That's a lot to deal with, Luke. Are you sure you know what you're taking on?' It's the wrong thing to say: Dan realizes this as soon as the words have left his mouth. 'I didn't mean it the way it sounded.'

'Patronizing much? I think you did,' Luke says coldly, turning to walk away.

'Wait, Luke, please, let's talk this through.'

'I'm not one of your clients.'

'I know. I'm sorry. Truly. I just don't want you to get hurt or caught up in something that seems . . . complicated.'

'Fine. Look, I've got to go. Am I still allowed to have Fitz or is he too much responsibility for me to take on?'

'Don't be like that, please.' Dan holds out his hand for their shake. For a moment Dan thinks Luke isn't going to do the finger-wiggle, but then he does. Dan lets out a breath he didn't know he'd been holding.

Walking back to his flat, he tries to work out what just happened. Luke has never been like that with him before. He worries about it until his phone flashes with Atticus's name, and then Luke and real life are forgotten.

Lizzie

(You've done this before, haven't you?)

LIZZIE HAD ONCE READ a memoir by a survivor of Jonestown. A story about a woman getting out of a bad marriage, joining the cult in blind faith, and fleeing shortly before nine hundred people were forced to drink poison at gunpoint. She had done a lot of research after that memoir. It seemed too unbelievable but, then, Margaret Atwood hadn't included any scenario in *The Handmaid's Tale* that hadn't already occurred in some time or place.

Lizzie thinks of these things as she gets up and makes the bed, as she trots down the stairs and joins the other women. It's her turn to do breakfast duty. She gets out the spoons and lines them up neatly beside the bowls. The women say good morning to her now, but she's still not in the gang. She feels alone, as she always has, and sad, which is new, as she washes the dishes. She feels like the handmaid Offred. Maud seems to sense her mood and lies on her feet. Lizzie is grateful for the warmth.

Today she is meeting the careers-advice lady, Jackie. Jackie is pretty, in an overly made-up way. Long hair curls down her back. Her feet look swollen in her high heels. 'Hello, Lizzie, lovely to meet you,' she says, in a quiet voice, as they go into Tess's office. 'Sorry it has to be under these circumstances.'

'Me, too.' Lizzie means it. She can tell this lady feels awkward and almost guilty for not being one of them.

'Where would you like to sit?' Jackie asks. Lizzie chooses a chair by the window. 'Can I get you anything before we start?'

'No, thanks. I'm fine,' Lizzie says, shifting in her seat. She doesn't deserve this niceness, this compassion. What would Greg think if he could see her now?

Jackie pulls out paperwork from her bag and orders it in neat piles on the table. She pushes her hair back from her face, and a long nail gets caught in a honeyed strand. 'I love them,' she says, looking at her perfect manicure. 'I can't fit in half the clothes I want to wear, but I can have nice nails. Daft, I know.'

'You're damaging them with those long extensions, though,' Lizzie says, surprising herself by reaching out and taking one of Jackie's hands in her own to inspect the nails closer. 'Our primate ancestors had claws, over two and a half million years ago, but over time we evolved to have nails. The little white crescents are called *lunulae*, meaning "little moons".'

'Little moons,' Jackie says. 'How lovely.'

'Nails don't keep growing after you're dead either,' Lizzie adds, dropping her hand. 'That's just the base of the nail retracting.'

'Urgh,' Jackie says, wrinkling her nose and laughing.

Lizzie is so used to thinking of facts to impress her son that she forgets not everyone is interested in the grotesque. 'Sorry, my son loves all that kind of thing.'

'I have an eight-year-old daughter who's obsessed with sharks,' Jackie says. 'I have to watch *Jaws* almost every night.

She draws herself in a cage being dunked in the sea. I don't even like getting my hair wet, and she wants to swim with hammerheads and great whites.'

Lizzie laughs. She realizes that Jackie has relaxed her, and she likes her. She wishes they could be friends.

'What is your daughter called?'

'Bliss,' Jackie says. 'Your son?'

'Lenny.'

Lizzie imagines introducing them, then realizes it could never happen.

'Now then, enough about me. Tess said you were interested in charity work. There's an evening course at Sussex Uni. Sound good?'

'I love learning,' Lizzie says.

'Tess mentioned you used to be a teacher. Are you sure you don't want to go back? I could help you. We could fill in the forms together.'

A lump appears in Lizzie's throat. Jackie's kindness has caught her off-balance.

'I can't,' she says, her voice wavering. 'I wish I could, but I can't.' She cracks then, with the understanding that she will never be able to teach again. Her career is over. She can't go back to any of it. She'll have to start all over again.

'That's okay,' Jackie says. 'Don't worry. It's all going to be okay.' She passes Lizzie a tissue and pours her a glass of water.

Lizzie surprises them both by giving her a quick, hard hug. Jackie smells of berries and her jumper is soft. 'Bliss is lucky to have such a lovely mum,' Lizzie says.

'So is Lenny,' Jackie says back.

*

'I was thinking of going to college tonight to pick up some leaflets, maybe register for a course. Strike while the iron's hot,' Lizzie comments later that afternoon. It's not a good thing to say, one of the unspoken banned phrases, and she stiffens. 'I meant . . .'

'It's okay, Lizzie. I know what you meant,' says Tess. 'I must say, I'd rather you talked to the police first – we really do need to go through the official channels – but if you need the dangling carrot of the course to make you do what you need to do, then I'm happy to support you. I'll go and dig out the bus timetable.'

Maud stays close to Lizzie's heels for the rest of the day. Lizzie tells the dog she's fine, but Maud doesn't believe her, and follows her from room to room until Lizzie gives in, sits down on the sofa and lets Maud jump onto her lap.

'I'm going out, and you can't come with me,' Lizzie tells Maud later, but Maud doesn't budge. Lizzie sighs and says, 'I'll be back soon. Now move.' But Maud has one of her heads on and Lizzie is forced to open the door with Maud still against it. The terrier rolls along the welcome mat dramatically. Lizzie sighs again and says, 'Maud, stop it. I need to go.'

Lizzie doesn't take the bus towards the college. She plans to, but instead finds herself boarding a bus that heads in the opposite direction.

Luke opens the door wearing jogging bottoms and his school shirt. She's caught him off-guard. He's all rumpled and confused. 'Lizzie. What are you doing here? Sorry, I mean, come in . . . Wow, I wasn't expecting you.'

She'd been thinking about what it felt like to be in his arms. The sanctuary of them. How oddly safe he made her feel. The urge to be held again had been overwhelming.

He pulls the door open wide and she walks into the hall, where two dogs sit looking at her. A big yellow one with a pink nose, who wags his tail, and Wolfie, who barks. 'Stop it, Wolfie. Why can't you be friendly, like Fitz?' Luke turns to Lizzie and says, 'Fitz is my cousin's dog. He's here for the weekend.'

'Oh.' The yellow dog thumps its tail in response and rolls over for a tummy rub.

Luke drags a reluctant Fitz away from Lizzie's leg and puts him and a barking Wolfie in the living room, then shuts the door. 'Where's Lenny? Would you like a drink?'

'Wine? Lenny's with Tess. She runs the shelter.' Lizzie hadn't planned what she was going to say, and it comes out in a rush.

'Right.' Luke swallows. 'Cool. I mean, it's not cool . . .' Lizzie had told him about the shelter the night he saw her arms, but she hadn't given many details.

Lizzie watches Luke's Adam's apple bob and sees she's made a mistake. 'I shouldn't have come.' She thinks of Maud, the way she'd tried to warn her by blocking the door.

'No! I mean, yes. It's just a surprise. A great surprise. An I'm-your-father surprise.'

Lizzie frowns.

'*Star Wars?*' Luke says.

'Oh,' Lizzie replies.

They go to the kitchen and sip the wine awkwardly, their swallows loud in the silence. Lizzie hadn't planned it to be like this. She hadn't planned it at all. What had she been thinking? Why had she come? She should be at home now with her son, not here, pretending to be something she isn't with someone like Luke.

Lovely Luke, who looks at her like she's made of glass and he doesn't want to break her. She's broken already. She's jagged and she's going to cut him too. It's inevitable. Finally Luke puts down his glass and finds his courage.

He's too handsome not to have some kind of game, and here it comes, a finger on her wrist, turning it over, sending a shiver up her arm. The heat of him as he moves closer, taking her glass and setting it down with care. Eyes focused on her lips, head tilted to one side, then a pause, for her to nod or turn away. It's just science, really it is, but in that moment, when his warm lips meet hers, she almost forgets. They move to the bedroom.

'I need to hear you say yes,' Luke says, his fingers on the curve of her waist.

'Yes.'

'Are you sure? We don't have to do this. I'm happy to wait.'

Lizzie is impatient then. A woman's pain-killing response is triggered during orgasm and she badly needs some oblivion. 'Yes. Now. Please.'

Luke smiles at her and drops to his knees, and for a brief moment, everything is beautiful and nothing hurts.

Later, when Luke is asleep, Lizzie carefully untangles herself from him, gets dressed and goes into the bathroom to tie her hair into a ponytail. Then she opens the compact mirror with the bluebird on it and takes out a blade.

She uses the side of the bath to rest her leg on and pushes the razor into the skin at the top of her thigh. It bleeds well here and heals well too. Luke won't be expecting a repeat performance any time soon, and if he does, she'll tell him she's bleeding. It won't be a lie.

The blood flows fast and warm. She's gone deep and has to take her leg down and lean against the bath as her head spins. She lets it bleed for as long as she dares, as long as she can bear it, before she stems the flow. She's quick and efficient with the alcohol and the Steri-Strips. The homeless man was right. She'd make a wonderful doctor.

Dan

(Paris is lovely in the spring)

PARIS IS PERFECT. DAN will look back on the two nights and three days and know he experienced true happiness and will always be grateful for that.

Atticus has been before, of course, and whizzes him round galleries and cafés, filling him with culture and coffee as dark as treacle. They hold hands and kiss in public places. Dan has never been touched so much in his life. Atticus constantly has a hand on his knee, or the bottom of his spine. Dan jokes that he isn't going anywhere, but Atticus doesn't laugh, just holds him tighter.

On soft sheets in a breezy hotel room, Atticus asks Dan how often he's counted since they've been away. Dan says, 'A bit,' and tries to tell him how counting helps him, how it keeps him on the grid he likes to live in. When Atticus asks what his own number is on the map, Dan tells him he's no number, he's the winning coordinates in a board game of Battleships. Row C, line six. Hit.

'You sank my floating fortress, Atticus.'

He'll have to make up for the missed training sessions and the croissants when he gets home, but it'll be worth it. The *crème brûlée* and the *tartes framboise*, sweet and sour on his tongue, will always remind him of Atticus.

Atticus buys Dan a scarf that costs more than Dan makes in a week. He finds it in a shop full of scented candles and things that no one needs but people desire anyway: peacock feathers, glass coffee-tables, sheepskin throws. Dan tries to refuse but Atticus is adamant. He tells Dan it's to keep him warm when he can't, and there it is again, a brief acknowledgement of their impending doom. Dan doesn't have words to show what the scarf means, can only clutch Atticus to him by the Seine and think of how falling in love is a bit like drowning.

They wander until their feet ache, smiling at strangers. Dan wonders what they look like together. He sees them as an odd pairing, but when they lie together, their curves bend and fold into one another, as if they were two spoons cast from the same mould.

In a moment of bravery, Dan stops a pretty girl with long red hair and asks her to take their photo. They push their heads close together for the shot.

Just before the flash goes off, Atticus turns his mouth to Dan's ear and whispers, 'I'm so glad I didn't die before I met you.'

In the photo, Atticus's hair is blown back by the breeze, and although Dan's smile is slightly wonky, it is also wonderful.

They kiss goodbye outside Brighton station, Dan trying not to look like he's uncomfortable. On the way to Luke's to get Fitz, he promises himself he'll tell his cousin everything, but Luke is too full of Lizzie and the best sex he's ever had in his life for Dan to get a word in.

'Jesus, Mary and every single bloody saint, Dan. The way she—'

'*Aaand* that's enough.'

'How about you, man, did you get any action this weekend?'

How can Dan describe what he's seen? He felt like Armstrong stepping off the ladder onto the untouched surface of the moon. Like Columbus when he set sail. How could he put into words everything Atticus had shown him? 'It was pretty busy.'

'Good. Great. Lizzie told me we've been doing our training wrong. She says chocolate milk has the perfect amount of carbs.'

'She's wrong.' Dan is indignant.

'I doubt it, Dan. She knows everything. No more of your nasty whey protein. She said we should train barefoot too.'

'Has she done an Ironman?'

'No.'

'Well, then, I rest my case.'

'She's swum across the English Channel, though.'

'Oh.'

Dan feels out of sorts. He's only been away for two days but everything has changed. He thought only he'd be different, not Luke as well – Lizzie-this and Lizzie-that Luke. Dan feels replaced and recyclable and he doesn't like it.

George

(Where did you get that hat?)

GEORGE LIES IN BED and thinks about Betty. How she must have been clearing out the spare room all those times he was alone at the allotment. He thinks of her panting and puffing as she organized his wife into bags and boxes. Did she keep some bits for herself? He imagines her trying to cram her fat feet into Ellen's narrow slippers, like some pensioner playing Cinderella. He also pictures the people at the charity shop going through the boxes Betty dropped off. The comments, the sizing, the deciding if her underwear was good enough to pass on. Bits of his wife bandied about the village.

George flings off the covers with purpose, and Poppy scrambles closer to him for warmth. He needs to go and get it all back. Find the missing pieces of his Ellen jigsaw. He needs to remain calm and rational. He'll offer to buy back the stuff, if need be. Five pounds should do it. The main thing is to get it all back. He hopes it hasn't been sold, hopes he can remember what her stuff looks like. In his mind her slippers and dressing-gown whizz along a conveyor belt, like on *The Generation Game*. He needs to win back her china dogs, and her hairbrush, and that hat she loved. While he's very pleased Ellen never dressed like Betty, it would be easier to remember her clothes if she had.

George forces himself to take his pills after eating a stale bowl of cereal that's supposed to make him shit. He washes in the bathroom and gets dressed in clean clothes he laundered himself last week. Fuck you, Betty. I don't need you. They don't smell like they do when Ellen does them. *Did them.* He couldn't be bothered with the fabric softener or the clothes horse. He just hung them over the back of the chair in the kitchen, but they'll do.

Poppy wants to come with him, and he says no. 'Not today, dog. I'm going to have my hands full.'

George realizes what he's just said and worries he won't be able to get all the stuff back alone. He worries that he talks to the dog now. Then he wonders how Betty got it all out of the house. She must have had help. That scheming, planning, conniving bitch. What did she bribe them with? Did she bring that fucking Don round here? George decides he'll demand the people at the charity shop bring it back. They've stolen it, after all. It's up to them to return Ellen's things.

Poppy isn't talking to him, has turned her long body away from his goodbye. Betty's not even attempted to come round with a pie or a cake or an apology, and his wife's wardrobe is too bland to remember. Women, George thinks, as he sets off. Nothing but bloody trouble.

Dan

(Velveteen rabbit)

PARIS HAS BEEN AND gone, and Dan and Atticus are missing their holiday. To cheer them up, Atticus wants to take Dan dancing. 'I want to romance you, Count Danula. I want to buy you shiny shoes and a bow tie I can undo at the end of the evening.'

What can Dan say to that? He's only ever danced with Luke, at the front of noisy gigs in pubs with sticky floors. They didn't dance as such either, just jostled alongside the crowd, and Dan always got a cheap thrill when he pushed up against a pair of broad shoulders. Once, in a mosh pit, he was lifted overhead across the crowd. Hands on his buttocks, fingers digging into his ribs. It was euphoric and erotic. Dan had thought it would be the most dangerous thing he'd ever do.

But now here's Atticus, and he wants to hold Dan in his arms in a wine bar and croon into his ear. Then he wants to hold hands on the pier, on the fairground rides, scream to go faster. Dan wants to scream to go slower. Whenever Atticus touches him Dan blushes and Atticus laughs, and their intimacy is a whole other world in the sky.

Afterwards he floats back to earth, coated with a smear of

shame and the discombobulating sense that something changed while he was away and he can never go back. He is sure everyone is looking at him and he hates it. Wants to hide away in a small space and stroke his dog until people forget about him. Until he forgets about himself.

He remembers, as a boy, how his mum would march along the pavement, always in a hurry. Dan's legs were too short to keep up. 'Wait, please,' he'd say to her, but she never listened. She had things to do and places to be, and Dan eventually just learned to walk faster. That's how he feels now. Like a little boy trying to keep up.

'It'll be fun.' Atticus raises an eyebrow and Dan blushes at all the things the gesture has come to mean.

'I know. I just . . . I'm tired. It's been a long week.'

'That'll be all the training, wearing you out.' Here it comes, thinks Dan. Atticus has mentioned this before.

'I don't know why you're bothering. It's just a load of men in Lycra . . . Actually, *that* bit sounds good.' He looks at Dan and they smile before he carries on: 'But what does it actually mean? Who do you need to prove yourself to?'

'No one. It's not like that.' Dan tries to explain: 'I just want to know that I can do it, and I want to do it well. I like it, the training and the pressure. I don't know . . .'

'I don't know either. All that time you're wasting when you could be spending it with me.' Atticus sounds like a sulky child. It's almost adorable.

'It's not for much longer. I promise.'

'And then what? Another Ironman? A Goldman?'

'There's no such thing.'

'It really means a lot to you, doesn't it?'

'Yes. Sorry.'

'Don't be sorry. It is what it is. You want to be able to swim in the sea for miles, cycle for even more, then run a marathon. You can bear the pain and exhaustion. You just can't bear to be seen in public with me.'

'Atticus . . .'

'Please don't deny it, Dan. I'm many things, but I'm not stupid.'

'I'm not ashamed of you,' Dan whispers fiercely, and Atticus frowns.

'That's the saddest part of it all. I could handle you being ashamed of me. You're ashamed of yourself, and that's the bit that hurts.'

'I'm not.'

'Hide me, deny me, but don't lie to me.' Atticus isn't that much older than Dan, but in that moment, he sounds like he's lived a thousand lifetimes.

'I'm so sorry.' Dan's voice is a whisper.

'Don't be. Just tell me what I can do to help you.'

'I don't know. Maybe we should run away to Paris.' It sounds flippant, but Dan means it. He's been thinking about it. They could open an antiques shop. Spend the weekends driving to remote villages and the weekdays polishing chandeliers. 'Imagine it. Imagine how great it would be.'

'Daniel. I'll take you anywhere you want to go, but this would come with us and I couldn't bear it. You can be an iron man, but apparently you can't be a gay man.'

Dan gazes at Atticus and he sees lines on his face that weren't there before. His pale skin is stretched over his cheekbones. Is Atticus getting thinner? 'Are you losing weight?'

'Don't turn this back on me.'

'I'm not. I'm, just, God . . . I've no idea what I'm doing, Atticus. You're like the Fibonacci sequence. I'm constantly trying to work out your patterns. What you'll do next. I—'

Dan doesn't have any more words, so he kisses Atticus instead. It's desperate and fumbling and Atticus pulls away too soon.

'Don't distract me. Don't take me up there, because afterwards we'll just come crashing back down to earth.'

'I don't know what else to do.'

'Me neither.' Atticus reaches up and strokes Dan's cheek. A tear Dan didn't know he was crying sits on Atticus's thumb. 'My poor velveteen rabbit,' he says softly. 'If I love you enough, can I make you real?'

Lizzie

(I've got your number)

LIZZIE WALKS BACK FROM another school drop-off, another trek across the Beacon, where the windmill seems to have started following her. She swears it's getting closer, a black shadow behind her. Maud hasn't noticed. She does her normal routine, stopping to pee in the same places, barking at Lizzie now and again as if she wants to show her something, but there's never anything there.

Lizzie hangs up her coat, nods hello to Frankie and Sarah. 'Want a cup of tea?' Lizzie offers.

'No, thanks,' Sarah says. 'We've just had one. Kettle should still be warm.' She's frowning at a form in front of her. 'I'm applying to college – at least, I'm trying to,' she says. 'I'm rubbish at forms, though.'

'I'm good at them,' Lizzie says, then adds, 'I can help you, if you like. Later.'

'That would be great. I'll do your dinner duty in return?'

Sarah does something lovely with carrots and her mashed potato is always smooth.

'Deal,' Lizzie says, and they both smile.

Lizzie takes her mug into the office and turns on the

computer. She's not even logged in before the office door bursts open and Tess enters. 'Ah, good, there you are. I've set you up a meeting with our fabby liaison officer.' Before Lizzie can protest, a rowdy policewoman barges in and slams down a folder. She's a rectangle on legs that look like ham hocks. Her face is a balloon about to pop. Lizzie is instantly concerned about her cholesterol levels.

'Proof. *Proof* that men do it again and again. You have the power to stop it happening to someone else. You, Lizzie. Don't let the bastard win. You're no coward.'

Lizzie finds it ironic that this bully has been employed to help stop bullies. Everything about her screams barely repressed hatred, disguised with a Lego haircut and shiny metal-capped boots, worn, no doubt, to kick any man who dares step within a metre of her. Lizzie wonders who hurt her.

She rants at Lizzie. Promises protection for her and Lenny. A new name, a new life. A new start.

Lizzie tells Rowdy she'll think about it. Rowdy doesn't understand what there is to think about and tells her as much, tapping blunt square nails on the files she's brought. To her it's simple, and Lizzie is testing her patience. No doubt she'll go home and moan about Lizzie to anyone who will listen, or to Tess. She imagines how the conversation will go, 'Some people don't want to be helped.'

She knows Rowdy and Tess have had words about her and her reluctance to talk. She knows these sessions will carry on until she caves in. It's exhausting, staying strong. Every muscle stretched taut, ready for an attack. Sink or swim. Fight or flight. Rowdy urges her to start the process *soon*, before the scars fade. Lizzie wants to tell her there's no chance of that.

By the time Lizzie goes to get Lenny she's desperate for him. For that Marmite smell, the feel of his hair under her chin when she holds him. She grabs him and breathes him in, like oxygen.

'Mum, you're squashing me!' Lenny pulls away and stares at her. 'It's only been, like, six hours.' His words hurt Lizzie, who has watched the clock arm make every slow rotation after Rowdy left, waiting for the hour that would bring her boy back to her. She briefly wishes he'd catch a cold and they could lock themselves together in their room with a *DO NOT ENTER – CONTAGIOUS* sign on the door.

No chance of that, though. Lenny is full of life. He runs around with Maud, trying to teach her to tackle. Maud gets the ball a couple of times, and tears off across the grass with it, Lenny on her tail. Sometimes literally.

When they get back, Tess is waiting in the kitchen with a cup of tea for Lizzie and a Milkybar for Lenny. With Tess, tea is accompanied by a biscuit and a quick chat. She sends Lenny outside for a kickabout before sitting down.

'So, how did it go with the liaison officer?' Tess gulps at her drink. 'Aah. Tea makes everything better.'

Lizzie thinks of all the times Greg put the kettle on. 'No, it doesn't. Tea drinking is just a habit.'

Tess ignores this and says, 'So you'll be making your statement? It is your choice but you know it's for the best.'

'Soon.'

'As soon as it's done, you'll be able to start making plans to leave. You and Lenny can make a new life. You'll have a new name, a new identity. Don't you want that? Not always having to look over your shoulder? A proper garden for Lenny. His own room. A place where he could bring friends. What's holding you back, Lizzie?'

Guilt climbs up Lizzie's throat and she snaps at Tess, 'Leave my son out of this.'

Tess looks shocked, clears her throat and says, 'Well . . .'

Lizzie realizes she has gone too far. 'Of course I want all those things.'

Lenny walks in now, saving her. 'Why have I got to go to bed early tonight?'

'Because the *New Scientist*,' she waves the page at him, 'says a blood wolf moon is coming but you need to be up really early to see it.'

'A blood wolf moon? Sounds wicked,' Lenny says.

Tess frowns. 'Sounds gory to me.'

Frankie, who has come in and is making toast, peers over Lizzie's shoulder at the article.

'Why's it so special? It's just the moon.'

Lizzie turns to face her. 'It's so much more than just the moon. A total lunar eclipse happening at the same time the moon is closer than normal to Earth? It's amazing. We're so lucky to be able to see it.'

'You're a right old nerd, aren't you?' Frankie says, biting into her snack.

'Yes, I am,' Lizzie says, at the same time Lenny says, 'No, she's not.'

Frankie grins at him. 'Are you looking forward to seeing the dog moon?'

'Wolf moon. Super blood wolf moon,' Lizzie corrects her quietly.

'Yep. I am. It's going to be awesome,' Lenny says, 'and you shouldn't talk with your mouth full.'

'You should see it,' Lizzie says. 'Set your alarm. It's going to be amazing.'

'Hmm, maybe,' Frankie says noncommittally, and takes another bite.

Lizzie doesn't think much more about it, but when she and Lenny creep downstairs at four a.m. to make hot chocolate, Frankie, Sarah and two of the others are sitting round the table in their dressing-gowns, yawning over mugs of coffee.

'Oh!' Lizzie can't hide her surprise, or delight, especially when Tess also appears in her nightcap and slippers.

They settle on blankets in the back garden, a frigid wind snatching the wisps of steam from their cups and dispersing them into the navy sky. Within minutes, Frankie starts grumbling about being cold and wasting her time. 'The moon looks as boring as ever.'

'Shush,' Lenny whispers.

'Why? It can't hear me.'

'Maybe it can. You don't know.'

'Maybe it's made of cheese. This is a ridiculous waste of time and sleep. Come on, girls, let's—'

The sky darkens then, as the moon starts disappearing, sliver by sliver.

'Holy shit.'

'Language, Frankie!' Tess's voice is shrill in the night air.

'Don't mind me. I hear worse at school,' Lenny whispers cheerfully. The giggles die out as the moon becomes visible again, only this time as a glowing ruby ball.

'Holy *fucking* shit.'

'It's amazing.'

'Beautiful.'

'Isn't it?' Lizzie says, looking across briefly to see them, the shelter women, with Tess on the end, lying with their heads tipped back, silent and symmetrical, like a row of swans looking upwards, lost in the supermoon. A group of women, and for once she is part of it.

Later, when Lizzie goes to make a cup of tea, she finds a mug by the kettle with a huge red circle painted on it. Underneath is written 'Lizzie Supermoon'.

As she is making her way upstairs, she hears Frankie calling her. 'Oi, Luna, you coming in or what?'

They were all in the living room, with plates of toast and crumpets on their knees. In the middle is a space, saved just for her. 'Go on, then, put on your posh show,' Frankie says, and passes Lizzie the remote control.

Dan

(What did you call me?)

D AN WAS WORRIED WHEN Atticus started volunteering in
his local charity shop. Why did he want to waste his
time there, when his phone beeped and trilled non-stop with
work stuff? Dan was no Peeping Tom, but occasionally, as he
was walking past, he peeped at Atticus's messages. All of
them seemed to be pleas for him to call people back about
exciting projects, or from artists keen to meet him. Dan wondered why he was hiding among bric-a-brac and bunting
when he could be drinking champagne among paintings and
sculptures.

'I like it there,' Atticus told Dan simply, when he asked in
his best *not*-counsellor voice. 'It's a nice break from the fakery
of the art world.'

Dan, who didn't know the art world, couldn't argue with
this. All he could do was remind himself *not* to tilt his head
in the classic counsellor 101 move that Atticus knew all too
well. They'd only been seeing each other for three weeks but
already Atticus knew his moves.

When Atticus had first brought home bulging bin bags,
wanting Dan to help him sort out old ladies' clothes and price

up Marks & Spencer bedding, Dan was reluctant. 'They're full of germs,' he said. 'I don't want to.'

Atticus had laughed and blithely tossed everything into the washing-machine, and Dan, who adored his Miele washing-machine – which he may or may not have named 'Mr McWash' and imagined was married to 'Mrs McTumble' – was forced to pull the sheets out when they were done and iron them ready for the shop.

And before Dan knew it, he was dropping the laundry down to the charity shop himself, because after all that washing, stain-removing, pressing and scented-water ironing, he couldn't bear to see them tossed back into the same bin liner and hoisted over Atticus's shoulder.

Dan thought Atticus was being obtuse on purpose. He wanted to pull apart Dan's daddy-long-legs excuses for why he couldn't be seen in public with Atticus ('I'm too busy training'; 'I need to catch up on paperwork'; 'Charity shops make me feel sad'). He wanted them to have a row, a shouty one with door slams and dramatic hand gestures. Atticus was probably excellent at arguing passionately, but Dan's never done it before. He smooths people down like wrinkled sheets, says sorry to lampposts when he walks into them. He'd never had a lover before, let alone a tiff, and he was scared. He pictured Atticus walking away from him and not looking back, and Dan saying sorry, but Atticus saying it wasn't enough and never would be.

But just like the bedsheets, it all comes out in the wash anyway. Dan has been forced to deliver another load of laundry. Atticus had coerced him into it, telling him the clothes had been donated by a woman whose child looked like it had head lice. Poor Dan couldn't resist tweezing his way through them all, plucking at lint that might have legs. Neither could he stop himself airing them, pressing them and folding them neatly. And spritzing them with his own unique blend of fabric conditioner and essential oils.

So now they are wedged together behind the makeshift counter, putting clothes on hangers while Fitz sits by their feet, wearing a bonnet that Atticus put on him earlier.

They're talking about dinner plans when the door is pushed open with so much force it slams against the wall and knocks a row of DVDs off the shelves.

'Where is it all?' says an old man with white hair, like a dandelion clock. He is wearing tangled braces and a scowl. They both freeze, Atticus's hands still tucked into Dan's jacket. Before either of them can speak, the old man shouts, 'Are you deaf? I *said*, where is it all?'

Dan tries to remember what he learned on his conflict-resolution course. Do you approach with your hands out to your sides, or is that when you see a bear?

'Do you think he's trying to rob us?' Atticus whispers, as the stranger marches past them and starts pulling clothes off rails and flinging them over his shoulder, muttering, 'No . . . no. Fuck, I don't know . . .'

'I don't think so.' Dan realizes Atticus is still holding him, and gently steps backwards out of the embrace. 'I think he's looking for something.'

Atticus picks up the pricing gun 'just in case' and then says, in a loud faux-jaunty voice, 'Hello, sir, can we help you?'

'I want my stuff back. Where is it?'

'I'm sorry. I don't know what you mean.'

'It was brought in by *her*. By a fat, lumpy bitch with purple hair.'

'Betty?' Atticus asks.

'Who's Betty?' Dan asks, confused.

'She helps out sometimes – she always brings in cake.'

'Yes. *Betty*.' The man's face twists into a grimace as he says her name.

'Atticus, I think there's something wrong here,' Dan says, feeling the tingling in his fingers he gets around people who are not containing themselves.

'Where did you put it all?' The man has stopped searching now and is panting at them.

'What exactly are you looking for? Betty brought in some stuff a week or so ago, but it was all *ladies'* things.'

'Yes. *My* lady's things. Where are they?'

Atticus whispers, 'Ooh, a cross-dresser' to Dan very quietly, hoping to make him laugh, but Dan frowns and says nothing because the man looks too flushed, his eyes are too wide and his shirt is buttoned up wrongly.

He touches Atticus's sleeve gently, tries to pull him close enough to say, 'Be careful with him. I think he's delicate,' but Atticus is in one of his flamboyant moods and shrugs Dan off.

'I'm sorry. It's all gone. We did the most *wonderful* window display, and everything flew out the door in seconds. We could help you get something new, if you like?' He steps out from behind the counter and starts sifting through a rail of glitzy dresses in the corner, then pulls out a blue number with tassels and says, 'What size are you?'

For a second, Dan thinks the old man might have a heart attack. He coughs and splutters and his hands tremble. Dan is about to ask him if he'd like a glass of water when he squeals, 'You dirty bastard fags. You filthy stinking queers. How *dare* you?'

'Hey now . . .' Atticus stops looking through the dresses. 'There's no need for any of that.'

Dan feels the words crawl into his eyes and ears and burn him like acid. He's never been called a fag or a queer before, and it feels even worse than he imagined.

Suddenly the old man lunges at him. 'That's hers. I know it is. How fucking *dare* you wear it?'

He starts to tug at Dan's Parisian scarf, and it hurts, and he feels like he's being choked and then Atticus is there too, tugging as well, telling the old man to get off and let go. Dan is being pulled and pushed and called gay, and he thinks he might be having a panic attack but isn't sure. He spins and twirls and wrenches himself free, and, before the old man or Atticus can get to him, is out of the door and running towards home.

Fitz, who's been watching from under his bonnet, bursts out of the shop to join him. The bonnet slides off his head and lands in a puddle and he seems to consider going back for it, but he's never seen Dan run like that, not even when he's racing Luke, and he decides that nothing else matters.

When the bell rings Dan ignores it. The door opens a moment later and he hears footsteps on the stairs. Fitz lifts his head and wags his tail.

'Daniel?'

Atticus smells like an evergreen tree in a cold field but his hands are warm when they find Dan's face, under the covers, where he is hiding from the world. Dan wants to push him away, make him leave, make him no longer exist, but his body is a filthy traitor. It wants Atticus to crawl under the covers with him. Fag. Fag. Fag.

'It doesn't matter, what that old man said.'

'It matters to me.' Dan talks to his toes, counts the hairs.

'Why? It's the twenty-first century. We live in Brighton. Section Twenty-eight is no longer applicable.'

'I know,' Dan says weakly.

'Do you? Do you really know how we used to be treated? How we used to be beaten. Forced to live as recluses. Thatcher lumped us in with the paedophiles. Banned us from having a voice. Made us criminals.'

The words make Dan jump.

'People have died for being gay, Daniel. People have died protesting for our freedom, for us to be accepted. Respected. Read about our history. It's your history too, Dan. What we did together, what we do, in your bed, on your sofa, used to be illegal.'

Dan tries to let his words sink in.

'But it isn't any more. I refuse to hide, to pretend, to deny for a single second, Daniel. And in honour of all the people who couldn't, I will be as gay as the day is long. I am not ashamed of my sexuality. I am not ashamed of my feelings for you.'

He takes Dan by the shoulders. 'Daniel, my sun, I want to be your boyfriend.'

A firework goes off inside Dan. He feels it explode into a million sparkling stars fizzing in his veins. 'I want that too.'

'Not behind closed doors, though, Daniel. I won't go down that rabbit hole. I don't fit.'

'I'll be better,' Dan vows.

'Just be yourself.'

'I'm still working out who that is.' Dan lifts one of Atticus's hands from his shoulders, squeezes it in his own. 'Help me find out.'

Afterwards, they lie together, Dan's head on Atticus's chest. 'I've missed you,' he whispers to Atticus. 'I've missed you through all the years before I met you.'

It's the truest thing Dan will ever say to Atticus.

Lizzie

(Secrets and lies)

'I WANT YOU TO MEET my cousin, Dan.' Luke and Lizzie are in his kitchen making a roast dinner while Lenny watches *Hotel Transylvania* in the living room. There's crumble for dessert and the kitchen smells of cinnamon.

'Oh.' Lizzie doesn't want to. She doesn't want to meet anyone. 'The one you're doing the Ironman with?'

'Yep, he's my best friend. He'll love you and Lenny.'

Lizzie doesn't want to meet Dan. She wants to have Luke to herself. Likes the person she is around him. He looks at her like Greg used to. She misses that. She needs that, not group dinners with friends.

'So, shall I invite him over?'

Lizzie shakes her head to clear her thoughts and sees Luke is holding his phone. 'Oh . . . I . . . Now? It's a bit soon.' They'd only slept together for the first time a week ago.

'Well, we have enough food . . .'

Anger sits at the base of her spine. It runs fingers over her vertebrae, wanting to play, but all she can do is nod and say, 'Yes. Why not? Two hundred and fifty thousand tonnes of edible food go to waste each year in the UK. Meanwhile, eight point four million people struggle to afford food. That's the equivalent of the population of London.'

Lenny rolls his eyes and asks if he can go and play football.

'Sure thing, dude,' Luke says, opening the back door, then he walks over to Lizzie. 'You are so sexy when you talk statistics.' He kisses her, full on the mouth.

Greg used to say the same thing to her. She felt it, too, then – sexy, desirable. She doesn't feel that now and pulls away from Luke. 'The crumble will burn.'

An hour later, Dan is sitting across from them at the dinner table, chatting to Lenny and complimenting Lizzie on her roast potatoes. Fitz and Wolfie are in the living room, talking about their owners.

'We've earned these carbs,' Luke says, running a brick of Yorkshire pudding through a puddle of thick gravy on his plate, 'with all the training.'

'Bloody Ironman,' Lizzie says, then stops herself before she says more.

'You're sick of hearing about it, too?' Dan asks, then blushes and goes back to his dinner.

'Who's been moaning at you about training?' Luke says, moving on to his cauliflower cheese.

'Oh, just work people.'

Lizzie knows Dan is lying. She's the queen of it and you can't kid a kidder. They share a look while Luke attacks a piece of broccoli. He says, 'Broc me up,' as he does it. Lenny giggles and copies him.

Luke doesn't notice the suspicious glances between Dan and Lizzie. Happiness has blinded him. He's having a lovely roast dinner with two of his favourite people. Life is good for him. Lizzie has never envied anyone more.

'So, what do you do, Lizzie?' Dan has finished his dinner and is sitting back in his chair. Luke goes to answer for her, but she puts her hand on his leg under the table.

'I'm not working. Me and Lenny only moved here a short while ago.'

'Where are you staying?'

'With friends.' It's not a complete lie: she does have friends at the shelter. She knows she won't be able to keep them for long, and the thought saddens her. All her life she's wanted to be 'in', but never like this. She wonders why Dan is asking her this stuff, when she knows Luke will have told him all about her. She can tell from his pink ears that Dan is suspicious of her. He's protecting his cousin. The fact that he's right to do so also saddens her.

After dinner, Dan insists on washing up. Lizzie is propelled into the living room with Lenny and a cup of tea. When she's finished, she takes the cup to the kitchen. The sound of Dan and Luke's low voices makes her hover by the door.

'What do you think?' Luke asks Dan.

'She's slightly intense, and she knows a lot about vegetables.'

'She knows about everything. Sexy, isn't it?' Lizzie can't see Dan's face but she can tell he doesn't agree.

'Just go slow, okay, Luke? She's probably got a lot of stuff to work through.'

'I know,' Luke says. 'I'm not stupid.'

'I know you're not, dude. I'm just trying to protect you.'

'I don't need protection and, no offence, but you've never been in a relationship. You don't know how they work.'

'That's not fair,' Dan's voice is raised in anger, 'and actually I've been seeing—'

They're arguing because of her. Lizzie walks in before she realizes her legs are moving.

'I wondered if you needed any help.' She takes her cup to the sink and makes a show of rinsing it.

Dan and Luke take a step apart from one another. They both look annoyed. This is what Lizzie does best, ruin things.

'No, thanks, babe. I just want you to relax.' The endearment rolls off Luke's tongue easily, but Lizzie sees Dan stiffen. They both know she isn't a babe.

'I want to help. Let me finish the rest.' Lizzie tries to take the tea-towel from Dan's shoulder, but he moves away.

'Nothing to do.' Dan swipes the towel across the work surface with a slightly camp flourish before tossing it onto the floor next to the washing-machine. 'We were just coming in to sit with you.'

'We should really be going.' Lizzie tries to sound regretful.

'So soon? I thought we could watch a film with Lenny,' Luke says, from behind her.

'Lenny is very tired.'

'No, I'm not, and I don't want to go back to the shelter.'

'Lenny!' There's an edge to Lizzie's voice.

'We live in a shelter,' Lenny tells Dan, 'and I don't know why. I hate it there and I want to go home. I miss my dad.' Then he bursts into tears, his thin shoulders shaking.

Luke rushes over and says, 'It's okay, mate. It's all going to be okay.' He puts his arm round Lenny, and Lizzie can see that Dan is thinking how wrong it looks.

She goes over and positions herself between them. 'Come

on, Lenny. Let's go.' Lizzie needs to go home. The shame and guilt about the way they live now is too much for her. Dan and Luke are too nice, too normal, for her. She's going to mess them up, and they don't deserve it.

'Please don't leave on my account.' Dan frowns. 'Why don't we all sit down and watch a film?'

He looks at Luke, who says, 'I've got popcorn . . .'

Lenny looks up at that. Poor Lenny. So easily pulled and pushed across the chess board. A little pawn. 'I like popcorn,' he says, wiping a tear away with his sleeve.

'Me, too,' Dan says, going to the cupboard and pulling out the packet. Seeing how comfortable he is in Luke's home makes her understand she never will be. She should never have started this.

'It's the proper stuff,' Dan is saying. 'We can make it with butter and toffee sauce.'

Lizzie has never made popcorn with Lenny before. She's always thought it a pointless snack, nothing but air and indigestible kernel skin. What a useless mother.

'Is he okay to have sugar?' Dan says quietly.

He's not asking in the fake way her mother-in-law used to, as if the idea is ridiculous. He's being genuine, moving slowly, defusing the tension. He's a good person, Lizzie thinks suddenly, and is jealous Luke will get to keep him and she won't. Something in him makes her think he might understand. 'He's probably had more than his twenty-five grams today, but I don't suppose it will matter too much, with all the football he's been playing. Did you know it was first known as sweet salt?'

'Really?'

Lizzie checks to see if he's being sarcastic, but his face is open and even.

'Any other sugar facts?'

'Lemons contain more of it than strawberries. Too much sugar negatively affects your memory. Adding it to a vase of flowers makes them live longer.' Lizzie rattles them off on her fingers. 'It releases an opiate-like substance that activates the brain's reward system.'

'It doesn't cause tooth decay. The bacteria that feed off sugar cause that,' Lenny pipes up, from his spot in Wolfie's basket.

When Dan smiles, Lizzie can't help but twist her lips in response.

Dan pulls up a chair and he and Luke let Lenny hold the pan lid as the kernels pop and blister inside. Each clang against the metal makes Lizzie's teeth clench, but Lenny is laughing. He's laughing, and that laugh means he's not thinking about his dad. He's living in the moment. Lizzie wants to join in. Wants to tell them popcorn expands to thirty times its original size when popped, but she's scared what else she might blurt out. Dan is deceptively manipulative with that eye contact. She feels like she needs to clamp her lips shut to stop secrets spilling out.

'What's your favourite *Star Wars* film, dude?' Luke says, as they settle on the sofa.

'I've never seen them,' Lenny says, helping himself to popcorn.

Dan and Luke sit up so sharply their bowls almost tumble to the floor.

'What? Not seen a single *Star Wars* film? That's preposterous!' says Luke.

'A travesty!' Dan chimes in.

Lenny shrugs. 'Mum won't let me watch them. She says they're factually incorrect.'

'*What?*' Luke and Dan are agog.

'I might have said that once, Lenny.'

'No, Mum, you say it all the time.'

'Well, they are incorrect. All the planets only have one weather system. Tatooine is a desert, Hoth is all ice. Endor is a forest moon . . .'

'So you have watched them?' Dan asks.

'Once.'

'And you remember all that?' Dan looks impressed. Luke puffs out his chest as if he's personally responsible for Lizzie's intelligence.

'She remembers everything,' Lenny says sulkily, 'except where my dad is.'

George

(Downtown)

ELLEN'S STUFF IS GONE. The village is full of fags. It's been five days and Betty still hasn't contacted him. He wants to go round and shout at her again, but he told himself she was dead to him and you don't come back from the dead. Not even through letters.

George doesn't know what to do with himself. He can see Ellen's face in his head and she looks disappointed by the way he behaved in the charity shop, and disappointing someone is so much worse than making them angry. Especially Ellen.

He tried to do a nice thing – getting her stuff back – and all she can do is judge him from beyond the grave. He stands in the spare room with her Singer sewing-machine, where her other things should be. With them all gone, it's like she was never here at all. Now, more than ever, George needs something solid of hers to cling to. Her parrot umbrella would have been perfect.

He was so upset that he had left without looking at the shoes and hats. How could he have stayed, though, after what he'd said? That tall man had looked like he was about to punch him, and the smaller one seemed close to tears. George is worried he may be charged with assault. Can you be arrested for trying to steal a scarf? All he could do was mutter that he'd be 'complaining about this' and march out, emptier-handed than he'd gone in.

'Bollocks,' George says to Poppy, when he realizes that what happened will get back to Betty. She's going to know what he said and he feels so awful he wants to be sick. 'Fuck it,' he says then, and Poppy wags her tail in approval, having no idea what 'fuck it' means, but George sounds assertive again, which is good and might lead to a walk.

They don't go for a walk, though. Instead George gathers all of Ellen's letters, takes them to the shed, ties them together with twine, then puts them under his bed with his money stash. But what should he do next? He could go to the shop and buy himself some beer or whisky, but the manager in the off-licence looks a bit fruity and he's probably got a wanted poster with George's face on it up already.

He could go to the allotment and dig up the bulbs. Set fire to the ground and watch all his hard work turn into ash, but he likes those fucking bulbs, those trenches. He'll wait until his crops are ready to eat, then take them all home for himself. Fuck the church, the liars.

He could sit in his chair and listen to the cricket, but his thoughts yap away at him, like Poppy does at next-door's cat. It never used to be this way. His life used to be led by the slow hand of the clock. He didn't have to think: his wife did that for him. When the clock stopped, he put in new batteries and everything worked again, tickety-boo. He can't recharge his old life, though. He can't put batteries in Ellen.

What will you do, Georgy-boy? he thinks to himself. Will

you sit in your chair and starve, fade and stink, or will you get up and do something for yourself?

He thinks of Ellen, that Fats Domino number she used to sing on sheet-washing day, something about noise and pots and pans. She loved that song. She'd play it so loudly he couldn't hear his radio, and he'd let her because of the way her feet moved in her slippers and the sun came shining through, just like Fats promised.

My God, what's happening to him? He's going pulpy and soft like an over-ripe pear. He gets up and paces. Up and down the living room, in and out of the kitchen, up and down the garden path. *Think, George, think. What now? What next?*

'She's not coming back,' he tells Poppy, who's been faithfully following him on his road to nowhere. 'She's really gone, and it's just you and me now.' Poppy looks at him as if he's an idiot. She'd figured this out ages ago. She loves George, she really does, but he can be so dense at times.

George paces for another half-hour before hunger makes up his mind for him. 'Come on, dog, we're going out.' Poppy runs to the door and sits to have her lead put on. She's surprised when they don't take their normal left turn at the end of the road. She's never been the other way before. The high street is busy, and her legs are little, and George keeps walking faster and faster. At one point he starts running and Poppy pants to keep up with him.

'Fucking buses.' Poppy is scooped up and tucked under his arm as he drops change noisily into a tray next to the driver.

'Do you have a bus pass?'

'No.' George is indignant at the thought.

'Then it'll be five-fifty, please.'

'Daylight robbery.'

'Don't get on, then.'

But George needs to get on. He's hungry and he can't be seen in the village. He tosses more coins into the tray, tutting with each clank. The bus pulls away before he's settled in his seat and he and Poppy almost go flying. She yelps in alarm and he holds her on his lap where she whimpers quietly.

'It's all right, dog,' he tells her, but really he's telling himself. They both gaze out of the window as trees and bushes turn into the grey tarmac of the road along the seafront, where waves crash and smash against the marina. As they head into Brighton city, George sees cranes and lorries where buildings used to be. Traffic, and an abandoned shell in place of the old swimming-pool. Brighton needs some tidying up, George thinks idly. Betty could get it done in a flash. He rests his head against the window and closes his eyes.

The bus driver shakes him so hard his bones rattle. 'Hey, mate. It's the last stop. You need to get up.' George's eyes open slowly, and he looks around in confusion. This isn't his armchair. The person waking him up is not Ellen, or Betty.

'Where am I?' The bus driver looks cross. 'You're at Brighton station,' he says slowly, as if George is mentally challenged. 'Is there someone here to meet you?' George scowls at him.

'Do you need help getting off the bus?'

'No. I. Don't.' George lifts Poppy off his lap and sets her on the floor. It's covered with chewing gum. 'Your floor is filthy.'

'I don't clean the bus, I just drive it.' The driver offers George a hand, but he bats it away and wobbles down the aisle with Poppy at his side.

George hasn't been into the centre of town for a long time, even though it's only twenty minutes from Rottingdean on the bus. Everything is different here. There is a gym where an office used to be and a café that promises 'world-class coffee and cake'. George is suspicious, but hungry, so he heads inside.

The staff are patronizing and slow. The waitress wants to stroke Poppy. A boy at the next table pulls her tail and George thinks about stamping on his foot. The coffee is weak, and the cake is dry. He tells the waitress as much when he asks for the bill. She apologizes, and George asks if she made the cake. When she tells him no, he tells her not to apologize for it, then. She goes to get the manager but George doesn't want to speak to the manager. He doesn't want the credit note for a free coffee and cake either. 'The coffee is shit and the cake is dry. Why on earth would I want to come back?'

He doesn't pay the bill, just marches out, leaving a trail of crumbs that Poppy licks up behind him. They lumber down Queen's Road, and George remembers the old Brighton, when there weren't homeless people on every corner with signs that said 'Hungry but hopeful' and 'I'm allergic to cheese.' 'Get a job,' he grumbles at them, and tugs on Poppy's lead when she stops to sniff and wag her tail.

They take a left at Boots and head down into the Lanes. George used to deliver his tables to a market here. He wonders if it's still there. It's not. A fancy gift shop called Pussy has taken its place. 'Disgusting,' George says to Poppy, who barks in agreement.

George takes them in a circle back up to North Street.

There is a Sainsbury's on the corner and he stocks up on bread and milk, cheese and ham. Then he grabs a couple of chicken pies and a Swiss roll. At the last minute he goes back and gets two more. The person behind him at the till tuts and George is about to tell him to fuck off, but Poppy barks outside and distracts him. His fingers fumble with the bags, and a lady in the queue tells him he should get a portable shopping trolley, proudly showing off hers with a twirl. It's tartan. George hates it but he sees the value. Every-thing's going too quickly for him. He drops the receipt and has overloaded his bags. The cashier starts scanning the next customer's shopping before he's ready to take his from the loading bay. A drip of sweat trickles down his fore-head.

'Are you okay, sir?' the woman at the till asks, and he wants to say, 'No.' Wants to sit on the floor and crack open the cheese. Wants to tell everyone in the shop about Ellen and the dog and Betty and the charity shop and how none of it is his fault.

He does none of these things. Just nods once, grabs his heaving bags, and marches out with them.

Once he has collected Poppy, he flags down a taxi, but when the driver sees the dog he pulls away again. George has to stuff her inside his cardigan, then flag down another. He tells the driver his address and sits in the back of the cab, coughing each time Poppy yips.

It takes seventeen minutes to get home and costs him seventeen pounds. The world has gone mad since George last checked on it. He pays the driver with a twenty-pound note. 'Yes, I want my change. Why wouldn't I?'

Back at home with a cup of tea, George decides, overall, that the day was a success. He heats a pie in the oven for as long as his hunger will allow, then eats around the cold bits while Poppy licks the tin tray. Afterwards, George slices a Swiss roll like it's a lump of Cheddar. He eats off the knife and tells himself it's delicious.

Lizzie

(I walked into the door again)

IT HAS BEEN BUILDING up for weeks. The signs were there, but Lizzie had ignored them. The ache in her jaw from grinding her teeth at night. The pale white lines on her nails. The twist in her gut, and the lump in her throat that always preceded tears or violence. Lizzie's nervous system is flooded with cortisol, adrenalin, testosterone. She can feel it, burning like acid through her system.

She worries about Lenny. She used to be his only influence. Now friends at school dictate how his life is supposed to be. Now Lenny wears expensive football boots and wants to grow his hair into a quiff, like Luke's. He's been in a couple of fights in the playground. He's finding his edges and pushes away from Lizzie at night. Doesn't want to sleep in her arms. He wants to do his own thing, to stay after school and play football. Once, he told her to piss off. He meant it, too. She worries he won't understand, doesn't love her enough for what is coming.

There is no line between love and hate, not for Lizzie. It's the same thing. A loss of control, the same rush of blood to the head. When she first met Greg, she couldn't stop smiling.

She'd scrub at her mouth with a flannel, but the grin would remain. Something happened to her that she couldn't prevent. Then other things happened to her too. She could have prevented them, but she didn't. And now here she is, breaking into small pieces. And she's so tired. All she wants to do is sleep. She has been purified, like rock salt. Heated and stirred and reduced to small crystals. Tiny, bitter diamonds. She is exposed in a Petri dish. Soon everyone will see what remains of her.

The evening had started well. Lizzie had made chicken Caesar salad and garlic bread for Luke. He had eaten it all and asked for seconds. She'd washed up while he dried. Afterwards, she wanted them to go to bed, needed to be swept up in the white heat of oblivion. It was better than cutting or burning herself. No marks to hide.

But she didn't want to be out late. She'd promised Lenny she'd be home to tuck him in. She needed her sleepy boy, the one who didn't ask questions.

'What's the rush?' Luke had asked, with a smile, when she tugged him towards the stairs.

'No rush, just . . . come on.'

'Let's sit and watch a film for a bit?'

'I don't have time. I need to get back.' She'd tugged on his sleeve again, and Luke had pulled back.

'I can't believe I'm actually about to say this, but I kind of feel a bit used . . .' He sounded as if he was joking, but his face didn't match.

'Really?' Another string snapped. Lizzie was a violin, about to sing. She could feel what was happening, like she always did, but was powerless to stop it.

'What's going on?'

'Nothing.' Lizzie tried not to show how annoyed she was, but the mood was ruined and she just wanted to go home, before she did something she might regret. She needed her blade, a white patch of skin. 'I'd better go.'

'Why? You just got here.'

'Because. Lenny is at home and I've got stuff to do.'

'And I'm just an item on your to-do list? Christ, Lizzie. I just wanted to talk to you first. I was going to ask you to—'

'To what?'

Luke laughed, but it wasn't a nice sound. 'I was going to ask you and Lenny to move in with me.'

'Oh,' Lizzie said quietly, but Luke heard.

'Oh? Is that all you've got to say?' He looked embarrassed, exposed.

'I didn't expect that.' Lizzie cupped her face in her hands and tried to take back some control. 'It's too soon.'

'I know, and were you not living in a shelter, I'd wait, but I hate the thought of you and Lenny living there. I had it all planned. I even went out today and got this cut.' Luke pulled out a key with a football fob attached, then shoved it back in his pocket. 'You won't be needing it, though, will you? You just come here for dinner and sex, right? That's all I'm good for.'

And that was when Lizzie slapped him. Hard. A crack across his cheek that seemed to split the shaky ground she stood on.

'What the fuck?' Luke's hand went to his cheek and he looked at her in horror.

Time stopped for them briefly. They had paused in the moment, Lizzie's arm in mid-air, Luke's hand on his cheek. Slow motion. A shutter closing. A freeze frame.

George

(I miss you like I miss you)

GEORGE LETS POPPY OUT for a wee and a sniff in the garden. Asks her about the weather, then makes his own tea. One teabag for him, one for the pot. Ellen used to say it out loud. The tea comes out hot and chestnut brown, the way he likes it. Poppy gets a slosh in the saucer. Like clockwork.

He eats brown cereal to match his brew. Walks round till it does its thing, and then sits on the toilet and does his. A quick flannel wash over the sink, hair wet and slicked back, whiskers tidied, then he gets dressed.

The iron is shit and he's given up. Funny how you care less about standards when you have to keep them up yourself. Plus he's learned that the creases come out in the end. Everything does. He writes a to-do shopping list in pencil, sharpened with the Swiss army knife he keeps in his pocket. Brighton is dangerous, these days. You never know.

In the village, he marches into the post office and demands a form. There is someone already at the counter, but George doesn't care. He is full of purpose and things that need to be done.

The woman serving him is old and bitter and smells of

Murray Mints, which reminds George to buy some. He likes the rustle they make in his pocket.

'How do I fill it in?'

'Just write in the boxes.'

'They're too small.'

'Put your glasses on.'

George isn't used to unhelpful women and it puts him on the back foot. He doesn't want to fill in the form himself. He wants someone (yes, ideally a woman) to do it for him.

'It says I need a photo.' George is hot and cross by this point and is tempted just to leave it. The thought of paying full price for the bus again is what stops him. The woman (nametag Pru) points at a machine in the corner, then goes back to stamping things. It takes George a while to grasp that he is supposed to get inside it, then press buttons. When he does, many times, nothing happens.

'Fuck's sake. Japanese shite,' he says to Pru, who ignores him.

The shop is starting to get busy and George is in the way, Poppy squirming in his arms. Finally, a lad behind him steps in to help and tells George he needs to put in two pounds fifty for the photos.

'Two pounds fifty? Daylight bloody robbery!'

'You put the money in the slot there and press this button when you're ready. I'm not sure you're allowed to have your dog in the photo.' George ignores him and clambers back in, Poppy under one arm.

At first, he can't find the slot for the money, so in the first photo he's squinting. In the second, Poppy's face is blocking his, barking at the camera. The final photo 'will do', according to Pru. Finally, form complete, photo included, George turns to leave.

'Wait.' Pru digs around in the drawer under her desk and pulls out a letter covered with crumbs. 'Been here for ages, was going to put it in the bin.'

George reads it on the bus into Brighton centre, his wrinkled hands smoothing out the crinkles.

Hello dearest,

What are you doing in the post office? Are you finally getting your bus pass? I do hope so. I love my trips on the bus. The photo bit is a faff and don't ask Pru to help you because she won't. She's been miserable since her husband left her for the baker. They are jolly good Scotch eggs, though. I like the thought of you and Poppy on the bus. I must warn you, town is very different from when you last visited. It's all offices and nightclubs and vegan restaurants.

Vegan? George looks at Poppy in confusion.

Vegans are people who don't eat meat or dairy. No milk or cream or cheese or eggs, imagine that! I wish I could see your face now. The Pavilion is still lovely and that pub you used to drink in after work has changed hands but still serves bitter. Don't have more than one, though, or they won't let you back on the bus! And don't be cross that everything costs so much, these days. The money under the bed is for spending. We've no one to leave it to, so make the most of it. Go clothes shopping, get yourself a new hat or Poppy a smart collar. Maybe take a trip on the Volk's railway for old times' sake. Do you remember our first date? You kissed me in the queue. I wasn't expecting it and I had to sort out my lipstick with your hanky. I never gave that hanky back to you.

George stops reading and lets himself remember that day and the blue dress Ellen wore, which billowed in the breeze. Her face full of life and excitement as she clutched his arm, making him feel like a man. She'd been talking when he kissed her, babbling on about how she'd lived in Brighton all this time and never been on the railway. It was a rubbish ride that went nowhere, then back again, but Ellen had been like a child so he'd tipped her back and laid one on her. His one and only romantic gesture, when his heart was a balloon on a string, no longer entirely his, but at the mercy of Ellen's breezy smile.

Come on now. No being morbid. We had our years, our wonderful years. Remember, you're not a widower, you're a bachelor, and when you get your new hat you'll be quite the man about town! The ladies will all love Poppy and I will always love you.

Your Ellen

When they get into town, George decides to visit the railway. He stands in the queue and thinks about his wife. The train isn't popular any more. Who wants to go on a train when they can ride on rollercoasters on the pier or take a trip up the i360? He and Poppy stare at the faded lettering and the litter that has collected in the tracks. Red Bull and Monster Energy drinks. Is the whole world on drugs?

To cheer himself up, George buys a pair of expensive golf shoes. He's only played once and hated it, so has no need for the white-and-fawn tasselled trainers, but he loves the tappy sounds the spikes make on the polished floor of the shop. On the way out, he steals a pair of fingerless gloves to make amends. To feel like himself again.

They go into the Pavilion tea rooms for a cheese sandwich. The girl on the till is wearing a badge that says 'I'm new' and is flustered and nervous when he places his order. She spills his tea and gets his change wrong. George tells her to go back to school and two pink dots appear on her cheeks. It reminds him of Betty the last time he saw her.

Because of this he says no more. He just watches the girl, closely. Half an hour later (half an hour? What were they doing – churning the bloody butter by hand?), a long white-and-brown 'thing' appears on his plate.

'What the hell is this?'

'Your cheese panini?' The girl says it like a question.

'A what?'

'A panini?'

'Have you got a stutter?'

'No?'

'I asked for a cheese sandwich. What the bloody hell is a pan wotsit?'

'It's Italian, I think.' The girl looks as if she's about to wet herself.

'I didn't order this. I ordered a cheese sandwich.'

'This is a cheese sandwich. It's just a toasted one.'

'I don't want it. I want one with bread. Normal *British* bread.' The girl goes to remove it, but George stops her. 'Leave that there and get back to the kitchen.'

After she's scuttled behind the counter, George pulls the plate towards him and sniffs. Poppy does the same. George breaks a bit off and gives it to her. 'You can be the canary down the mine.'

When Poppy has chewed, swallowed and doesn't drop dead, George takes a tentative bite. The bread is crisp and warm, slightly salty. The cheese is rich and gooey and strings of it land on his chin as he chews. When *I'm new* finally returns with his plain cheese sandwich, George waves it away and gets to his feet.

'I don't want it.'

'But you ordered it?'

'Well, it's too late now.'

'You'll have to pay for the panini?'

George stopped mid-coat zip. 'What?'

'The panini?'

'I never ordered it.'

'But you ate it?'

The girl looks confused, and George, full of carbs and salt and warmth, ploughs on: 'Don't know what you're on about. Bloody teenagers, all on drugs.' Then he sweeps out with crumbs on his coat and a bit of cheese on his cheek. 'Paninis, eh?' he says to Poppy on the bus home. 'Who'd have bloody thought it?'

Dan

(I just called to say)

A S PER HIS PROMISE to try harder, Dan is standing in the chemist's, trying to pick condoms. He plans to surprise Atticus by being the prepared one, but it's not going well. He's been here for fifteen minutes already, peering at them discreetly, while Fitz, bored, whines outside.

Just pick one, Dan thinks to himself, but he can't. He likes twos, but the second row is dedicated to ribbed condoms, and Dan can't see how many ribs there are. There might be nineteen. He hates the number nineteen. He moves to the sixth row along, sixth row down, but they are flavoured. Nope. He tries eighth across, eighth down, but they are extra-lubricated. Is that what Atticus buys, or will he be insulted? Is extra lubrication good or bad?

'Can I help you, sir?' A girl is standing in front of him with a 'Here to help' badge on.

'No, thanks,' he says. 'I'm fine.'

The girl smiles at him. 'Honestly, you can ask me any questions. I don't mind.' She points to the ribbed condoms. 'I like these ones.'

'Right,' Dan says. 'Good stuff.'

'And these ones,' she says, pointing to Durex Invisible. 'You can hardly feel them at all.'

'Great,' Dan says, his face on fire.

Fitz barks twice. SOS.

'Got to go,' Dan blurts out. 'My dog is barking.'

Outside the shop, Fitz looks at Dan. Dan knows that if he could speak, Fitz would say, 'Really? All that time and you come out with nothing? Lame, dude. Super-lame.'

'I know.' Dan thinks of Atticus's disappointment and groans.

'Fine. Wait there.' He marches back in and picks up the Invisible, ribbed *and* strawberry Durex, tossing them onto the counter with a tube of lube.

The girl smiles and says, 'Lovely selection. I've not tried the strawberry. Maybe you'll let me know how you get on with them.'

As Dan is stuffing the condoms in his backpack, the girl holds out the receipt and says, 'Hey, are you Luke's brother?'

'Cousin.'

'Oh, you look so similar. How is he?'

Oh, shit, not this. Dan realizes he's been talking to Smurf-girl, only now her hair is peach. He tries to remember if Luke slept with her or not. Did they date? Who dumped whom?

'He's, um, good. We're training for an Ironman. It's hard work. He's very busy. I hardly see him,' Dan blathers, getting the rucksack zip caught in the plastic bag in his haste to be out of the shop.

'Ironman? I bet he's looking good. Send him my regards.'

'Okay.'

'He uses the ribbed condoms too,' she adds, as Dan is walking to the door.

Dan is so surprised that he walks into a rotating display of sunglasses.

'I got you something,' Dan says later, after dinner.

'How exciting.' Atticus shuts his eyes and puts out his hands. Dan tips the condoms into them.

'Open,' Dan says shyly, wringing his hands.

'You brought me condoms?' Atticus says, slightly confused.

'Yes. I brought you condoms,' Dan says slowly, 'because I love you.'

The last time Dan told someone he loved them, it was his father, before the cancer claimed him. Of course he tells his mum he loves her, in that exasperated 'Yes, Mum, love you too' way sons do. This time is different, though. This is a declaration, and it is one Dan doesn't make lightly.

'I've never . . . done this before. Never been *in* love, only loved objectively.'

'I love you too. I have from the first moment I saw you,' Atticus says, grinning.

'Really?' Dan hates how needy he sounds, but really?

'Yes. Fuck, yes.'

The next morning Dan wakes Atticus up with a black coffee ('Has it been passed through the bowels of a golden elephant? I won't drink it otherwise') and a kiss, then Atticus punches Darth Vader on the head and Dan calls work to tell them he's got a bug and won't be in.

They spend the morning in bed and the afternoon

wandering round Kemp Town buying vinyl records. No one takes any notice of them. They are nothing special in this area, where men dress as women and the boys wear tight jeans and quiffs even slicker than Luke's. Here there is the full rainbow spectrum: old, young, black, white.

They stop for food and share crispy Chinese duck and sticky ribs. Atticus is effervescent, a shot of vitamin C in the leg. The air is fizzing with the pair of them. When the food is finished, and their sticky fingers have been cleaned in bowls of steaming-hot water and lemon, they sit back, full of each other and good food and, for one giddy afternoon, the unlimited possibilities of their life together.

They discuss what kind of restaurant they'd run in Paris. Dan wants a deli, autumn-coloured salads served out of blue-and-white enamel bowls. Atticus wants an upmarket bistro, where the waiters wear smart red coats and a pianist plays blues on a polished walnut piano. It's the difference between them and always will be. Atticus is not going to change. He is who he is, whole and complete. Dan is still in training.

It's not Paris, not quite, but it's a good day. They leave in high spirits, stopping at the Taj supermarket for dinner ingredients. Atticus, inspired by all the talk of restaurants, wants to make *boeuf bourguignon*. They stand side by side in front of the vegetables, squeezing lemons for no reason and making jokes about firmness.

The shopping swings between them at the bus stop. When the bus arrives, Paris-Dan clambers upstairs to get the best seats at the front. Atticus joins him, and they ride home with their feet up.

*

'So, you don't like this Lizzie, then?' Atticus says later, over dessert (peach parfait). Dan has told him about the awkward dinner at Luke's.

'It's not that I don't like her, there was just something off about her.'

'How so?'

'Well, from what Luke told me, she fled her husband and now lives in that women's refuge. You know the one?' Atticus nods and Dan says, 'Apparently he beat her pretty badly. Luke has seen the scars.'

'But you don't believe her?'

'Of course I believe her. I'm just surprised. She's not what I thought she'd be like. She's confident and kind of intimidating.'

'So, all battered women are meek and mild and deserve what's coming to them?' Atticus says, raising an eyebrow.

'Not at all! No one knows what goes on behind closed doors. No cases are ever cut and dried.'

'You see her as a case?'

'I can't help it.'

'Dear Daniel, wanting to save the whole world.'

'Stop it. You know what I mean. I did a couple of modules on abuse.'

'Anyway,' Atticus says then, 'perhaps Luke has just fallen in love.'

'Love? Luke is the king of crushes. It's so out of character.'

'Like you holding hands with a boy in public?' Dan blushes and Atticus grins. 'People don't always present their truth, Daniel. Sometimes they project something entirely different. The lies we tell others are nothing compared to the lies we tell ourselves.'

'Plato? Pushkin?' Dan asks.

'Derek Landy, actually.'

Later, after Fitz has licked the bowls clean, Dan lights a scented candle and puts his feet on Atticus's lap. 'Why don't we ever go to your house?'

'We do,' Atticus says evenly.

Dan wriggles his toes. 'Don't take it the wrong way. I love having you here. I just wondered if you wanted to be at home more. I don't mind going over there.'

'It's not really mine. It's my parents' flat. I just live there. I feel more at home here, with you, plus it's easier for me to get to work.'

'The charity shop?'

'Tsk, don't laugh. I love it.'

Dan hasn't been back since the old-man incident. He still washes the sheets and clothes, and if Atticus brings board games home, he makes sure they have all their pieces. He even bags up the outside bits and inside bits of jigsaws, but he never drops them into the shop any more. He doesn't really like the shop, truth be told. He still can't understand why Atticus would rather spend time there, among the eighties Charles and Diana wedding plates, when he could be in glass galleries in London. When he could be talking about art. He was so alive that night in the gallery. If asked the right question, he can wax lyrical for hours. 'And did you know, Dan,' he'd say, his voice full of admiration, 'Emin challenges everything. Every norm. People asked her if she got lost in her art and she said, "The kind of work I do, you're not going to lose yourself. You're going to be digging yourself up."'

Dan still didn't really understand art, but he loved Atticus's face when he spoke about it. Art ran through his veins, so why was he hiding away from it in a tiny shop in a wonky village, off the map of Brighton?

'Don't you want to do more gallery work? Your phone is always ringing with people wanting you to work with them.'

'I don't have the same energy for it I used to have. Artists are arrogant. Most good reviews are written by palms that have been crossed with silver.'

'Hasn't it always been like that, though?'

'Yes.'

'So what's made you dislike it now?'

'You. Since I met you, I've not found a painting I like better, or an artist worth leaving you for.'

'You can have both, Atticus, me and your career. You're so good at it.'

'I've had enough of one, and I'll never get enough of the other.' Atticus skirts the question expertly.

'It's impossible to get a straight answer out of you. Have you ever thought about becoming a politician?'

'Often. Now, would the honourable gentleman care for a game of Yahtzee?'

'Damn you. You know I can't resist Yahtzee. Will you ever learn how to play it properly?'

'Probably not, no.'

Lizzie

(I'm ready now)

LIZZIE'S HAND IS STILL sore when she wakes the following day. From the slap, and then the kettle when she got back to the shelter. She holds the hand close to her side now, telling Lenny it's just a touch of arthritis. 'I'm fine,' she tells him, when he looks worried. 'It's nothing.'

'But it's all red. I don't want you to get old,' he says. 'I don't want you to die.'

'I'm not dying!' she says, trying to laugh. 'I'm fine, and I'm not going anywhere.' It's a lie.

The Beacon is waking up. She sees buds and birds as they make their way to school. Maybe they've been there for some time. All she ever used to see was the lack of places to hide. Now that it no longer matters, she realizes she'll miss it here. She wonders what it will look like in the height of summer, alive with bees and buttercups, and feels a stab of sadness that she'll never know. She watches Lenny run and roll with Maud and says a silent goodbye.

They arrive at school half an hour early. She tells the receptionist she has a doctor's appointment, and would it be okay if Lenny sat in the office for a little while? Linda says, 'Of course,' and Lenny frowns and asks Lizzie if it's about her hand. Lizzie says yes. She's off to get some magic cream to make it better. 'Nothing to worry about. I'll be here at pick-up.'

Her breath catches on the last word. She kisses him hard and holds him even harder, and he doesn't complain as he usually would. He senses, perhaps, that she needs this. They have always had this unspoken telepathy. When he was a baby, she'd walk into his room seconds before he woke. Her breasts would harden with milk in the moment before he cried. Her body was made to look after his. She has failed them both. All she can do now is let him go with a smile that hurts more than the kettle, the blade, the car door, and say, 'See you soon, my darling boy,' and make the sign-language shape for 'sorry'.

Lizzie and Maud march back to the shelter and Maud doesn't pause once to wee or sniff. She knows what's coming, is as keen as Lizzie to get it over and done with. When Lizzie stops briefly, to take a breath, Maud barks at her to keep going.

When she gets back to the shelter, Lizzie strides into the office and says, 'I'm ready to talk to the police.'

Tess is both surprised and delighted. 'Well, then, how about that.' She picks up the phone. 'Twelve o'clock. Lovely, thank you. Yes, we'll be here. See you soon.' She puts the receiver down. 'You're doing the right thing. I'm so proud of you, Lizzie. We're all here to support you.'

Lizzie writes a letter to Luke while she waits for Rowdy. It says sorry and not much else. She doesn't have anything else to give him. She never did: all she ever did was take. She was a leech, sucking blood, drawing what she needed from him.

The oldest form of medicine. She tells him it was all her, not him. Forces herself to underline it. 'You are perfect,' she scrawls, in shaking script, unable to hold the pen steady. She licks the envelope and thinks about putting money in for the football boots, but doesn't because she's hurt Luke enough in every way. She can't do that to him too.

Once the letter is written, Lizzie turns to the packing. There isn't much to take. All she has are the contents of the small bag she and Lenny arrived with. The bracelets and scarves don't belong to her. They belong to the Lizzie she created, so she leaves them all neatly laid out, like evidence, on the stripped bed.

Lenny had put up a couple of posters, which she takes down and rolls carefully. He has his football boots with him, takes them everywhere, and Lizzie hopes he'll be able to keep them.

When she hears the doorbell ring, she makes her way downstairs, adding to the scuffs on the carpet one last time.

'Would you like me to sit in with you?' Tess is desperate to know the details Lizzie has never told her. Wants to join the dots and see what picture they make. Lizzie is too tired to protest and simply nods.

'Wonderful. I'll make tea.'

Lizzie and Rowdy sit in the office, listening to Tess clatter with cups and saucers. Every time they make eye contact, Rowdy smiles at Lizzie. It's a reassuring smile, like everything's going to be okay. Lizzie doesn't smile back because it isn't. When Tess finally comes in with the tray, Lizzie grabs the mug and relishes the way it scalds her. She gulps at the steaming tea, chasing the burn.

When she looks up from the empty cup, Tess and Rowdy seem slightly alarmed. Good. Best to warn them, prepare them for what's to come.

'Okay, Lizzie. Are you ready?' Rowdy's smile is bright as she clicks record on her device and sets it carefully on the table between them. Tess squeezes her hand and Lizzie lets her. Then she starts talking.

George

(Not ruddy likely, George)

THE FIRST *WISDEN CRICKET* magazine had arrived a week after Ellen died. No letter, just a thick glossy pamphlet that landed on the mat with a heavy clunk. George had ignored the package, assuming it was Ellen's *People's Friend* or some other shite. Poppy had pissed on it soon afterwards and it had been tossed into the bin.

Betty rescued the next one and put it on George's coffee-table. He hasn't opened it, though. Cricket is for the radio. He listens to matches on long wave, interspersed with the shipping forecast. '... And now the shipping forecast, issued on behalf of the Maritime and Coastguard Agency at 17.54 GMT today. Low, north-west Malin 1002, slowly losing its identity by 1900 Tuesday.' He has no idea what any of it means, but it's comforting, and reliable, four times a day, every day. He used to think Ellen was reliable, but then she bought him a dog and died.

Rockall. Malin. Dogger. Fastnet. German Bight. Ellen.

George used to silence her if she tried to talk to him while it was on. 'Ssh, woman. Can't you see I'm listening to the shipping forecast?'

'George, you've never even been on a boat.'

'I won't need one, if I listen to the shipping forecast.'

Now George has to keep going, steer his solo ship on the treacherous seas of life. At least he has Poppy as his second-in-command. For a while he had Betty, too, his deckhand, but he had made her walk the plank.

The first time George had gone back to the allotment with his spade, he'd wondered if she might have left him a gift by way of apology, but there was nothing where Betty used to be. Just the smell of peat and manure. The sweet tang of weeds. A fork sunk in the ground where he'd left it. He picked it up and carried on digging more trenches, like a soldier in Flanders fields.

Today, the sun dials around him, hot on his neck, then his face. It's heavy, sweaty work. No tea, no doorstop sandwiches. George is very good at feeling sorry for himself. He potters around until hunger drives him to the baker's, where he buys all of the Scotch eggs, slips a sweaty two-pound tip into Till-girl's hand, then walks out without a word.

The first two Scotch eggs see him home, where George sits in the bath and holds the shower over his head, watching the mud under his nails dissolve in the warm water. His skin is papery and wrinkled, sliding off his bones. He lifts a heft of belly flab and watches it droop and resettle, like custard falling back into the saucepan from the spoon. He studies himself objectively, with neither disgust nor pride. He is intrigued that his internal machines and cogs whir on, while Ellen's have stopped. Why do the people who deserve to be alive always die, and the ones who don't are preserved, like a jar of pickles in brine? Why is he still here? he wonders.

*

He dresses in a clean shirt and trousers, adds socks and braces, then goes to the kitchen. To accompany the remaining Scotch eggs, he adds a thick wedge of cheese, some sliced apple, a dollop of salad cream and tomatoes. He fancies himself quite the cook, these days.

When he's finished, he claps his hands together and picks up the most recent magazine. When he sees the front cover has a women's team on it, he almost tosses the magazine to the floor, but a story about Victor Trumper catches his eye. 'Ah. Proper cricket. That's more like it.'

George rips off the cellophane and, for no reason other than that Ellen used to do it, he sniffs the pages. Satisfied the magazine smells good, he dives in and spends the next three hours devouring the *Wisden* with his magnifying-glass, stopping only to tell Poppy about the real Sylvester Clarke. 'He was fearsome,' George tells her, thinking how much he and Clarke had in common. 'People were petrified when he came up to bowl. He knew the battle between batsman and bowler was a trial of strength and character. He could bowl at one hundred miles an hour.'

Poppy has no idea about speed so she just barks.

'He died when he was only forty-four,' George carries on. 'I never knew that.' George thinks about how he got fifty years with Ellen and feels almost lucky.

As always, the sky around his house, his little sanctuary, slowly darkens. He's used to Ellen not coming home now. It doesn't hurt less exactly, it just is and there is nothing George can do about it. He has his dog, and he can empty his own washing-machine. His dinner was fine, and he's only had one glass of beer. It's not the life he wanted, but it is a life. A little one.

He's about to put the magazine down and go to bed when he spots it – the fixtures for a cricket tour. Kensington Oval to St Lucia and all the places in between. On a cruise ship. He reads about the boat, with three bars and a swimming-pool. It even has a theatre. Ellen always wanted to go to the theatre.

Come to think of it, Ellen had wanted to go on a cruise. George had told her to forget it: 'Waste of time and money. Like being on a floating council estate with food poisoning.' He says to Poppy, 'There are three restaurants on the *Crystal Esprit*,' he tells Poppy. 'Three!' One of them promises *the best of British* and George thinks of pie and mash and lamb chops, none of that foreign muck. 'That boat will be full of people thinking they know about cricket.' George pictures himself telling them how wrong they all are. It's a wonderful thought.

'I'm not going,' he says to Poppy, who has jumped on his lap now and is looking at the boat suspiciously. She has short legs, she doesn't tackle long grass in wet weather, so he can forget the sea!

'Too bloody expensive anyway.' George looks at the price and his eyes bulge. All that money. All that cricket, though . . . The sound of leather on willow . . . There's nothing else like it. 'Come on, dog. Wee and bed for the both of us.' Poppy jumps down and runs to the back door, barking.

Later, teeth brushed and put into the bedside glass of

water, George closes his eyes and pictures the ship. Him in a tiny cabin, being rocked to sleep. Rockall. Malin. Dogger. Fastnet. German Bight. A pile of sausages, fat and crispy. Cricket whites hanging out to dry in the sunshine. The sound of balls being tossed and caught, dropped and saved. Howzat, eh, George?

Dan

(Five-star review)

'GET UP, ATTICUS! I'M taking you to Bournemouth.' Dan surprised himself when he booked the tickets, but the Ironman is so close he's tapering down his training and can think of nothing better than Atticus and a hotel room for the weekend, before the big day.

They stay in a dog-friendly hotel called the Martory Inn. It smells of mildew and the woman on Reception frowns when she sees Dan, Atticus and Fitz wagging their tails, wanting to check in. The room is cold and doesn't look like it's been cleaned since the last guests departed. Two lumpy singles are pushed together with a yellow candlewick counterpane draped lopsidedly over the top. A doily-covered bedside table, with a lamp that doesn't work and a *Bournemouth* magazine, six months out of date, complete the decor.

Atticus wants to iron his shirt, but the woman on Reception tells him there is only one iron and she's already lent it to 'someone . . . perhaps room fourteen'. Atticus spends half an hour meeting all the hotel guests, and their dogs, but returns *sans* iron. Dan apologizes for it not being the kind of place Atticus is used to.

'Shut up, Daniel-sun. I bloody love it.'

They go out and eat fish and chips from newspaper on the beach. Fitz runs in and out of the tide, barking at the waves, and Atticus kicks off his loafers and wades into the sea, his feet blue with cold when he emerges.

After two frankfurters with ketchup, no mustard, and an hour of ball-chasing, Fitz is ensconced in a nest on the bed, with *Countryfile* on in the background, while Dan and Atticus go to a nightclub on the seafront.

'Fancy wiping your feet on the rhythm rug, Daniel?' Atticus says after a triple gin and tonic.

Dan does his best to join in, though he's stiff and mechanical and feels like an idiot. But then Atticus copies his awkwardness, and they look like they're having a robotic dance-off and suddenly Dan's stomach hurts in the best way and his face aches from laughing.

Dan knows it's a forever memory. That one day, when he can no longer bend and snap, this moment will still bring him to his knees. Him jerking and winding his hands like a clock. Atticus doing the worst moonwalk in his pink loafers, bumping into people, spilling his drink and giggling. Them being exactly who they are in that moment: two young men in love.

'Four of your worst shots, please, good sir,' Dan says to the barman, with finger guns.

'Frightful, disgusting,' Atticus declares after the first, before licking salt from Dan's hand and taking another. 'Keep 'em coming, cowboy.'

Dan slaps a note on the bar.

'More dancing, Danula?'

'Lead the way, Atty.'

They don't leave until closing time, Atticus dragging Dan, dopey and delightfully drunk, back to the hotel room, where he needs help getting up the stairs. When they go into the room, they see the two single beds have been pushed as far apart as they could be and a Bible has been placed on the bedside table. Fitz has been relegated to a cardboard box that once held industrial-sized soap and is clearly not impressed. The television is off and a note about keeping residents awake with 'howls and barks' has been left under the miniature kettle with no plug.

Dan just laughs. Bumps into the walls, into the door, and finally into Atticus, who undresses him and puts him to bed while Dan mumbles on about the Bible and Bournemouth being out of date.

Initially, Fitz was cross with Dan for being home late, for the mean lady telling him he was a menace. But who could stay cross at Dan when he's all slippery like an eel with happiness, and his eyes so full of adventure? Fitz can't help but yip and groan with glee, to hell with the consequences.

When Dan wakes the following morning, with a dry mouth and an aching head, he sees Atticus is sitting in the threadbare chair scribbling in his notebook. Fitz is by his side, snoring lightly.

'He wakes,' Atticus declares, as Dan sits up and groans. 'Don't move too quickly. I'll get you some water.'

There's no glass, though, only a small vase with green mould encrusted in the bottom, which Atticus offers to Dan, who shakes his head. He says, 'Ouch. No, thanks,' and gets up slowly to stand under the shower, where the trickle of cold water does nothing to make him feel much better.

'Why aren't you dying, like I am?' Dan groans at breakfast, over a plate of pale cold toast and a lukewarm coffee.

'Pshh, we didn't drink that much,' Atticus says, looking out at the sea.

'Yes, we did.' Dan thinks of all the shots. 'You're not hungover at all. It's as if you didn't have a single drink.'

Atticus looks at him quickly, then back to the tide. 'I used to drink more than I do now.' It's unusual for Atticus to allude to his past like this. He normally jokes that nothing happened to him until he met Dan, which was 'the first day of my life'.

Dan wishes he felt better. He would like to snip and prune at this hint about a drinking problem. His face must show it because Atticus says, 'No counselling, please. I said I used to. I don't any more. Does it seem like I have a drinking problem?'

'No,' Dan is forced to admit.

Atticus leans over and kisses him on the cheek. 'Get up, Count Danula. Sea air and a brisk walk is all you need. You'll be fine. And I should know, right, raging ex-alcoholic that I am?'

All Dan can do is tuck away the little titbit, like a squirrel with a nut in its cheek, something to gnaw at later.

They pack their bags and Atticus writes a long message in the visitor book about how well he slept and how delightful he found the service. 'I'll be sure to book the same room for our honeymoon,' he tells the receptionist, then offers her a high-five, which she refuses. Dan sleeps all the way home on the train.

The whole weekend was so oddly strange and weirdly wonderful that Dan hasn't looked at his phone once. He finally gets it out as the taxi pulls up outside his house, and it is only then that he sees all the missed calls from Luke.

Lizzie

(I told you so)

LIZZIE IS NOT ARRESTED. She's told to call her husband. She'd have preferred the handcuffs.

Rowdy, cross at having her time wasted, puts on her hat and gives Lizzie a final look of disgust before letting herself out.

'Can I have some time alone?' Lizzie's voice is small. The voice of a broken woman.

'You have five minutes.' Tess's tone is clipped. The voice of a woman barely holding in her anger. That used to be Lizzie's voice. Now they've switched roles.

Lizzie wishes she didn't know the number off by heart, but she does. She hasn't forgotten a thing. The phone rings twice before it's snatched up. Greg's voice is desperate.

'Beth?'

She realizes he must have been answering the phone this way since the day she left him.

'Greg.'

His voice sounds the same, gravelly, northern, perfectly pitched at ninety hertz.

'Where are you? Where's my son? Are you safe?'

Safe. He's still worried about her, after all this. 'Yes. We're in Brighton.'

'Brighton? Where?'

Beth can't bring herself to say she's in a shelter. 'With a friend.'

'You don't have any friends in Brighton.' Greg sounds like a man who hasn't slept, hasn't lived, since the night she bundled Lenny into his coat and fled.

'It's complicated.'

'No, it isn't, Beth. It really isn't. You took my son away from me.'

'He's my son too.' Her voice is cracked and thin, a car skating on black ice.

'You don't deserve him.'

'I know.' Tears run freely down her face. They burn like acid, hurt more than a kettle or a cigarette ever could. Tess is in the doorway and she's seeing everything come undone. That burns too.

She grabs the phone from Beth and barks the shelter's postcode into it. Then she hangs up and turns to Beth, who has crumpled to the floor.

'Get up.'

'I can't.'

'You can, Beth, and you will. Women who have actually been battered get themselves up, so *you* can too. Your husband got up, didn't he?' The words land on Beth, like a slap, and she forces herself to her feet.

'You'll stay here until he arrives. I want to make sure

you don't run off again. I'll get Lenny from school if need be.'

Beth just nods. The reins have been taken from her and it's almost a relief. Now she'll be told what to do and where to go. Now she won't be left alone with herself. She wants to cling to Tess's skirt and thank her. She's grateful, at last.

George

(Small china dog)

GEORGE FINDS THE LETTER when he gets home from the allotment. It's tied to a small china dog. The writing isn't Ellen's. George is so disappointed he has to sit down.

This handwriting is scratchy. It looks like a pigeon walked over the paper with a gammy leg. He can make out his name and then inside, after a bit of study with the magnifying-glass, the words appear.

Hello George,

It's me, Betty. You seem to accept things better in a letter so here it is. I'm sorry that I didn't tell you about Ellen's letter to me and I'm sorry for giving her belongings away. I should never have done that. Bill's things were stained with guilt and I couldn't bear to look at them. I tried so hard to make him better, you see, and I couldn't. The doctor told me to give him morphine when he asked for it. He asked for it all the time, and I gave it to him. Sometimes I feel as if his blood is on my hands. I administered that last dose, Sunday evening, six p.m., after a bowl of stewed apple with brown sugar.

The doctor told me it wasn't my fault. It wasn't the morphine that killed him, it was the cancer, but I still feel like I failed him.

That was not the case for you, though. You didn't fail your Ellen, and her things could've offered you comfort when enough time had passed. I was only doing what she had asked me to do. It's hard to deny a dying woman, though I never took that lovely Singer. It would have felt like payment and I never wanted or needed that. Getting the odd laugh out of you has been rewarding enough. Seeing you fall in love with that little dog.

Anyway, I'm doing all I can to get Ellen's things back. I've only found this dog so far. The vicar bought it to use as a paperweight. I think Barbara bought some clothes that she'll never get into.

I never came to see you out of pity or duty. You are a rude, grumpy, cantankerous, ungrateful old sod. You have terrible dress sense, and a potty mouth, but you make me laugh, and I like you.

Betty White

Bloody women and their bloody letters.

George imagines Betty writing it at the table he mended. Other than Ellen, George hasn't been surrounded by people for most of his life and has never minded. Betty isn't used to it, though. She's lost all the people she loved and solitude is punishment to her. George strokes his chin with one hand and the dog with the other. The letter isn't written on posh paper, like Ellen's were. This paper is cheap and George can see where Betty has pressed hard on her pen in some parts. He can imagine her writing it. Smearing her make-up with tears. Or does she bother with make-up any more? Now there's no one to see it.

Sympathy is new to George and he doesn't like it. He's rarely felt sorry for other people before, except Ellen and those tissues in her apron. He felt sorry then. Maybe it was his fault he couldn't get her pregnant. It had made him feel less of a man. He wishes now that he'd been able to tell her how much it had hurt him to see her tears, those chocolate wrappers. He'd never found the right moment, or the right words. George had sat in his shed instead and held the woodworking tools he had wanted to hand down to his son. He had put money into a wedding fund for a daughter he'd never have, so she could marry a man who would never be good enough for her. He'd carried on adding to the fund for years, even when it became obvious there would be no son, no daughter. No wedding. Like a table leg on his lathe, the disappointment shaved and moulded him, made him knobbly.

This sympathy for Betty is new, though, because he *can* do something about it. If he wants to. Does he, though? He has the bus now, and those paninis, and he can do his own washing. He doesn't need Betty. There's a bakery on Sydney Street that makes cupcakes as big as his fist.

George leaves the letter on the kitchen table for three days. It stares at him as he washes up. It gets covered with pickle from his sandwiches and a spilled slurp of tea blurs the confession.

On day four, he picks it up, folds it neatly and puts it into his pocket, clips on Poppy's red lead, and they walk out into the lemon-yellow sunshine.

The flowers he has picked from his garden (and other gardens in the village) are wilting slightly by the time he marches up the path, noticing the lack of weeding and the overgrown grass. Betty has let herself go.

He rings the bell twice. It takes a while for Betty to appear behind the frosted pane and, when the door finally opens, she's dressed all in black. She even has a small veil covering one eye.

'Are you going to a funeral?' George asks.

'No. I'm in penance.' Betty looks older, and sadder.

'Stupid cow. Come on, get the unlucky bastard.'

'I've told you not to call my dog that.'

'It suits him. Black doesn't suit you. You look like Bertie Bassett.'

Lucky and Poppy sniff, reacquainting themselves with one another.

Betty and George watch them for a while and then she notices the flowers. 'Merlin's beard. Are those for me?'

'No. We're off to the graveyard. We have some ghosts to lay to rest.' He offers an arm and she takes it.

They make quite a sight: George in his smart braces and Betty all in black, Lucky and Poppy on the outside, happily reunited. They pass the baker, who runs out of her shop while her pasties burn, to tell the florist that GEORGE AND BETTY are OFF TO GET MARRIED at the church. Curtains twitch and the rumour mill grinds as they pass by, arm in arm, along the busy pavement, by the pond and over the road to the church, where Betty pats George lightly on the arm and indicates with her head that Bill is 'that way'.

Ellen is at the back, underneath a yew tree. Light filters between the leaves, speckles the grass around her modest white grave. The inscription is simple: 'Ellen Dempsey 1943–2018'. Nothing else. George forbade it. Barbara had wanted 'loved and missed' and George had told her to fuck off.

Now he regrets it. His wife was so much more than Ellen Dempsey. She was all the seasons. He should have put that. Instead he puts his knees into the grass and his forehead against the stone, which has been warmed by the sun.

'Hello, wife,' he says. 'Hello, my lovely old wife.'

George manoeuvres himself so he's sitting with his back to Ellen's headstone, his legs stretched out, filling her space with himself. Protecting her. Poppy sits on his lap, a solemn little face on little brown paws. George is grateful for the warmth of this dog, his little hot-water bottle.

He lays the flowers down next to him, then pulls out the letters, the ones he'd hidden under the bed. The ones he'd decided always to have to hand. He opens the first with the care with which he'd have cradled the baby they never had, and slowly, haltingly, he answers all her questions.

Dan

(Things are not always what they seem)

THEY ARE IN BED when Atticus tells Dan he's going to work, at a friend's gallery opening. Dan is surprised then pleased that Atticus is going back to work. He wants to know all about it, but Atticus is vague. 'It's only small. He's been nagging me to help him.'

Dan wonders who 'he' is and how he's been nagging Atticus – via letters, emails, texts? Shit. Texts. He pulls out his phone and calls Luke again, but Luke doesn't answer. 'He must be at work already. I wonder what he wanted,' he mutters to Atticus. 'I had a load of missed calls from him.'

Atticus is distracted and doesn't respond. Dan wonders if he's nervous about the gallery opening as he shoots a text off to Luke: *You okay? Ring me. You'd best not be pussying out of the Ironman, dude!*

Dan puts the phone down and rolls over. He doesn't have a client till ten, so he reaches for Atticus, but Atticus pulls away and slides out of bed, reaches for his jeans instead.

'Sorry. I've got to go.' Atticus never turns Dan down. Disappointment and insecurity crest on waves inside his stomach as he watches Atticus dress with brisk efficiency. When his belt is done up and his shirt buttoned, Atticus leans down and kisses Dan on the forehead, takes a deep sniff of his hair, then turns and jogs down the stairs.

'Bye, Daniel,' he calls, as he opens the front door. 'I love you.' It slams behind him and the sound hits Dan in the face. What just happened?

Fitz runs downstairs and barks at Atticus to come back, but he doesn't listen. Fitz dithers, trying to choose the perfect present to cheer Dan up. He can't decide between Dan's old Spurs sock or the parrot. In the end he grabs both, and pads carefully back up the stairs, his nametag tinkling.

Bournemouth had been brilliant, but Dan wonders now if Atticus's oddness is because of the drinking confession. Did he feel he'd given something away? He decides to go to work early and go through the old notes he made on Atticus, brief as they were. See if he can join up any dots. But life gets in the way, and Alan is there waiting for him when he arrives. 'Ah, good, you're here early. I have an emergency case for you.'

Dan doesn't have time to eat, or to spray his lavender. He manages a quick text to Atticus: *Dinner at mine? I'll cook* and another to Luke: *Call me*. Neither replies.

Dan sees a woman who wants to leave her husband but not his money, followed by a teenager who wants to go to university, but his parents want him to run their shoe shop in Haywards Heath, as every man in their family has done before. He sees an overweight teenager who has been self-harming, a company director addicted to phone sex. He gives couples therapy to a pair of lesbians who both want to be mothers but neither wants to be pregnant.

By the time Dan gets home, he has nothing left to give anyone. Neither Atticus nor Luke answers his phone and he's secretly relieved. He eats a mountain of pasta and pesto, watches *The Empire Strikes Back* and falls asleep on the sofa with Fitz, who is being especially clingy.

Lizzie

(All coming out in the wash)

Beth sits in the office, like a prisoner. She doesn't need handcuffs, she's shackled by shame. She lets her shoulders sag under the weight of her self-hatred. She's exhausted. Could sleep for the first time in forever.

Tess is working but, really, she's just watching Beth, making sure she doesn't run. Lenny is outside, playing football with Frankie. Oblivious. Maud is sitting by her feet, her nose on Beth's shoe. Beth scoops Maud up and holds her close, grateful that she's a dog and will never know what Beth is really like. Maud knows, though. Of course she does, and she always did. She didn't judge her then and she doesn't judge her now. Dogs love unconditionally, not because they don't understand life, but because they understand it the best.

Beth pulls at a piece of skin on her wedding-ring finger, near the nail. It hurts enough to make her say, 'I had a miscarriage, after Lenny.' Tess doesn't look up, but her pen stops moving.

'Lenny was so perfect. Ten fingers, ten toes. Do you know how lucky that is? How often things can go wrong in pregnancy? First the twenty per cent chance of miscarriage. Then the background rate for birth defects. Then the risk of pre-eclampsia. Going into labour too early. Underdeveloped lungs. A complication giving birth, shoulder dystocia. Nuchal cord and birth asphyxia . . . Thirty-seven thousand billion chemical reactions take place per second in the human body. That's without a baby growing inside it.'

Maud sighs heavily. She'd thought it might be something like this. Sorrow has a certain smell.

'Greg wore me down. He kept on about how sad it would be for Lenny to be an only child and what if we died in an accident . . .' Beth pinches her thigh, quick and hard. 'When I stopped using birth control, I got pregnant straight away. The morning sickness was awful. The scans showed a healthy baby, but I knew it wasn't. Lenny came along with us to watch. He was fascinated. He asked if that was what he had looked like too. He didn't. The other baby looked like a prawn. It kicked and scratched at me. It wanted to get out.'

Beth looks out of the window, watching for cars, for the end. 'It stopped moving at thirty-six weeks. I knew it was dead, but I didn't tell Greg. I didn't tell anyone. I knew there was no chance I could be lucky twice. I carried it for another week before the blood came. Greg rushed me in, thinking the baby could be saved, but I already knew. They offered to knock me out, but I wanted to give birth to it. I refused pain-killers. I felt every second. He didn't arrive easily and the doctors told me I could never have another baby, but I already knew that.'

Beth feels Tess's hand on her arm. She hadn't even noticed her moving closer. 'I just wanted to go home and forget about it. I didn't go to the check-ups or take the tablets to stop my milk. I let it come and I let it hurt and I still didn't feel anything.'

Beth falls silent for a while and Maud has to nudge her gently to tell her to carry on, to get it all out.

'I first hit Greg six weeks after the baby died. He had been pushing me to talk about it. He wanted to hold me and cry over our loss. Lenny didn't understand what was going on. I'd left it to Greg to tell him. I didn't want my boy to know I'd failed. He was looking forward to having a brother.'

Beth's voice is flat and detached. Tess rubs her hand as if she's trying to warm her up, as if Beth's just come in from the cold.

'Greg said nothing to start with. He assumed the fact I didn't want to talk was just my way of dealing with things. I felt like he deserved it, that it was all his *fault*. He'd pushed me to have the baby, so I pushed him back. Then one day I slapped him, too. He just stood there. He didn't respond or retaliate. Not once.'

Tess and Maud sigh together. You didn't often hear about decent men in their shelter. 'I did it again, then again. Never in front of Lenny, but that just made it worse. The tension would coil up inside me all evening, like a snake, and as soon as Lenny went to bed, I'd force a row, just so I could snap. Greg would grab my arms, beg me to stop, to get help . . .' Beth is rambling now, a runaway train. The wheels have come off, the rails are shot to pieces. 'He sent Lenny to a sleepover one night, so we could talk, but he hadn't asked me first. I threw my hot coffee at him. He had to go to hospital. That was it. He told me if I did it again, he'd report me. He told me I'd lose Lenny.'

'Quite right,' Tess says sadly.

'I packed while he was at the doctor's for a check-up. My stuff and Lenny's. I thought I'd have time to get away before Greg got back. God, his face when he saw our bags . . . I had to grab Lenny and force him into the car. He didn't want to leave. He was screaming. Greg was screaming. He grabbed my arm and pulled, trying to stop me.'

'Your sore shoulder . . .' Tess's voice is quiet.

'It's the only time Greg ever laid a finger on me in anger. The rest was all me.' Beth rolls up her sleeve. 'One for every time I hurt him. An eye for every eye.' She pulls the sleeve down and looks back at the window. 'I'm sorry, Tess.'

'I believe you,' Tess says. They sit in silence until the knock at the door comes.

'I'll go,' Tess says. 'No men allowed in, remember?'

Beth realizes she's compromised their safety, Tess's birds with broken wings. Another broken rule. Another thing to add to the list. She casts about for something, anything to draw blood, but then the door opens and Greg walks in.

Beth looks at his strange, familiar face, and feels the slap she'd landed on Luke. Greg is so handsome, she thinks, seeing him as if for the first time. Strong lines, proud jaw, erect spine. Clean hands. He is decent, holds himself with restraint. He is all the things that Rudyard Kipling said about being a man, and he is her enemy.

'Beth! Thank fuck. Lenny? Where is he?'

'He's here. I just – please. Please, can we talk?'

'I've nothing to say to you. You took my son away from me.'

'I'm sorry.'

'Lenny is just outside, Greg,' Tess says, in her everything-is-going-to-be-okay voice. 'I'll go and get him. I promised him

I'd go in goal for a bit, so we'll be *five* minutes, if that's all right? I'd like to say goodbye, if I may?'

Beth looks at Tess and finally sees her for who she is. A woman who loves too much.

'Yes, of course. Thank you.' Even now, here, Greg can't help but be polite.

When the door closes, though, he turns on her. 'Do you have any idea what you've put me through?'

'Why didn't you call the police?' Beth has to know.

'Because you are still his mother. I didn't want him in the newspapers. I didn't want him being hunted.' Greg hunches his shoulders and says, 'You aren't well.'

'But you knew I'd never hurt him?' It comes out like a question, like a prayer.

'I didn't. I just hoped you'd come back, hoped you'd realize that you were wrong to take him.'

'Are you going to report me now?' A part of her wants him to. She can't punish herself enough. Lord knows she's tried.

'No. I'm going to take Lenny and go home. You're going to the doctor to get help. Proper help.'

'Then can I see him?'

'Why should I let you? You took my son away!' His voice is loud in a room where no men are allowed. It reaches all the corners and for the first time Beth fears her husband. 'I lost everything I loved. I lost a baby. He was mine too. You never cared about that bit, did you? I lost him, I lost you, and then you took Lenny. I've been dying, Beth. Dying.'

'I'll get help. I'll do anything.' Beth actually means it this time.

'No. We're done. You can call him. That's it.' Beth goes to

protest, and he stops her with a hand. 'It's more than you gave me.'

Beth can't argue with that, so she just nods in defeat.

'We'll tell him you have a job here and can't come back for a while.'

'I don't have a job.'

'I don't care. Lie. You're good at that. I assume you lied to him about where I was?'

'I said you were away, working.'

'I was at home, living by the phone.'

'I slept with someone else. While I was here.' He has to know the extent of it all.

For a moment Greg looks like he might be sick. 'I don't care.'

'It was Lenny's teacher, at the school. Then I hit him, too. I need help. I *know* I need help. I think I have postnatal depression, at the very least.'

'Fuck, Beth, what do you want me to say? You've broken me in every single way a man can be broken. How dare you tell me this now – look at me – like you think I can fix you?'

Tess knocks once at the door and they both straighten. Beth wipes her eyes and Greg clears his throat. Beth can see a vein pulsing in his neck, as he races to the door and pulls it open.

'Lenny. Lenny. My boy. My *boy*.'

'Dad! You found us!' Beth has to look away from their reunion. Greg saying hello to his son, like a soldier returning from a war she started.

Then it is time for her to say goodbye, to rip her heart from her chest so it can remain with her son. 'Play along,' Greg hisses in her ear, when she goes to hug Lenny.

Beth chokes back her sobs, and holds her son, and promises him she'll see him soon and tells him to be a good boy. 'Show your dad how good you are at football, won't you?'

She doesn't go out to the car. It's too much. She might throw herself under it.

George

(You can keep the hanky)

GEORGE CHATS TO ELLEN for an hour. Rambling thoughts spill from him, like marbles from a jar. 'Paninis, Ellen. They're the future. Should have taken you on that cruise. Your eggs were perfect. I miss your slippers by the back door. The dog lies down when you click your fingers.' Eventually he stands up and dusts himself off.

'Come on, dog. Time to do some digging.' George leaves Ellen with a gentle pat on the headstone and a promise to be back soon, then goes to find Betty. 'Need a hand, you old wench?'

She's tugging at a particularly resilient weed with both hands, but still no luck. George joins in and they re-enact the front cover of *The Gigantic Turnip*, with the two dogs urging them on.

'Mary and Joseph,' Betty wheezes, while Poppy digs at a patch of earth nowhere near the weed and Lucky runs round with a pink rose he stole from Iris Fielding's grave.

'Shouldn't laugh,' Betty snorts, when they finally uproot it, falling back and almost losing her footing. 'God save the

Queen!' She sits back on her bottom and lets out a giggle that has no place in a graveyard.

'Tougher than one of my bloody nose hairs, that was.' George brushes away some mud and shines up the stone with his hanky. He offers it to Betty, when he sees she's gone a bit runny and rheumy.

'Wow. Thanks.' She looks for a bit without dirt on it and dabs at her eyes. 'You're a true gent.'

'Feel better for coming?'

'Yes, oddly. Who'd have thought you'd be right about something?'

'I can see why you'd want to forget.'

George has been thinking about it. About having to see Ellen like that, wasting away, all her faculties gone. All the things that had made her Ellen missing. Nothing more than a body that needed wiping and rolling over. He pictured himself in the bed, Ellen being the carer. How he'd hate that. Her feeding him with a spoon, wiping his arse. Making him the baby she'd never had. He'd drink the morphine down in gulps until it did the trick.

'I bet your husband hated it. I bet he wanted to die from the shame.' They are walking out of the graveyard.

Betty stops and looks at him. She's got mud on one cheek and her lipstick looks as if a child painted it on. 'That's it. That's how he looked. Ashamed.'

'You didn't kill him, Betty. You gave him nothing but kindness. That doctor was right – it was the cancer that did for him.'

Betty sniffs and smiles and links her arm in his. When

they've walked a little further, she says, 'Thank you, George,' very quietly.

And George, who likes to shoplift and insult people, who relishes old ladies slipping in wet weather and cats being stuck up trees, pats her arm and says, 'You're all right, Betty,' and he means it.

Dan

(I could do with a friend right now)

DAN IS UP AT five on the day of the Ironman. He goes downstairs and wakes Luke, who's half on the sofa and half off it. He had turned up with a fading red cheek and a broken heart the night before. 'She hit me, Dan,' he said. 'She really hit me.'

'Shit.'

Lizzie was obviously complicated and not at all suitable for Luke. Dan couldn't help thinking his cousin had had a lucky escape. He didn't tell him that, of course. He tried to be a friend, and a counsellor, but he had problems of his own. Atticus had slipped off the radar. Was it something Dan did, or didn't do? Was Atticus bored with Dan? Had he met somebody better? Dan had found himself staring at his phone while Luke wittered on about how he was sure Lizzie 'had been the one' and they'd had 'a real connection'. She obviously wasn't, and they obviously hadn't. But, then, if Luke knew about Atticus and Dan, would he be thinking the same of them?

What a pair they were, sitting on the sofa, sharing shots of tequila, nursing broken hearts and bruised egos.

He'd texted Atticus yet again over twelve hours ago:

Atticus. I love you. Please be at the finish line of the Iron-man tomorrow to meet all my family. As my boyfriend. As my future. Love, Daniel xx

Again, Atticus hadn't replied. He'd left Dan hanging and it was killing him. Dan wanted to go round to his flat but Luke would wonder where he was going. Luke, his cousin. His best friend. He couldn't abandon Luke in his hour of need. All he could do was stare at his phone, hoping it would ring.

The drive to the event is full of curt sentences about preparations, and when they arrive there is no more talking. This is what they have trained for. Their big moment. Dan is going to do the Ironman, and then he's going to tell his family he's a gay man. He imagines Atticus at the finish line. Atticus waiting for him every night. Atticus moving his stuff in, or Dan moving to his place. Atticus wearing a thin gold band on his ring finger.

The Ironman, the hardest thing Dan thought he'd ever do, seems easy now. He had all that time to prepare. It's the things you can't prepare for that are hard, he realizes. They are the true test of character.

By the time Dan gets to the marathon, he is flat out, giving it everything he's got. He sprints towards his future, the image of Atticus eating away the miles.

Luke and Dan finish hand in hand as the speaker calls out their numbers. They fall into one another, crying and laughing. When they look up, they see their family. Luke's mum and

Dan's. Helen and Dave are holding a banner that says 'Luke and Dan are Irons'. Dan's mum is taking photos on her camera. When Dan and Luke approach, Helen drops the banner and pulls party poppers from her pocket. Their faces are coated with glitter.

But Atticus is missing. The adrenalin wears off and the cold sets in. Dan takes the foil blanket being offered, and the glucose drinks, but he doesn't feel or taste them. Where is Atticus? Dan waits while the crowd thins. His family are impatient. They've been standing for hours and they want to go and have lunch. The table is booked.

'Who are you looking for?' Luke finally asks.

'Atticus.'

'Who?'

'Atticus. My boyfriend.'

Dan doesn't turn to look at Luke's shocked face. Alarm bells are ringing. Atticus is not here. He didn't reply to the text and he's not here waiting.

Dan doesn't even say goodbye to his family. A taxi would be quicker, his legs are shot. He's running on empty, but his feet refuse to stop. They pound the pavement and Dan can feel that his socks are slick with blood. It makes no difference. He just has to get to Atticus. Dan takes the stairs to Atticus's flat two at a time. He doesn't knock. He uses the key Atticus hides under the doormat, fingers shaking in the lock, lungs screaming for oxygen.

Dan opens the door and solves the mystery. Who killed Atticus? It wasn't Professor Plum in the bedroom with the candlestick. It was Atticus himself, with the hook that held a chandelier, in the living room with a rope. The first time Dan came here, he had wanted to be Sherlock Holmes and work out all the clues. Now he has. 'When you have eliminated the impossible, whatever remains, however improbable, must be the truth.'

Dan collapses then, right under Atticus, whose feet swing above him. He's wearing the pink loafers, which dangle dangerously from his bare feet. There is no danger any more, though. The worst thing that can happen in the whole world has happened. All Dan can do is lie down and weep.

Later, much later, Dan sits up and looks around. Atticus is still there. Still dead. Dan sees that the chandelier has been taken apart, each glass tear wrapped neatly in tissue paper. He thinks of the hours it must have taken Atticus to preserve it so carefully, before he used the hook to end his life. There is an envelope hanging from one of the tears with his name on it.

Daniel. I couldn't go on any longer. I chose to stop. Don't do the same. You are going to change the world.

There are phone calls to make and things to do, but Dan is undone. He manages one text to Luke. Atticus's postcode with shaking hands. *LUKE. I NEED YOU. BRING FITZ.*

When he can bring himself to move, he carefully slips the loafers from his lover's feet and stands cradling them like newborn babies in his arms.

Lizzie

(I want my mum)

BETH SLEEPS ON THE train. The drugs the doctor has given her make her tired. She has been diagnosed with post-natal depression, which is complicated by her autism. There is a letter tucked into her bag. She isn't surprised. Knew it, deep down, but it's so much easier to swim with the tide instead of against it.

The doctor had undressed her with his probing questions. She was naked before he made her lie on a paper-covered bed under a spotlight so he could peer at her cuts and burns. Catalogue them. The last time she'd lain on a bed like this, she'd given birth to a dead baby with a head of dark hair. A baby who'd been healthy enough, at some point, to grow ten perfect fingers and toes, all the phases of the moon. The midwife had pressed them into soft white clay to take an imprint.

The last time she'd been touched was by Luke, in reverence. This was nothing like that. Beth was swiped and dabbed at with ointments and words that stung.

'You can't cut your thighs any more. They won't heal.'

'You're lucky this one didn't get infected.'

'This should have had a skin graft.'

'How have you even been able to walk with all these on your feet?'

The man's detached coldness made Beth think maybe she'd make a good doctor after all. She'd never speak to someone like this, though. She might lack small-talk, but she would never be as removed as he was. The human body, the whole world, is too full of wonders for her ever to feel neutral.

Villages and fields blur past her window. Her eyes can't take it all in. She has to close them, find Lenny's face behind her eyelids, let the weight of him keep her in her seat, on the train, moving forwards.

She walks to her mother's house. It's a long way from the station. The house she lived in with Greg and Lenny is closer. They must be back there now. She thinks of her son in his bedroom, the bedroom she and Greg had painted together. The same clouds above her head are over his too. That is all she can share with him right now.

Beth keeps her head down, not wanting to be seen. Her family home is small, wedged between two bigger ones, like an afterthought. The door is blue. It always was and always will be. Her mother will never move, never become unmoored, like her daughter did. The doorbell sounds and Beth thinks of Luke's *Star Wars* chime. How it made him smile.

Her mother is expecting her, and a small suitcase where Lenny should be.

'About bloody time, too,' her mother says. 'We've all been

worried sick.' She looks Beth up and down. 'The state of you. You're bones, just bones.'

Beth drops her bags and walks into her mother's open arms. They close round her like an envelope, like unconditional love. 'Come on in, Beth. Come home.'

George

(The king of grief)

GEORGE AND BETTY GO to see T20 cricket, the Sussex Sharks versus the Durham Jets. It's Betty's idea and George doesn't like it. People wear silly hats with blue hair poking out of the bottom. Music plays between each over and there are fireworks at the end. The man sitting next to him keeps declaring he'd rather be a chicken than an egg, rather be a parrot than a carrot. It makes no sense and drives George mad, but Betty loves it and joins in, making up lines of her own: 'I'd rather be a hat than a scarf.'

'Stupid daft cow,' he says to her, when she finally sits down, flushed and sweating in a too-tight shirt.

'Shut up, Sulky Susan. It's great fun.'

George harrumphs and refuses to join in. Instead, he keeps the scores in a little book. Dots and dashes, like Morse code. Betty talks to anyone and everyone, dragging George into conversations with people who know nothing about cricket and put him off his counting, as do the players in their bright kit. Cricketers should wear white, not these out-fits like pyjamas.

Betty can't understand it. 'Hey, Fanny Adams, why don't

you just enjoy the game?' she says, as another over ends and 'Sweet Caroline' blares out from the speakers.

'I am enjoying it,' George says, and discovers he means it. At some point during the last innings, he's stopped being annoyed by the cheering and chanting.

They stay well into the summer evening, as the smell of hot dogs fills the air, making George feel young again. Although there is a moment, when the man next to him tells George how funny his wife is, that he starts to feel sick and wants to go home.

Betty will never be his wife. George had one of those and will never have another. Betty is something else. She is his friend. So, instead of losing his temper and storming off, he simply says, 'Yes, she was, but that's not her. That's Betty. Shall I put in a good word for you?' The man laughs and George's cheeks go rosy pink with it all.

He feels slightly drunk by the time they wind their long way home. He's never talked so much, not belly-laughed in as long as he can remember. When he realizes this, George feels guilty that he's so full of life while his wife lies dead. That he has forgotten her for a moment and remembered to be happy. George thinks that grief is like a paper crown that slips over your eyes and gets pushed up over and over again. Sometimes it covers his eyes completely and he can't see a thing, it's lighter now, tissue thin and pale yellow, but still there, and wherever he goes he shall be wearing it. George, the King of Grief. He rather likes that.

Dan

(I'll never forget you)

ALL THAT TIME DAN had spent worrying about coming out, while Atticus had been fading away. All those hints that Dan, the counsellor, had never picked up on. *Why did you come to counselling, Atticus? Because I was lonely, I felt bereft, I don't sleep. I'm tired of my work. I feel like Tracey Emin. Because everything ends.* Those dark purple bruises he'd get under his eyes. *I used to have a drinking problem. To remind me I could stop. I'm so glad I didn't die before I met you.* All along, Atticus had been trying to tell him he was drowning at sea, when Dan had thought he was waving.

He had always been so busy digging into other people's weeds, he had forgotten to look for the seed in Atticus, things growing, pips of pain and deadly thoughts. Vines that crept and twisted and strangled.

After Atticus died, Dan spent a long time at home with his dog. He thought about how Fitz would eat, and wee, and poo and grow a summer coat that he would shed everywhere, and a winter coat that would do the same in spring, and how Atticus wouldn't be there to see it. He was behind the glass, pinned like a butterfly. Beautifully fragile, and always was.

Atticus's death didn't stop the summer rolling by, and the sound of bees stung Dan. The long, hot nights tortured him. He used to love the smell of freshly cut grass, but after Atticus, he felt the pain of each blade as it was decapitated. Dan felt every tiny death in the world. A discarded cup, a fox killed along the roadside. The bottom of a bread bag. Completion wounded him. His skin hurt as it flaked away and died, while all around him the world came to life. Helen's wedding passed in a blur of alcohol, Luke propping him up, his mother straightening his tie. He had walked Helen down the aisle, then Luke handed Dave the rings. It was a small wedding. Atticus should have been there, dancing with Dan. Making a speech, mocking Dave. Instead, Dan took Fitz as his plus-one and fed him marzipan and pigs in blankets. He looked at his dog when Helen and Dave shared their first dance. Fitz looked back, love shining in his eyes, tail wagging. He even wore a dicky bow. Atticus would have loved it.

Atticus.

Fitz was as good and loyal and constant as a dog could be. He didn't leave Dan's side, didn't eat till Dan did, or sleep till Dan slept. He watched over his human with absolute unconditional adoration. He could smell Dan's sorrow, licked it from his face when it came as tears, and from his bare legs when it came from running with the hope he could burst his broken heart. Fitz fitted into spaces far too small for a big dog, just so that Dan wouldn't be alone. He left his scent all over the Beacon, dribbled Morse code for help. Dogs dropped balls at Dan's feet in sympathy. In solidarity for his loss.

Dan didn't count the balls. His counting had died with Atticus, and for a long time, he simply didn't have the energy for it. He didn't need it as a coping mechanism, because he didn't want to cope.

Perhaps because of that, he ended up coping without it.

Atticus's mum and dad came to see Dan before the funeral. They were nothing like the people Atticus had described. His version of them was just another of his fabrications. His mum didn't drink and never had. His dad was tall and dark, like his son. He had the same walk and the same eyebrow waggle.

They'd sat Dan down between them and held his hands. Told him Atticus had tried to kill himself before and would have tried again if he hadn't been successful. They told him that, like terminal cancer, Atticus's mind had slowly mutated, the sad thoughts splitting and multiplying inside him. Dan had shouted at them then, demanded to know why they had left him, why they had abandoned him. Why they had given up.

'Don't you think we tried, Daniel?' his mum said carefully. 'But what sort of a life would it have been, being watched the whole time? With no knives being allowed in the house and doors that can't be locked? The only chance Atticus had of being happy was by making a life for himself. We couldn't babysit him. He had to live for himself.'

They'd filled the flat with bits and pieces for him, all of it intentional. All of it to make the place seem like a home. Memories of them, records to play, books to read, spoons and dishes to cook with. Nothing had worked.

'I failed him,' Dan whispered to them. 'I killed him. I didn't give him enough to live for.'

'No, son,' his dad said. 'Atticus killed himself. It had nothing to do with you. He'd tried a few times, and we knew he'd try again. It was always going to happen.'

'I thought I made him happy,' Dan said.

'Dan, people can be happy and still want to stop.'

Dan called them a week later. 'You might have to tell me that last bit again, please,' he said.

'We'll tell you as many times as you need.'

Atticus left Dan the flat, which he didn't want and wasn't Atticus's to give, but his parents insisted. 'You made him so happy, Daniel. He was his best self with you. Make it something wonderful.'

In time, Dan will come to understand they were telling him the truth. Atticus had always felt too light, too insubstantial. Not here to stay. Not Dan's, or anyone else's.

In time, Dan will turn the flat into a counselling practice. He didn't and couldn't save Atticus, but Dan will save others from suicide, and many more things besides. He will save Tony, who calls the helpline number Dan has attached to the top of railway bridges. He will talk him down and talk him home. He will save John, who wants to jump in front of a train because his wife left him. Dan will save many people. Necks won't break because of him. Bones will remain intact. Rigor mortis will not set in. He will save people who will go on to do great things and nothing at all. He will even save a man who wears loafers to pretend he's fine and life's a game. Over the years, Dan will save hundreds of people, and each time a tiny bit of him will come back to life.

The charity will grow, and it will win awards, and Dan will be revered. He will happily tell people he's gay. He'll flirt by the water-cooler. He won't be shy or embarrassed and will imagine Atticus laughing at him as he strides past.

And then he'll meet Tom on a walk with Fitz. Tom will be nothing like Atticus. He will be shorter than Dan and utterly ordinary and won't have a clue about art. His puppy, Albert, will be naughty, though, and Dan will teach Tom how to train him to come back. Well, Fitz will, but he'll let Dan think it was him.

In return, Tom will retrieve a little bit of Dan's heart – not the whole lot, because Cat Stevens was right: the first cut is the deepest. Atticus was Dan's Emperor Penguin. For him, Dan would have stood in the freezing snow, surviving on nothing but ice and love. He would have held Atticus's fragile egg-like life on his feet, protected it from the wind.

Dan cannot offer that to anyone else. His poor heart is too tired. It has stopped a couple of times, been too lost in pleasure to remember its beat. It has been coated in iron and hung from a hook. It is bruised and scarred, and Dan will never not be aware of it any more. He feels it ticking away inside him like the Tin Man's. He has learned that the heart is not a muscle but a clock, which can stop short, never to go again.

Dan doesn't have much to offer Tom, just his company and his quirkiness. He will care about his day, think about him when it's dark and he's not home yet. One day he will even find enough love to move in with him and hang his *Star Wars* poster on their living-room wall. Luke and Smurf-girl will come over on Sundays and rainy days, and for quiz nights and taco Tuesdays.

The photo of Dan and Atticus in Paris will always live on his desk, though, and Dan will look at it just before the door opens on a new client, and he will think, I'm glad you didn't die before I met you.

Beth

(Moving on)

B ETH IS LEARNING WHO she is. Not Lenny's mum or Greg's wife. Not a woman with postnatal depression. Not a liar or a beaten wife or a husband-beater. Not a cheater. Not Lizzie. She's just who she is – a woman who was ill and is getting better. She takes the pills, lining them up like dominoes, but instead of falling, she's standing up.

She feels the selective serotonin reuptake inhibitors marching through her system, like stern matrons from the 1940s. Trampling down her receptors, cleaning her veins, checking her vitals, topping up her internal water jugs. She can feel herself getting better. No longer needs word searches to keep her occupied. Her mind is getting clearer each day, like sheets drying in the sun. She is thawing.

Her mother pulled some strings and got her a job in the local pre-school, where she presses fat star-shaped hands into primary-coloured paints and marvels at the prints they leave behind. She cannot do it without thinking of her dead son's fossilized feet, nor can she do it without thinking of Lenny.

For the first month, when she got home, she pressed her thigh onto the blade with the same gentle precision, but as the tablets kicked in the blade was abandoned. The pain of acceptance is a dull ache compared to the sharp release of blood, but it is constant and reassuring. As long as Beth still feels bad, she doesn't need to cut. If she feels remorse, she isn't a monster. She doesn't need to punish herself with a weapon. All she needs to do is remember.

At the pre-school she wears ice-cream colours and plaits her hair back off her face. She counts up to twelve and back down again, then the same in French, cheers when her small group gets it right. Brings in snails and leaves and conkers. 'Did you know, did you know, did you know?' The children didn't know but they want to. Her encyclopaedic brain turns like the windmill on the Beacon, looking for facts to fascinate. She feels a small surge of pride that she can still teach. In the afternoons she reads *The Very Hungry Caterpillar* and *The Tiger Who Came to Tea*.

When she first read that book, she thought about herself. How she was the tiger, who came and took everything and left nothing behind. She had wanted to drop the book and run, but remembered she didn't do that any more, and then Annabelle, a small dollop of a child who smelt of Play-Doh, climbed onto her lap, and rested her head on Beth's shoulder.

Beth was frozen initially, by the downy hair of a child under her chin, the warm weight of tiny vertebrae pushing into her chest. How she had missed Lenny then, and her razor, the kettle, blood flowing. Annabelle, oblivious, just snuggled closer, and Beth had stayed and faltered through the rest of the story.

There have been more Annabelles, and Berties too. Little stout boys in stout shoes who kick balls solemnly to her, like

Lenny used to. It hurts and unhurts her over and over again. Her therapist says she is healing, tells her to embrace all her emotions, to let them out as tears, or laughter.

At work Beth is busy, consumed with slicing apples, and sorting out a row over who gets to play with the digger first, but at home there are only her mother, the TV and the space where her son should be. In the evenings, when there is nothing else to do, she reads out-of-date medical journals from the library, preparing for an exam.

After wrapping her wellies in a jumper to try to re-create the weight of Maud on her bed, Beth goes to the local RSPCA and adopts a wiry ginger dog, with one leg missing. The dog reminds her of herself now that she no longer has Lenny. It is right down at the bottom of the kennels, with its fat back to the world, and doesn't even bother to get up when Beth walks by. The dog is as surprised as the volunteers when Beth declares her perfect.

'Really? She's not very friendly, and she's terrible on or off the lead,' one helper says, while the other nudges her elbow and raises her eyebrows as if to say, 'Shut up! We're finally about to get rid of her.'

The dog is dragged out, dishevelled and blinking wildly. She hasn't seen the full sun for a long time. There will be no Nelson Mandela speech for her, though. She will not thank friends and comrades or stand unevenly before them as a humble servant. She lies down instead, and licks a bald patch at the base of her tail, which doesn't wag.

'It says here her name is Christmas?' Beth says, as she fills in the paperwork.

'Aye,' says a volunteer with dreadlocks, in a green bib, 'she was brought in on Boxing Day. We thought Christmas was slightly kinder.' Beth has nowhere to go with that logic.

Christmas is thrust at Beth with 'You are doing a truly wonderful thing' and 'We won't charge for the spot-on flea treatment.' All that comes with her, except her name, is an old orange towel full of holes. Christmas stares at Beth with the look of someone who's learned to disappoint first, before being disappointed.

Beth reaches out and gently turns one oversized ear the right way around. There is a patch of silky pink skin there, veins like a bright pink cauliflower. 'I'll treasure her,' Beth promises, paying for a water bowl and a lead.

Christmas refuses to walk, so Beth has to carry her, ripe and repellent, all the way home. Christmas does nothing to make the trip easier, refuses to bend into shape. Beth thinks of Lenny's arched back when she used to try to strap him into his pushchair. Christmas growls into Beth's armpit.

Beth readjusts her weight and continues on her journey. Christmas protests, nipping at Beth's collarbone. She smooths a long ginger wire from Christmas's eyebrow. The dog's mouth smells sweet and fruity. Beth makes a mental note to have her tested for diabetes.

'I'm going to look after you, and you are going to look after me.'

Beth gets up every day at six to walk the dog before work. Christmas barks at cars, people, trees and lampposts. She doesn't like the colour red, in fact she hates it, and she refuses to walk anywhere near a drain. But Beth loves Christmas as much as her broken heart will allow. She looks at her and sees herself, so takes the nips and sleepless nights when

Christmas howls at the moon. Beth even joined her once, throwing back her head and baying along.

On the early walks, Beth would wait patiently for Christmas to come back, which she always did in the end, if you didn't rush her. Maybe if Beth hadn't been rushed to have another baby so soon he might have lived. Maybe he wouldn't. These are the things Beth accepts as she waits for Christmas to limp back to her.

She tells Lenny about the dog when they talk on the phone and Lenny laughs when he sees the picture she texts him and replies, *OMG, Mum!* The text feels like the time she pulled off her little toenail, after stubbing it on the stairs. Fast, sharp pain, then relief. Greg wouldn't speak to her at all at first, just answered and passed the phone to Lenny, then hung up when she was done.

After a month, though, he asks her how she's getting on. He says it so quietly, she almost hangs up, thinking he's speaking to Lenny, but then he says her name. 'Beth?'

'I'm okay,' she stutters, 'I've been going to counselling. And taking the antidepressants. Almost a fifth of the population are on them. The number of prescriptions has doubled in the last ten years. Even children as young as six have been given them.' She pauses. 'It can happen to anyone.'

'I know, Beth,' Greg says quietly. He could have said he'd tried telling her that once but she didn't listen: she'd screamed at him instead.

After a month without seeing her son, Beth has started to live Greg's life. The agony of being childless but still a parent. Love like a river, like a sea, and nowhere to send it. A tsunami of pain.

Beth and Christmas don't walk far to start with. They are both weary, weathered by storms, as they shuffle round the park and the local pond, where she and Lenny once floated paper boats and collected frog spawn. The first couple of times they go, she wonders if she might spot them, Greg and Lenny, flying a kite or wading in the shallows, but by some unspoken agreement, Greg has stayed away from their old haunts. He lets Beth rediscover them and, in turn, herself.

Autumn falls on them slowly, and before Beth knows it, Christmas is diving into heaped piles of rust-coloured leaves while Beth laughs at her. Takes a photo to show Lenny.

She starts doing jigsaws with her mother. Trains, and cats in wicker baskets. She and Christmas hate them, but there is something to be said about starting from scratch. Sorting out the pieces, outside, inside, filling in the sky. It is the opposite of what she's done to Greg, dismantling their lives, piece by piece. Did she know what she was doing? Could she have stopped?

No, Beth realizes, with the clarity of chemical balance, sleep and no fresh scars. She was a train on a track heading towards disaster, imprisoned in her mind, but she isn't that person any more. It is over. She is living through the aftermath, grieving not just for her son and her husband, but also for herself.

'I forgive me,' she says one day to Christmas, as she rubs Bio Oil into the dog's scars and combs her bristly hair. She is getting shinier, and slimmer from all the walking, and has adopted a heartbreaking lopsided gait that makes Beth want to pick her up and carry her, but she doesn't.

'I forgive you,' she says, to the face in the mirror that stares back at her, unflinching. 'Life is a series of experiments and reactions to learn from. This has been another one.'

One day Greg calls to tell her Lenny is playing in a football tournament, then adds, 'He misses you,' in the flat voice of a parent trying to be a mum *and* a dad and finding he can't. The voice of a parent who wants to give their child the whole world but can only manage a sliver.

She stays hidden at the football match, Christmas bundled into her large bag, like a giant Brillo pad.

Greg spots her and nods, once. She does the same back, forces herself not to wave, prays for her legs not to buckle. They do anyway, when Lenny runs out onto the pitch and turns to look for her. He spots Greg first and throws up both arms – Look at me, here I am – then keeps looking, frantically, along the rows of legs, until his gaze lands on her Dr Martens. She sees his mouth make the shape of her name – *Mum* – and has to clutch the seat in front of her. She is still that. It can never be taken away from her. She is still a mother, to two sons.

When the match finishes, Lenny runs to her with arms wide and his dad's grin on his face. 'Mum, did you see my goal?'

'I saw it all. You were amazing.'

He throws himself at her then, knocking her backwards, and she clutches him until she sees Greg on the periphery, watching, and forces herself to pull back, wipe her eyes. 'You look great. Haven't you grown?'

Lenny beams as Greg comes over. 'Dad, Mum says I'm taller!'

Beth doesn't know what to say next or do with her hands, so she bends down to stroke Christmas, who has poked her ead out of the bag with a scowl. She can hear Beth's heart-beat, smell the salt of her nerves.

'Mum, have you finished your work at the shelter now?' Beth looks at Greg, not knowing what to say. Watches him look from her to their son.

'Yes. I have. I'm back now. Back and all better.' She looks at Greg as she says this.

He stares at her for a long moment, then replies, 'Come back for a cup of tea?'

Christmas yaps and Greg says, 'Right, yes. Sorry, I don't know your name . . .' He looks up at Beth, who mouths, 'Christmas.' He almost smiles then. 'I suppose you can come too. If you've nothing else on, of course?' Christmas grumbles but agrees, then goes back into the confines of Beth's bag, where she finds a half-chewed toffee.

When Lenny has said goodbye to everyone, they walk across the pitch to Greg's car, on either side of their son, like a pair of bookends. Lenny picks up his mum's hand, then his dad's, like he's a conductor of electricity, linking them together. Setting off the spark. Beth feels love shoot through her and light her up, like a pinball machine.

'Swing me!' Lenny demands.

And they do.

Postscript

I T'S COLD ON THE Beacon. There are lots of dogs up here. All their ears are inside out in the wind. Fitz doesn't mind, but Albert doesn't like it. Fitz waits patiently for his new friend to have them flipped back the right way, then they tear off together to see Wolfie. Albert has little legs and, although he's still growing, he's never going to be as big as Fitz or Wolfie, but they never make him feel bad about it. Sometimes they even let him get to the stick first.

Poppy and Albert are sort of a thing, but it's new and George isn't happy about it. Betty is, of course, and chats non-stop about the possibility of puppies. 'Oh, shush, George. It'd be lovely. You could name them all after pies.' Betty keeps her hand clasped firmly around George's arm when they pass Dan and Tom. George remembers the tall bloke from the charity shop and wonders what happened to him but senses it might be wise not to ask. There is something in the way Dan walks, like a man nursing an old injury, only slightly noticeable, and only in bad weather like this.

Luke and Smurf-girl have stopped walking, and Luke is fussing with her scarf. Wolfie does a long-legged lap, danger-ously close to her legs. Beth is visiting with Christmas, an odd collection of dog parts, and has taken Maud out with them too, for old times' sake. Maud is much slimmer now and s no trouble walking, but Christmas gets tired so Beth tucks her into a bag with her slightly bald nose poking out. Lenny isn't there, but Maud can scent him on Beth's coat. His happiness smells of washing powder and empty packets of cheese-and-onion crisps.

They are not a natural group of people to be together, not really. George and Betty, Dan and Tom, Luke and Smurf-girl and the woman who used to be called Lizzie, but dogs bring people together like this. They get people out in crazy weather, lifting an arm or tipping a hat to a fellow owner. Get people stamping their feet to keep warm so that the dogs can have one final loopy circuit together. When the dogs have shepherded their owners into a large, pen-sized cube, Betty lifts the lid off her Tupperware and the smell of banana bread rises sweetly.

'It's still warm, I've got napkins. Yes, Albert, you'll get some crumbs too.'

Luke is first in the queue, running back to his blue-haired girl with a wedge of sunshine-coloured cake. Dan is next. He eats the cake, breaking off a corner to share with Tom, who blushes with pleasure. Beth doesn't join the gang, but she and Luke take a moment that stretches between them, like taffy. Finally, Luke dips his chin at her, then lifts it back up, and Beth's heart follows it, like a bird on a gust of wind. Forgiveness. The lightest, sweetest cake in the world. Tess's letter to Beth, six months after she left, was tracing-paper thin, but hit her like an anchor dropping to the seabed: 'I hope you are better now, Beth. I hope you are beginning to recover from the past and find yourself again. I don't condone what you did but I do understand. Maud misses you.'

Dan watches Beth quietly, a fellow veteran of the war that is life. Fitz is by his side within seconds and pulls him back into the world with a wet nose in his palm.

'What is it, boy?' Dan asks, bending down to drop a kiss between Fitz's big brown eyes. Insane with jealousy, Albert bounds over, growling at Dan's trouser leg and, in seconds, all hell has broken loose as the dogs take off, zooming around the humans, crossing and uncrossing like maypole dancers.

'Stop that! Come back! Bloody hell. Grab his collar!'

George's napkin escapes from his grasp and dances up into the air. Betty takes a tumble in her wedge-heel fashion trainer. Fitz, Wolfie and Lucky make a fantastic three-pronged approach on the leftover cake, while Dan throws back his head and laughs. Beth smiles at the chaos, then slips off down the hill, back home to her boys.

Acknowledgements

This book would not have been possible without an awful lot of people.

Thank you, Kirsty Dunseath, for loving dogs as much as I do, for getting my sense of humour and for being the fairy godmother of all editors. I still pinch myself to be sure that this is real. I've been so lucky to have your eye on this book. Also massive thanks to all the team at Transworld and Doubleday.

Thank you, to infinity and beyond, to the coolest agent in town, Katie Greenstreet, for being amazing and for coping with me throughout this process. This book would not have progressed from a Word document to a novel without your patience, editing skills and insight. I am a very grateful grapefruit.

Big, fat, stinking love to Vicky Blunden, who looked at my first typescript and said, 'I think this will be picked up by agents, no problem.'

A massive thank-you to Sabrina at Faber for your guidance, and to the class of 2019.

What can I say to Helen Paris for your love and support?

ı are the Jack to my beanstalk. Can't wait 'til we are mess-
ıg about in boats again soon.

Thank you to all my friends and family who read early
drafts and helped shape the book. Fleur, Rae, Kelly, Judith
(your beat sheet changed my life), Pam, Sammy, Joe, Nula,
JD, Renx, Bex, Heather, Anne, Pat. There will be more, who
I have forgotten. I am so sorry.

Thank you to all the people who read my column and blogs
and said, 'You should write a book!'

Thank you to the NHS, especially the rheumatology
departments in Brighton and Haywards Heath, for your treatment and support. I couldn't have got out of bed, let alone
typed, without your incredible kindness and care. Big kiss to
you, Hilary on reception!

Thank you to my dogs, who I am sure secretly read my
work and improve it while I am asleep. Thank you for being
my constant, caring companions. Thank you for your wet
noses and wagging tails. Thank you for making everything
better just by existing.

I'd like to take a moment for Bryn Waters, who took his
own life, and made me realize what suicide was really about.
To his beautiful, brave sister, Linsey, and the people he left
behind – I hope this book lifts the lid a little.

Thank you, Mum, for taking me to libraries when I was a
kid. Thank you, Dad, for liking my first unedited poem about
the cat being run over more than the edited one. Thank you,
Brosie, and Brother John – not sure what for, because you
never read my work, but I know you love me anyway. Sorry,
I'm the favourite child now.

To Sara, Aunt Margaret and Maurice, who are not here but

ACKNOWLEDGEMENTS

should be. I miss you every day. I wish so badly that you could read this book.

To my daughters, Grace, Daisy and Bliss. If I can do this, you can do *anything*.

Last, but never least, eternal gratitude to my husband, James, for your unwavering support. When I suggested giving up my marketing career for a full-time journalist course, not only did you demand I do so, but you bought me a smoky old jalopy to get me there and back. Thank you for making me sign up for the Faber course, for showing me where it was on a map, and for all the meetings you had to leave when I was lost and late and panicking in the middle of London. Thank you for the million cups of tea and bags of pick 'n' mix and for listening to my middle-of-the-night plot problems. Twenty-one years ago, I wrote you an email. You replied and said, 'I didn't know you'd be so good at spelling.' Who'd have thought it, huh? Two no-good kids from the wrong side of the tracks, proving everyone wrong.

Daniel Shearing

ERICKA WALLER is an award-winning author who lives in Brighton, United Kingdom, with her husband, three daughters, and petting zoo. She's been writing since she was old enough to hold a pen.